By Margaret Truman

First Ladies
Bess W. Truman
Souvenir
Women of Courage
Harry S Truman
Letters from Father: The Truman Family's Personal Correspondences
Where the Buck Stops
White House Pets
The President's House

In the Capital Crimes Series

Murder in Foggy Bottom
Murder at the Library of Congress
Murder at the Watergate
Murder in the House
Murder at the National Gallery
Murder on the Potomac
Murder at the Pentagon
Murder in the Smithsonian
Murder at the National Cathedral
Murder at the Kennedy Center
Murder in the CIA
Murder in Georgetown
Murder at the FBI
Murder on Embassy Row
Murder in the Supreme Court
Murder on Capitol Hill
Murder in the White House
Murder in Havana
Murder at Ford's Theater
Murder at Union Station
Murder at The Washington Tribune
Murder at the Opera
Murder on K Street

MURDER ON K STREET

MURDER ON K STREET

A CAPITAL CRIMES NOVEL

Margaret Truman

 Ballantine Books • New York

Murder on K Street is a work of fiction. Names, characters,
places, and incidents are the products of the author's
imagination or are used fictitiously. Any resemblance to actual
events, locales, or persons, living or dead, is entirely
coincidental.

*For my son Thomas; my daughter-in-law Nina;
and my grandchildren Olivia and Truman*

MURDER
ON K
STREET

ONE

Washington smells good in springtime. The air is fresh and pure. The sweet scent of cherry blossoms is carried by gentle breezes from the Potomac and Chesapeake Bay, lifting spirits and promising renewal. Until . . .

Until spring fades to summer, turning the nation's capital into a domed stadium that traps the heat and humidity—as well as the stench of whatever political scandal might linger from the winter—and releasing foul vapors from the swamp on which the city is built, stinging the nostrils and eyes and erasing memories of springtime.

This was one of those summer nights in Washington, D.C.

The greenish, putrid outside air could be seen through the windows of the Mayflower Hotel's Colonial Room, where in air-conditioned comfort Illinois senior senator Lyle Simmons was winding up. Simmons was a speechwriter's dream: He was comfortable using the humorous asides sprinkled throughout his prepared text, delivering them as though they were impromptu. He had Johnny Carson's body language down to a T, and had mastered some of Jack

Benny's timing. Add to those techniques the widest, most engaging smile in the U.S. Senate, which he displayed with ruthless precision; his imposing height (two inches over six feet); a rich baritone voice; a full head of gray hair made less so with judicious use of darkening highlights; and a bespoke wardrobe, mostly from London, that draped nicely over his lean frame; and you had a potent package. His detractors and off-the-record colleagues felt that he talked too much, giving the impression that he was more comfortable speaking than listening—on-the-record journalists had occasionally used such terms as *motormouth* and *blowhard*—but most members of the press were kind: He worked hard at cultivating media approval, and reporters knew that for the most part, they would get the straight scoop from him. For the most part.

He stepped down from the podium and was faced with dozens of outstretched hands and eager voices. "Great speech, Senator," someone said. "Keep telling it like it is."

Simmons's chief of staff, Alan McBride, flanked the senator on one side, his press secretary, Peter Markowicz, the other, as they slowly navigated through knots of the faithful toward the room's exit. One of many lobbyists in attendance stopped Simmons, grabbed his hand, slapped him on the back lightly, and said into his ear, "You know what I'm waiting for, Senator?"

"What's that, Bruce?"

"The day when I don't have to call you Senator Simmons anymore."

"What?" Simmons said, adopting an exaggerated frown.

"I'm looking forward to when I can call you President Simmons."

Simmons's grin returned. "Not too loud, Bruce. Some blogger might think I'm running."

Bruce stayed close to the senator's ear as they continued toward the door. "Truman declared his candidacy right here in this hotel," he said. "Stayed here, too, for the first few months of his presidency." Closer to the ear now, and sotto voce. "I need time with you about the prescription bill."

"Call Alan tomorrow," Simmons said, breaking away from the lobbyist to greet others, his aides in lockstep.

They reached the Grande Promenade, the expansive lobby through which a Who's Who of political heavyweights had passed since the Mayflower opened in 1925: Truman; before that FDR, who lived there pre-inaugural and who wrote his famous "We have nothing to fear but fear itself" speech while in Suite 776; and the FBI's J. Edgar Hoover, who ate lunch at the hotel every day for more than twenty years, his daily menu choices never varying and considerably more bland than his personality—buttered toast, cottage cheese, grapefruit, salad, and chicken soup.

Simmons's final stop before reaching Connecticut Avenue was to greet a Senate colleague coming from the Café Promenade with his wife and daughter. "How did it go?" he was asked.

"Couldn't have gone better. Enjoy dinner?"

"The seafood buffet was superb," replied his wife.

"You two take care," Simmons said. "See you tomorrow."

Standing at the hotel's doors was McTeague. He'd been Senator Simmons's driver and bodyguard since Simmons had arrived in Washington years ago as a freshman member of the House of Representatives. A car and driver spoke of the family fortune that had been behind Simmons's successful run for Congress. There would be no scrambling to find inexpensive temporary housing, as many members of the House needed to do. Simmons and his bride had immediately purchased a three-story town house on the outskirts of Georgetown, where they quickly established themselves as frequent, lavish party-givers when Congress was in session. During his fourth term, they sold the house at a handsome profit and bought a sprawling, hilltop Georgian colonial in the Foxhall section, with sweeping views of the city. After almost a million dollars in renovations and additions, it had become a proper home for the congressman who would become the senator from Illinois.

Walter McTeague was a large man with a ruddy, puffy face and a nest of small gray curls atop his head. He wore what he always wore while on duty—black suit, black shoes, black tie, and white shirt. He saw Simmons and his aides approaching and pulled in his stomach and stood taller. Simmons dispatched McBride and Markowicz: "We've got that seven o'clock meeting on staffing. And don't forget to tell Chris Matthews or his producer that I want a more comfortable chair the next time I'm on."

He watched them greet McTeague and disappear through the outer doors.

"Hello, Walter," Simmons told his driver. "Sorry to have kept you. It ran longer than I anticipated."

"No problem, Senator," McTeague replied in a husky voice. Simmons knew that the former D.C. cop was a heavy smoker, which was all right as long as he didn't foul the air in the four-door black Mercedes, or in the house while waiting for him.

McTeague had left the Mercedes running to keep the interior cool.

"Hot as Hades," Simmons muttered as they stepped out onto Connecticut Avenue. "Washington should have thought of that when he decided to plop the nation's capital here."

McTeague laughed as he opened one of the rear doors and the senator climbed in.

"Home?" McTeague asked after he'd settled behind the wheel.

"As fast as possible. Put on the news."

Simmons leaned back against the leather seat, closed his eyes, and took in what the WTOP radio guy said. News but no news. Nothing earth shattering, nothing directly affecting him. But he silently reminded himself that if he did seek his party's nomination for president, everything would affect him, every niggling little incident across the nation and the world. Was it worth it? He was too tired at the moment to try answering that question.

They pulled into the long, circular driveway and came to a stop by the front door. Sensors picking up their arrival had activated a battery of halogen outdoor fixtures that bathed the front of the house in harsh white light.

"What's the schedule for tomorrow?" McTeague asked, turning on an interior light and twisting to face the senator.

"I have to be at the Capitol by ten to seven."

"Mind a personal comment, sir?"

"When have I ever minded a personal comment from you, Walter? Shoot."

"You're looking tired these days, sir. So is Mrs. Simmons. I saw her today when I delivered the dry cleaning. You and the wife ought to get away for a while. Rest up."

Simmons smiled, leaned forward, and patted McTeague's arm. "I'm sure Jeannette would agree with you wholeheartedly. I'll mention it to her."

McTeague came around, opened the rear door, and escorted Simmons up a set of wide marble steps. Simmons had given up trying to dissuade him from doing that; the former cop took his job seriously, both as driver and as protector. He was armed, his Glock nestled in a holster beneath his left armpit.

"Go on home," Simmons said. "Best to your wife. Sorry for the early start these mornings."

"Not a problem, Senator. You have a good night."

Simmons watched the burly McTeague drive off. He was happy to have the man. Wealthy members of Congress, such as himself, were able to provide and pay for their own personal security and transportation. Others were on their own.

He looked up at thousands of gnats and other nocturnal insects swarming around the halogens. *Constituents looking for favors,* he thought. Staring directly at the lights blinded him momentarily, and he shifted his gaze to the massive set of doors leading into the house.

He drew a breath, inserted his key, and pushed open one of the doors. The marble foyer, larger than the first floor of most people's tract houses, was dark; a chandelier at the top of a winding staircase cast a modicum of yellow light. He closed the door behind him. He didn't bother looking at the alarm system's keypad because he knew the alarm hadn't been activated. Jeannette seldom had it on when she was home, especially at night.

"What good is a security system if you don't use it?" he'd asked her repeatedly.

"Let the bogeyman in," she had said defiantly. It was the alcohol talking, he knew. Too many alcohol-fueled words lately.

He thought he heard something. "Jeannette?"

There was no reply.

He reached for a switch that operated the foyer lights, and flipped it up. The explosion of light from wall sconces and recessed fixtures and two chandeliers came to life so suddenly that it was almost audible.

He turned to go to the kitchen at the rear of the house where, if she'd remembered, she would have put the day's mail on a large island in the center of the room. He looked to his left. At first, it didn't register. He narrowed his eyes to bring *it* into focus, then took tentative steps in *its* direction. He closed his eyes and rubbed them. Opened them. Another few steps, his shoes sounding unnaturally loud on the marble floor.

He said nothing as he approached the body. He stopped a few feet from *it*, lowered his head and bit his lip. The air-conditioning provided what seemed to be an arctic blast of frigid air.

"Jeannette?" he said softly, leaning closer. He extended his fingertips in the direction of her face and neck, but withdrew before making contact.

"Good God," he muttered as he turned his back on *it* and went into a library off the foyer to his right, where he slumped behind the handsomely inlaid cherry desk. The outdoor lights poured through a window behind him. He switched on a desk lamp and stared at the phone. After drawing several deep breaths, he slowly removed the cordless unit from its cradle, dialed, and waited. He broke off, then entered another phone number. The ringing phone assaulted his ear.

"Hello?"

"Neil? It's Dad."

"Oh. Hi. How'd the speech go?"

"It went fine. Neil, there's been an accident here at the house."

"An accident? Are you all right?"

"Yes, I'm fine. It's Mother."

"What happened?"

"She's—she's dead."

"What? Dead? How? What?"

"Get over here, Neil."

"Are you sure?"

"Sure about what? That Mother is dead? Of course I'm sure."

"You—?"

"Yes, I confirmed it."

"It'll take me a few minutes. I'm in my pajamas and—"

"I don't give a damn about pajamas. Be here!"

His second call was to his chief of staff, who'd just walked through the door of his own home. There was no talk of pajamas with Alan McBride. Simmons instructed him to summon Press Secretary Markowicz and get him rolling.

He paused before making his third call, inhaling as though sucking in much-needed oxygen. He tapped his fingers on the phone before dialing a two-number direct-dial code.

"Phil. It's Lyle."

"This is a pleasant surprise," Phil said.

"But with unpleasant news. Jeannette is dead."

"Say again."

"It's Jeannette. She's dead."

"My God, Lyle," Rotondi said. "What happened?"

"I don't know. She may have fallen and hit her head. There's blood. Or someone might have bludgeoned her. I don't know. Can you come?"

"Of course. Have you called nine-one-one?"

He paused. "Yes," he said, fully aware that he hadn't. "They're on their way. Neil has been notified, and some of my staff. I need a friend, Phil."

"I'm leaving now."

Simmons returned to the foyer and cast a quick, sideways glance at his wife's body. He stepped outside and called 911. "This is Senator Lyle Simmons. I'm calling from my home." He gave the address. "My wife has died."

"Have you checked for vital signs?" the dispatcher asked.

"Yes. There's no sign of life."

"Do you know the cause of her death?"

"No. She's on the floor of our foyer. There's blood around her head. She might have fallen, or—or she's the victim of a homicide."

"I'm dispatching police and medical personnel immediately, sir. Please don't disturb anything at the scene and—"

Simmons disconnected the call. He returned inside, went into a powder room off the foyer, and checked his appearance in the mirror. Satisfied, he went outside again and awaited everyone's arrival.

TWO

Markowicz's arrival coincided with police and medical vehicles, six of the former, two of the latter, sirens wailing, lights flashing, tossing a garish red-white-and-blue kaleidoscope into the heavy, sullen night air. The official vehicles parked in the circular driveway, engines running; so did the press secretary's. Two officers jumped out and took up positions at either end to keep the uninvited from pulling in behind them. Two other uniformed officers were first up the steps to where Simmons stood, followed by white-coated EMTs.

"Where is she?" an officer asked.

"In there," Simmons said, nodding toward the door.

"It's the senator," one of the emergency medical technicians said to his partner, as though he'd spotted a rock star.

"I can't believe this," Markowicz said on reaching his boss.

"I know."

"I heard the call on my car monitor," Markowicz said. "The press will be here any minute."

"I'll need to make a statement," said Simmons.

"Negative, Senator. No one will expect a statement from you so soon."

"Still, come up with something."

A short, slender Asian American man approached; he was wearing a lightweight green suit, dark green shirt, and unfashionably narrow lighter green tie. "Senator Simmons?" he asked.

"Yes."

"I'm Detective Chang, MPD."

Simmons nodded and extended his hand; the detective didn't offer his in return.

"Is there anyone in the house besides the victim?" Chang asked.

Simmons's expression was puzzled. "No, of course not. Who would be there?"

"Staff? A housekeeper?"

"She's away. What does this have to do with anything?"

Chang ignored the comment. "The victim is your wife?"

"Yes."

"Excuse me," Chang said and entered the house, where the first two officers on the scene had secured the foyer.

"There's Alan," Markowicz said, pointing to the chief of staff's car that had just arrived. Other vehicles, including a TV remote news truck, roared up behind. "I'll head them off," the press secretary added, bounding down the steps in their direction.

McBride replaced him at the senator's side. "I'm so sorry, Senator."

"It's quite a shock, Alan. Quite a shock."

"She was murdered?"

"I don't know. There's a lot of blood. The police are inside now."

McBride looked down at other cops in uniform, who had fanned out to maintain a security line between the house and those arriving on the road below. Markowicz, with the aid of an officer, had corralled the press.

"She was—she was dead when you got home?" McBride asked.

Simmons nodded, his lips tight.

"Someone broke in?"

"I don't know, Alan." Simmons's annoyance at being asked a question for which he had no answer was palpable.

McBride had worked for the senator since his first six-year term, and read his boss. No more questions.

"I called Neil," Simmons said. "He's on his way."

"Good. What about Polly?" He knew that asking about Simmons's daughter was a mistake the moment the words left his mouth. She and her father had been noisily estranged for years.

"There's time for that," Simmons muttered.

Detective Chang emerged from the house as Neil Simmons arrived and joined his father and chief of staff. Chang looked at the two newcomers.

"My son, and my chief of staff," Simmons said, responding to the detective's questioning expression.

"May I speak with you, sir?" Chang said to Simmons. "Alone?"

"There's nothing I have to say that they can't hear," Simmons said.

Now Chang's hard expression didn't ask a question. Rather, it said he'd meant what he'd said—that he wanted to talk to Simmons without others present.

"All right," said Simmons.

"Dad, give me a few minutes first," Neil said. He turned to Chang: "I just got here. It's my mother in there. Surely—"

"I prefer that you and your father not talk before I have had a chance to speak with each of you."

"This is outrageous," Neil said, looking to McBride for assurance. McBride shrugged.

Senator Simmons walked with Chang to the bottom of the stairs. Chang flipped a small notebook to a fresh page and held a pen over it. "Tell me what you know, sir," he said.

"What I know? What I know is that I arrived home to find my beloved wife dead, her head bashed in, blood everywhere. You tell me what *you* know, Detective. Was it a murder?"

"What time did you arrive home, sir?"

Simmons was suddenly aware that photographers had trained their cameras from afar at him and the detective. He turned his back to them and said, "Can't we do this in a more private place? Inside the house? Out of this heat?" He was feeling soggy in his suit and tie. The detective appeared to be comfortable.

Chang responded by moving a few feet into a natural alcove created by a grouping of small evergreens. Simmons followed.

"What time did you arrive home, sir?"

Simmons gave Chang a thumbnail recounting of his evening, culminating with finding his wife's body. He ended with, "Look, Detective Chan, I—"

"Chang."

"Chang. I know you have a job to do, and I wish to be as helpful as possible. I'll be happy to sit down with you and answer any questions you might have, but right now I need to speak with my son and to my staff." He made a move to leave.

"Senator Simmons."

"What?"

"It was murder," said Chang.

"You're sure?"

"It was you who made the nine-one-one call?"

"That's right."

"Immediately upon coming upon the victim?"

"Look, Detective, I think that—"

"Excuse me," Chang said. He went up the steps and disappeared inside the house.

Simmons rejoined his son and McBride. Neil was attempting to look into the foyer past one officer stationed at the front door but without success. An assistant medical examiner arrived and began to take charge of Jeannette Simmons's body. The press, now numbering in the dozens, shouted questions from where they were sequestered.

"I wish they'd take her away," the senator said in a low voice to Neil and McBride. "This is becoming a circus."

"What did he ask you?" Neil asked his father.

"What time I got home. He's an unpleasant little bastard."

He'd no sooner said the words than Chang reappeared and said to Neil, "A word with you, please, sir."

Neil looked to his father, who said with a nod, "Go on, Neil."

After Neil and Chang had retreated to the area shielded by trees and shrubs, Simmons turned to McBride. "Why won't they let me back inside?"

"Just as well that you stay out here, Senator, until they've finished up what they're doing. It will take awhile."

"Before they bring her out, you mean."

"Yes."

"How could this have happened?" the senator asked no one in particular. "Who would have wanted to kill her?"

McBride didn't have an immediate answer to either question. "Some sicko," he finally offered.

"Yes, a sicko. I can't stay here tonight."

"You'll stay with Neil?"

He replied quickly. "No. Get me a suite at the Mayflower or the Willard."

McBride stepped away to place a cell phone call as Chang returned with Neil Simmons.

"He wants a statement from me, where I've been all night, things like that," said Neil. "You'd think I killed Mom."

Now Neil was able to see into the foyer at his mother's lifeless body. He turned away from the sight. What sounded like a gurgle came from his throat.

"I'll need to pack," the senator told Detective Chang.

"I'm afraid you cannot enter the house, sir, while my investigation is in progress."

"How long will that be?"

"Overnight."

"You can't expect me to—"

"The Willard, Senator," McBride announced, snapping shut his phone.

"I'll need a change of clothes, damn it!" Simmons snapped at Chang. "I have a day of important meetings ahead of me and—"

Hard stares from Chang and McBride stopped Simmons. He spoke more softly now. "I would appreciate it, Detective, if I could pack a bag for the night."

"I will see what can be arranged," Chang said, and left.

Markowicz broke away from the press contingent, which had continued to grow in size, and came to the front steps of the house. "I've got to tell them something, Senator."

"I can say that—"

"No, sir. A statement from you at this time would be viewed as inappropriate."

"Is *anything* appropriate at a time like this?"

"There'll be tremendous sympathy for you, Senator. No one, including the media, will be critical of you for not saying anything. I've formulated something in my mind. I can issue a statement that comes from you."

"Maybe you're right."

"I'll keep it short. Here's what I intend to say." He spoke the words into Simmons's ear. The senator nodded.

Chang returned. "Senator Simmons?"

"What?"

"If you wish to pack a suitcase, I will escort you inside."

"I don't need an escort into my own home."

Silence from the others mitigated Simmons's tone. "All right," he said. He told McBride to call Phil Rotondi on his cell phone. "He's on his way from the shore. Tell him I'll be at the Willard and to come directly there."

"I'll come in with you," Neil said.

"I'm afraid not, sir," Chang said.

The detective and the senator entered the foyer, where a temporary sheet had been placed over Jeannette Simmons. Evidence technicians who'd joined the flow of people into the house took still photographs, along with a video of the crime scene. Chang led Simmons on a wide path around them to the foot of the stairs. "Upstairs, sir?" he said.

"Yes."

Chang followed Simmons down a long hallway and into a huge master bedroom.

"I must ask you to not touch anything aside from the items you choose to take with you," Chang said.

"Yeah, sure," Simmons muttered. He opened one of many walk-in closet doors and turned on the light. As he stepped into it, Chang was two feet behind. "The suitcases are in here," said Simmons. Chang watched as Simmons chose a small leather carry-on case and matching leather hang-up bag. The senator turned and was face-to-face with the shorter, expressionless detective. "Excuse me."

Chang stepped back from the closet, allowing Simmons into the room. The senator moved to another closet, again followed by Chang, in which his suits were hung with precision on a long rack. He put one into the hang-up bag, added two ties from among hundreds on a battery-powered tie rack, and laid the bag on the bed.

"No, sir, not on the bed," Chang said. The detective picked up the bag and folded it over his arm.

"Don't you think you're taking your duties a little too far?" Simmons said.

Chang's response was, "Please, sir, finish what you are doing."

Simmons drew a deep breath of frustration, opened a dresser drawer, and removed items of clothing. "I need things from the bathroom," he said.

Chang preceded him into the immense master bath. Everything was white marble and ornate gold fixtures. Simmons filled a toiletries kit with what he needed. "Satisfied?" he asked. "I didn't touch anything except what I'm taking."

Chang said nothing as he stepped aside to allow Simmons to leave the bathroom and reenter the bedroom. "I will need a formal statement from you," Chang said. "You are going to the Willard Hotel?"

"That's right, but I'll tell you this. I'm in no shape to be giving you a statement, formal or otherwise. My wife has just been murdered, and I suggest you focus your investigation where it might do the most good. That doesn't include me."

Chang replied, "You said you were driven home by your driver. His name, please, and phone number." Before Simmons could respond, Chang added, "And names of those who were with you tonight at the fund-raiser you say you attended."

Simmons guffawed. "I can give you a hundred names," he said. "My driver is Walter McTeague." He rattled off McTeague's number so fast that the detective had to ask him to repeat it. "He's a former cop," Simmons added.

"Do you have everything?" Chang asked.

"I think so."

"Do you know anyone who might have wanted to kill your wife?"

"No. She was loved by everyone."

"Not everyone, sir."

THREE

By the time Phil Rotondi reached Washington, he'd learned what everyone else had learned about the death of Jeannette Simmons. The story led each newscast on his car radio. Details were sparse; rumors—"unconfirmed," or "according to reliable sources"—ran rampant. "Breaking news." On TV, breathless male and female anchors spoke. "The city was shaken tonight by the murder of . . ." "The police are treating the death of Jeannette Simmons as a homicide, according to information provided exclusively to this station . . ."

On one, dramatic music worthy of a DeMille epic preceded each report. "More on this developing story after these commercial messages."

Rotondi's left leg ached.

His mind ached, too.

He'd quickly packed a small overnight bag after Simmons's call. He let Homer, the fourteen-year-old mixed-breed dog—half German shepherd, half pit bull—whom he'd rescued as a pup from the streets, out into the fenced yard for a quick leg-lift, put the bag and the dog into the back of his Subaru Tribeca SUV, and was on his way within fifteen minutes. Packing to go to Washington was easy. He'd kept a portion of his wardrobe at Emma Churchill's Foggy Bottom town house for the past three years, adding to it on each visit; he now had more clothing there than in his condo on the Eastern Maryland shore.

He parked in front of Emma's town house and—stiffly—got out of the car. Although he'd made the trip in less than two hours, thanks to it being midweek and night, his skeleton had tightened up, especially his gimpy left leg. Opening the passenger's-side door, he pulled out his cane and bag, closed the door, and led Homer on his leash from the rear seat. Emma wouldn't be home, he knew. Her catering service had taken off in the past year, and she was out most nights overseeing her staff at multiple social or government functions, making sure the crab cakes were hot and the shrimp were cold, and reminding female servers to smile despite the hammy male paw on the rear end. Rotondi didn't know how Emma did it, being nice to guests who weren't—complainers with the taste buds of a mole, the D.C. posturing-and-maneuvering game in full sway night after night. He, Philip Rotondi, former Baltimore prosecutor with the bad leg, would have lasted just one evening, he knew, before wrapping his cane around someone's wattled neck, or over the head of a bastion of government or industry.

He opened the front door with his key and turned on lights—some were already on because of timers he'd purchased and installed. Let the bad guys think someone was home.

"Okay, buddy," he told Homer, who sat with his head cocked as though waiting for instructions. "Remember what I taught you about being a good houseguest. No barking, and no rummaging for food in the kitchen. Take a nap before Emma or I get back. *Capisce?*"

Homer whined, which Rotondi took as affirmation. After writing a note for Emma, he got back in his car and drove to Pennsylvania Avenue and Fourteenth Street, where he handed over the vehicle to a valet parker. He knew he wasn't dressed for the Willard—he'd left home wearing jeans, a maroon T-shirt, a blue chambray shirt, and deck shoes sans socks—but he'd decided that his presence was more important than his outfit.

"My name is Rotondi. Senator Lyle Simmons is staying here," he told a woman at the desk. "He's expecting me."

She'd obviously been well trained. Any doubt she had about him because of what he wore, and his five o'clock shadow, wasn't reflected on her pretty face. "One moment, please," she said with practiced pleasantness.

Rotondi grimaced against a shooting pain in his leg, and leaned against the counter to take some of his weight off it.

"Sir, the senator is staying here but hasn't arrived yet."

"Oh?"

"If you'd like to wait in the lobby, or in the bar, I'll see that you're paged when he arrives."

"Let's make it the bar."

Before entering the hotel's venerable Round Robin Bar, Rotondi called Simmons. No answer.

"A perfect Rob Roy," Rotondi told the bartender after taking a stool beneath a portrait of Calvin Coolidge, who'd lived at the Willard in 1923 while serving as Warren Harding's vice president. When Harding died in office, the hotel became the official presidential residence, and the official presidential flag flew from its rooftop until Mrs. Harding moved out of the White House.

The bartender placed his drink in front of him. Rotondi had no sooner picked it up for his first taste when a female staff member, pert and pleasant, entered the bar and asked for Mr. Rotondi.

"That's me."

She stepped close and said softly, "Sir, Senator Simmons has arrived and asks that you join him in his suite."

"Thanks."

"I'll have your drink sent up."

"Really? That'd be nice. Put it on the senator's bill."

He threw a tip down on the bar and followed the staffer. "We heard about the terrible thing that happened tonight," she said.

"Yeah."

"Are you—?"

"Just a friend. And slow down."

"I'm sorry," she said, now noticing his cane.

She escorted him up in the elevator to the suite, gave him a final look that said she was sympathetic, and left as Alan McBride answered his knock.

"Hello, Phil."

" 'Lo, Alan."

Rotondi followed McBride into the Willard's fifteen-hundred-square-foot Oval Suite. To his right was the elliptical-shaped parlor, its sunburst carpet inspired by design motifs in the White House.

"The senator is on the phone in the bedroom," McBride said. "I'll let him know you're here."

Rotondi stepped into the parlor and stood by large windows that afforded stunning views of the U.S. Capitol. McBride joined him. "He'll be out in a minute, Phil. Drink?"

"I have one being sent up, but thanks. I heard news reports on the way here. Anything new?"

McBride shook his head. He was shorter than Rotondi, and stockier, more a linebacker than a fleet wide receiver. His neck was thick, his features broad. Rotondi had always liked him, found him to be a straight-shooter with admirable loyalty to his boss that didn't preclude delivering bad news or contrary advice. He'd removed his jacket and tie; a tuft of reddish brown chest hair poked through the open neck.

"How's he holding up?" Rotondi asked, referring to the senator.

"Okay. He—"

Press Secretary Markowicz entered the room.

"Phil, this is Peter Markowicz," McBride said, "the senator's press secretary."

"Phil Rotondi," Markowicz said, shaking Rotondi's hand. "The senator talks about you a lot."

"We go back a little way," said Rotondi. He'd known Markowicz's predecessor but hadn't met this relatively new addition to the staff. "I suppose the press is all over this tonight."

"We thought we'd buy some time by coming here to the Willard," Markowicz said, "but they've tracked us down. The desk is holding all calls."

Simmons emerged from the bedroom wearing a hotel robe over shirt and pants. He crossed the parlor and gave Rotondi a quick embrace. "I am so glad you're here, Phil. So glad. Sorry to have disturbed your idyllic evening on the shore."

"You disturbed nothing, Lyle. Homer's not happy, though. He was watching his favorite show on Animal Planet."

"I owe him a dog treat."

A room-service employee delivered Rotondi's Rob Roy, along with an array of finger food ordered up by McBride and an assortment of liquor bottles.

"Is Neil here?" Rotondi asked.

"No," the senator said. "I told him to get home to his family. There's nothing he could do here."

Except to partner with his father in their grief, Rotondi thought.

"Have something to eat, Phil," Simmons said. "I have to return more calls, some of my Senate colleagues. But I do want to huddle with you later."

"I'm not going anywhere."

Rotondi watched TV along with McBride and Markowicz, who popped in and out of the parlor, leaving Rotondi to bring them up to date on what they'd missed. It was no surprise that the murder of Jeannette Simmons dominated every newscast, the competing stations pulling in anyone with even a tangential connection to Simmons for interviews and comments. A TV crew was camped outside Neil Simmons's home in Bethesda, as well as maintaining a vigil at the senator's house. The MPD issued a nonstatement: "We have no comment at this time." File photos and footage of Simmons with his wife, and some with his son and daughter, flooded the screen. Seeing

Jeannette's face caused Rotondi discomfort. At times, he looked away from the screen. Other times, he swallowed against a lump in his throat that seemed permanently lodged there. He kept adjusting his position in a chair to try to mitigate the pain in his leg, and massaged his thigh.

It was almost an hour later that the senator emerged from the bedroom and sat in a chair next to Rotondi.

"Have the police interviewed you, Lyle?" Rotondi asked.

"I suppose you could call it an interview. Some Asian American detective showed up and asked about my activities tonight. I don't think he knew what he was doing, Phil. Christ, I hope they put some better people on the case."

"I'll check in with friends over there," Rotondi said.

"Good. I suppose murder isn't as shocking to you as it is to me."

"Murder is always shocking," Rotondi replied, "especially when it's someone you know and love. Had Jeannette had any conflicts with anyone lately? A workman at the house? Someone in town? Had she mentioned anyone she'd had a run-in with?"

Simmons shook his head.

"What about you, Lyle? Any death threats lately?"

"No. There's always some nut who writes and says he'll kill me because of a vote I cast, or a speech I made taking a stand on a contentious issue. Nothing out of the ordinary."

"What about her sister?"

"Marlene? As crazy as ever."

"Even with the medication?"

"Not when she remembers to take it."

The latest report about the murder came on the screen: "According to sources within the MPD, an autopsy is being performed on Jeannette Simmons, wife of Senator Lyle Simmons, as we speak."

"Couldn't they wait?" Simmons said under his breath.

Rotondi said nothing. He was thinking of countless autopsies he'd attended while a prosecutor in Baltimore, and the vision of Jeannette's lovely body being unzipped from head to torso was grotesque:

all blood drained from her; organs examined one by one, weighed, and bagged; muscles severed in order to reach less accessible parts; nails clipped to see whether material from her assailant was on them; tissue samples snipped from a dozen places; stomach contents saved to be analyzed; and myriad other violations of her dignity, albeit necessary in the pursuit of justice.

He popped a Tum in his mouth.

Markowicz walked over. "Senator," he said, "I've had some calls asking about your schedule tomorrow. I assume—"

"I'll want to go to the house first, assuming that officious detective has finished his so-called investigation. If he hasn't, I'll make the staffing meeting and go to the house later. Call Walter and tell him to pick me up here at six. Find out when I can get in the house. Put out a written statement saying something like I intend to carry on the business of the American people in the midst of this tragedy—Jeannette would have wanted that—I hope her killer is brought to justice soon— maybe, or, I don't know, Peter, say that I'm cooperating with the authorities every step of the way, that I appreciate all the support and love I've been receiving and—"

McBride joined the conversation. He leaned close to Simmons and said just loud enough for Markowicz and Rotondi to hear, "Neil just called, Senator. Polly heard it on the news and called him. Maybe you should—"

"Call Neil and tell him to coordinate things with his sister. She'll want to get here, I'm sure. I'll pay any expenses."

Rotondi had sat silently during the exchange. Now he stood, grabbed his cane from where he'd hooked it over the arm of his chair, and limped to the window.

"That leg's really bothering you, isn't it?" the senator said.

"Sometimes worse than others."

"Let's go in the bedroom, Phil. We have some talking to do."

Simmons leaned back against the king-size bed's ornate headboard. Rotondi took a small club chair he pulled out from a French cherry desk.

"Why do I get the feeling that you're judging me, Phil?"

"Paranoia, probably. I don't judge anybody these days. I did plenty of judging people when I was putting away Baltimore's garbage, but that was then. Still . . ."

"Still what?"

Rotondi shrugged and smiled. "I think you ought to pull Neil and Polly in closer, Lyle, especially at a time like this. You need them."

Simmons chewed his cheek. His expression was unfriendly.

"The situation with Polly really tore Jeannette up," Rotondi said.

"I don't need to be told that, Phil. I heard it damn near every day for the past four years."

"Yeah, I know. Not my *problemo*. Look, I'm here to help in any way I can. I won't get in the way, but tell me what you need and I'll do it."

Simmons's face softened. He gave forth a small smile. "I'm sorry about Homer's TV show," he said.

"Maybe he taped it before we left." Rotondi came forward and leaned with both hands on the cane. "Mind a suggestion?"

"My driver, Walter, gave me one when he dropped me home tonight."

"McTeague? Good man. You have a lot of good people around you."

"Maybe Walter had a premonition. He said Jeannette and I should get away for a while, we both looked tired. If only."

"My suggestion is that you go with the flow of this tragedy, Lyle, and stop playing United States senator, at least until the right people get their arms around it. The so-called business of the people can wait."

"Easy for you to say. You're retired."

"Happily so, but that's irrelevant. I—" His cell phone rang. "Sorry." Simmons got off the bed and walked out of the room.

"Hi."

"Phil, I just heard," Emma Churchill said. "Jeannette Simmons? Good God."

"I'm with him now, at the Willard. Where are you?"

"Supervising the cleanup. I should be home in an hour."

"Homer's at your house. I swung by there on my way here."

"You'll stay with him at the hotel?"

"No. I'll meet you at the house. Frankly, I'm not sure why I'm here. He's in command—insufferably so."

"He needs your friendship."

"He needs more than that. What was the party?"

"A going-away bash for someone from Homeland Security."

"I hope you made them take off their shoes before entering."

He heard an exasperated sigh, coupled with an abbreviated laugh. "I'll see you later," she said.

FOUR

Rotondi had been awake for an hour but opted to stay in bed, enjoying his painless repose. The moment he placed his feet on the floor, the pain would stab his leg and stay with him throughout the day.

Emma slept sweetly next to him, on her side, facing away, one foot jutting out from beneath the rose-colored cover. Homer had co-opted a position at the foot of the bed, muscles twitching from a dream. Chasing cats? Being chased by a bigger dog? A lifetime supply of steak bones? A perpetual belly rub? Such simple pleasures.

Emma's body blocked Rotondi's view of the clock radio, but he knew it was early morning from the color of the outside light.

Rotondi's thoughts continued to be dreamlike, and apropos of nothing: contrails high in the sky—did only military jets fly high enough to create them?—chocolate-covered cherries; an egg frying on a D.C. sidewalk in its current heat wave; a cemetery where all the buried sat up, stretched, yawned, and sang "Oh, What a Beautiful

Morning"; a ten-foot-tall judge in black robes smashing Rotondi's hand with his gavel when he placed it on the bench; and occasionally more mundane matters such as wondering when Homer would wake up and have to be walked. He'd been trying to get Emma to fence in her postage-stamp-size backyard to no avail.

Homer stirred, lifted his head, looked at Rotondi, and flopped down again. Emma stirred, turned, and flung a leg over her lover.

"You awake?" he asked.

"No."

"Sorry."

Her movement had caused the cover to slide mostly off, revealing her in the oversize pale blue man's shirt she routinely wore to bed. Despite spending her waking hours preparing and serving food, Emma Churchill's figure didn't reflect that vocation. Not that she was the anorexic model type. Far from it. She packed a solid 145 pounds on her five-foot, seven-inch-tall body, her alabaster skin smooth and firm. A date had once asked whether she was a lesbian, citing coal-black hair that she wore extremely short and her dislike of makeup beyond absolute basic necessities. "Maybe we could do a threesome some day," he'd suggested, leering. It was their first and final date: "He was lucky I didn't deck him on the spot," she told Rotondi when recounting the story. "*Schmuck!*"

Emma and Rotondi had stayed up for hours last night after they'd arrived separately at her house, watching the news and providing their own commentary and analysis during breaks. Of course, aside from the murder itself, Rotondi had much more to discuss than the TV talking heads, who speculated on everything and knew little. He and Senator Lyle Simmons went back a long way together, a very long way. They'd been college roommates at the University of Illinois since their freshman year, inseparable friends despite a few incidents, one in particular that would have undoubtedly shredded other friendships.

He swung his legs off the bed and stood, giving out a customary groan as his left leg protested. He ignored the cane on the floor next to his side of the bed and limped into the bathroom, where he placed both hands on the sink and lowered his head, moving it in circles until he was ready to face the mirror.

"Good morning," he said to his reflection, not expecting a response. He wasn't *that* crazy. He stepped back and took a longer-range view of himself. Above his boxer shorts was a lean torso with plenty of dark chest hair. That he hadn't put on weight was more a matter of genes, he knew, than lifestyle, although he did work out regularly. His bad leg had put an end to his running routine, which he missed. He'd been recruited to the U of Illinois on a basketball scholarship—second-team All Big Ten his senior year—and had been a miler on the track team. After the damage to his leg, he'd had to content himself with weight-bearing exercises that toned the muscles in his arms and shoulders, along with painful, terribly dull trips on a stationary bike.

Below the shorts were legs slightly bowed. He yanked up one side of the shorts to reveal the wicked, eighteen-inch scar from groin to knee where the surgeons had done their best, cutting through muscle, tissue, and bone in an attempt to salvage what was left of the leg, and to avoid having to sever it from the rest of Philip Rotondi. They'd succeeded, for which he was grateful. His mind wandered, as it had while in bed, but the moment Kathleen's face joined the dozens of other conjured images, he turned it off as suddenly and easily as turning off an appliance, splashed water on his chiseled face, and returned to the bedroom, where Emma sat in front of a small television set to catch yet another report on the murder. Rotondi threw on some clothes, snapped on Homer's leash, and took the dog out for his daily ablutions. Back in the bedroom, he again stripped down to his shorts, slipped into a robe he kept at the house, and joined Emma.

"Anything new and exciting?" he asked. "Or true?"

"The police are still conducting their investigation at the senator's house. He evidently wanted to return there this morning but couldn't. They had a video of him entering his Senate office building. No comment from him, of course." She turned off the set with the remote. "Will you be seeing him today?"

"I'm sure I will. I told him I'd check in with friends at MPD to see how the investigation is *really* going. Lyle isn't impressed with the detective who arrived on the scene. There's not much else I can do for him."

"He needs a friend."

Rotondi nodded. "I wish I could intervene with Polly. He's always chalked up the problems between them to their political differences, Polly the raving left-wing liberal, her father, the U.S. senator, the calculating centrist. I've never bought it. You don't sever ties with a daughter just because she sees things different politically."

"Some would, Phil. Besides, she's been a vocal opponent of virtually everything he stands for. It's one thing to disagree with your father's political views, another to attack him in the press at every turn. You've said it yourself, how some of these liberal causes have taken advantage of her, put her out there whenever they wanted to make a point about an issue championed by her father."

Rotondi grunted and looked out the window into the haze of another hot one in Washington. "Maybe the funeral will salve things between them. Funerals sometimes accomplish that. I know that Jeannette would be pleased if that happened."

"What about the funeral?" Emma said.

"I don't know. I suppose they'll announce plans today. I'd better get moving." He started for the bathroom but turned. "As long as I'm in D.C., I'd like to catch up with Mac and Annabel Smith."

Mac Smith had been a top criminal defense lawyer in D.C. and Maryland for years, until on a rainy night years ago his wife and son were slaughtered on the Beltway by a drunk driver. The personal loss was, of course, devastating. But when a skilled fellow defense lawyer had managed to plea-bargain the drunk driver's case down to what Smith considered an insultingly small sentence—a slap on the wrist, and not a very hard slap at that—he'd lost his zeal for trial work, left the firm he'd established, and accepted a teaching position at George Washington University's law school.

His wife, Annabel Lee-Smith, had experienced a similar epiphany, although without the accompanying personal tragedy. She'd been a respected Washington matrimonial attorney with a thriving practice. But years of mediating between warring spouses, many of whom were willing to destroy their lives and those of their children in order to "be right," had taken a toll. She'd always loved art, especially pre-Columbian art, and dreamed of opening a gallery. She hadn't acted upon that dream until meeting Mac Smith and falling in love with the handsome, brilliant widower. He encouraged her to retire her lawyer's shingle and to follow her true passion. Together they found charming space in Georgetown where Annabel opened her gallery. The fulfillment of that ambition was closely followed by another, the marriage of Annabel Lee to Mackensie Smith. Life couldn't get any better for either of them.

Rotondi had butted heads with Mac in Baltimore courtrooms where he'd prosecuted cases, Smith defending the accused. Their courtroom confrontations were spirited, skillfully conducted, and often heated. But they'd simultaneously developed a personal friendship that transcended these professional bouts, and had nurtured that friendship to this day.

"I stopped in Annabel's gallery the other day," Emma said. "I'm catering an affair at the Mexican embassy and needed some advice on decorations."

"I'll set up a dinner."

"Great, only check my schedule. It's a busy month."

❧

As Rotondi got himself ready to leave Emma's home, Neil Simmons was in the midst of a domestic tornado. He hadn't slept all night. Both phone lines had rung nonstop and continued into the morning. His wife, Alexandra, had pleaded with him to turn off the ringers, but he was afraid he'd miss an important call from his father, or from someone else not associated with the media. Now showered and dressed, he sat with Alexandra in their kitchen.

Their two sons, ages nine and six, were excited about the large press encampment outside their front windows and repeatedly parted the drapes to peek, provoking an exasperated father to send them to their rooms.

Alexandra tended to be high-strung even when surrounded by calm, and chastised Neil for being so harsh with the children. He, in turn, reminded her that his mother had just been brutally slain, and that she should show some compassion.

"Maybe you should show some compassion for your own family." She was approaching the screaming threshold. "You're always so damn understanding of everybody else."

The muscles in his jaw gave away the anger he felt, but he avoided responding. Instead, he said, "I have to call McTeague about picking up Polly at the airport. He'll bring her directly here."

"Why here?"

"Please, Alex, let's not start on—"

"She's staying *here*? With *us*?"

"That's right."

"Put her in a hotel, for God's sake. It's a circus here already. She'll—"

"She wants to stay here."

"So tell her it would be better if she stayed in a hotel."

Polly Simmons and Alexandra Simmons had never been loving sisters-in-law.

"You're putting me in the middle again, Alex," Neil whined.

The nine-year-old snuck down the stairs and pulled aside a drape.

"Damn it!" Neil exploded. "I told you to—"

Alexandra rushed to the crying boy, wrapped her arms about him, and said everything was fine and that everything would soon be normal again and that Daddy didn't mean what he said and . . .

Neil picked up the ringing phone and shouted, "Hello?"

"Neil. It's Rick. I've been calling half the night."

"I'm avoiding the press. I don't know why I picked up this time."

"I'm sorry, man. About your mom."

"Yeah, thanks."

"That's all anybody's talking about. It's all over the news."

"I know. Jesus, do I know."

"I talked to Karl this morning. We're going to put up a reward for finding your mom's killer. We'll do it through CMJ." *CMJ* stood for "Center for American Justice," one of many front organizations controlled by the Marshalk Group, a leading Washington lobbying firm. The caller, Rick Marshalk, was the founder and force behind the firm despite Neil Simmons's title of president.

"Okay," Neil said.

"Can you get in here today?"

"I don't see how I can, Rick. I—"

"Look, buddy, no need to explain. It's just that we've got to put the finishing touches on the proposal for Betzcon. I'll call and tell them you won't be with us at the presentation. They'll understand. I mean, with what's happened to your mom and all. Hell, they'd better understand. This one's big, pal. I know you're under the gun, but if you could get in here for even an hour this afternoon, we could—"

Alexandra called for Neil from upstairs. "I'm on the phone with Rick," he shouted.

"Neil?"

"Yeah, sorry. I'll call you later."

"I'll be waiting, *ciao*! And I am really sorry about your mom, Neil. We're all in shock."

He next called the Hotel George, a small, chic hotel where he had a close friend in management. "Harry, it's Neil Simmons . . . yes, I know . . . thank you . . . it's devastated all of us . . . my dad? . . . holding up as well as can be expected . . . my sister, Polly, is flying in today from California, I need a quiet suite for her . . . sure, that would be fine . . . let's keep it under wraps, okay? She doesn't need a bunch of reporters camping out there . . . oh, right, you don't need that, either . . . thanks, Harry, I really appreciate this."

He dialed McTeague's cell. "We're doing okay, Walter," he said in response to the question. "Look, there's been a change of plan. Polly's not coming here to the house. I've got her a suite at the Hotel George on Fifteenth Street, Northwest. Take her there. She'll probably complain, but ignore her. Tell her I'll explain when I see her. I'd call now but she's in the air. Thanks, Walter."

He considered telling Alexandra that she wouldn't have to play hostess to Polly after all, but decided not to. *Let her stew.* He also didn't bother to tell her he was leaving. He didn't need another rant on his way out the door.

The press had been quiet as they maintained their stakeout. At the sight of him exiting the house, they sprang into action, shouting questions, cameramen and still photographers scrambling to get their equipment into place and rolling. He waved them off with a forced smile, clicked open the overhead garage door, climbed into his red Lexus, and carefully backed out to the street, mindful that to run over a member of the Fourth Estate would be efficient but not prudent. One female reporter screamed at him through the window, her face distorted with anger at his refusal to engage her. He managed another smile, thought of Alexandra, and pulled away, tempted to extend his middle finger but thinking better of it. *That's all Dad needs,* he thought, *a front-page picture in* The Washington Post *of his son, president of a leading lobbying firm, flipping the bird at a female reporter just hours after his mother's murder.*

As a young child, he'd been infatuated with the big, strong, sweaty men who picked up the family's garbage each week, and aspired to one day join their ranks.

Maybe I should have, he thought as he headed for the highway leading to downtown D.C.

FIVE

"Well, well, well, look who's here. The crusading prosecutor."

Morris Crimley, chief of the Washington MPD's detective division, looked up as Rotondi entered his cluttered office. During his years as an assistant U.S. attorney in Baltimore, Rotondi had served with Crimley on committees looking into crime prevention, and they'd forged a friendship outside those confabs, becoming fierce racquetball opponents and equally committed handball competitors. The physical aspect of their relationship ended, of course, after Rotondi's injury.

"Hello, Morrie," Rotondi said. "I'm still crusading, only now it's against irresponsible dog owners who don't pick up after their pooches." There was no hypocrisy involved in the comment. He'd picked up after Homer that morning. "Mind if I push stuff off a chair and sit down, or will that foul up your filing system?"

"I never argue with a man with a cane. Push away. How's the leg?"

"Lousy." Rotondi picked up a pile of file folders from a chair, plopped them on top of another pile on another chair, removed his blazer and added that to the mound, and sat. Although he knew he didn't have to wear a jacket and tie, he usually did when visiting Simmons's office, which he intended to do after leaving police headquarters. When in Rome . . .

"I hear there's a crime wave in D.C.," Rotondi said.

"It's the heat, Phil. The crime rate always goes up along with the temperature. Hell, you know that. "

"Simple solution. AC the city."

"I'll pass that along. You're here because your friend the senator is suddenly a widower."

Rotondi nodded. "Any progress?" he asked.

"Sure. That's for public consumption. For you, not much, but it's only been twelve hours for Christ's sake. Half the department is assigned to the case. Once the bad guys figure that out, the crime rate will go up even higher."

Rotondi's cocked head and raised eyebrows said he wanted to hear more.

"That's it, Phil," Crimley said. "We're working the case hard, all stops pulled out."

"Suspects?"

"Sure. This stays here?"

"If you want."

"I want."

"The senator says he doesn't like the detective who showed up the night of the murder," Rotondi said. "Chan?"

Crimley rolled his eyes up into his head. "It's Chang, Phil. Charlie Chang. He gets testy when anybody calls him Charlie Chan."

"His mother should have thought of that when she named him. He's lead on the case?"

"A lead. He's good, goes by the book, loves details. I wish more of my guys did. The problem with Charlie is that nobody wants to partner with him. The friendly gene wasn't available when he was born."

"What's he say about the murder?"

A shrug. "He finds it strange that the senator was dressed like he was ready to give a state-of-the-union address. He had given a talk that night, but no sign that he got down on his knees and wrinkled his pants to see whether the missus was dead. No blood, either."

"Lyle Simmons is a prissy sort of guy when it comes to his clothes."

"Even when your wife has her head bashed in? You know them both, Phil. How'd they get along, the senator and Mrs. Simmons?"

"Fine, considering their marriage was high-profile. Plenty of stress."

"I hear she wasn't much involved with his political career."

"Jeannette hated politics, hated politicians."

"Including her husband?"

Rotondi's shaking of his head wasn't convincing. He winced against a stabbing pain in his leg, shifted position, and asked, casually, "Is Senator Simmons a suspect?"

Crimley, a barrel of a man with a shaved head and wearing trademark, vividly colored suspenders, laughed. "He's the spouse, Phil. Always the first suspect. SOP."

"He was giving a speech in front of hundreds of people when it happened."

"He's always calling for a lowering of the unemployment level." Another laugh. "Maybe he hired somebody."

"Come on, Morrie. This has all the trappings of a stranger breaking in, or being invited in and killing her. No sign of a robbery?"

"No. Nothing missing as far as we can tell. No forced entry. We've got a couple of the types you're talking about. A handyman was working around the house yesterday, and there're a couple of local whack jobs we're looking at. Remember, Phil, what I say stays here."

"Sure. No alarm?"

"Turned off. At least that's what the senator says. According to him, his wife didn't bother activating it most of the time." Crimley came forward in his chair and pointed an index finger. "You working with the senator on this, Phil?"

"Working?"

"Poking your nose into it? Trying to take the heat off him? You're his best buddy."

"That's right. I don't know about best, but we are friends. That's why I'm here."

"What's he like, Phil? I mean, *really* like?"

"He's a—"

"Think he'll run for president?"

Rotondi laughed. "I feel like I'm on *Meet the Press*. I don't know whether he'll run, Morrie. If he does, I'll—"

"Think he killed his wife?"

Rotondi exhaled loudly and grabbed his cane from where he'd hung it on the chair's arm. "Do me a favor, Morrie."

"Sure."

"Keep me in the loop. Unofficially. I'd appreciate it."

"To the extent that I can."

"Can't ask for more than that. Thanks for letting me barge in. You can reach me at Emma's house. You have her number."

"Washington's Julia Child. How is she?"

"She's fine, Morrie, just fine."

Crimley got up and came around the desk. "Can't they do anything for that leg of yours?"

"They did all they could, Morrie. I'm lucky I still have it. Stay in touch."

A cluster of media that had begun to mill about outside police headquarters on Indiana Avenue when Rotondi arrived had swelled in size. They eyed him in the hope he might have something to offer about the Simmons murder, but decided he wasn't worthy of pursuit—until a female reporter called his name. Rotondi turned to see a familiar face closing the gap.

"Philip Rotondi," she said. "Remember me? Sue Carnowski from *The Baltimore Sun*."

"Oh, sure. How've you been?"

"Great! I'm with the *Post* now. You're retired, right?"

"Right. Good seeing you, I—"

"You and Senator Simmons are friends. Right?"

"A long time ago."

She narrowed her eyes, an all-knowing look. *Don't kid a kidder.* "Come on, level with me, Mr. Rotondi. What do you know about what happened last night? The murder."

Rotondi forced a smile. "Congratulations on your new job, Sue. The *Post's* gain, the *Sun's* loss. See ya."

She followed him to the curb and remained at his side while he looked for a taxi.

"You just happen to be in D.C. the day after the senator's wife is killed?" she asked in a voice that said she would accept only the reply she wanted to hear.

"That's right," Rotondi said, spotting a vacant cab and waving his cane at the driver.

"Have you spoken with the senator since last night?" she asked.

The turbaned driver pulled up, and Rotondi opened the rear door.

"How can I reach you?" the reporter asked as Rotondi disappeared into the cab.

"The Retired Prosecutors' Home in Florida," he yelled before closing the door.

"The *what?*" she mouthed without sound reaching him.

He grinned, blew her a kiss, and said to the driver, "The Dirksen Senate Office Building on First and C."

Another contingent of press was camped outside the Dirksen building when Rotondi arrived. Hopefully, it didn't include a reporter who remembered him from his Baltimore days. He nestled into a sheltered area formed by the building's façade and called Mac and Annabel Smith's number at their Watergate condo complex. Annabel answered.

"Phil Rotondi."

"Hello, Phil. I was just thinking about you. Emma stopped into the gallery and—"

"She told me."

"And, of course, because of the dreadful thing that happened to Jeannette Simmons. Are you in town because of it?"

"Afraid so. I thought we might find some time to get together. I don't know your dinner plans this week, but—"

"Free tonight?"

"As a matter of fact, we are. I checked Emma's calendar this morning. She's okay for tonight but tied up for the next four days."

"Perfect, if you don't mind a crowd. We're having friends in for dinner tonight. You'll like them. Ironically, he works for the Marshalk Group, the lobbying firm where Neil Simmons is president. I thought they might have to cancel because of what's happened, but they confirmed just a few minutes ago. Love to have you and Emma join us."

"Count us in. How's Mac?"

"Good. He's off playing tennis. I didn't want him to because of this heat, but he tends to be—how shall I say it?—he tends to be stubborn about some things."

"Glad he hasn't changed."

"So am I. Seven?"

"On the dot."

A quick call caught Emma as she was about to leave the house. Rotondi told her of the evening's plans.

"Great," she said.

"Give Homer a fast walk before you leave, huh? I'll be home by six."

He clicked off and thought of what he'd said—that he'd be "home" by six. *Home away from home. Her home. His home was on the Maryland shore.* Thoughts about *their* home were off-limits. They'd agreed soon after deciding they liked each other enough to share a bed that the subject of marriage was never to be mentioned, under threat of decapitation. They'd each been married once before. Rotondi's wife was dead. Emma's ex-husband was very much alive and living in New York, although there were times when the thought of attending his funeral was not unappealing.

A uniformed security guard in the lobby of the Dirksen building called Senator Simmons's office and was told to send the visitor up. Rotondi passed through a metal detector and rode the elevator to Simmons's floor. He entered the outer office and encountered a receptionist who'd been with the senator for as long as Rotondi could remember. Because of his seniority, Simmons had one of the largest and more attractive office suites in the building. It was a beehive of activity that morning, and the receptionist greeted him with a nod of the head while juggling multiple phone lines. Rotondi smiled and took a chair. When the receptionist caught a break, she said, "Hi, Mr. Rotondi. Sorry."

"I expected to see that phone catch fire in your hand," he said.

There was an eruption of rings again. "The senator's in a meeting. He should be back in a few minutes," she said. "Urrggh! The press! I'm canceling my *Post* subscription and cable TV."

Rotondi watched as she went back to handling calls. A succession of people, primarily young, passed through the outer office, moving with conviction and purpose. He'd always been interested in the allure of working for a member of Congress or other government bigwig. Rubbing shoulders on a daily basis with Washington's power brokers was obviously an aphrodisiac to the many young men and women who flocked to Washington in search of reflected importance. Rotondi had known plenty of them during his career, and decided early on that he preferred orgasms of the old-fashioned variety. His disdain for politics hadn't helped him advance in the Baltimore prosecutor's office, and he didn't care. His passion was going head-to-head with the best defense lawyers in the area, and successfully putting most bad guys behind bars. Philip Rotondi's conviction rate was the highest in the history of the Violent Crimes Section of the Baltimore U.S. attorney's office.

He picked up that day's copy of *Roll Call*, the publication covering congressional news—Monday through Thursday when Congress was in session, Monday only otherwise—and was into an article on the backstage machinations behind a contentious bit of legislation when Simmons burst through the door, followed by Press Secretary Markowicz, Chief of Staff Alan McBride, and three other staffers. Simmons stopped and said to Rotondi, "Philip, good to see you. Give me ten minutes. We need to talk."

Ten minutes later, Rotondi had finished the article he was reading. Simmons's personal secretary opened the door to his private office and motioned for Rotondi to come in. Simmons was in shirtsleeves and on the phone, his feet up on his immense, custom-crafted teak desk. The walls were filled with autographed photographs of him with a Who's Who of political heavyweights, top business leaders, and Hollywood, sports, and television celebrities. He motioned for Rotondi to sit, and ended the conversation he was having with "I'll be damned if I'll let that amendment sneak its way into the bill. Got that? Good!" He slammed down the receiver, withdrew his feet from the desk, and asked his secretary to leave. When she had, he asked, "What do you hear, Phil?"

"Nothing you haven't heard, Lyle. The investigation is barely twelve hours old. I stopped in to see my friend Morrie Crimley at MPD. He says the detective you mentioned, Charlie Chang, is good, a real stickler for details."

"I want him off the case."

"That's not your call."

"Don't count on it. I want back in my house. They tell me maybe this afternoon."

"That'd be good. Are funeral plans under way?"

"I suppose so. I'm leaving that up to McBride and Neil. Polly's due in today. I wanted her to stay with Neil, but he's got her at the Hotel George. I suppose that wife of his put the kibosh on Polly staying there. I never will understand what Neil saw in her."

Rotondi suppressed a smile. This was vintage Lyle Simmons, blustery in one situation, buttery smooth and conciliatory in others. It often occurred to Rotondi that he should be flattered that one of the Senate's most powerful members, and a potential future president, would be so open and candid with him, a mark of how close they were. But each time that notion crossed his mind, he reminded himself of Jonathan Swift's characterization of flattery, terming it "the food of fools." That his former college roommate was now a national leader meant nothing to him. They were friends, that was all, two men with wildly different views of most things, but with a bond born of time and shared experiences.

And there was Jeannette.

"Look, Phil, I've got my hands full with Senate business." Simmons sensed that Rotondi was about to comment, and quickly added, "I know what you're about to say, Phil, that this isn't the time for me to worry about things on Capitol Hill. But when *is* there a good time to put everything else aside and focus on grieving? You knew Jeannette. She was a no-nonsense lady who would have wanted us to forge ahead with our lives."

"What do you want me to do, Lyle?"

"Keep Polly on an even keel while she's here. I don't need her using Jeannette's death as a platform for one of her causes. Stay close to her and—"

Press Secretary Markowicz knocked, entered, and handed Simmons a sheet of paper. Simmons read it and handed it back. "Sounds fine, Pete.

"A statement from me thanking everyone who's shown kindness and understanding," Simmons told Rotondi, as though seeking approval.

"You say Polly's staying at the George. What time does she get in?"

"Plane lands at Dulles a little after eleven. She always liked you, Phil. I think she'll listen to you."

"All right," Rotondi said. "I'll head over to the hotel when I leave here."

Simmons walked him to the door, his arm over Rotondi's shoulder. "I need you, pal. I need someone around who I can trust." He looked down at Rotondi's cane. "You think about that night a lot, Phil?"

"Hard not to, Lyle. Nature has a way of reminding me. If I didn't say it last night, I'm sorry about your loss."

Simmons grimaced. "*My loss.* There are so damn many euphemisms for death and dying. But thanks. I know I'll get through this."

As Simmons opened the door and Rotondi stepped into the reception area, Neil Simmons arrived, accompanied by two well-dressed men, one white, one black. Neil greeted Rotondi.

"I'm just leaving," Rotondi said. "I'm going to the George to be there when Polly arrives." He looked back at the closed door to the senator's office. "Your father asked me to."

The younger Simmons nodded grimly. "Makes sense. I won't have any time, with funeral arrangements and all. The police want me to come in for questioning. I told that detective everything I knew last night, but they want more." He, too, checked his father's office door before saying, "Has he mentioned anything about Aunt Marlene?"

"No," Rotondi answered, not wanting to repeat what the senator had said last night about Marlene being crazy. He looked over at the African American, who'd stepped away to let them have a private conversation. "Jonell Marbury," Neil said. "I work with him at Marshalk."

Annabel Smith had mentioned that one of the dinner guests that evening was a Marshalk employee. One and the same? Probably not. The Marshalk Group, Rotondi knew, was one of D.C.'s largest lobbying organizations, with more than a hundred lobbyists and support staff.

"I'll call you after I hook up with Polly, Neil."

"Okay. I'm sure Dad appreciates everything you're doing, Phil. Just having you here is a great comfort to him."

Rotondi had never stayed at the Hotel George before, although he knew people who had and who were universal in their praise. He and Emma had eaten at Bistro Bis, the hotel's restaurant adjacent to the main building, and had enjoyed their visits. This morning, he entered the ultramodern entrance and paused in the lobby to allow the air-conditioning to wash over him. Dominating the space was a colorful Steve Kaufman portrait of George Washington, more a colorful collage against a blow-up background of a dollar bill. That Kaufman was a protégé of Andy Warhol surprised no one. At least it wasn't a soup can, Rotondi mused. He took a comfortable chair and picked up that day's paper. Looking back at him from the front page's lead story was a photograph of Lyle and Jeannette Simmons. Rotondi knew that photo only too well. He'd taken it.

Rotondi and his wife, Kathleen, had spent a long weekend with Lyle and Jeannette at a Delaware beach resort. The sight of them smiling as though at peace with themselves and the world caused their friend to close his eyes against what threatened to be tears, and to open them only after the threat had passed. Two additional photos accompanied the piece: one of the Simmons home cordoned off and draped with crime scene tape, another a more recent shot of the senator giving a speech sometime, somewhere. Rotondi read:

> Jeannette Simmons, wife of Senator Lyle Simmons, a potential presidential candidate, has been murdered . . . an anonymous source at MPD said that she was killed with a blunt instrument, a blow to the back of the head . . . her body was discovered by her husband when he returned from a speaking engagement . . . there are no suspects at this time, although the police are speaking with "persons of interest" . . . funeral plans have not been announced . . .

The article jumped inside the paper to chronicle Senator Simmons's career and point out that the couple had two grown children: Neil, president of the Marshalk Group; and Polly, a peace activist living in California.

He returned to the front page and gazed at the photo of Lyle and Jeannette, which triggered thoughts of another time and place.

❧

It was 1970, his senior year at the University of Illinois. Homecoming Weekend was in full swing. The football team had defeated Michigan State, a cause for celebrations on the Urbana-Champaign campus and in student hangouts in town. He had a second reason to celebrate. Earlier that week, he'd been named All Big Ten, second team. He'd called his father with the news.

"That's good, Philip, very good," his father said in his Italian-tinged English, "but remember, your studies are the most important thing."

Phil smiled at his father's admonition. Their conversations always ended with those words.

His father had come to America from Milan and set up a shoe repair shop in his adopted town, Batavia, New York, outside Buffalo. The shop generated enough money to support the family—two sons and two daughters—but left little for anything other than necessities. Phil and his siblings appreciated their father's hard work and helped out in the store whenever possible, pitching in with household chores. Unlike the father, their mother resisted assimilating into her new culture. She'd learned little English and kept to herself, limiting her social life to the small Italian American community that had sprung up in Batavia. She was a stern woman who ran the household with precision and an iron hand; the kids said—muttered, really—that she'd taught Mussolini how to keep the trains running on time. She always seemed to be cooking; memories of growing up in that modest home invariably included the smell of simmering tomato sauce and baking bread.

Philip was twelve when his mother died of a burst aneurysm, a congenital defect according to the doctor at the hospital. Philip's father, never a gregarious man except after consuming too much cheap wine, went into even more of a shell, spending virtually all his waking moments at the shop. Philip's two older sisters took over most of the household duties with help from their brothers. It was a difficult, challenging time, but the Rotondi children faced it head-on and made it work.

College was out of the question unless scholarships and student-aid packages were involved. The oldest sister felt it was her obligation to help support the family and took a job following graduation as a secretary in an accounting firm. She eventually married a boy she'd dated in high school who worked in his father's insurance agency. They'd had two sons and appeared happy.

The middle sister, only a year younger than the eldest, enrolled in a community college, supporting herself as a waitress. She excelled in school, and prior to graduating was offered a full scholarship to a New York State university. After a stellar career in college, she went on to law school and was now a corporate attorney in Cleveland.

Philip's brother, two years younger, floundered during and after high school, to everyone's disappointment, and ended up drifting through a succession of menial jobs. He eventually moved to Los Angeles, where he thought he might find work as an actor. The last Phil heard, he'd ended up in Las Vegas managing a pawnshop. Married and divorced three times, he'd virtually severed all relations with his family. Out of guilt or embarrassment? Phil and his sisters didn't know the answer, nor did they try very hard to come up with one.

It was no secret among the children that the father favored Phil, and viewed him as the bright and shining light that would make worthwhile all his years bent over stitching machines and rubbing polish into other people's shoes. His favoritism didn't cause resentment among the kids. They understood that their father was from the Old World where men succeeded in business, and women married and had babies. Phil was an outstanding high school student, both academically and athletically. He was energetically recruited in his senior year by a number of top colleges and universities, and chose the University of Illinois, whose aid package covered virtually everything apart from spending money. His father had never seen his son play basketball or run track in high school; nor did he ever venture west to see him at the university. After many attempts to coax the man to Urbana-Champaign, Phil gave up. He thought he knew why the old man wouldn't come. He was embarrassed at what he'd become, stooped, bald, his hands grotesquely swollen with arthritis, his breathing labored and voice hoarse from years of smoking. And so Phil contented himself with a weekly phone call to bring his father up to date—to make him proud.

This day in 1970, a Saturday, he sat drinking beer at a favorite student watering hole with his roommate. Earlier, he and Lyle had been to a party at their fraternity, Kappa Phi Kappa, and had driven to the bar in Simmons's new, fire-engine-red Ford Thunderbird. Rotondi had balked at joining a fraternity. He considered it an extravagance, one that neither he nor his father could afford. But the fraternity recruited him aggressively in his sophomore year the way all fraternities rushed star athletes. When he told them he couldn't afford the difference in cost between the dormitory and the frat house, they assured him they could work something out. It wasn't until he graduated that he found out that his dorm roommate, Lyle Simmons, who'd also pledged Kappa Phi Kappa, had agreed to pay the difference in order to have his new friend as a fraternity brother. It was too late to resent it. Nothing was to be gained. Lyle was his best friend.

Lyle had had considerably more to drink than Phil that day, and Rotondi became concerned about his driving. But they'd made it safely and were now ensconced in a booth in the noisy bar, B. J. Thomas singing "Raindrops Keep Fallin' on My Head" through the sound system.

"So, buddy, 'fess up to Uncle Lyle."

"About what?" Rotondi said.

"That delicious female creature you were with last night at the house."

Rotondi dismissed the question with a shrug and a slow grin, and sipped his beer.

Simmons reached across the table and grabbed his roommate's wrist. "Come on, pal, come on. You really scored. She's a knockout. An absolute knockout. Who is she?"

"Name's Jeannette."

"Jeannette what?"

"Boynton."

"Irish?"

"Alpha Phi. She's from Connecticut."

"So?"

Rotondi's expression asked a question.

"Did you score, do the deed?"

"Come on, Lyle. I only met her a week ago. She's in my political science class."

Simmons's leer was exaggerated, as though mugging for a camera.

Rotondi changed the subject. "You're definitely going to Chicago for law school?"

"Yup. And I'll never understand why you won't be coming with me."

"Money, Lyle. Just that simple. Maryland Law is giving me a free ride. The U of Chicago won't."

Simmons shook his head. "I told you I'd pay your tuition if you came with me."

"Yeah, I know, Lyle, but buying me a cheeseburger when I'm short of pocket money is one thing. Paying for law school is another."

"That's false pride, Phil."

"Call it what you will. I'm just not comfortable taking a big hand-out from a friend—from anyone for that matter."

Simmons sat back in the booth and flicked a piece of lint from the front of his argyle sweater. "You resent me, don't you, Phil?"

Rotondi had just taken a swig of beer and laughed, causing some to dribble down his chin. He wiped it with the back of his hand and said, "Why would I resent you, Lyle? You're my best friend."

"My money," Simmons said. "That I was born with a silver spoon in my mouth, as they like to say. I didn't choose that, Phil, and I'm not about to go to confession to ask for forgiveness."

"Cut it out, Lyle. You know I don't feel that way."

"Maybe you do, maybe you don't. But I want you to know, Phil, that I really admire you. I admire what you've achieved despite some pretty high hurdles."

"Thanks," Rotondi said. "I admire you, too." He laughed. "You say you want to be president of the United States some day, and I wouldn't bet against that happening."

"When I am, buddy, you'll be my attorney general."

"The hell I will. Politics turns me off, always have."

"We'll see," Simmons said, tossing bills on the table. "Let's go. I've got a date, a freshman, looks hot as hell."

As Rotondi was getting out of the Thunderbird in front of the Kappa Phi fraternity house, Simmons asked, "What did you say her name was?"

"Who?"

"The chick you were with last night. Jeannette something?"

"Jeannette Boynton."

"Yeah, that's it. Have a good night, buddy. Hit the books for me."

SIX

"Hi, Phil," Polly Simmons chirped as she crossed the lobby in Rotondi's direction. "No, don't get up," she said, seeing him struggle to extricate himself from the chair's soft cushions. He stood and they embraced.

"I'm sorry about your mom," he said.

"Thanks. I'm still in shock."

"Good flight?" he asked.

"Of course not. There aren't any good flights anymore unless you're a fat cat who flies first class. Pretzels and soft drinks. Ugh!"

Rotondi laughed. McTeague joined them carrying a small overnight bag.

"That's it?" Rotondi asked.

"She flies light," Walter McTeague said.

"Only way to fly," Rotondi said.

Polly looked around the lobby. "Fancy digs," she said.

Rotondi didn't bother replying. He knew that much of any conversation with her would involve swipes at the privileged class. He basically agreed with her on that issue, only he wasn't nearly as vocal or committed.

McTeague excused himself. Rotondi said to her, "Come on, let's get you checked in."

As she provided the desk clerk with the necessary information, Rotondi used the moment to take in the daughter of his friend, the senator from Illinois. He knew she was a dedicated vegetarian and exerciser; nothing other than "Certified Organic" passed her lips. Her figure reflected her healthy lifestyle. Her jeans were skintight, her blouse a little too small, which caused her breasts to strain against the silky blue fabric. She wasn't wearing a bra. One day, she might have to struggle with weight gain, but for now she was female perfection. Rotondi had always found the game of deciding which parent a child looks like, especially infants, to be, well, infantile. But he silently played the game anyway. Polly Simmons didn't look very much like either of her parents. She had her father's height, and there was something about her eyes that testified to being his daughter. Her nose and cheekbones were like Jeannette's, although not quite as refined. It was her hair that said she might have been adopted, which wasn't true. While Jeannette's brunette hair had had a hint of copper in it, Polly's was the color of cinnamon, and curly. *Where did* that *come from?*

They rode the elevator to her floor and entered the suite.

"Wow!" she said, doing a pirouette. "What does this go for a night?"

"Not your concern," Rotondi said as he opened the drapes and turned down the thermostat to make the room cooler.

"On Daddy's tab," she said absently. "Or some lobbyist's."

"He's trying to clean up some pressing business in the Senate, Polly, so he'll be free to—"

"Free to spend time with me in my moment of grief?"

"Yes."

She sat heavily on the couch and stared at Rotondi, who leaned on his cane in the middle of the room. Her mouth opened and she started to say something, but instead of words there was a torrent of tears. Rotondi put his arm around her.

"She's dead?" Polly said over and over. "Some bastard killed her?"

His answer was to pull her closer. He said nothing, allowing this outpouring of pain to run its course.

"I'm sorry," she said once the tears had subsided. Rotondi pulled a tissue from a small pack in his jacket pocket and handed it to her.

"I guess now that I'm here in D.C.," she said, "the reality has set in. Is there anything new? Have they found Mom's killer? Do they have leads? Anything?"

"It's too early in the investigation, Polly. I've been in touch with the police and they've promised to keep me informed. When was the last time you spoke to your mother?"

"Just yesterday." She shuddered. "The day she was murdered. In the afternoon, about four."

"Did everything seem all right? Normal?"

"Uh-huh. She . . ."

Rotondi waited.

"She sounded like she'd been drinking." Polly turned to Rotondi. "She had that problem, you know, Phil. I mean, not always, just the last couple of years. Don't misunderstand. Not falling-down drunk or anything like that. But I could always tell when I called."

Rotondi's silent nod said that he wasn't hearing anything he didn't already know.

"She's been so unhappy," Polly said.

"Do you know why?" he asked, already knowing but wanting her input.

"Everything. Getting older, I guess. She's been so disappointed in him."

"Disappointed in whom?"

"Dad, of course." She said it with a fleeting smile. "And Neil, too, for that matter."

"Disappointed in what?"

"What they've done with their lives."

"I'd say they've done quite well with their lives," Rotondi said. He got up and approached the minibar. "Like something, Polly? Soft drink, something stronger? Bloody Mary?"

"Bloody Mary mix, no booze."

"You've got it."

"I know what you mean," she said as she unlaced her sneakers and kicked them off. "Dad's a United States senator, a really big guy, huh? Neil's a lobbyist. Tell me, Phil, what does either of them do to make this a better world?"

"Well," he said as he handed her the drink—he poured one for himself from a can of lemonade—"your father has been behind some important legislation over the years that has made a difference in some people's lives."

"And how many deals did he have to cut to get that legislation through?" she asked angrily. "How many bad bills did he have to sign on to get what *he* wanted?"

"That's politics, Polly," said Rotondi, pulling up a chair on the opposite side of a glass coffee table. "Compromise and negotiation. In its purest sense, it's—"

"Purest sense?" she said. "Come on, Phil, you know there's nothing pure about politics. My mother really respected you, maybe even envied Kathleen for having you as a husband. You did what you wanted on your own terms, no compromise, no negotiation, just honor."

"You give me too much credit, Polly. There's been plenty of compromise in my life."

She ignored what he'd said. Instead, she said, "Look at Neil. All you have to do is pick up any newspaper on any day and read about the lobbying scandals, the payoffs to politicians, the fancy junkets, the sleaze. I don't think Neil ever wanted to take that job with Marshalk, Phil. It was Daddy who pushed him into it because it would help feather his own nest on Capitol Hill." She paused, head raised, index finger to her lips as though a sudden thought had come to her. "When Neil was a little boy, he wanted to be a garbageman." She laughed.

"Did he?"

"Yeah. Looks like he got his wish."

Rotondi let it go and sipped his lemonade. "Mind a bit of a history lesson, Polly, about lobbyists?" He didn't wait for a response. "Lobbying—in its purest sense—I know, there's the purity thing again, but many things start out pure and get corrupted along the way. Back when Ulysses S. Grant was president, he'd stroll over from the White House, sit in the lobby of the Willard hotel, enjoy a brandy and a cigar, and—"

"And be approached by men who wanted something from him," Polly said. "Grant called them lobbyists because they hung around the lobby waiting for him. Neil told me that when he took the job at Marshalk. I think he was trying to justify what he'd done, make it sound, well . . ."

"Pure."

"Yeah, pure. Neil gave me the standard speech that lobbying in its *purest* sense was an important part of the political process, that lobbyists help elected officials understand different points of view about a pending bill, that they bring expertise to politicians that the pols don't have time to research and understand. Poor Neil. He wants so much to be his own man, but he's never been allowed to. Politics! Purity! What a bunch of hogwash."

"Look, Polly," Rotondi said, "this is not the time to argue it. You and your dad and Neil have to pull together in this."

"To make it look like we're the all-American family? We aren't."

"That doesn't matter," he said, standing with the help of his cane. "I have to go. I told Neil I'd call him once I hooked up with you. Take my advice. Cool your jets when it comes to whatever hasn't been right between you and your father. Your mother deserves that."

She walked him to the door. He kissed her cheek. She wrapped her arms around him and squeezed tight. "I'm so glad you're my father's best friend, Phil. I think you're the only true friend he has."

He left wondering whether she might be right.

SEVEN

Everything about the Marshalk Group's offices was modern, including the support staff. Secretaries and administrative assistants had to possess the requisite skills—word processing, data input, filing acumen, and other routine office responsibilities. But they also had to be young, nicely made up, and with it—a 34-D cup wasn't overlooked when hiring took place—or young and handsome, slim, well groomed, and impeccably dressed among the men. Dark, wavy hair seemed to prevail; anyone who might accuse the firm of age discrimination, however, had only to look at some of the principals to be disabused of that notion. Those men and women had been recruited from the senior ranks of House, Senate, and administration staffs with the allure of big salaries—the average starting pay for a midlist lobbyist was three hundred thousand. Those who'd been there longest, and who had the most clout with their previous government employers, enjoyed multimillion-dollar paychecks along with hefty bonuses. Some were short and pudgy, others sported shining heads. There were the tall, slender patrician types whose gray hair indicated that they were of the age to have their prostates checked regularly, and middle-aged women who could afford tummy tucks and Botox injections, and for whom visits to the city's multitude of plastic surgeons were de rigueur.

What they all had in common was access to the most powerful of lawmakers in the House, the Senate, and the administrations. Access was everything in the lobbying biz. Those who had it—*really* had it—were aggressively recruited by the city's largest firms like star college athletes being drafted by professional teams. Some received so many offers once they'd announced that they were leaving government service, they hired attorneys to act as their agents, sifting through the pay and benefits packages and negotiating their deals. There are more than thirty-five thousand registered lobbyists in Washington, and more than enough special-interest cash for all.

The Marshalk offices occupied three floors in a steel-and-glass building on K Street, which had become known as Lobbyist Boulevard. The décor and furnishings matched the contempo style of the support staff, all chrome and leather and vivid modern art on the walls.

But there was another Marshalk "office" that wasn't quite as contemporary, a three-story row house on Eighteenth Street, a few blocks from the main office. The Marshalk Group had purchased it in 2004 for $2.6 million and turned it into a retreat in which to entertain clients and prospective clients, as well as lawmakers seeking to get away from the scrutiny of Capitol Hill. Decorated by a former girlfriend of Rick Marshalk who billed herself as an interior designer, it had what some in the firm said was the look of an eighteenth-century brothel, with its bloodred wall coverings and gold sconces, the furniture heavy, the artwork on the walls fox hunts and bistro scenes usually associated with restaurants attempting to establish a period mood. Interior design aside, it served its purpose.

This day, it was the scene of what Rick Marshalk hoped would be the final, definitive meeting with representatives of Betzcon Pharmaceuticals. Six months ago, the drug company had fired its D.C. lob-bying firm and made it known that it was shopping for a new one. Al-though considerably smaller than Merck, Lilly, or Pfizer, Betzcon had aggressively carved out a larger and larger niche in the intensely competitive pharmaceutical industry. Its commitment to, and fund-ing of, research was well acknowledged, and had paid off recently in a breakthrough drug for the treatment of high blood pressure that was already changing the medical landscape. Once the FDA had ap-proved it, Betzcon launched a multimillion-dollar campaign to win over physicians. A TV and print advertising blitz had patients pressing their physicians to prescribe the drug for them. The campaign suc-ceeded. The drug, Aorstat, was rapidly becoming the prescription of choice for cardiologists, turning Betzcon from a midsize upstart to a company with bulging profits and a bright future.

But while Betzcon's bottom line was fattening, trouble loomed in the halls of Congress.

"I know it's an understatement to say how shocked everyone is at the murder of Senator Simmons's wife," Rick Marshalk told those gathered in the town house's velvet-draped living room. With him were two other senior lobbyists from the Marshalk Group; Marshalk's administrative assistant, a stunning blonde who sat with long legs crossed and a notepad on her lap; and the group's vice president for security, Jack Parish. Representing Betzcon Pharmaceuticals were its governmental affairs VP and four of his staff. The only intrusions came from the house's elaborate kitchen, where three of Emma Churchill's catering staff ran Screwdrivers, coffee, and sandwiches to the living room. Emma had been there earlier but left to oversee an-other luncheon. Churchill Catering catered all of the Marshalk Group's business and social affairs, although as far as the IRS was con-cerned, there were no such things as personal and social gatherings. It was all business, all the time.

Marshalk continued: "We've arranged for a fifty-thousand-dollar reward for information leading to her killer. As you know, her son,

Neil, our president, won't be with us today for obvious reasons. Neil and his dad, Senator Simmons, are devastated by this horrendous loss, and the Marshalk Group stands ready to help in any way we can."

A few questions were asked about the crime and its investigation, and Marshalk turned to Jack Parish for the answers. "Jack is a former MPD detective," he told the Betzcon people, "and has maintained links to that agency. He's the one with the answers."

Nondescript was the appropriate description of Parish, average and medium in all ways except for a mouth that wasn't exactly straight-and-level. It started low on the left and slanted up to the right, giving him a look of perpetual skepticism. "There's not much to report," he said. "It's too early. But I have been told that they have a few suspects they're looking into."

"I hope whoever did it fries," a Betzcon executive said.

"Not here in D.C.," Parish said. "We don't have the death penalty."

"You should have," the exec snarled.

Marshalk had been sitting. He now stood and commanded the room. He was a large carton of a man in his early forties, his bulk mitigated by the cut of his custom-made British double-breasted suits. He was of mixed heritage; a swarthy complexion and coal-black hair honored his deceased Cuban mother. His father, a Caucasian American, had been a successful liability lawyer in Miami until dropping dead one sunny afternoon on a golf course at the age of fifty-six.

Their only child, Rick, graduated from Cal State with a degree in general studies, and went on to study screenwriting at UCLA. He found minimal success in Hollywood. Two of his scripts sold for the Writers Guild's minimum but were never produced. He had screenwriting credit on one film that actually made it to the silver screen, a low-budget horror movie that faded from public view within a month of opening.

But his time in Hollywood wasn't wasted. It was there that he'd learned a valuable lesson: Networking was everything. Who you knew paid bigger dividends than what you knew. The problem with applying that philosophy in Hollywood, he reasoned, was that once you met the right person, you still had to deliver a workable script. Better, he decided, was to be in a position where you were paid simply for bringing people together, without the need to deliver anything after that.

Who needs what? And who can deliver it?

He'd forged friendships with people in Washington, D.C., and made a series of visits to them. Their tales of how lobbying had made countless millionaires of former government employees intrigued the ambitious Marshalk. Business needed access to politicians to head off legislation that would be injurious to their companies, or to encourage laws favorable to their bottom line. Politicians needed money to win elections and to sustain their power bases. It was as simple as that. He picked up stakes in California and headed east. He never looked back. Washington was where he belonged, a place ripe for the picking for someone with his savvy.

The Marshalk Group was born.

Not that Rick Marshalk was the first to discover that becoming a lobbyist in Washington, D.C., could make a man rich. Influence peddling in the nation's capital had been alive and well for centuries, dating back to when President Washington traveled to Suter's Tavern in Georgetown to negotiate with local landowners the purchase of the properties on which the new "seat of empire" would stand. A century or two later, there were plenty of rich lobbyists in town. When Marshalk arrived, men—and some women—who knew their way around and were skilled at funneling money from clients into the political coffers of elected officials were ubiquitous. But he decided that he could, and would, do it better than they did. History proved him right. The Marshalk Group grew quickly and now occupied a preeminent position on K Street, which was why Betzcon Pharmaceuticals sat with Rick Marshalk and his colleagues that day in the red-and-gold town house.

"It should be obvious, Rick, that we've pretty much decided to go with Marshalk as our Washington lobbyists," Betzcon's VP said. "There are still a few loose ends to be tied up, which we can do here today."

"Need I say that you've made the right choice?" Marshalk said, laughing. "There's never been a more important time in our history for a company like Betzcon to have its voice heard in the halls of Congress and in the Oval Office. We know four or five months in advance of every bit of legislation that's apt to be introduced. Our intelligence is the best in town. And of course, the access we have to the right people is no secret. We'll put all of our resources to work for you to ensure that upcoming legislation not only doesn't hurt the company, but actually enhances your future growth and profitability. For example, we know that certain legislators in the House and Senate are considering introducing bills that could have a devastating effect on your pricing of Aorstat. We managed to head off in the Senate the previous attempt to force the Health and Human Services secretary to negotiate drug prices for the Medicare prescription drug plan. The House passed it, but through our efforts, primarily for your industry's trade associations, it stalled in the Senate. Now they're back on the case. This time, it will take an even bigger effort on our part to see that the bill never reaches the president's desk. We're poised to do that, but it will take every ounce of influence we have, to say nothing of money, to accomplish that goal."

"It's nonsense," said one of the Betzcon executives. "Screwing around with the free market is just plain wrong. It's—"

"Un-American," Marshalk said. "You're damn well right it is, and we have the clout to make sure that enough members of the Senate and House see it that way. I've already gone over how we plan to proceed. The writers we have on staff will begin turning out articles for medical and scientific journals, along with consumer magazines. We've established an impressive network of doctors and scientists who are willing to put their bylines on those pieces, giving them the credibility they need. There's nobody in town who's as good as we are at helping shape public opinion. I should also mention that there are members of the Senate Committee on Health, Education, Labor and Pensions—HELP. Neat acronym, huh?—who are facing tough re-election races, and their hands are perpetually out. You met one of them in Santa Domingo at the medical conference we hosted last month. We've already started providing them with the funds they need to beat back their opponents. All perfectly legal, I assure you," he added. "Our network of nonprofit organizations is solid and growing every day. The money you provide to help these deserving friends passes through those groups without a hitch."

Marshalk again sat. "Any questions?" he asked.

There were many, the answers to almost all of them satisfactory to the Betzcon questioners.

Dishes and glasses were cleared as the meeting was about to break up. There had been discussion about the fee Betzcon would pay to the Marshalk Group—forty-five thousand dollars a month—as well as contributions Betzcon was urged to make to some of the dozen nonprofit groups established by Marshalk, through which funds for "our friends on the Hill" could be dispersed. In addition, Betzcon's executives had agreed to pay fifteen thousand a month to a public relations firm recommended by Marshalk—and in which he was a silent partner.

"I would suggest that you make a donation to the fund we've established to find Mrs. Simmons's murderer," Marshalk told Betzcon's VP as they gravitated toward the door. "We're offering it through one of our affiliates, the Center for American Justice. Senator Simmons—he chairs HELP—will surely show his appreciation when we let him know of your generosity in helping find and convict his lovely wife's killer. We've offered fifty thou. If you could come up with half, it would be a welcome and much-appreciated goodwill gesture."

"We can do that."

"Great," Marshalk said, slapping him on the back. "I'm really excited about working with you to keep Congress on the right track. *Ciao*, my friend. And don't forget the golf trip to California. That's coming up in a couple of months. Senator Simmons has committed to joining us. This tragedy might change that, but I'm assuming he'll be ready for some R-and-R once the murderer is found and things get back to normal. Sorry Neil couldn't be with us today. I'll fill him in on everything."

With the Betzcon executives gone, Marshalk's administrative assistant dispatched back to headquarters, and the catering staff busy packing up in the kitchen, Marshalk sat with his colleagues in the living room. He punched the palm of one hand with the fist of the other. "Damn, that went well. Let's step up the pressure on those HELP committee pols." He said to his security chief, "Get me some inside info from the MPD that I can pass on to Simmons. I want to be his best source of information on the planet. Got it?"

Jack Parish stood, stretched, yawned, and said, "I'll see what I can do." The man with the crooked mouth left the room, his exit from the house heralded by the tinkling of a bell attached to the front door.

EIGHT

That afternoon, a group of MPD detectives gathered in a large, scarred room at police headquarters on Indiana Avenue, Charles Chang among them. Morris Crimley led the meeting. Behind him was a blackboard. Earlier that day, a female officer had written notes on the board pertaining to the Jeannette Simmons case. Working from a yellow legal pad containing Crimley's handwritten comments, she was chosen for the task because of her neat penmanship. Besides, she was the only one on the Simmons task force who could decipher Crimley's scribbles. Her future at MPD was bright.

One section of the board contained the names of every possible suspect in the murder. In this early stage of the investigation, no one was excluded—for any reason. Senator Lyle Simmons led the list, followed by his son, Neil; daughter, Polly; Jeannette Simmons's sister, Marlene; the housekeeper, Gina; the senator's driver, Walter McTeague; some of the Simmonses' neighbors; a handyman who often did work at the house; a slightly demented homeless man who'd found a space beneath a small bridge a few blocks from the house to his liking (he'd been picked up early that morning and was being held on a vagrancy charge to make sure he stayed around); and a dozen others, none of whom was a viable suspect but all of whom had had some connection, however tangential, with the deceased.

Another section of the blackboard contained a summation of forensic evidence that had been gathered at the house by crime scene investigators. It was a short list. A variety of fingerprints were being analyzed and compared with the FBI's central database. Hairs had been collected and sent to the crime lab, along with two shoeprints found on the foyer floor, formed by someone who'd stepped in stone dust created by the handyman as he'd repaired a stone wall near the front entrance.

The third and final chart linked the names of the detectives and the suspects they'd been assigned to interview.

"All right," Crimley said from the front of the room, "points for good list making. Let's put this thing in gear. Simmons's son, Neil, is in my office. Charlie, you've already talked with him at the scene, so follow up with the formal interview. Amanda, you work with Charlie on that." He ignored the exaggerated rolling of her eyes. "Same with the senator. You'll have to accommodate him, do the interview where he's comfortable, his office, house, some dark and seedy bar, whatever." He glanced back at the board. "Amanda, add that lobbying group the son works for to the list. Probably nothing there but let's touch all the bases. Matt Bergl, the U.S. attorney himself, is heading up the prosecution. I'll coordinate with him and his people, so I want whatever you come up with in real time, no surprises. I don't want to be blindsided. Herb and Bruce, you get over to that Marshalk lobbying group and see what someone there might come up with. Who wanted her dead? That's the piece we need right now. Motive! We can scratch the housekeeper from the list. She went home to Costa Rica three days before the murder. Still, it wouldn't hurt to try to contact her through authorities there. Public Affairs says nobody—and that means nobody—talks to the press, on or off the record, unless cleared through them. Anyone want to be famous?" Silence. "Any questions?"

There were a few but none significant. The group dispersed. Crimley returned to his office, where Neil Simmons waited with a man who hadn't been there earlier. Neil introduced him to Crimley as his attorney, a seasoned D.C. hand known for cutting deals for clients before their cases ever progressed beyond that stage.

"Your client doesn't need an attorney," Crimley said. "We just want to see if he can help us identify someone who might have had it in for his mother."

The attorney smiled, displaying an abundance of white teeth. He'd heard that sort of disclaimer from detectives too many times before to buy in. As far as he was concerned, Neil Simmons was a suspect, and anything he said could, and would, be used against him if he was eventually charged. "I'm just along for the ride, Detective," the lawyer said. "Neil is ready to answer any questions you might have."

"I'm not doing the interview," Crimley said. "Detectives Chang and Widletz are."

"The Asian detective who spoke with me at the scene last night?" Simmons said.

"Right. Here they are."

Charlie Chang and Amanda Widletz entered the office and were introduced to the attorney and to Neil. "Use Room Three," Crimley instructed the detectives. "I've cleared it."

They'd been gone for only a few minutes when U.S. Attorney Matt Bergl arrived. Bergl had recently received considerable press coverage for changing the way assistant U.S. attorneys were assigned to prosecute homicides in the District. Until his appointment to the post by the president, the District's three hundred assistant U.S. attorneys had been assigned geographically, each attached to a specific police precinct, which meant handling all crimes occurring in those jurisdictions—fraud, robberies, rape, and murder. The result? Homicides were often prosecuted by attorneys who were inexperienced in that area of the law. The further result? While the murder rate continued to climb, homicide convictions had gone down considerably.

Under Bergl's reign, the system was changed. Assignments were now based upon experience and expertise. All murders, from every precinct, were prosecuted by an elite team of seasoned homicide attorneys. Recent results? The conviction rate had risen to more acceptable levels.

Bergl was well dressed, well groomed, and well mannered. He was a little too slick for Crimley's taste, but the chief detective also recognized that along with putting bad guys away, the U.S. attorney's other job was to remain in political favor. He was good at both.

"Got a minute?" Bergl asked.

"Sure," Crimley responded. "Grab a chair."

"I wanted to run something by you, Morrie."

"I'm listening."

"You're aware of the rumor about Senator Simmons."

"*The* rumor?" Crimley guffawed. "I've heard lots of rumors about him. Get specific."

"The one about his having a girlfriend in Chicago."

"Oh, *that* one. Sure. What about it?"

"A state's attorney out there—a friend—tells me that the senator's extracurricular squeeze has connections with the wrong people."

"Mob?"

Bergl nodded. "Not the sort of woman a United States senator ought to be sharing a bed with."

"Your friend in Chicago, he—"

"She."

"She validates the rumor?"

Another nod. "The Chicago AG is buttoned up, sharing nothing with us."

Crimley slipped fingers between buttons of his shirt and scratched an itch. Relieved, he smiled at Bergl. "You think the senator's wife might have been killed by someone out there?"

"Far-fetched, right, Morrie?"

Crimley shrugged and attacked the itch again. "Yeah, far-fetched," he said. "Then again—"

"I just thought I'd toss it into the mix. I'll be finding out more."

"That's good. In the meantime, I don't think I'll add it to my list of possibles, if that's okay with you."

"Fine with me." Bergl stood, took a few steps toward the door, stopped, turned, and asked, "You're a friend of Phil Rotondi, right?"

"Yeah. Phil was in earlier today."

"Was he? He and the senator go back a long way, college buddies."

"Roommates."

"Think he might know something we don't?"

"Ask him."

"You ask him, Morrie. I wouldn't want it to get back that I'm questioning a senator's love life."

"Politically incorrect," Crimley said.

"Something like that. I'm holding a press conference at six. Your chief will be with me."

"Give him my best."

"I certainly will. Let's do this one by the book, Morrie. I don't want some defense attorney finding holes in whatever you come up with. See ya."

Crimley watched Bergl leave. He sat back, arms behind his head, and had two immediate thoughts.

The first was that Bergl's suit looked good on guys built like that.

The second thought was also unpleasant, and he grimaced against it. He'd investigated plenty of high-profile cases in his twenty-three years on the force, but this one—the murder of the wife of a U.S. senator and rising presidential possibility—was in a class by itself. Having turned down early retirement suddenly didn't seem like such a smart decision after all.

NINE

Earlier that day, Rotondi had called Neil Simmons.

"Neil, it's Phil Rotondi. I just left Polly at the Hotel George."

"How is she?"

"She's fine. Where are you now?"

"At the office. The press won't leave me alone. I ducked in here to get rid of them."

"Have you spoken with your father?"

"A couple of times. He wants to see you."

"I was there this morning."

"He wants you to call him."

"As soon as I hang up on you."

"I have to go to see the police this afternoon."

"Uh-huh."

"I'm bringing a lawyer."

"Can't hurt, although you probably don't need one at this stage."

"You're saying I will later?"

"Bring a lawyer, Neil. Look, I have to run. I'll call your dad. Anything I can do for you?"

"Yes. Make it all go away."

"If only I could."

Rotondi had called Neil Simmons's cell phone from the District ChopHouse and Brewery on Seventh Street, where he'd settled at the bar and enjoyed a beer and a cheeseburger. Although the restaurant was crowded and noisy, he felt very much by himself. He was good at that, creating solitude in the midst of chaos. Kathleen used to comment after leaving a party that he seemed in his own little world. To which he invariably replied, "I was, and it was a more pleasant place than the party." He wasn't necessarily antisocial, nor was he a stereotypical loner. But he treasured his inner spaces, and his ability to summon them when it suited.

He called Senator Simmons from outside the restaurant.

"Oh, Mr. Rotondi, the senator is waiting to hear from you. He's in an important meeting, but he said to put you through."

The senator's voice broke in. "Hello, Phil. Polly arrived all right?"

"Yes. She's at the hotel. I'm sure she'll be calling."

Would she?

"Hold on a second, Phil." Rotondi heard Simmons ask those meeting with him to leave. When they had, he came back on the line. "Phil. I need a favor from you."

"Sure."

"The police have told me that I can go back to the house. I'd like you to come with me."

Rotondi hesitated. "Sure you wouldn't rather have Neil and Polly?" he said.

"I'd like you with me."

Another pause from Rotondi.

"Please, Phil."

"Okay. Emma and I are having dinner with friends tonight at seven. Other than that—"

"Come by the office at five. Walter will drive us."

"I'll be there. Oh, Lyle, by the way. I spoke with Neil a few minutes ago. He's giving an interview to the police this afternoon."

"I know. He was going without a lawyer. I told him to get smart. I'm negotiating now for a convenient time and place for them to interview me. It's bad enough when you lose your wife, but they're making it doubly hard. I can't even arrange for a proper funeral for Jeannette. The medical examiner says he won't release the body for God knows how long. See you at five. And thanks, Phil. I knew I could count on you."

Rotondi went to Emma's house, where he took Homer for a walk. He intended to make it a long one, but the combination of the heat—when would it break?—and his aching leg precluded that. He settled on the couch and watched the ongoing TV news reports about Jeannette's murder. He tried to focus on what the talking heads were saying, but it was a lost cause. Images of times past dominated, rendering the words from the TV nothing more than a drone. He turned off the set, closed his eyes, and allowed his thoughts to take him where they wanted him to go, back to his senior year at the University of Illinois.

Back to when Jeannette was alive.

༒

It had been two months since Rotondi first got up the courage to ask Jeannette Boynton out. He'd dated little during his first three years at the university. Between his studies, and basketball and track practice, there didn't seem to be time for the opposite sex. At least that's what he told himself. He often closed the library at night, and was the last athlete to leave the gym and weight room.

Not that he'd failed to notice the multitude of attractive coeds in his classrooms and around the campus. Nor was he a virgin. The sexual freedom of the 1960s was pervasive on campus, as it was across America. As a freshman, he'd had sex with a "townie," a young woman from Champaign-Urbana. The experience had been revelatory. He wasn't sure what he'd learned, but it had been pleasurable aside from the fear that she might become pregnant, which as far as he was concerned would ruin his life. Fathering a child out of wedlock, before his education was completed and he'd become a married man, would devastate his father. His relief was palpable when she called one evening to advise that she'd had her period. He didn't see her again after that.

There had also been a woman back in Batavia, a waitress ten years older than he was, with whom he'd ended up in bed—twice. These brief encounters happened one week apart while he was home on the Christmas break during his junior year. She provided protection, and told him after their second experience that she was going back to her husband. Her decision made him happy.

None of these encounters was particularly memorable; nor had they piqued his masculine interests the way Jeannette did. When attending one of two political science classes he'd enrolled in early in his senior year, he often found himself tuning out the lecturer and looking at Jeannette, who sat one row in front and to his left. Objectively, she wasn't any prettier than many other young women at the university, but there was something different about her, an intangible quality that tripped his male synapses and caused warm feelings from head to toe. They barely spoke in that classroom, nothing more than pleasant greetings and farewells.

Their first real conversation occurred in the coffee shop of the school's Student Union. He was sitting alone at a booth studying for an English lit exam when she suddenly appeared at his side.

"Hi, Phil. Mind if I join you?"

"What? Oh, sure. Please do."

"Studying?" she asked.

"Yeah. English lit."

"Can I help? That's my major."

"It is? Thanks, but I don't think so. Just have to finish this assigned reading and—"

"I saw the game last night. You were terrific."

"Thanks. We almost lost it."

"You scored the winning basket."

"I got lucky."

"You're too modest. Where are you from?"

"Upstate New York. A small town called Batavia."

"I know it."

Her perfume was intoxicating. So was her smile. It was that smile that he'd first noticed in class, wide and genuine and full of life. She wore a powder-blue sweater over a white blouse, a simple gold chain, and gold earrings in the shape of tiny birds. Her large, hazel eyes said she was thinking of nothing but him.

"You do? Where are you from?"

"Greenwich, Connecticut."

"Oh." He'd heard that Greenwich was a wealthy place. "Connecticut's pretty, huh?"

"It is. I like it."

"Why did you decide to come to school out here?"

"My father thought it would be good for me to see another part of the country. I'm glad I did." She moved as though she was about to leave. "I'll leave you alone with your book," she said.

"No, no, that's okay. Want a cup of coffee or something?"

That smile. "I'd love it," she said.

They spent the next half hour learning a little about each other. When she announced she had to leave, he stood.

"That's so nice," she said.

"What is?"

"That you stood. It's so—so old-fashioned." She sensed he might have taken it as a criticism and quickly added, touching his hand, "I like the old-fashioned way. There isn't enough of it these days."

"I'll walk you home," he said.

As they stood in front of the Alpha Phi house, he said, "We're having a party Friday night at the fraternity house. I was wondering whether you'd like to go."

"I'd like that very much, Philip. See you in class."

She was gone, but only physically. The vision of her, her voice, her scent lingered far into the night as he sat in his room at the fraternity house and tried to finish the book he'd been assigned. It was after midnight when his roommate arrived.

"There you go again," Simmons said, "hunched over a book. All work and no play—"

"I am doing some playing," Rotondi said, allowing a sly smile to emerge.

"You are?" Simmons said, exaggerating how impressed he was. "A girl?"

"Yeah, a girl. Now shut up and let me finish before I flunk the exam tomorrow."

Simmons laughed. His roommate was always expressing concern that he would do poorly on exams, but seemed never to receive anything but straight A's.

The Friday-night party at the Kappa Phi Kappa house turned boisterous, as such parties often did. Beer flowed freely from a keg in the basement rec room, and there was a lot of male posturing for the benefit of the females. Lyle Simmons was absent for most of the party. He arrived a little after eleven, saw Rotondi sitting with Jeannette, gave his roommate a wink, and disappeared, not to be seen again that evening. Some of Rotondi's fraternity brothers, including a few who were there without dates, spent time talking to Rotondi and Jeannette, and a few of their comments were inappropriate in Rotondi's opinion. One frat brother in particular made a crude reference to Jeannette's bosom. When he walked away, Rotondi muttered, "He's such an ass, pardon my French."

Jeannette laughed and grabbed his hand. "You don't have to apologize, Philip. I've heard all the four-letter words, and three-letter ones, too."

"He shouldn't have said it in front of you," he countered.

"It's okay. I've heard worse. Want to dance?"

Despite being a skilled and graceful athlete, Rotondi knew he was a clumsy dancer, and told her that. His protestation went unheeded: "There you go being modest again," Jeannette said. "Come on, just move with me."

A slow tune came through the speakers, "Close to You" by the Carpenters. He was self-conscious not only because of his perceived shortcomings as a dancer, but also because he was in front of his fraternity brothers. He moved awkwardly to the strains of the music, enjoying the soft feel of her, her cheek against his, the sound of her humming along with the tune. When he developed the telltale sign that he'd become aroused, he pulled slightly away. She pulled him back, and he no longer fought the pleasure.

They left the party shortly after that dance, and he walked her home.

"Thanks for a nice evening, Philip," she said.

"Thanks for coming with me," he said.

"I really like you," she said.

"I, ah—I really like you, too, Jeannette."

She pulled him close and their kiss lasted for what seemed an eternity to him. When they disengaged, she asked, "When will I see you again?"

He caught his breath. "In class and—"

"I mean like this, silly, on a date."

He grinned. He was in control of his senses again. "As soon as possible," he said. "Next week?"

"Sure."

"How about dinner? I think I can borrow a car."

"Whatever you say."

He floated back to the fraternity house. But once there, a set of conflicting emotions gripped him. There was euphoria. There was also a vague sense of dread. Jeannette Boynton was out of his league. She was from Greenwich, Connecticut, which a fraternity brother told him was one of the most expensive zip codes in America. Another classmate, also from Greenwich, knew of the Boynton family whose father, Charles Monroe Boynton, founded and was CEO of a

New York City venture capital firm. Rotondi's stomach tightened when hearing these things. This was never going to work, and he practiced what to say when telling her that it wasn't a good idea for them to see each other again outside of class. He was certain that he'd come off the way he'd felt all evening, unworthy, bumbling, *old-fashioned*—yet she'd encouraged him to ask her out again. He was supremely confident on the basketball court and during track meets, and carried that confidence into his classes. But with her . . .

"I was wondering if tomorrow night would be good for you," he told her when political science class ended on Monday.

"Sure."

"I'll see if I can borrow a car. Otherwise—"

"It doesn't matter," she said. "If you can't, we'll grab a bite at the Union."

"Okay," he said. "I'll call you tonight."

At noon, he went to the fraternity house, where he found Lyle Simmons in their room hunkering down with a textbook.

"Nice sight, if rare," Rotondi said. "Got a minute?"

"This is all gobbledygook," Simmons said, closing the book.

"I was wondering whether I could borrow your car tomorrow night, Lyle."

"Tomorrow night? Sorry, pal, but I'll need it. I've got a date. Hey, are you taking out that beauty—what's her name?—Benson?"

"Boynton," Rotondi said. "Jeannette Boynton."

"How about this?" Simmons said. "We'll double-date."

"I don't know, Lyle, I—"

"Cynthia and I thought we'd catch dinner at that new Italian restaurant outside of town. We'll make it a foursome." Cynthia was a redhead he'd been dating for the past couple of weeks.

"I hear it's expensive," Rotondi said.

"Hey, pal, it'll be my treat." He held up his hand against the expected protest. "I insist. What's a few bucks when I can play Cupid for my best buddy? We're on?"

Rotondi smiled. "Yeah. Thanks, Lyle. We're on."

The restaurant was faux Venice with murals of gondolas plying the canals and statues of nymphs spouting water through their mouths. Simmons was in his usual gregarious mood during the drive there, and continued to dominate the conversation at the table as a succession of courses were delivered; wineglasses were never empty.

"What does your father do?" Jeannette asked Simmons at one point in the conversation.

"Real estate in Chicago. He owns half of Lake Shore Drive."

"Will you be going into business with him when you graduate?" Cynthia asked.

"Not me. I'm off to law school, U of Chicago. I tried to get my buddy here to come along, but he's heading for Maryland. After that, who knows? I like politics."

"Law school?" Jeannette asked Rotondi.

"Yup."

"What does your dad do, Phil?" Cynthia asked.

He deflected the question with one of his own. "What's your goal after graduation?" he asked.

She laughed loudly. "To marry a rich guy, have a bunch of kids, and live happily ever after."

"How about you, Jeannette?" Simmons asked. "Same goal?"

"I'd like to teach English back home for a while," she said. Her laugh was gentler. "So my dad doesn't think he wasted money on my education. But sure, someday I'd like to be married and have a family." She said to Simmons, "You want to go into politics?"

"I think so."

"He'll be president someday," Rotondi said.

"Will you really?" Cynthia said with mock awe.

"Maybe," Simmons replied. "Politics is where the action is. Everything that happens comes out of politics."

"A lot of bad things," said Cynthia.

"I like politics," Jeannette said. "I worked back home in Connecticut on some local campaigns."

"I bet you were good at campaigning," Lyle said.

"I worked hard," she said.

"The way I see it," Lyle said, "I . . ."

The discussion of their respective goals went on for the rest of the meal. Rotondi, always a good listener, took in what they said without offering many comments of his own. His goals, he decided, weren't worth discussing. He'd always been a tightly focused person, comfortable dealing with the here and now and convinced that overall success was achieved by a series of smaller successes, one upon another—excel on today's exam, win today's game, chase the next goal, and face the next challenge as each came, one at a time. The others at the table spoke in more sweeping terms about their futures than he preferred to contemplate. He recognized that his approach to life might be termed shortsighted by those with distant visions. Having money helped fuel grandiosity, he knew. For him, there hadn't been the luxury of dreams beyond the day's challenge. And that was all right. He was comfortable with it—and with himself.

Later, Rotondi and Simmons sat in their room.

"Thanks for treating us," Phil said.

"My pleasure," said Lyle.

"Cynthia's very nice," Phil said.

"She's okay. She's not the brightest bulb in the drawer but it's not her brains that attract me. Speaking of brains, you've landed yourself a real winner, all that beauty—and brains, too."

"I really like Jeannette."

"That's pretty obvious, Phil. I assume you'll be seeing her again."

"She's—well, I'm not sure she's for me."

Simmons laughed. "You talk like you're thinking of marrying her."

Rotondi joined the laughter. "The last thing I'm thinking about is getting married, Lyle. I've got law school ahead of me and getting a career started before I marry anyone. I just like being with her."

"She's obviously money, Phil. Getting hitched to her could make getting through law school a breeze and set you up with a nice, fat law practice."

Rotondi searched for something on his desk rather than responding. Lyle often viewed things from the perspective of money, which made Rotondi uncomfortable.

"Well, I'm glad you finally hooked up with a nice gal, Phil. I was getting worried about you. *Is my roommate queer?* I wondered."

"Say you didn't think that," Rotondi said.

"Of course I didn't. Just having some fun." Simmons stood. "Time to hit the sack."

"I've got a couple of hours with the books before I do that," Rotondi said.

Simmons changed into pajamas and retired to the dormitory that took up the entire third floor of the house. Rotondi started to study but found his mind wandering, which bothered him. He'd meant what he'd said: Marriage was the last thing on his mind. But he couldn't help envisioning being married to Jeannette Boynton. He fell to the floor and did a series of push-ups to clear such visions from his mind. Tomorrow's exam took center stage, and he studied until three.

TEN

His cell phone rang as he was about to call a cab from Emma's house.

"Mr. Rotondi, this is Walter McTeague."

"Hello, Walter. How are you?"

"Just fine, sir. The senator thought you might like to be picked up. I know you're meeting him at five."

"I'd appreciate that."

"Where shall I pick you up, sir?"

"I'm at my—at a friend's house in Foggy Bottom." He gave the address, and was standing at the window when the car arrived.

"Any idea when this heat wave is supposed to break, Walter?" he asked McTeague as they headed for First and C streets.

"Maybe tomorrow, according to the radio. But frankly, Mr. Rotondi, I don't put much faith in the forecasts."

"Neither do I," Rotondi said.

"We'll be picking up the senator away from his building,"

McTeague said, "out back near the entrance to underground parking. Too many press people out front."

"Smart move. Have you heard anything new about the investigation?"

"No, sir, I haven't."

"You knew Mrs. Simmons," Rotondi said.

"Oh, yes, I certainly did. A nice woman, a really good person."

"Had you seen her lately? I mean, in the days leading up to her murder?"

McTeague maintained eye contact with Rotondi in his rearview mirror. "Yesterday, as a matter of fact."

"Oh?"

"The senator asked me to pick up some dry cleaning and deliver it to her."

"What time was that?"

"A little after two, I think. I'm sure the police will want to know about it. They're questioning me tonight after I get off work."

"You were MPD. You'll probably know who's doing the questioning."

"I'm sure I will. A waste of time on their part. I would never harm that woman, not for a second."

"Just routine."

"I know, but it bothers me that anyone might even think I would."

"What frame of mind was she in when you last saw her, Walter?"

"Oh, I don't know. She was tired, that's for sure. I suggested to the senator when I dropped him home last night that they get away for a while, take a little vacation."

"What did he say?"

"He agreed, and said Mrs. Simmons would probably agree with me."

"Was she depressed, as well as tired?" Rotondi asked.

"I wouldn't know, Mr. Rotondi. I don't know how you can tell that sort of thing about another person."

Rotondi wanted to extend the conversation about Jeannette, but

McTeague changed the subject. They parked on the street in the back of Dirksen and talked about things other than murder until Simmons, accompanied by his press aide, Peter Markowicz, joined them.

"We're going to the house, Walter," Simmons told McTeague.

He pulled away and joined the flow of traffic.

"Nice of the police to allow me to enter my own house," Simmons grumbled.

"I've seen investigations where family members were kept away for months," Rotondi said.

"I'm sure the press will still be camped at the front door," Simmons said.

"I'll handle them, Senator," Markowicz said.

"There ought to be a law against them hounding people in a time of personal tragedy," said the senator.

There ought to be a law against a lot of things, was Rotondi's thought.

Simmons turned to Markowicz. "Phil Rotondi and I go back to our college days, Peter. We were roommates at Illinois."

"I know that, Senator. It's great that you've retained your friendship over so many years."

"He was second-team All Big Ten. Basketball."

"*That* I didn't know," the press secretary said. "You didn't try for the pros?"

"No," Rotondi responded. "I was good enough to make the team at Illinois. The NBA was beyond any ability I had. Besides, it didn't interest me."

Simmons sighed, leaned his head back, and closed his eyes. He opened them and said to Rotondi, "God, that was a long time ago, Phil, wasn't it? You knew Jeannette before I did. You introduced me to her."

Don't go there, Rotondi thought.

"When was the last time you saw her?" Simmons asked.

"A month or so ago. When she came down to the shore for a long weekend. We had dinner."

"That's right, you did. She needed a break. She'd been acting, well, strange, under the gun, unhappy. She seemed a little happier when she came home. She needed to get away, touch base with her girlfriends there."

"It was good seeing her," Rotondi said, glad that they'd reached the house.

"There they are," Markowicz said, referring to the press corps still camped on the road. As they pulled into the long driveway, they saw that a few reporters were also sitting on the front steps of the house.

"What the hell are they doing there?" Simmons demanded as McTeague came to a stop halfway up the drive.

"I'll handle them," Markowicz said, getting out of the car and sprinting toward the reporters.

"What's that other car?" Simmons asked, pointing to a green four-door sedan parked near the front.

"Looks like an unmarked police vehicle to me," Rotondi offered.

Markowicz herded the reporters away from the front door and back to where their colleagues waited on the road, then waved for McTeague to continue. Simmons and Rotondi got out of the Mercedes and walked to the front door. Simmons tried it. It swung open. "They didn't even bother to lock it," he complained as he stepped inside, followed by Rotondi. The air-conditioning was going full-blast; the foyer felt like a walk-in meat locker. The house was still, the only sound the whoosh of air coming from vents in the ceiling. Rotondi closed the door and waited for his friend of many years to make the next move.

"She was right there," Simmons said, pointing to the faint chalk outline of Jeannette's body. Whoever had tried to remove it from the floor hadn't done a good job. "Right there," Simmons repeated. "It was horrible, Phil." They'd done a better job of cleaning up Jeannette's blood; all that remained was a shadow.

Rotondi thought of what Crimley had told him about Detective Chang's reaction to the senator's appearance the night of the murder, neat as a pin, very much together, no sign that he'd tried to revive his wife or even touched her to determine if she was dead or alive. Rotondi stepped closer to the outline and tried to process what he was seeing, and what might have happened. She'd been struck in the back of the head, meaning she'd been moving away from her assailant. Running away? Walking away to fetch something for the attacker? There hadn't been any sign of a break-in. Chances were she knew whoever killed her and had willingly allowed him or her into the house.

"They haven't found the murder weapon?" Rotondi asked.

"Not as far as I know," Simmons replied. He stepped into the library and stood in the middle of the room. No lights were on, and the shades were drawn. Rotondi observed him from the foyer. It was as though his friend of many years had entered some sort of hallowed sanctuary, a sacred place where a voice from above might provide answers to his questions. Rotondi said nothing, did not interrupt whatever Simmons was thinking at that moment.

Both men turned suddenly at the sound of voices from upstairs.

"Who's here?" Simmons asked, returning to the foyer and standing at the foot of the stairs. "Who's up there?" he said in a louder voice. There was no reply. He started up, stopped, and looked back down at Rotondi. "Coming?"

"Go ahead," Rotondi said. "I'll be along."

Simmons disappeared at a turn in the elaborate staircase. Rotondi ascended slowly, favoring his leg and using the banister to help pull him up. He was almost to the top when he heard Simmons say, "Polly!"

She said, "Hi."

"What are you doing here?" were her father's next words.

Rotondi was startled at Simmons's tone. *That's no way to talk to your daughter*, he thought as he reached the second-floor landing and looked into the master bedroom, where Simmons stood with Polly. Behind them was an Asian American in a tan suit, white shirt, and skinny blue tie.

"This is Detective Chang," Polly said pleasantly.

"I know who he is," Simmons barked. "I ask you again, what the hell do you want? I was told your investigation here is over."

"The investigation will be over when we find the person who killed your wife," Chang said flatly.

"The detective was here when I arrived," Polly said. "We've been having a nice chat." She looked past her father. "Hello, Philip."

Simmons closed the gap and reached out to hug his daughter. She allowed him to kiss her cheek, but avoided a clinch. "How are you?" he asked, sounding as though it was the only thing he could think of saying.

She adopted a cheery, singsong voice. "Oh, as good as can be expected for someone whose mother has been murdered. How are you, Daddy?"

Simmons ignored her and turned to Chang. "Would you please give me the courtesy of spending time with my daughter? Alone? We haven't seen each other in quite a while."

"So I understand," said Chang.

Simmons glared at Polly, who turned her back to him and crossed the room to a nightstand on which small framed photographs stood. She picked one up and examined it, put it down and chose another. Rotondi couldn't tell whether she was sincerely interested in the pictures or simply busying herself to avoid conversing with her father.

Simmons told Detective Chang, "I'm asking you again, Detective, to leave this house."

"Of course, sir," the short, slight detective said. He approached the bedroom door where Rotondi stood. "Excuse me," he said. Rotondi stepped aside to allow him through, but he turned and said to Simmons, "One thing, sir. I would like to arrange for us to sit down together at your earliest convenience. When might that be?"

"Call my office and arrange a time and place."

"I will be happy to do that," said Chang. "Oh, one more thing, sir."

"Yes?"

"I spoke with your son this afternoon, Mr. Neil Simmons."

"So I heard."

"He indicates that your marriage might not have been—how shall I say it?—had not been especially happy. Is that true?"

Simmons glared at him.

"We can discuss that, and other things, when we meet," Chang said. He nodded at Rotondi—almost a slight bow—and went down the stairs, pausing in the foyer to bend over the faded chalk outline of Jeannette Simmons's body and examine the wall next to it. Simmons and Rotondi watched until he finally closed the front door behind him.

They turned to face Polly, who had come to the door to listen.

"He's nice," she said.

"What did you talk to him about?" Simmons demanded.

"A few things. Don't worry, Daddy, I didn't tell any tales out of school."

"You heard what Neil told him?" Simmons said.

"Poor Neil. He's in for it now."

Simmons pulled his cell phone from his pocket.

"It's true, isn't it?" Polly said.

Simmons stopped punching in Neil's cell phone number. "What's true?"

"That you and Mom didn't have what you'd call a happy marriage."

"This is neither the time nor the place to be having this discussion, Polly."

"What is a good time, Daddy, the Senate floor where you can orate about family values and the sanctity of marriage? God, how hypocritical!"

Rotondi thought that Simmons might lash out physically at his daughter, and prepared to head it off.

"Don't you have any sense of what's appropriate, Polly. My wife, your mother, has been killed and—"

She spun around, entered the bedroom, and slammed the door.

"Go on downstairs," Rotondi told Simmons. "I'll join you there in a minute."

Rotondi went into the bedroom, where Polly sat crying on the edge of the bed. He handed her his handkerchief. She dabbed at her eyes and gave it back. "You understand, don't you, Phil?" she said.

"What I understand is that you're acting like a brat, Polly. I don't care what's gone down between you and your father, he happens to be right. This is not the time or the place to get into it, and it won't be the time or the place until your mother's killer has been found, and she's properly laid to rest."

His harsh words hit as though she'd been punched. She pushed away from the bed and went to a window. Rotondi followed. "He's hurting, too, Polly, only he may not show it the way you'd like him to. What's important is not what you think and feel, but what your mother would have wanted. She deserves some dignity, if a murder victim can ever truly find that, and you owe her that. Shelve your feelings about your father and do what's right for your mother. Suck it up and act like a grown-up. Got that?"

She sniffled and said, "I know you and Daddy are friends, but I didn't think you'd take his side."

"The only side I'm taking, Polly, is your mother's. I suggest you do the same."

"You're right," she said. "I'm sorry."

"Nothing to be sorry for," he said. "Just do the right thing while you're here. And stay away from the press. They'll take what you say and chew you up."

"Yes, sir!" She gave a halfhearted salute.

Rotondi grinned. "Good girl," he said. "What are your plans for tonight?"

"I don't have any."

"Why not suggest dinner with your father?"

"Oh, Phil, I don't know. I—"

"Suit yourself. You'll have to spend time with him at some point."

"I know. Phil?"

"What?"

"Mom really liked and respected you."

"The feeling was mutual."

"She talked about you a lot, especially in the past couple of years. Did you and she . . . ?"

Rotondi placed an index finger against her lips. "Go down and spend time with your father. I have to pick up Emma—you remember her—we have a dinner date with friends. Here." He pulled a card from his pocket and wrote Emma's number on it. "Call me anytime, Polly."

"Thanks, Phil."

The senator was sitting in his darkened library when they came downstairs. Polly went into the room and said, "Dad, would you like to have dinner together?"

He'd been slumped in the chair. He came up straight, started to say something, paused, and said finally, "That would be nice, Polly. Yes, I'd like that." He saw Rotondi standing in the foyer. "You have an engagement, Phil."

"Yes. I'd better get moving."

"Walter will drive you."

"I'll call a cab."

"Walter will drive you," Simmons repeated. "Polly and I will spend some time here until Walter gets back. Thanks for coming with me, Phil. I know it's not easy for you, either."

"You two take care," Rotondi said. "We'll catch up tomorrow."

As he sat in the Mercedes's backseat, he was flooded with thoughts. Simmons was right. This wasn't easy for him, and he had the sinking feeling that it would soon become even harder. He considered packing it in the next morning and fleeing back to his condo on the Eastern Shore. But he knew he couldn't do that, wouldn't do that because—and he was loath to admit it—he was part of the emerging puzzle of Jeannette Simmons's murder, and of the dynamics of the Simmons family.

Neil had wanted it all to go away.

If only. If only.

ELEVEN

Annabel Lee-Smith's dinner conquered the oppressive heat. The entrée was lobster salad, the lobsters shucked and chopped with loving care by Mackensie Smith. Gazpacho was first on the table, accompanied by fresh French bread. Key lime pie would top things off.

"You look splendid in that apron," Annabel told Mac as they awaited the arrival of their guests.

"Thank you, ma'am. You look pretty good yourself."

"It's a shame we can't have cocktails out on the terrace. The ice wouldn't last a minute out there. Neither would we."

"I'll have to hoist a toast to Mr. Carrier tonight."

"Who?"

"Willis Carrier. He invented air-conditioning more than a hundred years ago."

"And why do you know that?"

"In case I end up on a quiz show. Want to know who invented the chastity belt?"

"No."

"Suit yourself."

The front desk called to announce that Mr. Marbury and Ms. Coleman had arrived. A few minutes later Mac, Annabel, and Rufus, their blue Great Dane, greeted the couple at the door and led them into the living room, where Mac's small bar was set up in a corner. "Drink?" Mac asked. "I have the ingredients for most concoctions. Just don't ask for a pousse-café."

Jonell Marbury's laugh was a rumble. "I was counting on one of those, Mac, but I'll settle for a gin-and-tonic." The woman accompanying him, his fiancée, Marla Coleman, opted for the same.

Once everyone was settled with drinks and hors d'oeuvres in hand, the conversation almost immediately turned to the murder.

"I thought you might have to cancel, Jonell, because of it," Annabel said.

"There's really not much I can do," he replied. "We all feel terrible for Neil Simmons. He was so close to his mother."

"A terrible loss," Marla said.

Marbury's Caribbean roots were evident in the slight but discernible lilt to his voice. Considerably darker than Marla, who hailed from Savannah, Georgia, the thirty-seven-year-old was a man who turned heads and commanded attention when he entered a crowded room. Mac had met him when Jonell was chief of staff to an African American congresswoman from California. He'd established a reputation as one of the most effective staffers on the House side, and his influence in drafting legislation was considerable. He was, among other things, especially skilled at working with lobbyists who had a stake in a pending bill, weaving their input and legitimate concerns into the finished product. And he kept them all legitimate. Then, a year ago, he'd told Mac over lunch that he'd resigned from his post with the congresswoman to take a job with the Marshalk Group on K Street. His decision was not, he admitted, popular with Marla, an executive with the National Urban League in D.C.

She, his fiancée, was equally attractive. She'd been cited by

Washingtonian magazine as one of the city's up-and-coming influence makers; the photograph of her in the magazine was stunning. This night she wore an off-white linen suit that hugged her tall, slender body. Jonell's suit was light gray and nicely cut. Seeing the couple featured in the pages of a fashion magazine wouldn't have surprised anyone. One thing was certain. They'd outdressed their host and hostess, who wore casual clothing.

"Rick Marshalk is putting up a fifty-thousand-dollar reward," Marbury said.

"That might generate some leads," Mac said. "Do the police have any suspects yet?"

"Not that I know of. I was talking to Rick today and—"

Another call from the downstairs desk informed Mac that Phil and Emma had arrived.

"We invited another couple to join us tonight," Annabel said as she stood to get the door. "I think you'll enjoy them. Phil Rotondi was an assistant U.S. attorney in Baltimore, and Emma Churchill runs a top catering service here in Washington."

"She caters all of our affairs at Marshalk," Marbury said.

"Phil is a close friend of Senator Simmons," Mac added. "They go back a long way."

Rotondi and Emma were introduced and joined the group in the living room.

"I understand you and Senator Simmons are close friends," Marbury said to Rotondi in his deep, well-modulated voice.

"That's right. College roommates."

"You should be on the radio," Emma said to Marbury.

"I was. The college station."

"The senator must be devastated," Marla said.

"Of course." Rotondi turned to Marbury. "Annabel tells me that you work for Neil Simmons."

"Yes, I do. I've been there about a year now." He turned to Marla. "Marla thinks I've sold out."

"I never said that," she said.

"Not in so many words."

"Jonell used to be chief of staff to a congresswoman on the Hill," Annabel said.

"Congresswoman Dustin," Marla added.

"She's a firebrand, I hear," Emma said.

Marbury laughed. "She can be tough. I loved working for her."

"Marshalk recruited you?" Rotondi asked.

Marbury nodded. "They offered me a deal I couldn't refuse, like *The Godfather.*"

"Money," said Marla.

"Nothing wrong with that," Marbury said, defensively.

"I never said there was anything wrong with being paid more," Marla said. "It's just that—"

"Lobbyists have taken a beating lately," Mac tossed in. "Refills anyone?"

"Sure," said Rotondi, holding up his empty beer stein, which had been frosted in the freezer before use.

"They deserve to," Marla opined.

"Oh, come on now," Jonell said. "Lobbyists play an important role in the legislative process."

Only in its purest sense, Rotondi thought.

"Had you ever met Mrs. Simmons?" Mac asked Marbury.

"Yes. A few times. In fact, I saw her yesterday afternoon."

His statement caused a hush to fall over the room.

Rotondi broke it. "How was she?" he asked.

"Fine. I mean, I was only there for a minute or two. I delivered something for the senator, an envelope. Rick Marshalk asked me to drop it off. I handed it to her at the door."

The conversation veered from that to a discussion of a developing scandal with a member of the House of Representatives that had made the papers that day. From there, it was on to some amusing stories from Emma Churchill about unusual catering situations she'd recently experienced, and Marla weighed in with the tale of a politician who'd fallen asleep during an Urban League–sponsored round-table discussion on the state of race relations in America. Although Marbury and his fiancée, and Rotondi and Emma Churchill had never met before, they quickly fell into the sort of easy conversation typical of old friends. When Rotondi got up to fetch a plate of hors d'oeuvres, Marla asked what had happened to his leg.

Rotondi shrugged. "It's a long story," he said.

"When you were a U.S. attorney in Baltimore?" Marbury asked.

"Yeah. A creep I put away decided to get even when he got out."

&

He hadn't wanted a retirement party, and had made his feelings known to his bosses and fellow U.S. attorneys. But they weren't about to be deprived of putting on a grand farewell for their iconoclastic colleague, and so the night was chosen and the site reserved—Caesar's Den, Rotondi's favorite haunt, on South High Street in Baltimore's Little Italy.

Ninety men and women showed up that evening. Spirits ran high, the liquor freely. Rotondi ordered his usual twenty-ounce veal chop, a house specialty. His wife, Kathleen, opted for mussels in a white wine sauce. In Rotondi's eyes, she looked especially beautiful that night, although there had never been a day in their sixteen-year marriage when he hadn't felt that way. Her long hair was naturally blond, and she wore it simple and straight. She had a surprisingly dusky complexion for an Irish girl from Annapolis; her grandmother had been French. All Rotondi knew was that she was as kind and gentle as she was attractive, coolly efficient in court, loving and playful when away from the black robes and stuffy decorum of the courtroom.

They'd met on the job. A new addition to the criminal section, she was assigned to work with Rotondi on some high-profile cases he'd taken on. At first, she found his personality to be off-putting. He attacked every day with the zeal of a man possessed; smiles and relaxed moments were few and far between. But as the weeks went by, she began to see something in him that he wasn't totally successful in hiding from public view—at least not from her, though he tried hard.

And while he never veered from his professional approach, she also sensed a growing flicker of male interest.

One night, after a particularly grueling all-day court session that lasted into the early evening, she suggested they grab a bite together.

"Sure," he said without hesitation, which surprised her. She'd assumed she would have to cajole him into accepting. "I'll take you to my favorite place," he added.

That was the first of many nights at Caesar's Den, where the owners greeted Phil with open arms and extended the same warm welcome to the lovely lady who now regularly accompanied him. Conversation on their first few evenings together consisted primarily of office talk—lawyer talk—hashing over cases in which they were involved. But as the days extended into weeks, his defenses slipped, and his more personal side peeked through.

". . . I used to think I'd never marry," he told her one night. "I was immersed in my studies at law school, and joined the office here right after graduation. What about you?"

"Me? I think marriage is wonderful, provided you meet the right person. I've seen some of my friends settle because they're convinced they have to get married by a certain age. I think that's dumb."

"Dumb?" He laughed.

"Well, maybe *ill advised* is a better term."

"No," he said. "I like *dumb*." He swished the red wine remaining in his glass. "Maybe it was the thought of having kids," he said to the wine. "I don't think I'd make much of a father."

"Why do you say that?"

"Just knowing myself. You might have noticed that I'm a little self-obsessed."

"I've seen hints of it now and then," she said with a smile. "I suppose I'd like children someday. But like getting married, I don't think it's something you have to do. There are so many pressures on us to do what others expect. Marry by a certain age. Have two and a half children, one and a half dogs. You might have noticed that I'm somewhat self-obsessed, too."

"I've seen hints," he said, lightly. "So tell me about your family, Kathleen."

She obliged. Her father was a carpenter at an Annapolis boatyard. "He works hard," she said. "He's my hero, no pretensions, no posturing, just hard work every day. My mom is a receptionist in a dentist's office. Every cent she made went into a college fund for me and my brother."

"What's your brother do?"

"Bart's two years older. He teaches earth science in a local high school. His wife's a doll. She teaches, too. They have one and a half children, no dog. I grew up with a border collie named—ready?—Lassie. I love animals."

"Why don't you get one?"

"Too busy. Wouldn't be fair to the dog. What about you, Phil? I showed you mine. Your turn to show me yours."

"Not a lot to show, Kathleen, or to tell." He talked about his sisters and wayward brother, and his deceased parents. He found it difficult to discuss such things, and there was a moment when Kathleen thought he might cry. But he didn't, and eventually he even smiled when recounting a few intimate—intimate in his mind—details of family life. "Like I said, not much to tell."

"Your father sounds like he was a wonderful man."

"Yes, he was. His Old World views caused some tension between us now and then, but nothing major. I had a couple of fights with kids in school who made fun of the way he talked." He laughed. "I won."

"I don't doubt that. Were you a religious family?"

"Not formal religion. We were brought up Catholic, and I was baptized and confirmed. So were my brother and sisters. My father, he believed in individual faith but was distrustful of organized religion. I suppose I feel the same way. He taught me a lot of things, Kathleen, including the importance of always standing for something, standing tall. I like to think I practice that advice."

They closed the restaurant that night and went to his apartment, where they made love for the first time. The next morning, they both knew without saying it that they were in it for the long haul.

"We should take a weekend and visit my folks," she said. "You'd like them. My dad is every bit as hard-ass as you are."

His thoughts flew back to the University of Illinois and to Jeannette Boyton, but only for a moment.

"I'd like that," he said.

They made that weekend trip two weeks later. Kathleen had been right. Rotondi liked her parents and brother, felt very much at home with them. The wedding took place three months later. Phil's sisters and their families attended the small ceremony; his brother sent his regrets but wished him well. Their honeymoon consisted of a long weekend at the acclaimed Inn at Little Washington, in the foothills of the Blue Ridge Mountains in Washington, Virginia, where they got to know each other even better. Four days later, they were back in the courtroom.

❧

Kathleen had come directly to Phil's retirement party dressed in her all-business tailored black suit and white blouse. Had she been able, she would have chosen a dressy outfit for this special occasion honoring her husband. But she'd spent the day in court arguing before a notoriously dim-witted judge who moved things along slowly in order to keep up with what was going on. Kathleen Moran-Rotondi was a highly respected assistant U.S. attorney, as much at home in a courtroom as she was in the kitchen of their high-rise apartment in Baltimore's Inner Harbor development.

"Come on, Phil, 'fess up," a colleague yelled from across the table. "You use some kind of superman drugs, right?" His comment caused others to laugh, and to follow up with the same accusation. Rotondi was the star player on a once-a-week recreational basketball team that pitted prosecutors against defense lawyers. His intensity on the court matched his concentration in the courtroom, and although some joked about how seriously he took the games, few failed to appreciate his talent, on the court and off.

"All right, all right," Rotondi said, standing and holding up his hands for silence. "I admit it. I've been taking steroids every morning with my granola. But even if I hadn't, I'd still outplay all of you clowns."

Kathleen looked up him and beamed. He'd started the evening stiff and reserved, but the drinks, and the outpouring of goodwill from everyone in attendance, had loosened him up. He was thoroughly enjoying himself.

Over dessert, Rotondi was roasted. It became raunchy as the evening wore on, but it was all in good fun, and the room roiled with laughter, Phil and Kathleen leading the charge.

Farewells took forever. Everyone wanted to shake Phil's hand on the way out of the restaurant, and hug him, tell him how sorely he'd be missed, and warn Kathleen that having a retired husband was a recipe for marital disaster, wishing him many happy years of leisure and warning him to drive home safely lest he end up with a DUI and sully the department's reputation.

"I'll see you in the morning," Phil told them. "I've got the Jensen case on the docket tomorrow. My retirement doesn't kick in for another month."

"Know what I'd love?" he told Kathleen after everyone was gone and they stood alone on the sidewalk in front of Caesar's Den.

"What's that?"

"A cigarette. Can you imagine that? I've never smoked in my life but I have this urge to puff on a cigarette."

"Well, get over it, my dear," she said.

"Maybe you'd be willing to substitute another vice when we get home," he suggested.

She gave forth with a wicked laugh. "I've been planning that all evening," she said. "Come on. I parked around the corner." She'd dropped him off at the office that morning and driven to the courthouse for her appearance.

He put his arm around her and held tight as they walked down the street, their gait a little rocky from all the wine, their spirits equally as intoxicated. They turned the corner, waited for passing traffic to clear, crossed, and proceeded down a deserted, dimly lit street.

"It's down there," she said, indicating the cream-colored Toyota Camry parked at the end of the block. When they'd almost reached it, Kathleen pulled keys from her purse. "You okay to drive?" she asked.

"Yeah, I'm fine."

They were within a few feet of the car when a man's voice said, "Hey, Rotondi!"

Phil and Kathleen turned in the direction of the voice, which came from behind a tree. Its owner stepped out of the shadows. "Hey, Rotondi," he repeated. "Remember me?"

Phil ignored him and moved Kathleen closer to the car.

"You bastard!" the man said.

"Look, fella, I suggest that—" Rotondi said.

The man moved quickly to cut off their path to the Toyota. Now the handgun he wielded was visible.

Rotondi squinted to better see his face.

"You put me away six years ago, Rotondi. Remember? Paulie Sims?"

"Get in the car," Rotondi said to Kathleen. He said to the gunman, "Yeah, I remember you, Paulie. What the hell do you think you're doing with the gun? Put it down before you end up in bigger trouble."

"You and your cop buddies planted that evidence on me and used it to put me away."

"The hell we did," Rotondi said. "You did the crime and you did the time. Now wise up and get out of our way."

Sims raised the weapon and pointed it at Rotondi's head. Rotondi growled at Kathleen, "Get in the car, Kathleen."

She didn't move.

He turned to Sims. "You've got a beef with me, Paulie, fair enough, but this is my wife. She had nothing to do with your case, so let her get in the car. You and I can talk this out." Rotondi extended his hand. "Give me the gun, Paulie. Give it to me!"

The tranquil silence of the side road exploded with gunshots, one after the other, a staccato barrage of bullets, the smoke and smell of cordite drifting up into the still night air. The *pop-pop-pop* of the gun was replaced by an anguished scream from Kathleen and a tortured groan from Rotondi as pain pulsated through his leg, causing it to collapse beneath him. He hit the sidewalk face-first, breaking his nose and taking the skin off his cheek. He twisted his head to see their assailant run out of sight. Rotondi turned in Kathleen's direction. She was sprawled on the sidewalk six feet from him, on her back, legs akimbo, hands crossed defensively over her face.

"Kathleen," Phil said. He tried to stand but his one leg was useless. He crawled toward her, a hand outstretched, saying her name over and over. He hauled himself on top of her body and pushed her hands away from her face. "Kathleen, say something. Say something, damn it!"

No words came, nor would they ever come from her again.

◈

". . . and so I spent two months in rehab for my leg," Rotondi told those gathered in Mac and Annabel Smith's apartment. "They arrested the punk the next morning. He's doing life without parole. My sentence? They almost had to take the leg off, but the surgeons were great."

Mac and Annabel knew about Rotondi's wife but respected his decision to leave out that part of the story.

Emma squeezed Rotondi's hand. His telling of the tale never failed to send chills through her, and to make her nauseous.

"What a horrible thing to go through," Marla said.

"Yeah, but it's history." Rotondi turned to Annabel: "Hey, when's dinner, sweetheart? I'm starving."

As they enjoyed their dinner, a violent thunderstorm roared into the city. Blinding shafts of lightning were like strobe lights outside the glass doors to the terrace, and sharp cracks of thunder caused them to start. It was over as quickly as it had arrived.

"Maybe it'll break the heat wave," Emma commented.

Mac went to the sliding glass doors and opened them. "Heavenly," he announced. "It must have dropped ten, fifteen degrees."

The key lime pie was a hit, along with cups of cappuccino Mac brewed in the kitchen. He offered after-dinner drinks in the living room, but Rotondi and Emma declined. "I've got a seven o'clock breakfast at Homeland Security to cater," she said. After they'd left, Mac, Annabel, Jonell, and Marla strolled onto the terrace.

"Turned out to be a lovely evening," Annabel commented, taking a deep breath of the cooler air.

"Everything's lovely about this evening," Marla said.

"Phil left out the part about his wife," Annabel said. "She was killed when that released criminal started shooting."

"How sad. Poor man."

"I think he preferred not to put a damper on the evening," said Annabel.

The women stayed outside for a few more minutes before Annabel cleared some dishes; Marla followed her inside, leaving Mac alone with Marbury. "I imagine the police had plenty of questions for you, Jonell, about having been at the house the day Jeannette Simmons was killed," Mac said.

"I haven't spoken with them, Mac."

"They'll get around to questioning you."

Marbury hesitated before saying, "I haven't told them I was there."

Mac looked at him quizzically. "I assume you intend to," he said.

"I, ah—I'm not sure I should bother, Mac. I have nothing to offer. I rang the bell. She came to the door. I handed her the envelope and left."

"Still, you have an obligation to tell them you were there. If the police come up with it on their own, they'll focus in on you as a suspect."

"I'm sure that's good advice, Mac. Thanks. I'll take care of it."

Later that night as Mac and Annabel got ready for bed, Mac told her about his conversation with Marbury about his not having gone to the police.

"I hope he listens to you," she said.

"I do, too, Annie. I had the feeling that it wasn't because he considered himself irrelevant. It's almost as though he had a more concrete reason for his decision."

"Well," she said, "if he's smart, which we know he is, he'll do what you suggested. The evening was a success, wasn't it?"

"It always is with you at the helm."

A kiss good night, then lights out.

TWELVE

The next morning, Jonell Marbury sat in Rick Marshalk's office with Marshalk and the firm's president, Neil Simmons. "What time is the press conference?" Marshalk asked Simmons.

"Noon."

"It's a good move," Marshalk said. "You say your sister will be with you?"

"According to Dad, and I was happy to hear it. They haven't always gotten along."

"Sometimes tragedy brings families together," Marbury offered.

"Glad everything went well with Betzcon," Neil said.

Marshalk snapped his fingers. "Piece o' cake. Couldn't have gone better. They've got deep pockets and are willing to fund whatever we suggest. They're putting up half of the reward money through CMJ. I talked to them this morning. They've committed to underwriting that rock concert in New York next month." His laugh was snide. "Can you believe those clowns in Congress? They pass all those new ethics rules so we can't buy a congressman a hamburger, but they open it up for us to pay thousands for their fund-raisers. The concert will cost Betzcon sixty grand, and we net half. That's a bargain for Betzcon considering the political clout they're getting."

Neil stood and removed his suit jacket from where he'd hung it on the back of his chair. "I have some things to do before the conference," he announced.

"How'd the interview with the cops go yesterday?" Marshalk asked.

"Okay. They kept asking about Mom and Dad's relationship, whether they had problems. I mean, Jesus, doesn't every couple have problems? That's what I told them, that my parents fought once in a while like every other married couple." He shook his head. "Dad was all over me on the phone last night for telling the cops that. They've got this Chinese detective doing the questioning. I feel like I'm back in a nineteen-forties black-and-white movie."

Marshalk laughed; Marbury was silent.

"I'll check in later," Simmons said.

Marshalk turned to Marbury after Simmons was gone. "You said you had something to talk to me about. Shoot."

"The murder," Marbury said. "I know you and Jack say I shouldn't bother mentioning to the police that I was there at the senator's house the afternoon of the murder, but I'm uncomfortable with that."

"Why?"

"Because I might have been the last person to see her alive."

"Oh, come on, Jonell, you come off like some knee-jerk do-gooder." He leaned his elbows on the desk. "You have nothing to offer the cops. So you were there delivering something for us. Big deal. You heard what Jack said. He should know. Christ, he was with MPD for twenty years before coming over here. He told you that if you volunteer that you were there, all it will do is open up a can of worms where you're concerned, and cause problems for the firm. I'm sure you wouldn't want to do that."

"I had a conversation last night with Mackensie Smith."

"Who's he?"

"He used to be a top defense lawyer here in D.C. He teaches law at GW now. He suggests that I go to the police immediately."

"You told him that you were at the Simmons house?"

"Yes."

Marshalk sat back and sighed.

"I just want to do what's right," Marbury said.

"Sure. So do I." Marshalk leaned forward again. "Look, Jonell, give it a day or two before you make a decision. Fair enough?"

"I talked to Marla about it last night. She thinks I should go to the police today."

"Marla's not an attorney, or a cop." Marshalk came around the desk and slapped Marbury on the back. "All we all want, Jonell, is for the police to find who murdered Jeannette Simmons and bring that person to justice. Agreed?"

"Of course. Thanks for listening, Rick."

"Hey, buddy, that's what I'm here for." He walked him to the door. "Call that rock promoter in New York and make sure everything's on schedule. Free for lunch?"

"Yes."

"Great. Morton's. My treat."

In his office, Jonell read that morning's paper. The Simmons murder was still page-one news, as expected. Most of the lead article was a rehash of what had been written in previous editions, with a healthy dollop of rumor and innuendo thrown in for spice. He was pondering the conversation he'd just had with Marshalk when a woman knocked on the door and opened it.

"Hey, Camelia," Marbury said. "How goes it?"

"It goes okay," she said, plopping in a chair. "You?"

"So-so. I was just reading the latest about the murder."

"Poor Neil. He seems lost."

"To be expected. He and his mom were close. So, all ready for your farewell bash?"

"I think so."

Camelia Watson had resigned from the Marshalk Group after two years. Before becoming a lobbyist, she'd worked at the Justice Department in its governmental oversight department. While there, she had developed close relationships with myriad top officials in Congress and in a variety of federal agencies. Her relationship with them was what had attracted Rick Marshalk, and he'd aggressively pursued her to come to work for him, dangling a series of large salaries and bonuses until she'd succumbed. While she enjoyed the money and lifestyle it afforded her, she'd never found her comfort zone lobbying former friends in Congress and at various agencies, and finally decided to return to her old job at Justice—if they'd have her. They didn't hesitate: "Welcome back, Camelia." She was that good.

Marshalk had been unhappy when Camelia turned in her resignation, and tried to entice her to stay. She resisted. The more he persevered, the more she grew resentful of his attitude that he could buy anything, including her. While she'd kept her mood upbeat throughout the process of leaving, her disenchantment with Marshalk and the firm had become increasingly pervasive, and she often confided her negative feelings to Jonell. He served as her sounding board and confidant, their bonding enhanced by their African American roots.

His relationship with Camelia had caused occasional bouts of jealousy with Marla, who saw Camelia as a romantic threat. Both women were extremely attractive, but in different ways. Marla was fashion-conscious, her tastes running to designer clothing and spa treatments, which Jonell sometimes kidded her about—"Pretty highfalutin for somebody working at a leading agency for social change and justice like the Urban League," he would say, but not too often. To which she would reply, "Working nonprofit doesn't mean taking a vow of poverty." Interest from a modest trust created for her by her father, a deceased Atlanta physician, provided her "play money" with which to indulge some of her whims.

Camelia Watson, on the other hand, lived a simpler lifestyle despite the lofty salary Marshalk had been paying her. She was no less attractive than Marla, just packaged differently. Her understated sexiness appealed to Jonell, including—especially—the oversize, round, red-framed eyeglasses she wore. He'd told her he thought the glasses were sexy, and she'd made it known, subtly, of course, that she wouldn't have minded a romantic relationship with him. But it never went beyond that sort of office flirtation. Jonell might have lusted for her, but only, as a former president of the United States once famously said, in his heart.

Her face turned serious.

"Something wrong?" Jonell asked.

"It's Marshalk. He insisted on taking me to dinner last night and—"

"What's wrong with that?"

"Nothing wrong with going to dinner with your boss. It's what he said that bothers me."

"I'm listening."

"He—he basically threatened me, Jonell."

"Threatened you? With what?"

"About what I've learned about Marshalk Group since I've been here. He's afraid that by going back to work at Justice, I might use my inside knowledge of how things work here to bring some sort of legal action against him and the firm."

"That's ridiculous."

"He doesn't think it is. It was creepy, really creepy. He was all smiles and happy talk during most of the meal. But then he got serious, *very* serious, and gave me this lecture on how he expected me to treat what I know as sacred, and that . . ."

"And that *what*?"

"And that he'd hate to see something terrible happen to me."

"He *said* that? I mean, those were his words?"

"Yes, that's exactly what he said. Oh, he couched it with lots of flowery talk about what a great career I have in front of me, and how much he's appreciated the work I've done here. But when he said that—when he threatened me—my blood ran cold." She looked behind her to confirm that the door was closed. "Jonell," she said, "the Marshalk Group breaks the law every day. That's one of the reasons I'm leaving. This place is a legal train wreck waiting to happen."

Marbury forced a laugh. "Come on, Camelia," he said, "it can't be that bad."

"It's worse, Jonell. Want some good advice?"

"Sure."

"Listen to Marla. She wants you to leave. You don't want to be on this train when it goes off the rails."

⁂

That same morning, Detective Charles Chang sat in an interrogation room with his partner, Amanda Widletz. Across the table from them was the handyman who'd worked on the Simmons house the day Jeannette Simmons was killed. He was a stout, barrel-chested man, almost totally bald, and had the red nose and whiskey veins in his cheeks often associated with heavy drinking. His name was Lou Schultz.

"Am I a suspect?" he asked.

"No, sir," Chang said. "Absolutely not, sir."

"We wouldn't be doing our job if we didn't talk to everyone who knew the victim," Widletz added. "By the way, thanks for coming in like this."

"I want to help."

"Of course you do," said Widletz.

"You were doing repairs on the Simmons house two days ago," Chang said.

"That's right."

"Were you their regular repairman?"

He nodded. "I was recommended to Mrs. Simmons by a neighbor about two years ago. She liked the work I did, and I've been there ever since, part-time, general repairs, things like that, painting, wallpapering, fixing up outside. It's a really nice house.

"But no major projects, no additions or things like that. I like to keep it simple."

"Were you there all day?" Widletz asked

"Got there early in the AM. I wanted to start early 'cause of the heat."

"And you worked there all day?"

"Pretty much. I took an hour, maybe a little longer for lunch— Mrs. Simmons paid me by the project, so there's no problem with taking off time now and then."

"You ate there?"

"No. There's a bar and restaurant about a mile away. I go there regular. Everybody knows me. Mrs. Simmons offered me a cold drink about noon and wanted me to come inside where it was cool. I didn't want to do that. She was one nice lady. I can't believe somebody did this to her."

"Aside from offering you a cold drink, Mr. Schultz, did you have other conversations with Mrs. Simmons?" Widletz asked.

He rubbed his chin. "A couple of times. She came out once and admired the work I was doing on a stone wall." He laughed. "She said it was a work of art. That's what she said. A work of art. Oh, and when I took a break in the afternoon, I told her I'd be gone for about an hour. She told me to come inside to cool off, but I was uncomfortable doing that, so I went back to where I had lunch and enjoyed a beer. Boy, that heat was tough. Cleared up really good though, with that storm that came through last night. Some difference, huh?"

"What was the last time you saw Mrs. Simmons?" Chang asked.

"When I took my break late in the afternoon. Can't say exactly when that was."

"Your best estimate, Mr. Schultz," Widletz said.

Another rubbing of the chin. "I'd say I left there about three thirty. Yeah, that's about right. Three thirty."

"And you returned when?" Chang asked.

"Was gone an hour, so it was probably four thirty, give or take a few minutes. Like I said, I can't remember exactly. That's one of the things I like about being on my own. No time clock to punch." He hoped they hadn't taken offense. He was sure they punched in and out.

"Did you see Mrs. Simmons when you returned at four thirty?" Chang asked.

"I didn't say it was four thirty exactly," Schultz replied.

"Approximately four thirty," Chang corrected.

"Right. Approximately. No, I didn't see her again. I really didn't stay around long, just cleaned up, grabbed my tools, and went home. I was pretty upset, I'll tell you that."

"Why?"

"I couldn't find my favorite hammer. Somebody must have stole it. You wouldn't think that sort of thing would happen in a fancy neighborhood like that. You can't leave anything lying around these days. I really liked that hammer, had it for years."

Chang noted the missing hammer in the notes he was taking. "You went straight home after work?"

"Right. Well, no, not exactly. I stopped off for a beer."

"Not exactly," Chang said.

"Right. I want to be as accurate as possible for you folks. I know you've got a lollapalooza of a murder case on your hands."

Widletz readjusted her posture in the hard wooden chair and said, "While you were working at the house that day, Mr. Schultz, did you see anyone else there? Were there any visitors?"

"Oh, boy, let me think about that." Again, a hand to the chin.

Could anything ever grow on that chin? Widletz wondered.

"The mailman," Schultz said. "He came while I was there."

"Anyone else?" Chang asked.

"Let me see. Oh, sure. Walter arrived with some dry cleaning."

"Walter?"

"Walter McTeague. He's the senator's personal driver. Body-guard, too, I think. Hey, he was one of you guys as I understand. A former cop."

"Did he go inside the house?"

"Sure. He shows up there lots of times. Usually goes inside."

"What time did he arrive?"

"That's a tough one. Let me see. I think it was just before I left for my break at three thirty. *About* three thirty."

"How long did he stay?" Chang asked.

Schultz shrugged. "I don't know. He was gone when I got back."

"Who else?" asked Chang.

"Hmmm. Mrs. Simmons came out after I got back from lunch and asked whether I'd seen her sister. I guess she was supposed to visit."

Chang glanced down at his notes. "Marlene Boynton?"

"That's her."

"You didn't see her?"

"Nope. She stops by the house often. She doesn't live far away. She's . . ."

"She's what?" Widletz asked.

"Well, no offense to her, but she's a little—" He rotated his index finger against his temple. "I don't listen in, mind you, but I've heard them get into some pretty bad arguments. So loud it comes right through the closed doors and windows." He raised his hand. "Wait. I don't want to be wrong here. It's always the sister who does the screaming, not Mrs. Simmons. She's too much of a lady to do that."

"But she didn't show up that day?" Chang said.

"Not as far as I know. Of course, I was gone for a while. Okay if I go now?"

"In a few minutes," Chang said. "No one else visited the house that you can remember?"

"Wait a minute, wait a minute. There was somebody else, arrived just as I was leaving for the day."

They waited for him to elaborate.

"Never saw him before. He pulled up in a fancy car, a Mercedes—or maybe it was a BMW—I can't tell one of those expensive cars from another. Might have been a Lexus. I know it wasn't an SUV. Anyway, I was pulling away in my panel truck when he arrived, pulled right up in the driveway to the front door and got out."

"You saw the driver?"

"Yes, I did."

"And?"

"He was a tall black fella. Real dark. Had on a suit."

"And you'd never seen him before."

"That's right."

"Think you'd recognize him if you saw him again."

"Probably not. I only got a glimpse of him."

"Did he go inside?" Chang asked.

"Sure. I mean, I didn't see him go inside because I was on my way, but I assume he did. Why would he be there if he wasn't going to go inside?"

"What color was the car?"

"Light-colored. White, I think. Maybe gray. But light. Are we finished? I promised my wife I'd get home early today."

Or his buddies at the bar are waiting, Widletz thought.

"Sure," she said. "You're free to go, but we may want to talk to you again. No trips planned?"

"Nope. We've got a cabin in North Carolina. That's about the only place we go."

"Where do you keep your tools, Mr. Schultz?" Chang asked.

"In my truck."

"You have it with you, sir?"

"Sure. I drove it over here."

"Would you mind showing me your tools, sir?"

"What for?"

Chang stared at him.

"Sure. Happy to show you whatever I've got. Nice meeting you, ma'am. Hope you find whoever killed Mrs. Simmons. She was some nice person, a real lady."

When Chang returned twenty minutes later, his partner asked if he'd found anything.

"He has many tools that might have been used to kill Mrs. Simmons. I want a warrant for evidence technicians to test them for blood."

"Do you really think that's necessary," Widletz said.

"Yes, I do, Detective Widletz."

"Hey, Charlie, do you think you could call me Amanda? We've been working together a long time."

"I prefer not to," he said.

"Suit yourself," she muttered, adding under her breath, "*You officious little twerp!*"

⟨✽⟩

Emma Churchill returned to her Foggy Bottom house, where she and Rotondi lunched on choice leftovers she'd brought home from that morning's catered breakfast. They turned on a small TV in the kitchen and watched the news. A press conference by Senator Simmons and his family was scheduled to begin at noon. Ten minutes before that, the newscaster said, "Our Jane Willis is standing by at the Dirksen Senate Office Building with some breaking news. Jane."

The familiar face of a local reporter filled the screen. "While we're waiting for a statement from the senator and his family, I've been told by reliable sources within the MPD that the marriage between Senator Simmons and his deceased wife was a troubled one. According to these sources, there had been marital problems for a number of years, and separation and divorce had been discussed."

The anchor said, "Jane, are the police considering this significant as far as the investigation of the murder is concerned?"

"I haven't specifically been told that," replied Willis, who stood in front of the bank of microphones that would be used by Simmons and the family, "but we have to assume that it will figure into their probe. Back to you until the senator makes his appearance."

"*Breaking news* indeed," Rotondi grumbled. "Breaking *rumor* would be more like it."

"You've indicated in the past that their marriage was rocky, Phil," Emma said.

"They had their ups and downs."

"You should know."

He did know a lot about the marriage between Lyle and Jeannette Simmons, far more than he'd ever confided to her, or anyone else for that matter.

The scene on the screen shifted from the anchor desk to the press conference. Lyle Simmons stood in front of the bouquet of microphones, flanked by Neil and Polly. Dozens of reporters surrounded them. The senator looked good, Rotondi thought, tall, tanned, sadness written on his handsome face, his gray hair promising wisdom in all things. Polly looked as though she'd suddenly found herself in an alien land and was desperate to escape. She hadn't bothered to dress for the cameras; she wore what she'd had on when she'd arrived in D.C. It was Neil, however, who especially captured Rotondi's attention. He was certainly a good-looking young man, no surprise considering his parentage. He wore clothes well. But there was a softness about him, Rotondi had always felt, not physically but in spirit and character, a man who harbored few convictions about himself or the world.

The senator spoke: "Thank you for coming here today. My son, Neil, my daughter, Polly, and I suffered a terrible tragedy a few days ago. The brutal murder of my wife, and of their mother, has shattered our lives, as you can imagine. There has been speculation as recently as a few minutes ago about the state of my marriage to Jeannette. I was shocked to hear the sort of vicious rumor reported just prior to this news conference. Nothing could be farther from the truth. We enjoyed many happy years together. That happiness has been taken away at the hand of a murderer, and as a family we are working closely with law enforcement to bring that killer to justice. Polly has flown in from California—" He put his arm around her, causing her to visibly flinch. "—and we ask all of you in the media to do what you can to help find Jeannette's killer. I would also like to express our sincere appreciation to all those people who've sent us e-mails of sympathy, and prayers. The American people are the most generous in spirit in the world, and their support during this ordeal has sustained us. Again, thank you for coming—"

"Are you going to run for president?" a reporter yelled.

"There will be no questions," Simmons said. "And frankly, I find that particular question to be inappropriate considering the reason we are here today."

That didn't stop the press corps from shouting other off-message queries as the three of them walked away from the microphones and disappeared from the room.

"Nicely done," Rotondi commented to Emma.

"He's smooth, that's for sure. What about the sister? No one's mentioned her, and she wasn't at the press conference."

"Marlene? I imagine they're keeping her under wraps. She's always been intensely jealous of Jeannette. Marlene is two, three years younger than her sister. She tried to make it as an actress in New York but didn't get very far. I've always felt that she sees Jeannette—*saw* her married to a powerful U.S. senator and felt she was the one who should be in that role."

"She never married?"

"No. She's spent time in a few mental institutions when she's gone off the deep end. She's a strange lady, Emma. She goes through life as though she's constantly auditioning for a role. One day she's Blanche DuBois, the next she's Mary, Queen of Scots. She never seems to connect with reality." He smiled. "I suppose there are other actors and actresses who have that problem."

"Maybe some."

"Uh-huh. Anyway, Marlene has been supported by Lyle and Jeannette for much of her adult life. They pay for the condo she lives in, buy her cars, and pay most of the bills. She hasn't worked in years."

"What an unhappy life."

"That it is."

"Do you think that she might have let her anger at her sister boil over and . . . ?"

"Anything's possible. She's volatile. I've been with her on a number of occasions when she's erupted. One minute she's as pleasant as can be. Then, without warning, she blows. She seems unable to control her emotions, especially her anger."

"Have you ever seen her attack her sister?"

"Once. Kathleen and I were away for a weekend with Lyle and Jeannette. Marlene came along. She'd just gotten out of a stay at some mental health facility, and Jeannette wanted to treat her to a pleasant, relaxing weekend. I don't recall what triggered it, but all of a sudden she started ranting about how their mother favored Jeannette. When Jeannette tried to calm her, Marlene lunged at her and pushed her over a chair. Lyle and I physically restrained her. After a couple of minutes, she was calm again and talking as though nothing had ever happened." He looked out the window. "Funny," he said.

"What's funny?"

"Marlene and I always got along. She's clearly unbalanced, but I never thought she could be homicidal."

"*You* weren't a threat to her."

"I suppose. At any rate, I'm sure the police are taking a close look at her."

"Phil, let me ask you something else."

He cocked his head.

"Do you think it's possible that the senator killed his wife?" Before he could answer, she added, "Or had someone kill her?"

"God, I hope not, Emma. I really don't know."

✐

Detectives Chang and Widletz had been in the crowd at the press conference. They left quickly, got in the vehicle they'd checked out of the motor pool that morning, and drove away. Widletz would have preferred to drive, but knew that Chang didn't feel a woman's place was behind the wheel—didn't feel, it seemed, that a woman's place was anywhere except in front of a stove or folding laundry. He drove the way he lived his personal and professional life, slowly, deliberately, by the book. He'd never met a yellow traffic light that he didn't observe. There was no racing to a crime scene with Charlie Chang behind the wheel.

"Where are we going—Detective Chang?" she asked.

"Back to headquarters. Detective Crimley is bringing up the vagrant we've been holding. We can't keep him much longer without charging him. And the senator is coming in at five."

"I hope they cleaned him up, and somebody gave him deodorant. Man, he smelled to high heaven when we brought him in."

Chang said nothing as a light ten feet ahead turned yellow, and he hit the brakes hard.

"I meant the bum, Detective Chang, not the senator."

"I know what you meant, Detective Widletz."

༺

Rotondi and Emma cleared dishes following lunch.

"What's on your agenda?" he asked while placing glasses in the dishwasher.

"A couple of jobs coming up. I'm catering a C-SPAN event tonight, and there's a going-away party tomorrow night for someone at the Marshalk Group." She checked the clock on the wall. "I'd better get over to the kitchen and make sure everything's going okay for tonight. One of my new chefs has a heavy hand with the salt. You?"

"I thought I might swing by Marlene's condo this afternoon."

"Just to say hello?"

"No."

"To satisfy yourself that she didn't kill her sister? Or that she did?"

"Let's just say there are some questions I'd like answered."

"No matter where the answers take you?"

"You might say that." He kissed her. "Tell your chef to go easy on the salt, Emma. You don't want to be responsible for some bigwig having a coronary from your latest concoction." He laughed. "*Death by Sodium*. Not a bad title for a murder mystery."

THIRTEEN

The vagrant, whom the cops knew as Gerry but who asked that he be called Gerard, looked considerably better upon being escorted into the interrogation room than when he'd been picked up. He was freshly showered and fed. His jailhouse jumpsuit was without stains or tears. His slip-on slippers with rubber soles were fresh out of the box. And he was now sober. Gerard gave his age as thirty-three. He claimed to have been an inventor whose inventions were stolen from him by corporate thieves. He was short and sinewy; the muscles on his pale biceps were surprisingly defined. His last name, he claimed, was Lemón, with the accent on the last syllable. "Lemon's a fruit," he told the booking officer. "I'm no fruit."

He was seated at the table by a uniformed cop, who waited until the detectives arrived.

"Want me to stay?" the uniform asked.

"It's not necessary," Chang replied.

Chang sat opposite Gerard. Widletz leaned against an air-conditioning unit that hadn't worked in months.

"So, Mr. Lemón," Chang said, "tell us about yourself."

Lemón was pleased to be asked such an open question and launched into a lengthy, disjointed biography. Chang and Widletz didn't interrupt. When Gerard paused for a breath, Widletz asked, "When did you first meet Mrs. Simmons?"

"Who?"

"Mrs. Simmons. She has a home near that bridge you were sleeping beneath every night."

"Mrs. Simmons? Mrs. Simmons?" He shook his head. "I don't know anybody like that."

"What have you been doing with yourself the past few days, Mr. Lemón?" Chang asked.

Gerard shrugged. "Just hangin' out, looking for a job."

"We're told you stand on the corner with a sign asking for money. True?"

"Yeah, sometimes I do that. But I don't just ask for money. I say I want a job, any kind of job. I'm no bum. I can work if somebody lets me."

"Let me show you something, Mr. Lemón," Widletz said. She opened a file folder in front of him on the table. It contained color photographs of the front of the Simmons home taken by a police photographer. "Recognize this house?" she asked.

He leaned forward, brow furrowed, and picked up each picture. He dropped the last one on the pile and said, "Can't say that I do."

"But you've been there," Widletz said.

"No I haven't."

"Oh, come on, Mr. Lemón, you've been seen walking around this neighborhood by many people."

"Nothing wrong with taking a walk."

"That depends on what you do during your walk," Chang said. "It has been very hot lately. Didn't a woman from this house come out and offer you a cold drink?"

"I don't think so. I mean, maybe somebody did, but I don't remember."

"I don't think that's the sort of thing someone would forget," Chang said.

"I can't remember anything in all that heat. It makes you crazy."

"Were you crazy, sir?" Chang said.

"Me?" He laughed, displaying neglected teeth. "Some people say I am, but I'm not. I'm as sane as you or anybody else."

Chang looked down at the notes he'd made during the questioning of Lou Schultz, the handyman. "Do you do carpentry?" he asked Lemón.

"I can do carpentry. I've done some work like that."

"Do you own a hammer?"

For the first time since the interrogation had started, Lemón appeared to be flustered. He'd met the detectives' eyes while answering their questions. Now he evaded their stares.

"Do you own a hammer, Mr. Lemón?" Chang repeated.

"I had one. Tossed it away."

"Where?"

"I don't know. Somewhere."

"When did you throw it away?"

He shrugged.

"Why did you throw it away?"

His laugh was forced. "Had no use for it. Don't do carpenter work no more."

"Do you think if we went with you, took a pleasant ride, that you could show us where you threw away the hammer?"

"No."

"Was it your hammer, Mr. Lemón, or did you take it from someone, someplace, maybe a man who was working on this house?" He slid one of the photos closer to Lemón.

"No, no, I didn't steal nothing from nobody. I swear it."

Widletz, who now stood behind him, placed her hand on his shoulder. "Do you have a family, Gerard?" she asked softly.

"I did have, a wife and kids. They sided with the ones who stole my ideas, so I told 'em all to go to hell."

"I really wish you'd try harder to remember where you tossed your hammer," Widletz said.

Morris Crimley, who'd been observing the questioning through a one-way glass, stepped into the room and motioned for Chang to come out into the hall with him.

"We just got this back from the lab, Charlie." He handed him a sheet of paper.

"It matches," Chang said.

"Looks like it. Thought you might like to see what he has to say about it. He ask for a lawyer yet?"

"No."

"I'm not surprised. Probably the best sleep and meals he's had for a while."

Chang returned to the room and showed Widletz the paper. Her eyebrows went up as she came around the table and took a chair next to her partner. "Gerard," she said, "we have proof that you were at the house in the pictures."

"Proof?"

"Yes. Stone dust found on the bottom of your shoes matches the dust that the workman made when he was fixing the stone wall in front of the house. And it was found inside the house near the body."

"The *body?*"

"The woman who owned this house was murdered. Did she show you some kindness and offer you an iced tea or lemonade, invite you inside where it was cool?"

He wrapped his arms about himself and pressed his lips together. "I don't want to talk anymore," he mumbled.

"We'll be back," Chang said, and motioned for Widletz to follow him outside, where Crimley waited.

"What do you think?" asked their boss.

"I think we have enough to hold him," Chang said.

"I agree," said Widletz.

"I'll call Matt Bergl at the U.S. attorney's office and tell him what we have," Crimley said. "I think he'll go along."

The uniformed officer who'd escorted Gerard Lemón in for questioning was told by Crimley to return him to his cell. "And cuff him this time."

FOURTEEN

Rotondi pulled up in front of Marlene Boynton's condominium complex, parked on the opposite side of the road, and looked around, surprised that no media types seemed to be in the vicinity. They'd either decided that she wasn't of editorial interest, or learned that she wasn't there.

He got out of the car and walked into the cluster of attached, gray-shingled, three-story town houses. A dog barked from a window; a Hispanic man tending shrubbery that lined the walkway didn't look up as Rotondi hobbled past and found Marlene's unit at the rear, where a man-made creek gurgled behind another row of condos.

He pressed the button and heard the bell sound inside. A tall, narrow strip of glass ran down the side of the door. Rotondi peered through it and saw nothing. It occurred to him that Lyle and Neil might have whisked her out of town to some secluded hotel or spa where the media couldn't get to her. He was about to turn and leave when he saw shadowy movement inside. He rang again. After a long time, she came to the door and peered at him through the glass.

"It's Phil Rotondi," he said loudly.

She hesitated, as though his words had to cross a gap, like the time between lightning flashes and thunder. He heard interior locks being undone. The door opened a crack.

"It's Phil," Rotondi repeated, giving her his best smile.

"Philip?"

"Yeah. It's me, Marlene."

The confusion on her face faded into recognition. "Hello, Philip. Why are you here?"

"Just visiting. I was in Washington and—"

"Do you want to come in?"

"I was sort of hoping for that."

She opened the door farther and stepped back to allow him to enter. The house was cold; the AC was cranked up to its maximum setting. Marlene wore jeans and two sweaters, a cranberry-colored one beneath a tan cardigan. She looked good, looked together. Her auburn hair had the gloss of recent shampooing, and her makeup had been judiciously applied. That she was Jeannette Simmons's sister was unmistakable. Though aging had predictably changed the facial landscape, the sisters' natural beauty shone through.

"Come in, Phil. Sit down. Would you like a cold drink, maybe some tea or coffee? I have coffee left over from this morning."

"Coffee would be nice, black, no sugar."

He followed her into the spacious, spotless kitchen. The multitoned granite countertop was uncluttered, everything in its place, a single cup in a dish drainer. He sat on one of two stools at a movable island in the center of the room while she poured coffee from an insulated carafe into a pretty ceramic mug with flowers on it. She placed it in front of him and took the other stool.

"Thanks," he said. "Nothing for you?"

"I've had enough coffee for the day."

He broke the ensuing silence. "Have you talked to Lyle or Neil since what happened? Polly? She's in town."

"Polly called. She said she's staying at the Hotel George. Pretty ritzy."

"Yes, it is. You haven't spoken with Lyle?"

"Oh, yes, of course I have. He called and told me to stay inside and not to answer the phone."

"Has the press been bothering you?"

"A few called. I hung up on them."

"No one knocking on your door?"

"I've heard a few people outside, but I didn't answer. I just let them bruise their knuckles."

Rotondi laughed. "Good for you, Marlene."

The flesh around her eyes turned dark, and she pressed the knuckle of her hand against her lips. "It's true, isn't it, Phil? Jeannette is dead."

"Yes," he said, aware that she was simply stating what she already knew. He changed the subject. "I'm glad Polly called. She's always been fond of you."

"She's a good girl." She laughed. "Not a girl anymore, is she? She's a young woman."

"And a very smart and attractive one. Tell me more about Lyle's call to you."

"Oh, him? I don't know how he sleeps at night."

"Why do you say that?"

She looked at Rotondi as though he were demented. "Really, Phil, I expect better of you."

"I know that you and Lyle haven't been the best of friends over the years, and that you've had your problems with Jeannette, too."

"Poor Jeannette," she said, slipping into a theatrical voice. "What a mistake she made marrying Mr. Lyle Simmons, the distinguished United States senator." She emphasized the latter part of the statement to indicate her disdain. "What a fraud he is."

A *generous fraud*, Rotondi thought, *paying for your condo, your car, and almost everything else.*

"You don't think poorly of me for saying that, do you, Philip?"

"Of course not, although I'd like to know *why* you said it."

"That's right. You wouldn't have the same view of him, would you, being his college buddy."

"Are you speaking of him politically?" Rotondi asked, taking a sip of his coffee which was turning cold.

She waved away the notion. "I don't care about his politics, Philip. Do you?"

"Depends upon how his votes impact me."

"He wants to be president."

"So I've heard."

She looked past him to a place only she could see. "I wonder whether people would vote for a murderer."

"Marlene?"

"A man who murdered his wife."

"Whoa, Marlene. Hold on. Why would you say something like that?"

"He killed Jeannette."

"You know this for a fact?"

Her voice became dreamy. "Oh, no, he's too clever for that. But he killed her. He's been doing it for years."

"Mentally?"

"Uh-huh." She nodded vigorously for emphasis.

He gathered his thoughts, but she spoke again, too fast for him to express them. "Jeannette was such a fool marrying him, Philip. She was infatuated by his money and his ambition. You know that."

"Their marriage was like any other marriage, full of ups and downs." *At least in the beginning*, he thought but didn't voice.

"She was always starstruck," Marlene added. "There he was, the rich, handsome lawyer consumed with power. Lyle loves power, loves controlling people. He controlled her like she was his puppet, and she accepted it because she didn't want to lose her lofty position, la-di-da. The senator's wife! But even she finally saw through him. She hated him."

Rotondi didn't reply. To argue with her would accomplish nothing. More important, he knew that she was right.

"Polly knows it, too," Marlene continued. "She stood up to him and wouldn't let him bully her the way he did Jeannette. Good for her! Good girl!"

"Let me ask you a question, Marlene."

Her tone suddenly shifted. She grabbed his hand and asked in what could only be considered a little girl's voice, "Do you think I'm insane, Philip?"

"I—"

"Lyle does, and he convinced Jeannette that I was. Do you think I'm insane?"

"Whether someone is considered insane, Marlene, often depends on how many people they annoy."

She pondered that. "Ooh, I like that," she said. "Lyle put me away, you know."

"I know."

"He said it was for my own good, but I knew differently. He did it because he's so cruel."

"Marlene—"

"Jeannette was, too."

He cocked his head.

"She was cruel, too. She always went along with him whenever he sent me to one of those places."

"I'm sure she had your best interests at heart, Marlene." He staved off another interruption by saying quickly, "Did you see Jeannette the day she was murdered?"

She nodded, sat back against the back of the stool and encircled herself with her arms. "I did."

"And?"

"And what, Philip?"

"How was she? What did you talk about?"

"She was drunk."

"How drunk?"

"Not stumbling around, if that's what you mean. Jeannette wasn't a perfect person. She drank too much, you know."

He knew.

"She used to go with him to those fund-raising dinners where all they do is drink. Washington! Nothing but whiskey and payoffs. It's disgusting. Polly wanted me to move to California."

"Did she? When?"

"Oh, now and then she'd mention it. I should have gone, too, gotten as far away as possible from the distinguished senator and my cruel big sister."

"They've been good to you, Marlene," Rotondi said, not sure why he felt the need to defend them.

"They've controlled me," she snapped. "Do you know what Jeannette said to me the other afternoon when I visited?"

"No."

"She said I was jealous of her."

Which was true, Rotondi knew.

"She said I was pathetic. A *pathetic creature*, is what she said exactly."

Somehow Rotondi couldn't envision the Jeannette he knew saying anything that harsh to anyone, especially to her sister. How drunk had she been? Maybe it'd been the booze talking. He made a mental note to check with Crimley on the autopsy to see how much alcohol she had in her system, although the passage of time between her death and the autopsy would cause the level to drop.

"What time did you visit Jeannette?" he asked.

"Does it matter?"

"It might."

She waved her hands in the air to chase away the importance of the question, and answer. "The afternoon. I went in the afternoon."

"Was anyone else there?"

She snorted. "Nobody ever visited Jeannette except me. After she got fed up with having to be at the distinguished senator's side night after night, she decided to stay home. Like me." A laugh. "What a pair the Boynton sisters are, a couple of recluses, two old bags sitting around the house studying their navels."

Rotondi glanced up at a clock decorated with colorful birds. "I think I'd better go, Marlene."

"So soon?" The little girl voice again. "Please stay. I haven't seen you in a while, and I need comforting. My poor sister is dead. I didn't ever hate her, Philip. It's just sometimes I—"

He stood and stretched his leg, grimacing as he did.

"Poor dear," she said. "I hope the man who shot you rots in hell."

"He's close to it," he said. Rotondi had never been in favor of the death penalty: As far as he was concerned, life behind bars was a fate far worse than having a needle stuck in your arm, delivering you to a more peaceful place.

He'd started toward the living room when she stopped him with, "Jeannette should have married you, Phil. You were the one she loved."

He turned and leaned on his cane.

"She told me that many times," said Marlene. "She told Polly that, too. She should have married you."

"I'll stop by again, Marlene," he said and continued to the front door.

She came to him. One hand went to his cheek, her fingertips caressing it.

"You take care, Marlene. Everything will work out."

He left quickly.

FIFTEEN

"The war was a mistake to begin with."
"They say we had to take a stand somewhere against Communism."
"My father says that if we hadn't gone to war in Vietnam, the whole area would've fallen to the Communists."
"The domino theory."
"That's what he called it. The domino theory."
"We went into Vietnam because we were misled. The Gulf of Tonkin was a deliberate lie to justify sending in troops. Our involvement in Vietnam isn't justified on the grounds of vital national interest, or of moral commitment. The government says we had to go in because North Vietnam was aggressively attacking the south. That makes it a civil war, and we have no right injecting our national will into a civil war. Not only that, Vietnam was one nation until it was temporarily split by the Geneva Accords of 1954. There were supposed to be national elections to unify the country, but it was the South Vietnamese president, Ngo Dinh, who violated that agreement."

"That may be true, but—"

"Besides, we've never had a treaty agreement to defend South Vietnam. All SEATO did was to establish a structure through which its members would get together and talk about Communist aggression in the region. It didn't dictate military action by us or anyone else."

Lyle Simmons laughed. "I see why you're the captain of the debate team, Phil. You guys won the tournament, right?"

"You bet we did."

Rotondi had returned a month earlier from a four-day Midwest collegiate debate competition on the campus of the University of Wisconsin. He'd joined the team as a sophomore, and had been elected captain at the start of his senior year. He considered the debate team a natural extension of his studies as a pre-law major; it would provide valuable experience for arguing cases in courts of law.

Rotondi, Simmons, and Jeannette Boynton were having this discussion about Vietnam on a gentle, warm afternoon in May 1971. They'd driven to an idyllic knoll a few miles outside the campus and had spread a blanket. It was a sunny day, with a hesitant breeze that put leaves, and their hair, into motion, hardly a time and place for arguing over a nasty, controversial war.

But this was May 1971. Only one year earlier, on May 4, 1970, the nation's universities and colleges had erupted in protest over the killing of four Kent State students by the Ohio National Guard. The students had rallied against the Vietnam War and President Nixon's decision to send troops into Cambodia. By May 4, more than three thousand protesters had flooded the university and downtown Kent. When the wind caused tear gas to float away from the crowds, the Guard opened fire. The torch had been lit, banners raised high.

Two days later, almost five million students at 850 colleges and universities across the nation, the University of Illinois among them, went on strike, the only national student strike in U.S. history.

"I don't know what to think sometimes," Jeannette said. "It's all so confusing."

Rotondi was tempted to break through her confusion with another speech against the war, but thought better of it. Lyle had adopted his usual stance of seeing both sides without committing to either.

Phil and Jeannette had been seeing each other on a fairly regular basis since the previous fall. They were "an item" to some, the handsome basketball and track star and budding attorney, and the strikingly lovely daughter of a wealthy Connecticut family. But it hadn't all been smooth sailing.

Like many seniors, Jeannette viewed her final undergraduate semester as a time to kick back and soak up springtime after four long years of study. Her grades were slightly above average, more than good enough to graduate. She wanted to be with Rotondi every waking minute—at least it seemed that way to him—which wasn't possible. Unlike many of his peers, he considered his senior year to be the time to really turn it on academically, to raise his grade point average as high as possible. He felt an obligation to Maryland University's law school, which had granted him a scholarship. They were putting their faith in him, just as his father had, and he was not someone to take that lightly. Added to that commitment were the debate team's demands and extended, strenuous track team practices and meets.

Which left scant time for Jeannette. She wasn't happy about that, of course, and had become open in expressing her dissatisfaction to him. While she admired his drive and commitment, she had her own needs to satisfy, and many a night at the sorority house found her sharing her growing frustration with sorority sisters. The prevailing, giggle-inducing subject was, of course, sex.

&

Their first full-fledged sexual encounter occurred shortly before they were to leave campus on their Christmas break. There had been frantic grappling on local lovers' lanes in Lyle Simmons's Thunderbird, which Rotondi managed to borrow on occasion. Jeannette found these moments to be immature, the stuff of freshmen. She was, after all, a senior, a grown woman about to leave behind sophomoric back-seat fumbling. The libidinous 1960s were not long gone.

Philip was not without sexual experiences of his own. But Jeannette was different. Those few other women had meant little to him in a personal, caring sense. They'd come and gone. Making love with Jeannette Boynton transcended the physical for him. This was love in all its glory, which was precisely why he had trouble initiating sex with her.

"Why not?" she asked. They'd been necking in the car, juices flowing, frustration levels nudging the unbearable. She suggested taking a motel room.

"I'm just not sure that we should," he said, his breathing labored.

"Why not?" she repeated, discarding the bra that he'd pulled down to her waist.

"Because—because I love you, Jeannette."

His words dumbfounded her. She said, "That's exactly why we should make love, Phil, *because* we love each other."

"I just don't want you to think I'm with you because of sex, because I'm after your body. I want you to know that I love you, the person. It's more than sex, Jeannette. At least it should be."

Does he have a sexual identity problem? she wondered. That had been a recent topic in her class on human sexuality.

In any event, his rationale didn't appease her. She put herself back together, turned from him, and stared out the passenger's side window.

"I want us to sleep together," he said, touching her shoulder.

"Then why won't you?"

"I—I will. I have to get the car back to Lyle."

"Call him. He'll understand."

The way she said it pricked him. It sounded as though she was making a comparison with Simmons, one not favorable to him.

"All right," he said.

They drove to a motel that posted a VACANCY sign. He told her to wait in the car while he registered for a room, and used the pay phone in the lobby to call Lyle.

"Lyle, is it okay if I keep the car overnight?"

Simmons's laugh was pointed. "Why do I think my best buddy is about to shack up?"

"It isn't that. Well, anyway, can I bring the car back in the morning?"

"Sure. Have fun, pal. I'll be thinking of you."

Philip and Jeannette awoke at three the following morning. Their lovemaking had, at first, been tentative. But it soon became intense— and wonderful for both.

"I have an idea," she said, sitting up against the headboard.

"What's that?"

"Why don't you come home with me for Christmas and meet my folks."

He turned on his side, rested his head on his hand, and looked up at her. "I can't," he said. "I promised my brothers and sisters that I'd be with them over the holidays."

"You don't have to spend the whole break with them, Phil. Batavia, or whatever the name of your town is, isn't that far from Greenwich. You could drive down and at least spend a few days with us."

He swung his legs off the bed, which positioned his back to her. He felt her fingertips on his neck, then her lips. "Please," she said. "For me?"

"I don't know, Jeannette. Probably not. I made a lot of promises to the family, things to do, stuff like that. And I planned to write a paper that's due when we get back."

She pulled away, got out on the opposite side of the bed, and disappeared into the bathroom. The grayness of the room matched Rotondi's mood. He knew he wouldn't go to visit her over Christmas—couldn't go. What he'd said was true, that plans made with his sisters and their families would take up some of his time while at home. But not that much. It was also true that he intended to write a paper to get a jump on things when he returned from the break.

He knew that those reasons for not going were just rationalizations. The truth was that he did not feel comfortable spending time with

Jeannette's wealthy parents, to be judged by them, to be asked questions about his own family. Was he truly in love with Jeannette Boynton? The answer to that was beyond debate. He was, and desperately so. At the same time, he was convinced that he wasn't worthy of her. It wasn't a matter of self-loathing. It was just that his feelings of love seemed always to be tempered by a need to disengage—for her sake.

He was terminally confused.

⁂

As winter surrendered to spring, they continued to date, although less frequently and with diminished urgency. There were a few more nights in motels, pleasurable physical experiences but with both instinctively realizing that the fire had lost some of its intensity—not extinguished by any means, but banked. Phil became less and less accessible, taking refuge in his studies and finding pleasure in the physical exhaustion that followed workouts and track meets.

Now, on this lovely day in early May 1971, he shared a blanket with the woman he loved, and with his best friend.

"What are you doing for the summer, Phil?" Simmons asked.

"Working back home. I've lined up a job in a local factory. Not the sort of job I wanted, but it pays better than anything else. I'll need the money at Maryland."

"Like I told you, buddy, you can come to work for my father in Chicago. Wouldn't hurt a future lawyer to learn something about the *real* real estate business."

"I appreciate it, Lyle, but I'd rather be home." He glanced at Jeannette, who was on her back, her arms folded over her eyes against the sun.

"You look beat," said Simmons. "Man, you should back off the books a little."

"Not much longer to go," Rotondi said. "I think I can ace a straight four-oh this semester."

"All work and no play . . ."

Rotondi grinned and stood. "You think I'm a dull boy, Lyle?"

"Hell, no," Lyle responded. "You're the most interesting guy I've ever known. I'm just saying that—"

Jeannette sat up abruptly. "I have to get back," she said, rising to her feet and gathering her belongings.

Lyle and Phil looked at each other, knowing what the other was thinking. She'd been in what could only be termed a foul mood lately, not finding things as funny as she would have a month or two earlier, and exhibiting an uncharacteristic short temper.

That night, Rotondi sat in his room boning up for an upcoming exam.

"Need the car tonight, Phil?" Simmons asked.

"No, thanks, Lyle. I'm in for the duration. You're not using it?"

"No. I'm going out with some of the guys to do a little bar-hopping."

Usually, he would have invited Phil to join them. He didn't.

"Have fun," Phil said. "Drive safe."

Simmons slapped Rotondi on the back and started to leave the room. He stopped, turned, and said, "Maybe you ought to give Jeannette a call."

"Why?"

"Oh, I don't know. She's uptight lately."

"Not tonight," Rotondi said. "Maybe tomorrow."

Simmons had been gone less than ten minutes when the hall phone rang. It was Jeannette.

"Hi," he said.

"I know you said you were going to spend the night studying, Phil, but I really need to talk to you."

"Can't it wait?"

"No, it can't wait, Phil. Please. Pick me up in an hour. I know you have Lyle's car."

Why did she assume that? he wondered.

"Okay, Phil? I just need to see you."

"All right. I'll be there in an hour."

He parked in front of the Alpha Phi sorority house and rang the bell. One of Jeannette's sorority sisters answered. "I'll get Jeannette, Phil," she said. "Come on in."

He waited in the small foyer until Jeannette came down the stairs. "Hi," she said, smiling.

"Hi. Ready?"

"Sure."

"Where to?" he asked once they were in the car.

"Let's go someplace where we can talk. The Lane?" She was referring to a secluded dirt road on the outskirts of the campus, a popular lovers' lane for college couples looking for privacy.

"Want some coffee?" he asked.

"No, thanks. I need to talk, not coffee."

They drove in silence until reaching their destination. Phil maneuvered the Thunderbird into a spot between two other cars with steamed-up windows. He turned off the ignition and faced her. "I have a feeling I'm not going to like what you're about to say."

She looked straight ahead, saying nothing. He reached for her but she deflected his hand.

"I'm pregnant, Phil."

He sat back and exhaled loudly. Although hearing it from her was shocking, the silent truth behind it wasn't. It was one of the two things he expected: that she wanted to break off their relationship, or that she was pregnant.

"Are you sure?" he asked, not sure of what else to say at that moment.

"Yes."

"I'm sorry," he said, then quickly added in case it had been the wrong thing to say, "I mean, I'm sure it's not what you want."

"I don't know what I want, Phil." She looked at him, and tears streamed down her cheeks. He pulled her close and wrapped his arms around her, his chest muffling her sobs. Eventually, she pulled away and placed a hand against his cheek. "I love you, Phil Rotondi. I'm so sorry."

"No, no, no, it's okay, Jeannette. I always used protection, but maybe there was a problem with one. It's fine. I'm surprised, of course, but it's all right. We'll just have to work this out."

His mind raced, his thoughts pragmatic. What would this mean to his immediate future? He certainly hadn't planned to be married while attending law school, but that could be managed. He thought back to what Lyle had said about Jeannette's rich father supporting them. He didn't want that, but maybe—

"We don't have to work it out, Phil. I've made a decision."

An abortion?

"No, Jeannette," he said. "I don't want you to—"

"Please listen to me, Phil."

He silently waited for her to continue.

"The baby isn't yours."

Again, he sat back, this time as though having been shoved physically against the seat back.

"It's Lyle's," she said softly.

"Lyle's? How can that be?" He recognized immediately that it was a ridiculous question.

"We—you and I—haven't been together much lately, Phil."

"You and Lyle have been seeing each other?" His voice was hoarse.

She nodded. "Not a lot, just a few times when you weren't available."

"And you . . . ?"

"Yes, we slept together. Twice. You were away at the debate competition in Wisconsin. I was feeling lonely and pretty down. I know that's not an excuse, but it's the truth."

"And you called Lyle?"

"No. He invited me out for a few drinks. He said he'd promised you he'd take good care of me while you were gone. I was angry, Phil, angry at you. It seemed I always came last on your schedule. Lyle and I went out and had some drinks, and then a few more. He provided a shoulder to cry on and I needed that. Then—oh, I don't know—then one thing led to another and we ended up in a downtown hotel for one more drink and . . ."

"And you ended up in bed with him."

Her silence confirmed it.

He was struck with simultaneous conflicting thoughts, as he'd been when learning of his father's death. His father had been sick for a long time, and had suffered. Phil's reaction to the news was both grief, and relief.

As he sat in a car on an Illinois lovers' lane, his mind was again operating on multiple tracks. He was angry, of course, and felt all the emotions of someone having been betrayed by those he trusted. At the same time, it was as though a weight had been buoyed from his shoulders. These were not unexpected reactions to what he'd just been told. He understood them while feeling them. But a third response elbowed aside the first two. For the first time, he felt superior to Lyle Simmons and in control of that relationship.

"Let's go back, Phil," Jeannette said.

He started the engine but didn't slip the shift into gear. "I want you to know, Jeannette, that I'm not angry with you. Surprised? Sure. Disappointed? That, too."

"You have every right to hate me, Phil."

He put the Thunderbird into reverse and backed out of the spot. As they drove to the sorority house, he mentally grappled with the question that had taken center stage—could he ever be comfortable being married to Jeannette and raising Lyle's child? By the time they reached the house, he'd concluded that if that was what had to be, he'd do everything in his power to make it work.

"Thanks for being so understanding," she said.

"There's really not much of a choice, is there?"

"You could have exploded."

"Which would accomplish nothing." He forced a smile. "Tell you what, Jeannette. Let's sleep on this and talk again tomorrow after we've had a chance to digest things. I somehow think that—"

"Phil! Lyle and I are getting married."

SIXTEEN

The Cirilli Group sure as hell isn't being suttle about going after
X-M Shipping as a client. Let's cut them off at the legs. Rick.

I t wasn't fair, of course, to judge a man's character and personality by a misspelling in a memo. But in Rick Marshalk's case, it
seemed apt. *Subtle* wasn't a word in his vocabulary, correctly
spelled or not; nor was it a part of his makeup. He'd navigated the
treacherous shoals of Hollywood, and although his years there could
never be considered a success, he'd learned plenty. Subtlety! That
was for losers. His full-frontal-attack philosophy had served him well
since arriving in D.C., and he saw no reason to change or even question it.

He'd called a meeting that afternoon at his high-rise condo over-
looking Washington Harbor. It was the largest unit in the building,
with splendid views of the water and of the complex itself from its
wraparound balconies. Present were two of his top lobbyists, as well as
the Marshalk Group's head of security, Jack Parish.

"I wanted to meet here," Marshalk said, "because I'm getting paranoid about talking in the office." He turned to Parish. "I want the place swept again, Jack."

"I had it done only a couple of weeks ago."

"Do it again, every day if you have to."

"It might not be a bug," one of the execs said. "Maybe somebody at the office is leaking information."

"Any ideas who that might be?" Marshalk asked.

His colleagues looked at each other. Parish, who sat on a window seat in front of a floor-to-ceiling window, had been examining a discoloration on the back of his hand. He looked up and said, "You want it straight, Rick?"

"Of course I do."

"I've got my suspicions about a lot of people in the firm."

They waited for him to elaborate.

"Neil," he announced flatly.

"Why do you say that?"

Parish shrugged and grimaced against an unseen kink. "He's a weak sister, Rick. He's got a flabby mind."

"*Flabby mind?*" someone asked.

"No strength," Parish explained. "I know he's the president and all, but I just have this uneasy feeling about him."

"Who else?" Marshalk asked.

"The one who's leaving, Camelia. She's gotten cozy, real cozy, with Jonell, and I've never trusted him, either."

Marshalk, who'd been standing behind an elaborate bar in the living room, moved around it and approached Parish where he sat. "I agree about Camelia Watson," he said. "She's been warned. But Neil has been loyal, at least as far as I can tell. Hell, he knows what side his bread is buttered on."

Parish looked up at his boss and smiled crookedly. "It wouldn't take much to get him to say anything, Rick. Believe me, I know his type. I dealt with lots of them when I was MPD. He's weak."

Marshalk knew that his security chief was right. Bringing Neil

Simmons on board hadn't been motivated by wanting a strong presence in the firm's presidency. It had been more pragmatic than that. Neil assured Marshalk of a strong pipeline to his father, one of the most powerful men in the U.S. Senate. Neil's weakness was a plus as far as Marshalk was concerned. He was easily manipulated, not one to stir the pot and cause trouble. Potential clients responded favorably, even enthusiastically to having Lyle Simmons's son working on their behalf in the halls of Congress, and in offices of top people in every government agency.

Marshalk turned to the others. "We tighten things up from now on. We bring people into the loop on a strictly need-to-know basis."

"Right," affirmed the two-man chorus.

"Okay, let's get down to what we have to do to land the X-M Shipping account. Cirilli's been telling X-M that we're under investigation by Justice. That's all they've got to offer, crap like that. We've got the people in Congress who can kill that new legislation requiring shipping companies to set up their own port security procedures. It'll cost them a fortune. Homeland Security's pushing it on the basis of national security. So what else is new? I want an all-out blitz on X-M and Cirilli. Get our writers to start grinding out op-ed pieces, and make sure they emphasize our experience in lobbying for shipping company interests. Feed info to the columnists and bloggers we've got in our pocket about a pending congressional hearing into Cirilli and its paying off of lawmakers. Get some of our House members to put it in the *Congressional Record*, tip off the press. Put Kelman from the National Security Committee together with X-M's execs. Tell Kelman we'll bankroll another fund-raiser for him if he'll lean on X-M to come with us. He owes us plenty." He turned to Jack Parish. "You've got the goods on Cirilli's number one guy, Clauson. Right?"

"About the bimbo he's got stashed away in Georgetown? Yeah, I've got it."

"Leak it! X-M's people won't want to get in bed with a potential scandal."

Marshalk's minions took notes.

"Questions?" Marshalk asked.

There were none.

"Okay, let's move." He asked Parish to stay behind.

"Look, Jack," Marshalk said when they were alone. "I had a conversation with Jonell about his being at the Simmons house the day of the murder. He's wavering about going to the police. I think I convinced him to cool it for a few days, but he may need a stronger message than that."

"I'll take care of it," Parish said.

∾

When Rotondi left Marlene Boynton, he intended to go straight to Emma's Foggy Bottom home to walk Homer. But he stopped on the way at Kinkead's and nursed a drink at the sparsely populated downstairs bar.

His visit with Marlene, and her parting comments, had opened a torrent of memories of that senior year at the University of Illinois, memories he was almost always successful at blotting out. He recalled the conversation with Jeannette in Lyle's Thunderbird as though it had happened the night before, and the knot in his gut was equally as fresh—and painful.

∾

After dropping Jeannette at the sorority house, he'd driven aimlessly, the windows open, the radio loud as a local station spun the day's hits. "How Can You Mend a Broken Heart?" by the Bee Gees was on at the moment, and the lyrics had meaning to him for the first time. He knew he should be feeling a litany of emotions—rage at Lyle, extreme disappointment in Jeannette, a sense of betrayal to rival Caesar's, hatred, disgust, maybe pity. But he was unsuccessful in summoning any of those feelings. He wanted to cry; wasn't that the appropriate reaction? But he didn't. Couldn't. Mitigating all those human emotions was what had nagged at him ever since he first saw Jeannette

Boynton and fell in love with her easy laugh, her beautiful face, her stunning body, and all the other good womanly things.

He wasn't right for her.

And wished he were.

Where was his competitive spirit? He attacked every basketball game as though it would be the last one he ever played, tenacious, focused, eyes set on winning above all else. Or those track meets in which he viewed each opponent as a threat to his very existence, summoning up every last ounce of energy and fire to finish first. Always finish first.

Love was different, he now knew. There were no referees to call foul, no umpires to set the rules. No one counted the number of times you stole the ball from an opponent, or how many seconds you shaved off your personal best in the quarter mile. Love was no game. It had to do with how lifetimes would be spent, and who would spend them together.

He returned the car a little before midnight. Simmons looked up as Rotondi walked in, laid the car keys on Simmons's desk, stripped off his shirt, tossed it on a chair, and sat at his desk. "Thanks for the car," he said.

"Anytime, pal."

Rotondi opened a textbook.

"You know, right?" Simmons said.

Rotondi swung around in his chair. "Yeah, I know. Jeannette told me. You knew she planned to tonight. That's why you gave me the car."

Simmons shrugged. "I figured it was better coming from her than me."

"You mean *safer,* Lyle?"

"No, of course not. She's the one who's pregnant, not me." It was an ugly attempt at a laugh.

Rotondi turned away. Simmons rolled his desk chair across the floor to his roommate's side. "Look, Phil, I know this comes as a hell of a blow to you, and I'm sorry. I truly am sorry for the way it worked out."

"Drop it, Lyle."

"I can't drop it. You're my best friend, damn it! You're the last guy I'd ever want to hurt. You know that, don't you?"

Rotondi faced him. "What I know is, Lyle, that you and Jeannette are getting married. I'm square with that. I wish she weren't pregnant going into it, but that's not my concern. You're right. I am your best friend. I thought you were mine."

"I am, I am, Phil, and this shouldn't get in the way of that friendship. It's not as though I planned it. It just—it just happened, like these things sometimes do. By the way, this is no shotgun wedding. Jeannette and I have really fallen for each other, and it's because of you. You spotted her first. Man, you've got good taste."

Rotondi sprung out of his chair, grabbed Simmons by the throat, and propelled him across the room and into the far wall, spilling chairs and knocking things from desks en route. He held him against the window, the venetian blinds falling and tangling Simmons in the slats and cords. Rotondi cocked his right fist and held it in front of his roommate's face.

"Go ahead," Simmons gasped. "Take a shot, pal. Beat me bloody. I deserve it."

An animal growl came from Rotondi's throat. His hand shook as though the nerves in it had short-circuited.

"Go ahead, Phil," Simmons repeated. "Break my nose. Get it over with."

Rotondi loosened his grip on Simmons's throat. He lowered his hand and took a step back, hyperventilating. Simmons rubbed his neck and slumped to the floor. Rotondi backed away and fell into his chair.

"Lyle," Rotondi said.

"What?"

"We have a month before graduation, and I don't want to hear another word about this. Okay?"

"Yeah, sure, but I don't want it to destroy a great friendship."

"It won't, Lyle, if you'll just shut up. The best man won and—"

"Oh, no, my friend, *you* are definitely the best man. You will be, won't you?"

Rotondi stared at him.

"Be my best man. You're the brother I never had, Phil. Please. We'll be planning a quick wedding in Connecticut. Kind of necessary, you know? I'll pick up all the expenses for you to come. Bring a gal."

Rotondi slowly shook his head and was unable to stifle a smile. "You know what, Lyle?"

"Tell me, brother."

"You *will* be president of the United States some day. You've got the cojones to pull it off."

⟋⟍

The week after graduation, Rotondi drove one of his sisters' cars from Batavia to Greenwich, where Lyle put him up in a suite at a local motel. He arrived two days before the wedding, in time to attend the bachelor party at a historic pub in the center of town, and the rehearsal dinner that was catered at Jeannette's home, also the site of the wedding itself.

There were a dozen men at the bachelor party, including Lyle's father, with whom Rotondi had spent time over the course of his four years at the university. The elder Simmons, a gruff, no-nonsense sort of man for whom laughing appeared to be painful, was overtly uncomfortable in the midst of the over-the-top, forced masculine gaiety. It was evident to Phil that the father was not pleased that his only son had opted to marry straight out of college. He confirmed that to Rotondi later in the evening when they found themselves apart from the others.

"Lyle's got himself a great wife," Rotondi said.

"She's nice," Mr. Simmons said. "I like her. But I would have preferred for them to wait until Lyle's established in his career."

"Well," Rotondi started to say, "there's—"

"I know, I know. There's a kid coming. Four years of college and he's never heard of condoms." He laid a large hand on Rotondi's shoulder. "You ever need anything, Phil, you come to me. I consider you and Lyle brothers. Call anytime. Got that?" He walked away, his posture less erect than when Rotondi had last seen him.

The number of toasts Lyle made during the party increased with the consumption of drinks. He directed a few at Phil, which made him uncomfortable. At one point, he announced, "When I'm president of the United States, you're looking at my attorney general, Mr. Philip Rotondi, my best friend." Glasses were raised to Phil, which he halfheartedly acknowledged.

When everyone spilled out of the pub and into the street, Lyle tried to coax Phil back to Jeannette's house to continue the evening.

"Not tonight, Lyle," Rotondi said. "See you at the rehearsal dinner."

He sat in his suite and watched a made-for-TV movie, *River of Gold*, with Ray Milland and Suzanne Pleshette. His attention kept shifting from the screen—*Why would someone like Ray Milland get involved in such a stupid film?* he asked himself—to his thoughts about the wedding and his being there. Jeannette's parents seemed like nice people, wealthy but not ostentatious. He wondered whether things would have turned out differently if he'd agreed to accompany her home over the Christmas break. Probably not. They'd turned out the way they had because deep down, it was what he wanted.

He felt awkward during the rehearsal dinner. Jeannette had mentioned earlier in the year that she'd told her parents all about him, and had showed them a photograph of the two of them taken at a school function. Were they comparing him with Lyle during the dinner? He felt they were—and wished they wouldn't. He left as soon after dessert as proper etiquette allowed and went back to the hotel. *One more day*, he thought.

The following afternoon, he fulfilled his assignment as Lyle's best man. The ceremony was held on the Boynton family's sprawling estate on a picture-perfect June day. Jeannette looked, of course, radiant in her gown; the dressmaker had artfully arranged the layers of silk and satin to camouflage the beginning of a bulge in her belly. At the appropriate time, Rotondi dutifully handed the ring to Lyle; he joined the applause after the minister had pronounced Lyle and Jeannette man and wife, and suggested that the groom could now kiss the bride.

A wooden dance floor had been set up on the grounds by the caterers, and an offshoot eight-piece band from a leading society orchestra provided nonstop music. Rotondi hung around one of the bars and took in the festivities. The newlyweds would leave that evening for the British Virgin Islands on their honeymoon. Bride and groom danced with others, and with each other. When the band changed tempo to something slower and more easily navigated, Jeannette came to Phil and asked him to dance.

"You know I'm not very good at that," he said.

"Oh, come on, Phil. Please?"

They took to the floor and moved stiffly. The feel of her against him was exquisite, and his thoughts raced back to those times when they'd been intimate.

"Thank you, Phil," she said into his ear.

"For what?"

"For being here. I know it's not easy."

"It's not hard, Jeannette. Your folks and friends are nice people. I'm having a good time."

"That may be," she said, "but I'm sure that if I—"

"I'm happy for you and Lyle," he said, cutting off what he knew she was about to say. "I just hope we can stay in touch."

"You bet we will, Phil. Count on it."

She kissed him lightly on the lips as Lyle cut in and swept her away.

❧

They did stay in touch. Rotondi graduated at the top of his class from Maryland's law school, and Simmons received his law degree from the University of Chicago. The announcement of the birth of Lyle and Jeannette's first child, a baby boy they named Neil, arrived in the mail, followed by a phone call. And there were other announcements from the Simmons household, most having to do with Lyle's rise through the Chicago and state political ranks, as well as news of the birth of their second child, a girl named Polly.

Rotondi settled into the U.S. attorney's office in Baltimore and eventually sent out a personal announcement of his own, of his marriage to Kathleen. Simmons's election to the U.S. House of Representatives brought the family to Washington, close to Baltimore where Phil and Kathleen lived, affording the couples time to get together on a regular basis, parties at Simmons's D.C. home, occasional weekends away, and dinners at favored restaurants. Phil had never told Kathleen about his college romance with Jeannette Boynton and how it ended, concerned that it might taint her view of Lyle and Jeannette. His continuing friendship with the rising political star and his family was important to him. But his reluctance to share with his wife that portion of his life also had to do, he knew, with not wanting to have to answer what would undoubtedly be her first question: *Why would you want to remain friends with someone who did that to you?* Although he didn't have to answer that question for her, he silently knew the truth. His friendship with Lyle Simmons was based, in large part, on his fascination with the man. He enjoyed being close to an increasingly powerful figure without having been sucked into his vortex, able to stand aside and observe, offer advice and not give a damn whether it was taken or not. All of this was selfish, of course, including the reflected importance he felt as the one to whom members of the powerful man's family frequently turned.

Better that Kathleen not have reason to raise that question than have to honestly admit to those weaknesses.

&

"A refill?" the bartender asked Rotondi.

"What? Oh, no, thanks. Time I was going."

He'd paid his tab and was on his way out the door when his cell phone rang. It was Lyle.

"Phil. Glad I reached you. I'm on my way to the Willard to meet with the detectives. I arranged for a suite."

They won't be impressed, Rotondi thought.

"Can you meet me there, Phil?"

"They won't want me in on the interview, Lyle."

"After they're done. The medical examiner is releasing Jeannette's body. We need to plan a memorial service. I told Neil to call Saint John's Episcopal on Lafayette Park."

St. John's Episcopal, Rotondi thought. The Church of the Presidents. Every U.S. president since James Madison had attended services there; Pew 54 was reserved as the "President's Pew." Jeannette was never particularly religious, but when she did attend church services, Rotondi knew, it was at All Souls Unitarian, which she liked. Not enough cachet for a potential future president.

"I'm sure you'll want to confer with Polly, too," Rotondi said.

"Of course. I'll get hold of her. Can you come by at six? We'll have dinner."

Had Emma not had a catering assignment that evening, he would have declined. "All right," he said.

He clicked off the phone and left the restaurant. It had clouded up during the time he'd been at the bar, and the humidity level had risen. There was a moment while standing on the sidewalk that he considered going to Emma's house, packing up Homer, and heading home.

But he knew he couldn't do that. There were things he knew about Jeannette and Lyle Simmons that he'd been suppressing since heeding Lyle's call the night of the murder. It was time he took the lid off them and followed where they led.

SEVENTEEN

After taking Homer for a walk and feeding him, Rotondi changed clothes, left Emma's house, and drove to the Willard hotel, where he passed the time by sitting in the opulent lobby and watching the parade of well-dressed humanity passing through. His vantage point gave him a view of the elevators. At a few minutes before six, two people emerged from one and walked his way. The man, of Asian descent, was dressed in a suit and carried a small briefcase. The woman wore a black pantsuit. *The detectives*, Rotondi reasoned as they disappeared from view. The interview was over. He called Simmons's suite on a house phone and was told to come up.

He expected to see the senator surrounded by his usual entourage, but the man was alone in the suite. He looked tired, and older than a day ago.

"Sit down, Phil. Drink? There's a minibar and—"

"Nothing, thanks. How did the interview go?"

Simmons, who was in shirtsleeves, the knot of his tie pulled down, plopped in a chair across from Rotondi. "Insulting, that's how it went. You'd think I was a serial killer the way that obnoxious little Chinese detective talks. I have a call in to the police chief. I refuse to be treated this way. The detective made a lot out of what Neil told him, that Jeannette and I had a rocky marriage. Why the hell Neil would have offered such nonsense is beyond me. It was a good marriage, Phil, no better or worse than any other. Maybe being a senator put an extra strain on it at times. You know, me being away a lot and Jeannette rattling around alone in the house. I tried to get her involved in my activities, but she just kept retreating into a shell. I suppose I can't blame her for wanting to stay clear of politics. It can be a rough business, Phil, a nasty business."

Rotondi listened patiently, something at which he'd always been good.

"She was having trouble with booze," Simmons announced.

"How much trouble?" Rotondi asked, knowing the answer.

"It wasn't always evident," Simmons said. "It was being alone that contributed to it, that I know. That was one of the reasons I tried to convince her to join me in some of my travels. Showing up alone at fund-raisers always raised eyebrows with the press. I suppose the detectives who were here heard the rumors, too, and are making a big deal out of it."

"You said the ME is releasing Jeannette's body, and that you're setting up a memorial service. Any idea when that will be?"

"After I get back from Chicago. That's what I wanted to speak with you about, Phil. I'm due out there day after tomorrow to meet with an exploratory committee, and to attend a fund-raiser."

"Exploratory committee?" Rotondi said. "For a run?"

Simmons nodded. "Strictly preliminary, Phil, and hush-hush. Surprised?"

Rotondi's laugh was sardonic. "Why would I be surprised? You've been running for the White House since poly sci one."

"What do you think?"

"About you running for president? Sure, why not?"

"That's hardly a ringing endorsement."

"I'm not into ringing endorsements these days—for anything."

"You know the problem with you, Phil?"

"I have a leg that doesn't work the way it should."

"Besides that. Your problem is that you know me too well. That should make me uncomfortable."

"It doesn't?"

"No. You're the only person in my life who won't let me get away with anything, and that's good. I need people who'll be straight with me, tell it like it is. Want to work on my campaign?"

"No."

Simmons laughed. "Maybe you'll change your mind down the road. Come with me to Chicago."

"Why?"

"Give you a chance to see our old stomping grounds. How long since you've been back?"

"Six months."

"I'd love to have you with me, Phil. I'd really appreciate it. I'm staying at the Ambassador East. That's where we'll have the exploratory committee meetings. But it won't be all work. There'll be plenty of time to enjoy a drink in the Pump Room. Remember the nights we spent there downing a few?"

"Nice place."

"So you'll come?"

"What about your staff?"

"They'll be with us, but that's what they are—staff. I need a friend."

While Simmons had been making his pitch for Rotondi to accompany him, Rotondi had been silently processing the request. He wasn't interested in tagging along for the ride just to be Simmons's listening post, but it occurred to him that there was another reason to spend time in Chicago.

"Sure, Lyle. Why not?"

"Great. Neil has arranged for a private jet through the Marshalk

Group. Sure you can tear yourself away from your lady friend–chef for a few days?"

"I never see her anyway," Rotondi said. "She feeds half of Washington."

"Marriage on the horizon?"

Rotondi ignored the question. "I spent time this afternoon with Marlene," he said.

Simmons screwed up his face. "Why?" he asked.

"What do you mean *why*? I always got along with Marlene and—"

"That doesn't say much for you. She's been nothing but trouble, always filling Jeannette with poisonous thoughts about me and our marriage."

Rotondi was mute.

"Despite that, I've been damn good to her, Phil, damn good! If it weren't for me, she'd be a bag lady out on the street."

"She was Jeannette's sister," Rotondi said, stating the obvious.

"Yeah, I know, you marry into a family you take the good and the bad, the bitter with the sweet. Well, believe me, my friend, Marlene Boynton is the bad and the bitter all rolled into one. Hungry?"

"Not particularly."

"Let's grab something anyway and talk about more pleasant things. Charlie Palmer's? I'm in the mood for red meat."

∾

While U.S. senator Lyle Simmons and former prosecutor Philip Rotondi, college roommates who loved the same woman, dined at one of Washington's signature steak houses—a truffle-basted filet mignon for Simmons, salmon with corn ravioli and corn ragout for Rotondi—another Simmons was sitting down for a family dinner at home. Neil Simmons's wife, Alexandra, had ordered in Chinese, which those reporters still stationed outside the house dutifully noted, and envied.

Neil had spent most of the day at his office at the Marshalk Group, trying to focus on business while fending off calls from the media. He'd almost lost it while approaching his driveway when a TV cameraman stood in his way to videotape him through the windshield. For a split second, he considered taking his foot off the brake and jamming the accelerator to the floor. But discretion overcame temptation, and he waited until the cameraman finally stepped out of the way.

"I can't take this anymore," Alexandra said as she and Neil emptied plastic containers into serving dishes.

"It'll be over soon," Neil said, giving a salad he'd made a final toss. "Once the memorial service is behind us, the vultures will go away."

His assurances didn't appease her. She fairly snarled as she touched the toaster oven in which she'd heated up General Tsao's chicken, and burned her finger. "This is so harmful to the boys' psyches," she said, running cold water over her burn. Alex Simmons had read virtually every book ever written on the psychology of raising children.

"They'll survive," he said.

"You don't care, do you, Neil?"

"Care about what, that some bastard murdered my mother?"

"I'm not talking about that. I am talking about getting the ghouls outside to go away. Jesus, Neil, your father is a United States senator. Why doesn't *he* do something?"

"What's he supposed to do, Alex, call out the National Guard to arrest them? Drop it. Like I said—"

"Your sister called today."

"When?"

"This morning."

"Why didn't you tell me?"

"I'm telling you now."

"What did she say?"

"The usual."

He stopped portioning out the salad and asked, "What the hell is that supposed to mean?"

"She has that phony accent and—"

"What accent? Polly doesn't have an accent."

"She puts it on, as though she's somebody special."

"Look, Alex—"

"You know what, Neil? Maybe she's the smart one, putting as much distance as possible between herself and your father."

Neil shouted, "Damn it, Alex, why do you always have to—?"

"Are you and Daddy fighting again," their older son asked from where he'd been watching and listening in the doorway.

Alex wrapped her arms about the boy. "No, darling, Daddy and I are having a discussion, that's all. A grown-up discussion." She glared at Neil and angrily carried plates of food to the dining room.

Later that night, after the dishes had been cleared and they had gone their separate ways within the house, Neil carried a snifter of brandy to a small room he used as a home office, closed the door, put on a CD of hits from the 1980s, raised the footrest in the recliner, and closed his eyes. He wasn't sleepy. Closing his eyes was like bringing down a curtain on a particularly unpleasant and distasteful stage play in which he'd recently starred.

⁓

His father's anger at him for having told the police that his parents' marriage had ups and downs was misdirected. He, Neil, had actually been kind in his gentle evaluation to the police of how Mom and Dad got along. In truth, their relationship had deteriorated dramatically in recent years, and their only son had a front-row seat.

His mother's increasing isolation and drinking had been of great concern to him. He hadn't confronted her directly about it, afraid that it would provoke anger. But he found himself dropping by the house more than usual, casual visits during which he observed her behavior. He considered bringing his concerns to his father, but opted not to do that, either. While his mother could demonstrate anger when provoked, it was a mild breeze compared with his father's tsunamis.

The chats he'd had with his mom over the past six months had been cursory, nothing substantive, passing-the-time sort of conversations. But two weeks before her murder, that had changed.

He'd called ahead and said he wanted to swing by to pick up a gardening tool from the shed at the back of the property. They'd talked on the phone for a few minutes, and he sensed, as he often had, that she'd been drinking, not enough to cloud her mind but sufficient to affect her speech. He parked on the drive in front of the house and let himself in with a key he always carried.

"Mom?" he called.

He didn't receive an answer, which concerned him. He walked through rooms on the first floor but didn't find her. He went upstairs and looked into the master bedroom. The door to a small room off the bedroom that she used as her office was slightly ajar. He approached and opened it more fully. She was seated in a wing chair, her back to him. No lights were on. The only illumination came through a window whose yellow drapes had been parted.

"Mom?"

"Oh, Neil," she said, turning.

"Are you okay?" he asked, coming to her and sitting on a hassock that matched the chair's upholstery. He reached out, took her hand, and looked into her eyes. They were moist; some of her makeup had run.

"What's wrong?" he asked.

She straightened as though a steel rod had been rammed into her back. Her eyes opened wide. She said in a strong voice, "Neil, I want you to listen to me."

"Of course I'll listen to you," he said. "I always do."

"You've got to get away from the Marshalk Group. Resign. Do it now!"

If he'd conjured a dozen things she might be poised to say to him, this would not have been on the list. He'd known since accepting the presidency of the Marshalk Group that she didn't approve, although she'd never said it directly. The scandals surrounding K Street's lobbyists, with disgraced lobbyist Jack Abramoff leading the way, had dominated the media and Washington conversation for many months. Pictures of corrupt members of Congress delivering staunch resignation speeches, or being photographed leaving courthouses in which they'd been convicted of crimes, aided and abetted by smarmy lobbyists, had brought them unwelcome fame. Neil's father vigorously defended his son's decision to abandon a good management job at a bank for the presidency of the Marshalk Group, citing lobbyists as valuable contributors to the legislative process. Unstated, but blatantly obvious to Jeannette, was the fact that the senator, her husband, had choreographed Neil's move to Marshalk for his own self-interest. She cursed both men in her life, her husband for manipulating his son for personal gain, and Neil for not having the backbone to stand up to his father and make his own decisions.

"I don't understand," Neil said.

"I know that, Neil," she said. "That's the problem. You don't understand what's likely to happen to you if you stay there."

His carefully blank expression told his mother that he still didn't understand, although that didn't necessarily reflect the entire truth. While he was kept out of the loop on many issues within the Marshalk Group—and resented it at times—he couldn't help but be aware of mounting tensions. The lobbying scandals that had rocked K Street had caused Rick Marshalk and his trusted lieutenants to become more secretive than usual. Jack Parish, the former MPD detective who headed up Marshalk's security operations, had ratcheted up internal security procedures, including frequent sweeps of the offices in search of electronic listening devices. A new set of rules had been enacted regarding the safeguarding of documents and e-mails. Everything was to be secured at night in new safes Parish had purchased and installed. There had also been a memo circulated in which the importance of not talking about Marshalk business outside the offices was stressed. World War II's "Loose lips sink ships" and the Las Vegas tagline "What happens in Vegas stays in Vegas" were quoted.

Jeannette Simmons slid forward in her chair and grasped Neil's hand in both of hers. Her expression and tone cried out for his attention. "I've learned things about your father and what he's been doing that upset me terribly." She sat back again and waved her hands in front of her. "I know, I know," she said. "Politics and politicians have to cut deals now and then to get legislation through and win elections. But your father has crossed the line, Neil, and he's using the Marshalk Group to do it."

"What are you talking about, Mom? Are you saying he's doing something illegal?"

"That's exactly what I'm saying."

"What?"

"He's involved with some very bad people, Neil. So is Marshalk."

"Who? What bad people?"

"It doesn't matter. What *does* matter is that you leave Marshalk as quickly as possible before you become tainted by it—or worse."

He stood, went to the window, and stared outside, his fingers kneading the drape's heavy fabric. Hearing that his father might be involved in something unlawful, and with unsavory people, was nothing new to him. Those rumors came and went with regularity in Washington, a city driven by such speculation. His father's legislative deals cut with fellow senators often raised eyebrows. His end runs around the ever-shifting Senate ethics and campaign contribution rules and regulations elicited cynicism, in some cases outright scorn, from those on the other sides of the aisle and like-minded press. And there was the salacious rumor about his having had an affair with a Chicago woman with reputed ties to organized crime, and allegations that as a result he'd gotten into bed not only with her but with *them*, too.

Until that moment, however, Neil had never been directly confronted with his father's transgressions, by anyone, let alone his mother. He turned and said, "I wish you'd be more specific."

"I will be if I have to. I have the proof, Neil. I know what I'm talking about. Believe me. Someone has given me documents that prove what I'm saying."

He cocked his head but didn't voice his next question. *What would prompt her to do that? When would she feel it was necessary?*

Believe her? I have no reason not to.

"I don't know what to say," he said as she walked him from the room and down the stairs to the foyer.

"You don't have to say anything, Neil. But you do have to act."

"Does Dad know how you feel?"

"Yes. We've been talking about a divorce."

Neil drew a deep breath before saying, "Can't you work something out short of that? There's his position in the Senate, and I think he's serious about running for president."

"Politics!" she sneered. "I don't care about politics. I care about my family. I care about you, Neil, and I'm perfectly willing to tell what I know if it means saving you and Polly."

"I'm sure it won't come to that," he said, kissing her cheek. "I'll do the right thing. I'd better be going."

"Don't forget the tool you wanted to pick up."

"The what? Oh, right. Yes, I'll get it. Mom, give this some thought, huh? Some real thought."

"I already have, Neil."

He looked into her eyes and knew that she meant it.

EIGHTEEN

Rotondi had been at Emma's house for an hour before she arrived.

"How was it?" he asked.

"Fine. Those C-SPAN people are terrific. Brian Lamb personally complimented me and the food."

"I've been complimenting you ever since we met."

"But you're not Brian Lamb. Besides, I expect compliments from you."

"I never thought you'd take me for granted."

"I take it for granted that you got through the evening without me."

"Had dinner with a United States senator."

"And? How is your buddy?"

"All right. I'm going with him to Chicago the day after tomorrow."

"Why?"

"He asked me."

"That's a good enough reason, I suppose. What's the occasion?"

He explained the purpose for the trip, adding, "The exploratory meetings are strictly between us."

"I've forgotten it already."

They changed for bed and sat in the den to watch news on TV. Homer had climbed up on the couch next to Emma, plopped his head on her lap, and closed his eyes.

Jeannette Simmons's murder was no longer the lead story, having slipped to second place behind coverage of a House committee hearing that day into the corrupting influence of lobbyists on the legislative and judicial processes.

"The influence peddlers are taking big hits these days," Emma said.

"They've brought it upon themselves," said Rotondi.

"I expect to see Neil Simmons's name on the news any day," she said. "Have you spoken with him?"

"Not lately. He's supposed to be putting together Jeannette's memorial service at St. John's Episcopal. I'm sure that's keeping him busy. Emma, remember the conversation at Mac and Annabel Smith's house last night?"

"Not much of it. Why?"

"I've been thinking about something the fellow who was there, Jonell, said about having been at Jeannette's house the afternoon she was murdered."

Emma screwed up her face. "Yes, I do remember that. Why?"

"I haven't seen or heard anything in news reports that mentions his name. He works for Marshalk."

"So?"

"So—so I'm wondering why."

"The police probably questioned him and decided he wasn't a suspect."

"Or he didn't tell the police he'd been there."

"Why wouldn't he?"

"That's what I'm wondering. I think I'll call Mac Smith in the morning and see if he knows anything. Jonell—what was his last name?"

"Marbury."

"Yeah, Jonell Marbury. Nice guy."

"I'm catering a going-away party tomorrow night for one of Marshalk's staff."

"You mentioned that. Maybe he'll be there. Where's the party?"

"Marshalk's satellite office. Eighteenth Street. A town house. You should see it. It's decorated like a New Orleans brothel."

Rotondi laughed. "Maybe it is."

"I wouldn't be surprised. Marshalk isn't one of my favorite clients. He and some of his male buddies have wandering hands."

"Take my cane. You can fend them off with it."

Emma reached for Rotondi and traced an index finger around his lips, which woke Homer and sent him off the couch. "I wouldn't fend you off," she said.

"I think I'm being taken for granted again," he said.

"And?"

"And—I love it. Come on, lady. I'm hungry. What's on the menu tonight?"

"It's not coconut shrimp," she said.

☙

Emma's nonculinary appetizers and main course sated any hunger Rotondi had been suffering. He awoke the next morning rested and satisfied. He looked over to Emma's empty side of the bed and heard the shower running. He got up, put on a robe, and went to the den, where he debated whether it was too early to call Mac Smith. The phone rang. He waited until the machine went into action, heard Morris Crimley's voice through the tinny speaker, and picked up.

"Screening calls these days?" Crimley asked in his gravelly voice.

"You might say that," Rotondi responded. "Then again, you might not. What's up?"

"Hope I'm not disturbing something pleasant."

"You're late for that."

"What do you have on tap today?"

"Thought I'd rob a bank, or assassinate somebody important."

"You shouldn't say things like that on the phone, Phil. Ever hear of the Patriot Act? The Secret Service will be there in fifteen minutes."

"Slow, aren't they?"

"Phil, I need to talk with you."

"Go ahead."

"In person. Come by the office later this morning?"

"Okay. Eleven?"

"I'll be waiting."

"Who called?" Emma asked as she emerged from the bathroom, body and head swathed in fluffy pink robe and towel.

"Morris Crimley at MPD. He wants to talk to me about something."

"You're out to solve Jeannette Simmons's murder, aren't you?"

"No," he said. "I just think there are things I know that others may not."

"Care to share them with this lowly caterer?"

"Not at the moment. What time's the Marshalk party?"

"Seven." She looked up at a wall clock. "I'd better get on my horse. I have two clients to meet with, and I need to do some shopping at Eastern Market."

"Keep your eyes and ears open tonight, Emma. You never can tell what somebody is likely to say to a ravishing woman in kitchen whites."

After she left, he took his time getting ready, reading cover-to-cover the newspaper that had been delivered. Showered and dressed, he called Mac Smith.

"Good morning, Phil," Smith said.

"Good morning, Mac. I wanted to run something past you."

"Okay."

"Remember what your friend, Jonell Marbury, said at your dinner party about having been at the Simmons home the afternoon she was killed?"

"Yes, I do. Why?"

"I haven't seen any mention of him in connection with the murder and was wondering whether the police know he was there."

"I don't have an answer for you," Smith replied. "I urged him to step forward. Whether he did or not is another question. I hope so. If the police come up with that knowledge on their own, he'll have some explaining to do."

"I was surprised he casually mentioned it that night, Mac. It doesn't sound as though he's trying to keep it a secret."

"I agree. I'll call him and ask. Free for lunch?"

"I'll be at MPD at eleven. Shouldn't be there more than an hour."

"How about twelve thirty at the Garden Café? It's in the State Plaza Hotel on E Street, between Twenty-first and Twenty-second, sort of a hangout for us GW professors."

"See you there."

Crimley was in a meeting with Detective Chang when Rotondi arrived. He saw the two men through a glass insert in Crimley's office door and recognized Chang from having seen him at the Willard. Chang left, and Crimley waved Rotondi in.

"How's the leg?" Crimley asked after Phil had taken a chair and rested his cane against it.

"Feels a little better today," he replied, wondering whether having spilled precious bodily fluids the night before had activated his body's natural painkilling endorphins.

"Glad to hear that. I'll get to the point, Phil. The detective who just left here, Chang, is lead on the Simmons case. We've run a check on the victim's movements for the two months leading up to her death."

"I'd be surprised if you hadn't."

"She didn't go many places, stayed pretty close to home. We've pulled her bank records, credit card receipts, E-ZPass usage, the usual."

Rotondi nodded

"It looks like she made only one trip out of town during those two months."

"Oh?"

"Yeah, she went down to the Eastern Shore."

Crimley cocked his head as though waiting for Rotondi to respond. When he didn't, Crimley added, "Looks like she made that trip to spend time with one Philip Rotondi."

"Let's be a little more accurate, Morris. She came to the Eastern Shore for reasons other than seeing me. While she was there, we had dinner together. Shocking? As you said, Jeannette and I were close friends."

Crimley pulled a receipt from a folder on his desk. "Nice restaurant," he said, handing the receipt to Rotondi.

"The best crab cakes in the area."

Crimley rubbed stubble on his face with the palm of his hand, and shifted to his eyes with his knuckles. "Phil," he said, "why are you in Washington?"

"I'm here as Lyle Simmons's friend."

"No interest in the case beyond that?"

"Not at the moment."

"We've been friends for a long time, Phil."

"We sure have."

"You asked me to keep you informed of how the investigation is going. I'm willing to do that. But it would be nice if it were a two-way street. You were probably closer to the family than anyone else around."

"You're probably right."

"We're holding a suspect."

"So I see on TV. The drifter. What's his name?"

"Lemón."

"He's convenient, but he didn't do it. It wasn't some down-and-out stranger who killed Jeannette Simmons, and you know it."

"Give me an alternative."

"I don't have one at the moment."

"*At the moment?*"

"I have some ideas."

"For the first time I feel you're leveling with me. We have prints."

"Anyone I know?"

"We don't have a match yet. Maybe by tomorrow." He slid an eight-by-ten photograph in Rotondi's direction, a close-up of a water glass. A fingerprint processed at the crime scene was evident on the glass.

Rotondi examined the photo before pushing it back to Crimley. "Sounds like you're making progress," he said.

"Slow but sure."

A shooting pain stung Rotondi's leg from hip to foot, and he grimaced against it. "Look, Morris, I have to leave," he said. "A lunch date. I promise I'll get back to you in a day or two and we can discuss this further."

"Sure, Phil. Thanks for stopping in. Oh, one more thing. After you and Mrs. Simmons enjoyed your crab cakes together, where did you go next?"

Rotondi knew what was coming.

"You've got alert neighbors in your condo complex, Phil. Real crime stoppers. It seems one of them saw you and Mrs. Simmons go into your condo unit in the evening and not come out till morning. They identified Mrs. Simmons from photos. Detective Chang and his partner not only interviewed that neighbor, they talked to a second one who confirmed what the first one said."

Rotondi stood, stretched, picked up his cane, and smiled at Crimley. "You missed your calling, Morris. You should be working for a tabloid."

"Just part of a routine investigation, Counselor."

"You should add me to your suspect list."

"I already have, but don't sweat it. I'll take you up on your offer to come back. In fact, I'll be damn upset if you don't."

He'd been exercising early one morning a month ago when Jeannette called.

"Hi, Phil, hope I'm not waking you."

"I've been up for a while."

"You sound out of breath."

"Doing some light weight lifting. How are you?"

"All right." She didn't sound terribly convincing.

"How's the family?"

"Everyone is fine. I'm coming down your way in a few days."

"What's the occasion?"

"I just need to get away. One of my classmates, Josie Williams, lives on the shore with her husband. He's retired. It would be nice to see her again."

"I remember her. A sorority sister."

"I thought maybe you and I could have lunch or dinner together."

"Love it. Are you staying with her?"

"No. I've booked a room at the Marriott. It's not very far from you."

They arranged a date for dinner, and he went back to his weight lifting. It would be good to see her. They hadn't spoken in a while. He'd been in Batavia visiting family and had returned only a few days earlier. He kept up with Lyle Simmons's activities through the press, of course, and had received a call just yesterday from Polly Simmons. The purpose of her call was to ask that he use his friendship with her father to persuade him to not go forward with a piece of legislation that she found offensive and unconstitutional, but otherwise palatable. While he agreed with her that it was a bad law if passed, he wasn't about to inject himself into Simmons's political life. He never had.

Rotondi chose a restaurant equidistant between his condo and the hotel where Jeannette would be staying, a lively neighborhood spot short on pretense and long on fresh seafood. He'd eaten there often and was by now a familiar face to the owners, a husband and wife who ran the place with Prussian efficiency. Mom and Pop stayed where they belonged, in the kitchen, except for occasional forays into the dining room to ask how diners were enjoying their meals. An attractive daughter manned the reservations podium.

Jeannette called early that afternoon from the hotel, and Rotondi filled her in on plans for the evening. He suggested getting together earlier for a walk along the shore, but she begged off: "I'm exhausted, Phil. A nice nap is appealing at the moment." He said he would pick her up at six.

She was waiting in the lobby when he arrived.

"You look rested," he said as they embraced. "And beautiful." He was being truthful. Jeannette was the sort of woman who would remain beautiful until her dying days. She had lost considerable weight, though, which concerned Rotondi. Had her drinking progressed to the point of not eating regularly?

"Hardly beautiful, Phil, but yes, I am rested." She stepped back and took him in. "And you look—well, you look terrific."

"Now that we've lavished compliments on each other, let's go."

"It's so peaceful here away from Washington," she said as they drove to the restaurant. She'd rolled down her window and leaned in its direction, allowing the breeze to whip her hair, which had grown darker with age but was lightened somewhat with streaks recently applied. It was a perfect day on the Eastern Shore, the sky cobalt blue, the air pleasantly warm. They entered the restaurant from the adjacent parking lot and were seated in a secluded booth Rotondi had requested when making the reservation. A young waitress asked if they'd like drinks.

"Extra-dry Beefeater martini, straight up, cold and dry, with a twist." Jeannette rattled it off like those silly disclaimers at the end of commercials. Phil ordered a glass of house red.

"I'm a purist when it comes to martinis," she said, laughing. "No vodka for me. Any martini not made with gin isn't a martini."

"So I've heard," he said.

Their drinks arrived and they touched the rims of their glasses. "Here's to you being here," he said.

"Here's to my being here," she repeated. "I'm so glad I am. How's Homer?"

"He's good. He hurt his rear leg the other day racing up the stairs and is limping around a little, like me. We make a wonderful gimpy pair when I walk him. No broken bones, according to the vet."

"What about your leg, Phil? The last time I saw you, you said you were considering another surgery."

"Ruled it out. The surgeon said it might not do any good, but he's willing to try. I'd just as soon not provide a practice session for him. How are Neil and Polly?"

Her mood darkened, but she took another sip and lightened up. "They're okay. Polly said she spoke with you recently."

He recounted the gist of Polly's call.

"She's so passionate about her causes," Jeannette said. "I admire that."

Rotondi nodded.

"I wish Neil had some of her passion for something—for anything."

"Different personalities, Jeannette. Always amazes me how kids from the same parents and upbringing can end up so different."

"What amazes me is how much Polly is like her father, yet they're always at each other's throats."

"Their relationship still rocky?"

"Worse than that. It breaks my heart."

"Maybe Polly ought to loosen up, accept Lyle for what he is."

"Don't you think I've lectured her about that? She's so stubborn."

"Like her father," Rotondi said.

Jeannette finished her drink and motioned for the waitress to bring her another. Rotondi was about to suggest that they skip a second drink and order, but she reached across the table, placed her hand on his, and said, "I lied to you, Phil."

"Oh?"

"I didn't come here to see Josie Williams. I came here to see you. I didn't want to tell Lyle that. And I didn't come just to enjoy a pleasant dinner."

Their second round was delivered and she drank. "I need your advice, Phil. I need your help."

"About what?"

"About what's happening with Lyle and Neil."

"I'm not sure my advice is worth much, Jeannette, but I'm a good listener."

The waitress returned to the table "Care to order?" she asked.

"Maybe we'd better," Rotondi said. "The place is filling up."

As Rotondi ate, he watched Jeannette push food around on her plate, taking an occasional nibble between sips of the wine she'd insisted on having with dinner. Aside from a slight thickening to her speech, she showed little effect from the alcohol. Whatever it was that she needed to discuss with him had been forgotten, at least for the moment, and their conversation centered on pleasant topics, nothing weighty. Rotondi proved his claim of being a good listener, going with the flow and reacting to things she said, humorous comments about Washington and how much she disliked living there, a few reminiscences about their college days—without getting into their tangled relationship—and other areas that didn't demand advice. It was over a rice pudding to share and cappuccinos that she brought the conversation back to something meatier.

"Phil," she said softly, "Lyle and Neil are in serious trouble."

"What sort of trouble?"

She started to explain, but he took note of tables in their vicinity that were now occupied. "Maybe we'd better have this conversation someplace more private, Jeannette," he suggested, motioning for a check.

The husband-owner intercepted them on their way out. "Was everything all right, Mr. Rotondi?" he asked.

"Everything was great," Rotondi said, slapping him on the shoulder.

"It was delicious," Jeannette said.

The owner beamed. "That is always good to hear. Come back soon."

Rotondi drove directly to his condo. Homer greeted them enthusiastically, one hind paw held slightly off the ground. "Poor baby," Jeannette said, roughing up the hair on his head and neck.

"I'll put coffee on," Rotondi said.

"I'd love a drink," she said.

"Maybe later."

He left her in the living room while he puttered in the kitchen. When he returned, she was perusing a series of photographs hanging on a wall above a desk, some of them with Kathleen.

"It's so tragic what happened to her," Jeannette said.

"I still sometimes have trouble believing it," he said, setting down on a coffee table in front of a couch two steaming mugs of black coffee, along with a small bowl containing packets of sugar and Sweet'N Low, and a pitcher of half-and-half. "Come, sit," he said, patting the cushion next to him.

"How is Emma?" she asked when she joined him.

"She's fine. Busy. Now, you said that Lyle and Neil are in trouble. What do you mean?"

She sat back, leaned her head against the back cushion, closed her eyes, and said, "I don't even know where to begin."

"Political trouble?"

She came forward. "There's always political trouble for Lyle, but he seems able to handle that. I'm afraid the sort of mess he's in goes beyond politics, Phil."

"Go on," Rotondi said, sipping his coffee. Jeannette's remained untouched.

"I received a call a week ago from someone in Chicago."

"Who in Chicago?"

"It was a man. I don't know his name. He sounded old."

"Old?"

"His voice was weak, raspy. Maybe he wasn't old. Maybe he had a sore throat. I don't know."

"What did he say? How did he introduce himself?"

"He didn't. I mean, he asked if I was Senator Simmons's wife."

"*Senator* Simmons wife? That's the way he put it?"

"Yes. He asked that, and I said I was."

"What happened next?"

She sighed and reached for her coffee, then withdrew her hand. "I really would love something to drink besides coffee, Phil. I know you think I drink too much, but—"

"Cognac?"

"That will be fine."

He brought her a small cordial glass one-third filled with Cognac.

"Thanks," she said, tasting it.

"Let's get back to what this man from Chicago said to you."

"He apologized for calling me. He spoke with a strange kind of formality, as if he wasn't an educated person but was trying to sound as though he was. He apologized to me for—oh, yes, for calling with such bad news."

"Was it bad news?"

She guffawed and finished the Cognac in a swallow. "It certainly was, Phil. This gentleman—and I'm being generous in labeling him that—this guy threatened me."

"Physically?"

"Blackmail."

"Over what?"

"Over what he claimed to know about Lyle and his dealings with the underworld."

"Whoa, wait a minute. He claimed that Lyle is tied in with organized crime?"

"That's right. But Phil, he didn't just claim that. He said he could prove it. He told me I would be receiving a package within a few days with the proof."

"And?"

• "It arrived a day later. FedEx, overnight delivery."

"What was in it?"

"Damaging evidence backing up what the caller claimed. Copies of checks and e-mails between these people in Chicago and Marshalk, transcripts of recorded conversations, all sorts of damning evidence. Good God, Phil, organized crime has been laundering money through the Marshalk Group, and a lot of that money has ended up with front groups that use it to fund Lyle's run for the White House."

"You say the package contained evidence. Can you trust it? Can you trust this man who sent it to you?"

"I don't know. I want you to see it."

Rotondi asked, "Why would Lyle get involved with this sort of thing, Jeannette? For money? He doesn't need money."

"To run for president of the United States? Come on, Phil. No one has *that* kind of money. It takes hundreds of millions to even have a chance. Besides, you know Lyle isn't as rich as he was when his father was alive. Before he died, his father made some dreadfully bad real estate investments that almost broke him."

Rotondi did know. Lyle had confided in him throughout the period of his father's failing fortunes, and he had attended the senior Simmons's Chicago funeral, where his bad investments dominated the conversation.

"Excuse me," Rotondi said. He returned from the kitchen carrying a glass of beer.

"Please," Jeannette said, indicating her empty glass.

"You sure?" he asked. He was torn. Still, withholding another taste of Cognac wasn't going to send her straight to AA. He obliged.

"There's more, Phil," she said. She put her lips to her glass, made a face, and put it down on the table. "Photographs."

"In the package?"

"Yes."

He knew what was coming.

"Pictures of Lyle with a woman. I've known about her for a long

time, not her name or anything, but I've been aware that he was seeing someone in Chicago. The photos are—oh, God, they're so disgusting. She's not the only one. I know that for certain. I can't stand
the thought of living with him any longer, Phil. I'm divorcing him."

"He knows?"

"Oh, I've told him, which sends him into a rage. Do you know
what he suggested? He suggested that we live separate lives but stay
married. He gave me permission to see other men, as long as I was dis-
creet about it and didn't do anything to reflect poorly on him and his
political future."

The pragmatic Lyle Simmons in full flower.

"Did you show him the package you received from this guy in
Chicago?"

"No. I was afraid of how he might react. I wanted to talk to you
first."

She'd been relatively calm up to this point, considering the subject matter. Now, suddenly, as though struck by lightning, she swung
around on the couch to face him. Her face was a fright mask. "It's
Neil," she said. "I've got to get him away from Marshalk. He'll be de-
stroyed along with the rest of them."

"Do you think Neil knows?" Rotondi asked.

"I haven't told him any of this, but I intend to."

"I mean about the Marshalk connections with the mob. He's
there every day. Hell, he's the president of the firm."

"He's a figurehead, Phil, that's all. Lyle put Neil at Marshalk the
way he puts other people at lobbying firms around the city. I don't
know, maybe Neil does know about the money laundering. I've got to
convince him to sever his ties there, run as fast as he can." She
wrapped her arms about herself and shuddered. "He—the man who
called—said that if I didn't arrange to pay him money, he'd destroy
the family."

Now tears came. Rotondi pulled her close and held tight until the
sobbing had ebbed. "I'm sorry," she said, accepting a tissue from him.
"I must look a wreck."

"You look just fine. How much money does this guy want?" he asked.

"He didn't say. He told me he'd be in touch after I received the package. I haven't heard from him again."

They sat in silence. It was now dusk; without lights on, the living room had grown dim, as though an emotional thermostat had sensed the mood and made adjustments.

"Where's the package?" Rotondi finally asked.

"In the trunk of my car. I hid it under a lot of stuff."

"I'll look at it, Jeannette. I don't know what good that will do, but maybe I'll think of something."

"It's all so evil," she said quietly.

Rotondi tended to view evil as having a religious basis, which he eschewed. He'd put away plenty of bad people during his career as a prosecutor, men, and some women, for whom human life was irrelevant. In many of those cases, defense lawyers brought in psychiatrists and psychologists to testify that the accused were mentally ill and therefore not responsible for the heinous acts they'd committed. Rotondi frequently brought in his own shrinks to counteract their testimony, including one in particular with whom he'd forged a close relationship. She'd been a practicing psychiatrist for many years, and possessed what Rotondi considered a healthy disdain for much psychiatric theory, including the definition of insanity. As she often told him, "We're too quick to label people who do bad things 'sick.' The truth is, there are plenty of people who aren't sick at all. They're just bad people, and labeling them as sick gives legitimate mental illness a bad name."

As Jeannette had spun her tale of the call from a man with a raspy voice, and the threat he'd issued, Rotondi couldn't help but focus on the genesis of the problem, his college roommate, Lyle Simmons. Had Simmons's lust for power carried him over that line separating unbridled levels of ambition from unlawful behavior—a descent into evil?

"Look," Rotondi said to Jeannette, "I'm sure this will work out. I'll take a look at what this guy sent you and figure out where to go with it."

"I have to talk to Neil."

"And you should."

"I don't know if he'll listen to me, Phil. If he doesn't, will you try to get him to see the light? He's always admired you."

"I'm sure he'll listen to you, Jeannette. Ready to go back? I'll drive you to the hotel and we can get that package for me."

She didn't respond.

"Jeannette?"

"I want to stay with you, Phil."

He sighed. He'd wondered from the moment he'd received the call from her whether they would end up together. It wasn't what he intended. But he certainly recognized that such a possibility existed, and had given considerable thought to what his response might be. In a sense—and he wasn't especially proud of this thought—making love to Jeannette would represent some sort of sweet justice where Lyle was concerned. But that wasn't Phil Rotondi's style. Nor was taking advantage of someone's vulnerability, and Jeannette had certainly joined the ranks of the vulnerable over the past couple of years. She'd confided her unhappiness to him before, never as directly as this evening, but her message was easily read by someone who knew her when—and now.

He'd finally concluded that no matter what transpired during her visit, it would not involve sex.

"Can I stay with you tonight?" she repeated.

"I don't think that's a good idea, Jeannette."

"Should my feelings be hurt?" she asked.

"No. You know I love you and have since the first day we met. But things didn't work out."

Her laugh was rueful. "And how did they work out, Phil? God, I was such a fool, getting pregnant by Lyle and marrying him. Why do we have to wait until we're old before we get wise?"

"I suppose that's the way it was planned by somebody."

"God? If so, he has a cruel sense of humor."

"Let me heat up some coffee for us."

"I want a drink, Phil, a nightcap."

"Now that you're older and wiser, you know alcohol isn't going to solve anything."

"It may not solve anything, Phil, but it sure eases the pain. Please."

They sat quietly in the dark until Phil announced he had to walk Homer.

"Go ahead," she said. "Don't be long."

He was gone fifteen minutes. When he returned, she'd stretched out on the couch and was asleep. He covered her with a caftan that his mother once used to cover him as a boy, tiptoed into the bedroom with Homer at his side, lay down, and allowed his eyes to close. When they opened, early-morning sun streamed through the window.

Jeannette was already up and sitting on a small patio at the front of the condo. He made them breakfast, showered—she said she'd wait until returning to the hotel—and drove her to her pale blue Lexus in the Marriott's parking lot. She opened the trunk, rummaged through paraphernalia, and came up with the FedEx package.

"Here," she said, handing it to him. She kissed his check and said, "Thanks for being wiser and stronger than I am, Phil. You always have been. I wish I'd married you."

He watched her walk quickly toward the hotel's entrance and disappear through the doors.

NINETEEN

"What's new with the Simmons investigation?" Smith asked Rotondi after they'd taken at a table in the Garden Café.

"Not much. Morris Crimley says they're making progress. They have trace evidence they think might be important."

"I see that they're holding some drifter."

"They have to hold somebody. They're getting a lot of pressure to solve this thing."

"How's the senator holding up?"

"He's holding up fine, no surprise. He always does. The press seems to be cutting him some slack, although they still keep harping on the state of his marriage."

"Objective journalism at its best," Smith muttered. "What's your take on the murder, Phil? You're obviously more than just a curious bystander."

Rotondi thought for a moment before responding. "I'm convinced, Mac, that Jeannette Simmons wasn't killed by some passerby. She was killed because of what she knew."

"Knew about what?"

"Not here. It's sensitive stuff. But I do want to run something past you later. Let me just say for now that Jeannette was in possession of information that could blow her husband's career out of the water, and take down their son, too, along with the lobbying firm he works for."

Mac exhaled and raised his eyebrows. "That's pretty heavy stuff. You will elaborate now that you've captured my complete and undivided attention."

"Of course I will. That's why getting together was so appealing to me. Let's get food out of the way first."

After lunch, they entered a nearby pocket park and sat on its only bench. A leafy elm provided dappled shade from the sun.

"You're pretty well connected in this town, Mac," Rotondi said.

"Not that I try to be."

"You've always had a reputation as a stand-up guy who doesn't tell tales out of school. You were the most honorable defense lawyer I've ever known."

"Are you saying I'm the best of a bad bunch?" Smith said, playfully.

"I'm saying that you're someone I know I can trust."

"I'll try to live up to that," Smith said. "Are you in legal trouble?"

Rotondi grinned. "Get right to it, huh? No, I'm not in any trouble, at least not yet. I'll get to the point, too. I have information Jeannette Simmons gave me a month before she died. It came from an unnamed guy in Chicago who called and said he was sending it, and that unless she came up with money, he'd use it to destroy the family."

"What sort of information?"

"Dirt on Senator Simmons and the Marshalk Group, ties to organized crime, money laundering through Marshalk that ends up in Simmons's coffers. There are photos, too, of Lyle with a woman in Chicago who has ties to the mob." Rotondi winced. "Pictures like that are supposed to be salacious and erotic. They're almost comical, all those limbs intertwined, the expression of the senator's face while in the heat of the moment. It would almost make you think that sex is overrated, unless you're a United States senator with his eyes on the White House. Not so funny then."

"How much money is this guy after?"

"I don't know. That's what's strange about this, Mac. Jeannette never heard from him again. I kept in touch with her by phone almost every day during the period between when she gave me the material and her murder."

"Not a very efficient blackmailer."

"Most criminals aren't that smart."

"Why did she give the material to you?" Smith asked.

"She wanted my take on it. Her main concern was Neil and what might happen to him if this information ever became public. She spoke with him about it a couple of weeks before the murder."

"What was his reaction?"

"According to her, he wanted to think about it. Last I heard, he hadn't brought it up again. He might have chalked it up to his mother's drinking."

"And the senator?"

"Jeannette claimed she hadn't told him about the stuff from Chicago, but did tell him she wanted a divorce. She was really conflicted, Mac. On the one hand, she wanted to protect her son, and she's not out to destroy her husband. I know—knew her pretty well. She'd become very vulnerable the past few years. I think she just wanted to bury her head in the sand and hope it would all go away. If Neil resigned from Marshalk, he'd be in a lot better position when and if the walls came tumbling down around him. As for the senator, he'd just have to accept the fact that he screwed up big-time and find another profession, provided he avoided doing time in some federal pen. She wasn't a vindictive woman, Mac. She just wanted out for herself and her family, and didn't know the best way to get there."

Smith grunted and looked up into the tree, squinting against the flickering sunlight. "No way to trace the package she got?" he asked.

"I'm working on it. I have a friend in Chicago who's checking with FedEx. I'm flying out there tomorrow with the senator. I'll catch up with my friend in person while I'm there."

Mac's expression was thoughtful.

"So, Counselor," Rotondi said, "the question I have for you is, What do I do with this information? It could have direct bearing on Jeannette's murder."

"Not much choice, Phil. Go to the police with it."

"And take down one of the most powerful members of the Senate and a possible future president, to say nothing of a close friend? I can't do that, at least not yet. I'm conflicted, too, Mac. Don't get me wrong. If Lyle Simmons's shabby dealings had anything to do with Jeannette's murder, I want him, and anyone else involved, to pay. I spent my professional career committed to that."

"All right then," Smith said, "confront the senator and his son. Convince Neil to walk away from Marshalk and be ready to cooperate with the authorities should this thing become public."

"Good advice, except that maybe it won't become public."

"I don't follow."

"Jeannette never heard again from the guy in Chicago. Makes me wonder if he's decided to drop it."

"But can you afford to take that chance, Phil? It seems to me that what you have to do is get out from being in the middle. Wanting to preserve a family's reputation, which includes a leading political figure, is admirable. But there's a limit."

Rotondi started to say something, but Smith cut him off with, "And there's the law."

Rotondi nodded, his lips pressed together, eyes narrowed. "You're right, of course," he said. "I'll give it a day and see what I can come up with in Chicago."

"Don't wait much longer than that, Phil," Smith said, standing. "This is the sort of situation in which the stakes get bigger every hour."

They left the park and started up the street.

"By the way, I tried to reach Jonell Marbury," Smith said, "but got his voice mail. I assume he'll get back to me this afternoon."

"Emma is catering a going-away party for Marshalk this evening."

"Who's leaving?"

"I don't know. The only people I know there are Neil Simmons and Jonell Marbury, thanks to you and Annabel." Rotondi stopped walking. "I'd better grab a cab, Mac. This leg of mine isn't good for any distance."

"Sure. I don't suppose you're willing to share the information Mrs. Simmons gave you."

"Not yet. I'd rather keep it locked up until I get a better handle on things."

Smith waved over a taxi, and Rotondi got in. "Thanks for lunch," he said.

"My pleasure, Phil. Stay in touch. I mean that."

Rotondi gave him a thumbs-up as the cab sped away.

TWENTY

Detectives Crimley, Chang, and Widletz sat in Crimley's office going over test results of forensic materials collected at the Simmons house that had just been delivered.

"It's an African American hair," Crimley said. "No doubt about that."

"The handyman, Schultz, said he saw a black man arrive at the house as he was leaving."

"But no ID," Widletz said. "Drove an expensive sedan, light-colored, white or gray."

"What's the foul-up with the prints?" Crimley growled.

"A computer problem," Chang offered. "They're working on it. There is something I wish to mention."

"Go ahead, Charlie."

"The glass in question. When I went back to the house, I looked at other glasses in the kitchen cabinets."

"Uh-huh?"

"The glass found on the counter doesn't match the glasses in the cabinets. There was water in the one on the countertop. Other glasses in the cabinets that might be used for water are different."

Crimley laughed. "So what?" he said. "You should see the glasses in my house. None of them match. You end up getting glasses from different places, different sources, giveaways, freebies, a glass that comes with a bottle of booze."

"All the other water glasses in the cabinets match," Chang said.

"What do you make of that, Charlie?" Widletz asked.

"I haven't come to a conclusion," Chang said.

"All your glasses match at home?" Crimley asked Chang. "No, forget I said that. I'm sure they do." He glanced at Widletz, who returned his smile. "When does the lab think they'll fix the computer?"

"Later today," Widletz provided.

"Maybe we'll get lucky. In the meantime, check out BMW and Lexus dealerships in the District. See if they can document the sale of a light-colored vehicle to a tall, dark African American man, well dressed according to Mr. Schultz."

"Might as well try Audi dealers, too," Widletz said, her tone indicating she considered the order a waste of time.

"Sure," said Crimley. "Audi, too."

A uniformed officer stuck his head in. "That bum, Lemon, wants to talk to you, Morris."

"It's Lemón," Crimley said. "Like he says, he's no fruit. What's he want to talk about?"

"Maybe he wants to confess."

"Wouldn't that be nice," Crimley said. "Have him brought up to one of the interrogation rooms. Let me know when he's there." He said to Chang and Widletz, "Start checking out the dealerships. I'll let you know if anything comes of my chat with Mr. Lemón."

Lemón was in the interrogation room with a uniformed officer when Crimley arrived.

"I understand you want to talk to me," Crimley said.

"Yes, sir, that's right. I certainly do."

"You're entitled to have an attorney present."

"I don't need no lawyer."

"Suit yourself. What's on your mind?"

"I lied to you last time."

Crimley glanced up at the officer. "Get a tape recorder in here." He turned to Lemón. "I just want to get everything on the record, Mr. Lemón. Sure you don't want an attorney present?"

"Nah."

A few minutes later, a tape recorder was rolling. Crimley sat across from the vagrant. "Okay, the floor is yours," Crimley said. "What did you lie about—how the woman, Mrs. Simmons, died?"

Lemón vigorously shook his head. "I don't know nothing about that."

Crimley's enthusiasm waned. "So?" he said.

"You know what I said about losing my hammer?"

"Yeah."

"Well, I lied about that. I never owned no hammer."

"Why did you say that you did?"

" 'Cause I stole it. It wasn't mine."

"You stole it?"

He hung his head. "Yup."

"You took it from the workman at the house where the woman was killed. Right?"

A solemn nod.

"What did you do with it?"

He looked up. "Like I said, I tossed it away, down by where I was sleeping. In that stream, only I made sure I got far away so nobody could find it and get me in trouble for stealing it."

"And you didn't use it?"

A slow shaking of the head.

"Sure the lady at that house where you took it from didn't come out and catch you in the act?"

"No, she did not."

Crimley sensed that he was telling the truth. The stone dust on his shoes was picked up when he approached the front of the house to swipe the hammer.

"Why did you bother stealing it, Mr. Lemón, if you didn't intend to use it?"

"I don't know. Sometimes I do dumb things."

You'll get no argument from me, Crimley thought.

"Do I have to go now?" Lemón asked.

"You don't want to go?"

"I don't mind being here, only there's things I've got to do, meetings to go to."

"Yeah, I'm sure there are. You willing to take us to where you ditched the hammer?"

"I'll do that."

Crimley left the room and told other detectives who'd observed the exchange through the one-way glass, "We'll keep him for a while. He's not making a stink about being held, so let's hang on to him. I don't think he killed her, but maybe the hammer will say otherwise."

⋯

Neil Simmons spent part of the day planning his mother's memorial service, then he and his sister, Polly, got together that afternoon and met for an hour with people from St. John's. Earlier, he'd consulted with the police about crowd control at the service, and had finalized a press release announcing the plans. Those necessary chores completed, he and Polly stopped at the Four Seasons Hotel in Georgetown for coffee in the expansive lobby, where an elegantly dressed woman sat behind a gleaming black grand piano and wove familiar melodies. It was the sort of serene scene Neil had been longing for all day.

He was dressed in suit and tie, Polly in jeans and a white T-shirt with STOP THE INSANITY emblazoned across its front. Neil had wished she'd dressed more conservatively, but knew it would be futile to suggest it, and would probably invite a rant on "empty suits" and a lecture on why people act like sheep and all dress the same.

"I think we accomplished everything we had to today," Neil said pleasantly as his coffee, and her Diet Coke, were served.

"It would be nice if Daddy gave a damn and got involved," she said. He started to respond, but she said, "What a sham having her service at Saint John's. She never went near that church. The only reason Daddy wants it there is because of his image. What bull!"

"Oh, come on, Polly, let's not get into that. You know how busy he is."

"Busy doing *the people's business*. I've come to the conclusion that the best thing Congress can do for the country is to stay home."

Neil laughed.

"I'm serious," she said. "All Congress does is take money from lobbyists and pass laws the lobbyists want passed. What kind of democracy is that?"

Neil started to respond but she cut him off. "I know, you're a lobbyist, Neil, but just because you're my brother doesn't make it right. You ever think of leaving?"

"Sure."

"No, I mean *really* think of leaving."

"It's not that easy, Polly. I have responsibilities, a family."

"That's no excuse. You were supporting your family just fine when you worked at the bank."

"It was hand-to-mouth. Marshalk pays a lot better."

She turned from him, recrossed her legs, and looked at the pianist. Neil drank his coffee and observed the formidable, sharply dressed men and women occupying other tables. They represented what he'd aspired to be, a smooth, confident player moving easily through the corridors of the nation's most complex capital city. What he was feeling at that moment was hardly that. He was confused and deflated, unsure of who he was—who he'd ever been.

The conversation he'd had with his mother two weeks before she died had stayed with him day and night, making sleep virtually impossible. He'd tried to lose himself at work, but there wasn't enough for him to do there to occupy his mind. Marshalk and his lieutenants had been busy wooing new clients and setting up fund-raising events for members of Congress with whom they had close ties. Simmons knew about the upcoming trip to Chicago on a private jet arranged by Marshalk, and had suggested to his father that he accompany him. "There's no need for you to come, Neil," the senator had said. "You stay here in D.C. and make damn sure the memorial service comes off the way I want it to."

He waited until Polly had turned to pick up her soda to say, "Polly, I am going to be leaving Marshalk."

"Really? When did you make that decision?"

"I've been thinking about it for a long time. Happy?"

"No. Why should I be? Proud? I suppose so. Have you told Daddy?"

"No, and I'd appreciate it if you didn't mention it until I've had a chance to."

She pressed her finger to her lips and said with exaggerated gravity, "My lips are sealed." Her eyes opened wide. "He will not be happy," she said.

"It's important that I be happy."

"You bet. What does the missus say?"

"I haven't told Alex."

"Boy, I'd love to be there when you do. There go her plans to redo the kitchen again."

"Lay off Alex, okay?"

"Whatever you say, big brother." She took in her surroundings, leaned close to him, and asked, "Do you think Daddy had Mom killed?"

"Jesus, Polly, how can you even think such a thing?"

"They were getting a divorce, you know."

"They were?"

"You didn't know?"

"I—I heard something."

"And you know what that would do to Daddy's political future."

"I don't want to hear this, Polly, this nonsense about Dad killing Mom."

"You may not want to hear it, Neil, but you can't just dismiss it out of hand."

He felt a rush of heat to his face and wondered if he had reddened. "Please, Polly," he said, "this isn't the time. Our mother has just been murdered. We have to stick together as a family and honor her by our actions."

"For Daddy's sake?"

"No, damn it, for her sake." He realized his voice had risen, and he looked around to see whether anyone had reacted. No one appeared to have. She reached for her glass, but he grabbed her hand en route. "It doesn't matter," he said, "who killed Mom. That's for the police to determine. It's our responsibility to stand tall and—"

"*Stand tall?*" she mimicked. "When have you ever stood tall, Neil?"

He released her hand and sat back.

"I'm sorry," she said. "I shouldn't have said that. I know it hasn't been easy being involved with Daddy. He's overbearing, my way or the highway. That's why I got as far away as I could, as soon as I could." She paused as she saw his eyes become moist. "I love you, Neil. I just wish . . ."

"I'd like to leave," he said, motioning for a check.

He drove her to the Hotel George and pulled up in front.

"You're really leaving Marshalk?" she asked.

"Yes. I'm going to give Phil Marshalk my notice. I have to be at a going-away party tonight. Maybe I can corner him there and break the news. Dad is leaving tomorrow for Chicago. Phil is going with him. As soon as I tell Marshalk I'm leaving, I'll get hold of Dad and tell him, too."

"Everything will turn out okay," she said, and kissed his cheek.

"I hope so, Polly. I hope so."

Simmons watched her skip into the hotel. Then he drove to Marshalk's headquarters. Jonell Marbury intercepted him on his way to his office. "Got a minute, Neil?" Marbury asked.

"Sure."

Marbury closed the door behind them.

"What's going on?" Marbury asked.

"About what?"

"About this place, Neil. Marshalk and Parish have turned it into an armed camp. You'd think we were some Defense Department think tank with top-secret information about where the next war will be."

Simmons shrugged and waved his hand. "I don't know, Jonell. I'm just the president."

"You've heard the rumors."

"Which ones?"

"About Justice investigating us."

Simmons nodded.

"You must know something about it, Neil." Marbury got up from his chair, leaned on Simmons's desk, and said, "I've even heard it might involve money laundering for the mob."

"Just a rumor, Jonell."

Marbury sat again. "I'm getting really worried, Neil. I had a conversation with Camelia the other day. She's bailing because she's concerned about what's coming down. I'm thinking of doing the same thing."

Simmons was poised to reveal that he, too, intended to leave the firm, but thought better of it. Although he trusted Marbury, he also knew that even the most closed-mouthed people in Washington ended up spilling things said in confidence, perhaps not deliberately, but inadvertently.

"Maybe you should" was the way Simmons put it.

"You mean that?"

"Look, Jonell, I'm as aware as you are of things here getting out of hand. I hear the scuttlebutt as clearly as you do. Do you have something else lined up?"

"No, but I'm not worried about that. I had a long talk with Marla about it. She's all for me leaving."

"Well," Simmons said, "Marshalk will obviously miss you if you decide to resign. You have to do what's right for you." Simmons rubbed his eyes and added, "We all do."

Marbury looked at Simmons quizzically but didn't say what he was thinking: that Simmons's final comment was intriguing, and troubling. He changed the subject: "Things shaping up for your mom's memorial service?"

"Yeah, I think so. My sister and I tied up some loose ends today."

"Going to Camelia's bash tonight?"

"Sure. You?"

"Right. I'm leaving now and stopping at home before the party. Is your wife coming?"

"No. Tough getting sitters these days. Teenagers don't want to bother anymore making a few bucks watching somebody else's kids. Mommy and Daddy give them all the money they need."

Marbury got up and laughed. "I know what you mean, Neil. If I have kids someday, I intend not to spoil them."

"I wish you well in that, Jonell. See you at the party."

Marbury left the building, and Neil Simmons went through a sheaf of papers without focusing on any of them.

At the other end of the long corridor, Jack Parish sat in his office with Rick Marshalk. He activated a small digital tape recorder he'd taken from a locked cabinet that had recently been delivered. Inside the cabinet was other electronic equipment all tied in to a system that delivered conversations from a series of offices in which listening devices had been installed simultaneously with the sweeping of those same offices for other bugs. Parish activated the recorder.

"What's going on?"

"About what?"

"About this place, Neil. Marshalk and Parish have turned it into an armed camp. You'd think we were some Defense Department think tank with top-secret information about where the next war will be."

"I don't know, Jonell. I'm just the president."

"You've heard the rumors."

"Which ones?"

"About Justice investigating us. You must know something about it, Neil. I've even heard it might involve money laundering for the mob."

"Just a rumor, Jonell."

"I'm getting really worried, Neil. I had a conversation with Camelia the other day. She's bailing because she's concerned about what's coming down. I'm thinking of doing the same thing."

"Maybe you should."

"You mean that?"

"Look, Jonell, I'm as aware as you are of things here getting out of hand. I hear the scuttlebutt as clearly as you do. Do you have something else lined up?"

"No, but I'm not worried about that. I had a long talk with Marla about it. She's all for me leaving."

"Well, Marshalk will obviously miss you if you decide to resign. You have to do what's right for you—we all do."

"Things shaping up for your mom's memorial service?"

"Yeah, I think so. My sister and I tied up some loose ends today."

"Going to Camelia's bash tonight?"

"Sure. You?"

"Right. I'm leaving now and stopping at home before the party. Is your wife coming?"

"No. Tough getting sitters these days. Teenagers don't want to bother anymore making a few bucks watching somebody else's kids. Mommy and Daddy give them all the money they need."

"I know what you mean, Neil. If I have kids someday, I intend not to spoil them."

"I wish you well in that, Jonell. See you at the party."

Parish looked at Marshalk after turning off the recorder.

"Play that recording of Marbury and Camelia again," Marshalk said.

"Something wrong?"

"It's Marshalk. He insisted on taking me to dinner last night and—"

"What's wrong with that?"

"Nothing wrong with going to dinner with your boss. It's what he said that bothers me."

"I'm listening."

"He—he basically threatened me, Jonell."

"Threatened you? With what?"

"About what I've learned about Marshalk Group since I've been here. He's afraid that by going back to work at Justice, I might use my inside knowledge of how things work here to bring some sort of legal action against him and the firm."

"That's ridiculous."

"He doesn't think it is. It was creepy, really creepy. He was all smiles and happy talk during most of the meal. But then he got serious, *very* serious, and gave me this lecture on how he expected me to treat what I know as sacred, and that . . ."

"And that *what?*"

"And that he'd hate to see something terrible happen to me."

"He said that? I mean, those were his words?"

"Yes, that's exactly what he said. Oh, he couched it with lots of flowery talk about what a great career I have in front of me, and how much he's appreciated the work I've done here. But when he said that—when he threatened me—my blood ran cold. Jonell, the Marshalk Group breaks the law every day. That's one of the reasons I'm leaving. This place is a legal train wreck waiting to happen."

"Come on, Camelia, it can't be that bad."

"It's worse, Jonell. Want some good advice?"

"Sure."

"Listen to Marla. She wants you to leave. You don't want to be on this train when it goes off the rails."

Parish turned off the recorder. His office was silent.

Marshalk, whose mouth was empty, moved it as though chewing something.

Parish looked at his boss.

"Nice, huh?" Marshalk said. "There's no honor anymore. You do the right thing for people, give them the best jobs they'll ever have, and they stick it to you in the back."

Parish returned the cassette recorder to the cabinet and locked it.

Marshalk got up and went to the door. He paused, turned, and said, "Traitors get hanged. They get strung up because they violated a trust that can take down a country. Nobody's taking me down, Jack. Nobody!"

TWENTY-ONE

Emma Churchill, caterer to Washington's A-list, liked to arrive at events at least two hours early to size up and set up at her leisure, and planned to do so for the party at the Marshalk town house. But as sometimes happens—fortunately not often—the stars in catering heaven had gotten out of alignment. Her roster of regular help had started calling earlier in the day to inform her that they wouldn't be available that evening. The bartender claimed he had the flu, although Emma suspected that he'd landed a better-paying job. One of her assistant chefs, a young woman, almost sliced her finger off doing prep work, and Emma ended up running her to the ER to be stitched and sedated. And a server, a dedicated animal lover, called to report that she had to rush one of her dogs to the vet. All this meant frantic, last-minute scrambling to find replacements.

With her patchwork crew finally assembled at the town house, and with an hour before the start of the party, Emma picked up the pace of preparation. The substitute staff worked fairly smoothly with her, although there were a few snags because of their unfamiliarity with her routine. But everything was eventually done to Emma's sat-isfaction, and she went outside to enjoy a few minutes of peace before the crowd started to arrive. She did what she always did at such mo-ments, wanted a cigarette. It had been ten years since she'd stopped smoking, but certain triggers remained. The lull between getting ready for an event, and the event itself, was one of them. Theater in-termissions were another.

She saw two limos turn the corner and head for the town house. *Time to get inside*, she thought, and returned to where her staff stood ready. "Showtime," she announced as people began coming through the door; the jazz duo, a pianist and bass player, launched into "Make Someone Happy."

She knew many of the Marshalk staff from previous events, and some of them greeted her. Jonell Marbury and his fiancée, Marla Coleman, arrived on the heels of Rick Marshalk and his date for the evening, a stunning brunette a few inches taller than him, wearing a silver sequined dress that might have taken an hour to get into.

"Hello, there," Marbury said to Emma. "Where's your compatriot tonight?"

"Home missing me, I hope," Emma said lightly.

"He'd better be, huh?" Marla said with exaggerated seriousness, followed by a wicked laugh.

"Where's the star of the evening?" Emma asked.

They looked around. "Not here yet," Marbury said. "Probably wants to make a grand entrance."

"The bar's over there," Emma said, pointing.

"Time for a drink," Marbury said to Marla, "but only to keep the bartender busy. Nothing sadder than a lonely bartender."

Emma watched them move in the direction of the bar and was struck by what a handsome couple they were. She thought about what most of the people in the room did for a living.

They were lobbyists, highly paid, nicely dressed, well-connected men and women who spent their days—and nights—courting those in government with something to offer in the way of legislation, laws, and rules that would benefit their clients' bottom lines. Lobbying had become a major Washington industry; the number of registered lobbyists in town had doubled since 2000, and—according to what Emma had recently read—the fees they charged to their clients had gone up as much as 100 percent during that same period. More than half of all elected officials and their staffs now turned to lobbying in their post-government lives.

She wondered how the intense scrutiny that lobbying had recently come under affected the lives of those at the party. Depictions of the city's lobbying corps in the press were less than flattering, particularly certain firms that were reported to have progressed beyond legal influence peddling. She'd seen Marshalk's name mentioned in some of the stories, but to her knowledge no charges against them had ever been filed.

Washington! Was there any other place in the world with as much intrigue on a daily basis, and with so much at stake? Perhaps so, but she couldn't imagine where. As a caterer, she had a different vantage point from which to observe the men and women who called the shots and determined the future. It would have been easy for her to become terminally cynical, and she regularly reminded herself not to be. It wasn't always easy.

As the living room filled, people fanned out to other rooms and to a brick patio at the rear of the house. Emma wondered who the evening's honoree was. All she knew was that her name was Camelia—a lovely name, she thought, evoking images of sultry summer days in Memphis or Savannah, a swing on a shaded veranda, and a tall, frosty, colorful drink in your hand.

A few minutes later, three latecomers walked into the room, led by an attractive African American woman who immediately became the center of attention.

Aha, Emma thought. *The lady named Camelia.*

Rick Marshalk approached the woman and embraced her. Emma focused on Camelia's face, which did not say that she particularly welcomed his gesture. Jonell Marbury also gave the departing staff member a hug. Emma glanced at his fiancée, Marla, whose expression also was not approving.

"Where's Neil?" Emma heard a young lobbyist ask a Marshalk colleague.

"I don't know. He said he was coming."

"I feel bad for the guy, having to bury his mother."

"They still don't know who did it."

"Lots of possibilities."

"Such as?"

They walked away, but one's trailing voice reached Emma's ears: "Her husband?" His friend punched him in the arm and laughed as they left the living room for another place.

One of Emma's servers came to her carrying an empty canapé tray. "If that bastard grabs my butt one more time, he's getting this tray shoved up his—"

"Avoid him," Emma counseled. "I'll send Millie in his direction." Millie, the only regular member of Emma's staff working the party, had a black-belt in karate.

The party had been going for almost an hour when Neil Simmons arrived. He looked lost to Emma, as though he'd walked into a roomful of strangers and didn't know whom to approach. Marshalk brought his date to meet him. Jonell and Marla also welcomed him, as did Camelia Watson and some of the guests with whom she'd arrived.

Emma looked over to where the groper with a fixation on the server's posterior was overtly drunk. He wasn't the only one, and Emma whispered to the bartender, "Go easy with him and some of the others. I don't need a drunk rolling out of here and wrapping his car around somebody."

She checked her watch. The party was booked from seven until nine. It was eight thirty. *Time for a break*, she told herself and headed for the kitchen to hide out for ten minutes. The room had two doorways, one leading into the living room, another on the opposite wall that opened onto a short hallway. She sat on a stool near the latter, allowed her flat shoes to dangle from her toes, and reached down to massage her feet. A conversation from the hallway captured her attention. She immediately recognized Jonell Marbury's deep baritone voice.

"You're acting like a fool, Marla," he said.

"Don't call me a fool," she said. "If you think I'm going to stand around while you cozy up to Camelia Watson, you've got another guess coming."

"I wasn't cozying up to her, as you put it. It's her going-away party, Marla. I'm just being nice, that's all."

Marla lowered her voice, but it was still audible to Emma. "You aren't kidding anyone, Jonell, especially me. You've had the hots for her for a long time. I'm not blind."

"Marla, I —"

"You'd better make up your mind, Jonell. You're not a Mormon. You get one wife, one woman. I'm going home."

"No, don't do that, Marla. A bunch of us are going to a bar after we leave here."

"Wrong, Jonell. Maybe *you* are going to a bar, *you* and Ms. Watson. I'm out of here."

Emma heard the click of Marla's heels on the hall floor. Jonell called out, "Marla, wait." Then there was silence from the other side of the door.

Emma exhaled a stream of air and shook her head. Romance. Men and women. Jealousy. *Never easy,* she thought as she slipped her feet back into her shoes and left the kitchen to help wrap things up.

"Great food, as usual," Rick Marshalk said as he and his date were leaving. "No surprise. You're the best, Emma."

Others passed along compliments, too, as the crowd thinned and the noise level lowered. Soon she was alone with her staff, and they attacked the cleanup.

"Thanks, everybody," she said as they gathered on the sidewalk after loading things into the extended minivan Emma used in her business. "Great job. And thanks for filling in at the last minute. Call my office in the morning if you'd like more work with me. You were all terrific."

As she drove to her office and kitchen across town, where she would park the van overnight and empty it in the morning, she thought about Neil Simmons's arrival; she hadn't seen him for the rest of the evening. She reasoned that it wasn't easy attending a social event on the heels of your mother's murder, and that he probably had made what was a mandatory appearance as Marshalk's president, skipping out at the first opportunity.

After parking the van, she got in her car and drove home to where Rotondi waited.

"How'd it go?" he asked after she'd changed into pajamas and a robe.

"It went fine. Big drinking crowd. Speaking of that, I need a drink. You?"

"No, thanks. Just some water." They went to the kitchen, where she poured herself a brandy. He drew cold water from the refrigerator's water dispenser and used it to wash down two painkillers.

"Leg's bothering you tonight?" she asked.

"Yeah." He tried to avoid taking the pain medication he always carried with him, but there were times when it was necessary.

"How was your day?" she asked when they were settled again in the den.

"Okay. I had lunch with Mac Smith. He says hello."

"What was the occasion?"

"No occasion. I enjoy spending time with him. He's savvy and straightforward. Refreshing. Were that fellow Jonell and his fiancée there tonight?"

"They sure were. I ended up overhearing an argument between them. She left the party without him."

"Uh-oh, trouble on the domestic front."

"You might say that. Marla thinks he's getting too cozy with the woman who's leaving Marshalk. The party was for her. Anything new on the murder?"

"No. Was Neil there?"

"He was, but I don't think he stayed long. At least I didn't see him again after he arrived. A group of them were planning on extending the night, going to some bar."

"There'll be a few hangovers at Marshalk in the morning."

"Afraid so. What time are you leaving for Chicago tomorrow?"

"Eleven. I'll walk Homer. Then let's watch something dumb and unchallenging on TV. I'm in the mood for dumb and unchallenging."

⁂

Rotondi hadn't detailed what was discussed at lunch that day with Emma, but Mac Smith was more forthcoming with Annabel. They'd had dinner out, and now sat on their balcony. He told her what Rotondi had revealed to him over lunch, and Annabel listened without comment. When he was finished, she said, "He sounds as though he's determined to resolve this himself."

"I suggested he confront Neil and the senator with what he knows. He said he'd think about that."

She was silent, the brandy snifter pressed to her lips.

"I know what you're thinking, Annie, that Phil is wading in deep waters."

"Maybe over his head."

"He's a tough guy, a straight shooter. I think he'll do the right thing. At least I hope he does."

⁂

Some of the Marshalk partygoers had moved the festivities to the Fly Lounge, a relatively new club on Jefferson Place, NW, arguably the city's most expensive and exclusive new watering hole. Marshalk had frequently hosted politicians there who enjoyed the atmosphere—including occasional bursts of liquid nitrogen blasting from the ceiling to create the sound of a jet engine's roar—and the bosomy young waitresses known as "Fly Attendants," dressed in tight black costumes and knee-high boots. The money Marshalk routinely dropped there— eighteen hundred dollars for the corner VIP section with its own volume control for the music, and a secret code assuring access to a private bathroom—ensured that his party was never made to wait in line outside where a bouncer ascertained whether those awaiting entrance "looked right" and had the "right attitude."

A dozen holdovers from the party sat in the VIP section and drank Black Cherry Martinis, which one of the Fly Attendants assured was a house specialty. Marbury was next to Camelia Watson, who should have declined the last drink offered. She was tipsy, enough for others to notice. Spirits were high, but the evening's alcohol intake had taken its toll on everyone. Fatigue trumped the determination to party well into the night, and the gathering broke up at eleven.

"You okay?" Marbury asked Camelia as they exited the club.

"Oh, sure, I'm fine," she said, tripping on a raised portion of the sidewalk and falling into his arms.

"How did you get to the party?" he asked.

"I took a cab with Sid and Marshall."

"I'll drive you home."

"No, that's okay, Jonell. Get me a cab and—"

"Absolutely not," he said, putting his arm around her and heading to where he'd parked his silver Lexus a few blocks away.

"I never should have had another drink," she said.

"Happens to the best of us," he assured, enjoying the feel of her hip against his.

He opened the passenger's door, and she slid onto the seat. He came around and got behind the wheel. "Seat belts," he ordered. She fumbled to find hers and he reached across to help, his elbow nuzzling into her bosom. He drew the belt across her lap, inserted the tongue into the sleeve, clicked it closed, and turned the ignition key. High humidity had fogged the windows. He turned on the defroster, and lowered and raised both front windows to wipe them clean.

There was little traffic that time of night, and he reached the apartment building in which she lived in less than ten minutes. He pulled up a few spaces from the entrance, turned off the engine, and looked over at her. She hadn't said anything during the drive; she looked sad.

"How you doing?" he asked.

"Okay." She shifted in the seat to face him. "I'm so sorry, Jonell."

"About what?"

"About Marla."

He forced a laugh. "Not to worry," he said. "She'll get over it."

"I never wanted to cause you any trouble."

He placed his hand on hers. "It's okay, Camelia, it's okay. You didn't do anything."

"Except encourage you."

"You did?"

"Of course I did. I think you're—I think you're a very attractive guy in more ways than one. To be honest, I'm the one who's jealous—of Marla."

"That's all very flattering, Camelia, and I'd be a liar if I didn't admit being attracted to you. But it's not to be."

"I know that, Jonell. I hate coming off the fool."

"You're anything but. Did you enjoy your party?"

"No."

"No?"

"It was nice and all, but . . ."

"But what?"

"Marshalk." Her affect had been flat. Now she was more animated. "He tried to buy me off."

"What do you mean?"

"Marshalk came into my office today and handed me an envelope. Know what was in it?"

"I can't wait to hear."

"A check for fifty thousand dollars."

"That's a nice going-away present," Marbury said.

"I didn't take it."

"How come?"

"It's dirty money, Jonell. First he threatens me over dinner, now he hands me fifty thousand dollars with the hope I'll keep my mouth shut about what I know."

"Maybe you're being too hard on him, Camelia. You're not the first employee to leave with a hefty check."

"Oh, come on, Jonell, one thing you're not is naïve. Have you given any thought to what we talked about the other day?"

"About my leaving? Sure. I discussed it with Marla. She wasn't happy from the get-go when I decided to sign on with Marshalk. She wants me to resign, too. I spoke with Neil this afternoon about leaving."

"You did? What did he say?"

"He didn't try to discourage me. In fact, I had the impression that he might be thinking of leaving, too. He didn't say so, but there was that vibe."

"And you?"

"Me? I still have to give it some thought. I'm not sure what to do. I think what bothered me most was Rick not wanting me to go to the police and tell them I was at Senator Simmons's house the afternoon his wife was killed."

Her eyes widened and she grabbed his hand. "What were you doing there?" she asked, her voice mirroring surprise at what he'd said.

"Rick asked me to drop off an envelope. He told me to take it there on my way home. I left early that day and dropped it off around four."

"What was in it?"

"I don't know. It had the senator's name written on it. I handed it to Mrs. Simmons."

"And Marshalk didn't want you to tell the police that you were there?"

"Right."

"Why?"

"He said it would only cause trouble for me, and maybe for the firm. I shouldn't have listened to him. It's been keeping me awake ever since the murder. I'm going to the police tomorrow. I might have been the last person to see her alive."

"I didn't know."

"It was stupid of me to listen to Rick about something like this."

The windows had fogged up again.

"I'd better get in," Camelia said. "Thanks for the lift."

"My pleasure. You feeling better?"

"More sober?" She laughed. "Yeah. I'll be fine."

She brought her face close to him and they kissed.

He walked her into the lobby of her building where a uniformed doorman sat behind a desk.

"Remember what you said you'd do tomorrow," Camelia reminded Jonell.

"I won't forget," he said. "Count on it."

The doorman left his post and disappeared through a door behind the desk.

"Careful home," Camelia said.

"I will."

"Best to Marla."

Marbury watched Camelia disappear into an elevator. He turned to say good night to the doorman, but he hadn't returned to the lobby. Marbury went to his car and drove to the row house he and Marla had shared for the past year.

⬥

Camelia let herself into her apartment. She'd left a single table lamp burning, which spilled soft yellow light across the floor. She kicked off her shoes, tossed her handbag on a chair, and padded over to the sliding glass doors that led to a small balcony. She pulled the drapes open and looked out over the city of Washington, D.C., her home for the past eleven years. She was swamped with conflicting feelings. Since moving to Washington, her social life had been full, her romantic life less so. Should she have made more of an attempt to forge a relationship with Jonell despite Marla's presence? That possibility had crossed her mind many times, and there were moments when she rationalized it to herself. Jonell and Marla weren't married, which made him fair game. At least that's what girlfriends counseled when Camelia confided in them about her feelings for Jonell. "All's fair in love and war," they said, or something along those lines. Their encouragement made sense when they expressed it, but it didn't last. Camelia would walk away from those moments filled with determination to make a serious play for Jonell, but that sense of purpose waned quickly, like a fading musical note. The truth was, Camelia had her own standards to live up to, and they didn't include stealing another woman's man.

She slid open the doors and stepped out onto the balcony. A breeze was only hinted at as she placed her hands on the railing and drew a deep breath. A wave of calm settled over her. It was over—silly flirtations with a man she couldn't have, and working for Rick Marshalk. A smile crossed her face as she looked up at a crescent moon that came and went behind low, gray, fast-moving clouds. Tomorrow would represent a new phase in her life.

She never heard the man who'd been hiding just inside her open bedroom door as he silently crossed the living room, came up behind her on the balcony, gripped her neck with his left hand, and brought his right hand up between her legs. She went over the railing headfirst and never made a sound as she fell eight stories to her death.

TWENTY-TWO

"**O**h, my God! Phil, come quick!"

Rotondi looked for his cane, remembered he'd left it in the bedroom, and hobbled to where Emma was standing in front of the television. Half his face was clean-shaven; foam obscured the other half. A towel covered his torso.

". . . Ms. Watson, who was found on the ground beneath the balcony of her eighth-floor apartment, had just returned from a party celebrating her leaving a Washington lobbying firm, the Marshalk Group. Police are treating it as a possible suicide. Stay tuned for further information as we receive it."

"She's the one they threw the party for last night, Phil."

"Did you talk to her?" he asked, grabbing the towel as it started to slip, and reknotting it.

"No. She might have said hello or something when she was served, but I don't recall it."

"Did you have a chance to observe her? Did she look suicidal to you?"

"How would I know whether someone I don't even know looked suicidal?"

"Strike that," he said.

"The only thing I did notice was her reaction when Rick Marshalk greeted her with a bear hug. She didn't look pleased."

"I'll be back." He returned to the bathroom to finish shaving and put on a robe.

"You said her name came up in that conversation you overheard between Jonell and his fiancée," he said upon returning.

"Right. She accused him of getting too cozy with this Watson woman and left the party."

"Who did Ms. Watson leave with?"

"I have no idea. No, strike that, as you lawyers say. I saw Jonell go out the door with her. I think she was drunk."

"Which could account for falling off her balcony."

"It could. Then again—"

His raised eyebrows asked the next question.

"I don't know what to think. Someone told me at the party that she used to work for the Justice Department, and was leaving Marshalk to go back there. What time do you leave for Chicago?"

"Eleven."

"I have to go unpack the van and get ready for tonight."

"Who are you feeding now?"

"A bunch of foreign dignitaries visiting the Department of Agriculture. Strictly organic, no trans fat, lots of soy. Inspiring, huh?"

"Makes me look forward to a Chicago porterhouse. I'll be back tomorrow. You'll have to cuddle up with Homer tonight."

"He snores worse than you. Love you. Got to run."

&

Jonell Marbury and Marla Coleman woke up that morning twisted around each other in bed. They'd stayed up late hashing out the source of that evening's contretemps, and as usual patched things up, leading to a physical affirmation that all was well again.

Marla headed for the shower. Dressed in his robe and pajamas, Jonell grabbed the newspaper from where it had been tossed on the tiny patch of front lawn and was on his way back into the house when two nondescript sedans pulled up in front. Marbury gave a cursory glance at the three men in suits, one green—green?—and one woman who exited the cars and was about to open the front door when one of them said loudly, "Mr. Marbury?"

Marbury turned and narrowed his eyes. The contingent, two abreast, came up the short walkway. One held out what looked like an official badge.

"Yes?" Marbury said.

"My name is Detective Chang, Metro Police, Mr. Marbury."

"Yes?" Marbury said again.

"We would like to ask you some questions," Chang said.

"About what?"

"We can discuss that once we are at headquarters."

"Headquarters?"

"Please, sir," Chang said, "just come with us."

"Now wait a minute," Marbury protested. It was at this moment that reality struck. They were there to ask him about having been at Jeannette Simmons's home the day she was murdered. They'd beaten him to it. He'd intended to go to the police . . .

"May we come inside?" the sole woman in the group asked.

"Yes, of course. No! My fiancée is in there and—"

"Then you can come with us the way you are," she said.

"What is this about?" Marbury asked.

Marla, who'd emerged from the shower, came to the front window and saw the scene transpiring outside. She opened the door. "What's happening?" she asked.

"These are detectives," Marbury explained. "They want to speak with me."

"Why?"

Marbury faced the green suit. "I'd like to get showered and dressed," he said.

"You can get dressed, sir," Chang responded. "No shower."

"All right," Marbury said and led them into the house. Chang followed him to the bedroom. So did Marla.

"What's going on?" she demanded. "Are we in some sort of trouble?"

"Please leave the room, ma'am," Chang told her.

She looked to Jonell, who nodded that she should heed his advice. She left, confusion etched on her face.

"Is it really necessary that you watch me get dressed?" Marbury asked Chang when they were alone in the room.

"Yes, sir, it is. Please hurry."

The thought of not starting the day with a shower was anathema to Marbury, and he asked again if he could.

"No, sir. Please dress quickly."

He put on chinos, an open-neck white shirt, socks, and loafers, and placed items from a nightstand into his pockets. Chang opened the bedroom door and escorted him into the living room, where Marla waited with the other detectives.

"It's okay," Marbury said to Marla, kissing her on the cheek. "It's all a mistake, that's all. I'll be home soon."

She watched him get into one of the cars with the Asian American detective and his female partner, her fist jammed against her mouth to keep a cry from erupting. The minute they pulled away from the curb, she started pacing the room, myriad scenarios and actions racing through her head. As though someone had suddenly injected a dose of wisdom, she picked up the phone.

⚘

Marbury tried questioning the detectives during the ride to police headquarters but received nothing in response. He considered blurting out that he'd been at Mrs. Simmons's home the day she was killed, and that he'd planned to tell them that morning. But something told him to wait until they were in a more formal setting. The backseat of an unmarked car didn't seem appropriate, or useful.

He was taken to an interrogation room and told to sit at a table in one of three straight-backed, hard wooden chairs. A few minutes later, the detectives entered the room. Chang and Crimley took the remaining two chairs; Widletz leaned against the wall.

"I'm Detective Crimley," the chief said to Marbury. "You've met detectives Chang and Widletz."

Marbury didn't bother correcting Crimley that he hadn't been introduced to the woman. It seemed irrelevant.

"Why am I here?" Marbury asked.

"We have some questions for you, Mr. Marbury," Crimley said.

"I know what this is about," Marbury said.

"Do you?" Crimley said.

"Yes. It's about the murder of the senator's wife, Mrs. Simmons."

Crimley's hard stare challenged Marbury to continue.

"I was there the day she was killed," Marbury said. "I work for the Marshalk Group. I'm a lobbyist. My boss, Rick Marshalk, gave me an envelope to deliver to the Simmons house that afternoon. That's what I did. I drove there and handed the envelope to Mrs. Simmons."

"What time was that?" Crimley asked.

Marbury shrugged. "About four, give or take a few minutes."

"You went into the house?"

"No. Mrs. Simmons answered the door. I told her who I was and gave her the envelope. It had the senator's name written on it."

"What did you do then?"

"I left."

"You never went inside?"

"Never. Look, I know it was foolish of me to not come forward right away. I wanted to but . . ."

"But what?"

"It didn't seem important—at the time. I planned to come here this morning, but your detectives arrived at my house before I had the chance."

"What was in the envelope?" Chang asked. Round, rimless glasses magnified his small brown eyes.

"I have no idea," Marbury replied. "It was sealed."

Silence descended over the room.

Marbury broke it with, "You can ask Rick Marshalk whether he sent me with the envelope."

"We have," said Crimley.

"So?"

"He confirmed it. Let's go back over why you decided to not come forward with this information."

"Rick suggested that I . . ."

Crimley came forward. "He suggested *what?*"

"That I not tell the police I was there."

"That's not what he says."

A cold sweat broke out over Marbury. "What did he say?"

"He says that he encouraged you to come forward."

"That's not true!"

More silence, more sweat.

"Why would he tell you that?" Marbury asked, more of himself than the others.

"Doesn't make much sense, does it?" Crimley said.

Marbury didn't have an answer.

"Doesn't make sense for him to tell you *not* to tell us you were there."

"I don't understand," Marbury said, weakly.

"We would like a DNA sample from you, sir," Chang said.

"DNA?" Marbury said. "Why?"

They didn't elaborate.

"Am I suspected of something?" Marbury asked. "All I did was deliver an envelope and—"

"We can hold you for impeding an investigation," Crimley said.

"That's ridiculous," Marbury snapped.

"About the DNA?" Crimley said.

"This is getting out of control," Marbury said.

"We have reason to believe that you went inside the Simmons

house that afternoon, Mr. Marbury. We have your fingerprints from the scene."

Marbury fought to maintain control of his emotions, unsuccessfully. He slapped his hand on the table and said in a loud voice, "I have never been inside that house. *Never!*"

"Where were you last night?" Widletz asked from across the room.

"Last night? I was home."

"Before that."

"I was—I was at a party. Someone from the firm was leaving, and we had a party for her."

"Camelia Watson?" Crimley said.

"Yes. Camelia Watson. What does she have to do with this?"

"You were with her last night?"

"Of course I was. I was at her party and—"

"What about after the party?" Widletz asked. She'd now come to the table and stood directly behind Marbury, and close.

"I don't know what you mean."

"Oh, come on, Mr. Marbury," Crimley weighed in. "You drove her home, didn't you? You left the party with her, went to the Fly Lounge, had a few more drinks, and drove her home."

"I wasn't drunk," Marbury quickly said.

"We are not talking about driving drunk, sir," Chang said.

"Then what *are* you talking about?"

"About her death."

Marbury felt as though a javelin had pierced his midsection. He searched for words, stumbled, and finally managed, "Camelia is dead?"

"You didn't know?" Chang asked.

"No, of course not. She was alive when I last saw her."

"When was that?"

"As you said, I drove her home from the Fly Lounge and walked her into the lobby of her apartment building. We said good night and I left. You can ask the doorman."

"We did," said Chang. "He says that he did not see you leave the building."

"That's ridiculous," Marbury protested. "He . . . wait a minute. He disappeared from the lobby before I left."

"Uh-huh," Crimley muttered.

"He left through a door behind the desk," Marbury added.

"Right," said Crimley.

Marbury looked from detective to detective, his expression a melding of concern and pleading. "I don't believe this," he said, growing smaller in the chair as though air had been released from his body. "Camelia dead? You think I was in the house when Mrs. Simmons was killed. This is a nightmare."

"Care to change anything you've said so far, Mr. Marbury?" Crimley asked.

Marbury didn't reply.

"The DNA," Chang said. "We will be able to get a court order if you do not cooperate."

"Of course I'll cooperate," said Marbury. "I have nothing to hide."

Crimley was summoned from the room. When he returned, he announced that questioning would stop. Marbury's lawyer had called.

"Who?" Marbury asked.

"You travel in good company," Crimley said. "Mackensie Smith says he's representing you. He's on his way." Crimley motioned for Chang and Widletz to follow him from the room. "Relax, Mr. Marbury. We'll be back once your attorney arrives."

Smith and Marla Coleman showed up twenty minutes later. She was told to wait in the reception area while Smith was brought to the interrogation room.

"I can't believe what's happening to me," Marbury told him. "They say I was in the Simmons house the day she was murdered. That's not true, Mac. And I just learned that Camelia Watson died last night. They think I might have had something to do with it."

Smith, who was about to leave his apartment for a tennis game when a frantic Marla called, had changed into a blue blazer, white shirt, slacks, and tie. Marbury started to elaborate on the situation but Smith stopped him, glancing up at the two-way glass. "Not here," he said. "Have they charged you with anything specific?" he asked.

"No. They said something about impeding an investigation because I didn't freely tell them that I'd been at the house delivering an envelope. I meant to do that this morning."

"Okay, Jonell," Smith said, standing. "Let me go talk with them." He found Crimley just outside the room.

"Microphone's turned off, Counselor," the detective said.

"I wouldn't expect any less," Smith said. "Where can we talk?" They settled in Crimley's office.

"What've you got?" Smith asked the barrel-chested detective.

"Plenty. We've got his print off a glass in the kitchen of the Simmons residence, but he says he's never been inside the house. He was there late afternoon the day she was killed but doesn't bother to tell us that little fact until we pick him up. He says his boss, Rick Marshalk, told him to not come to the police with that information, but Marshalk says otherwise, says he encouraged him to do it.

"We've got a hair from the downstairs bathroom, African American hair. He says he'll be happy to give us a DNA sample. Wanna bet he matches up with it?

"And last night, a lady he drives home from a party falls, or jumps, or is pushed off her eighth-floor balcony. Some folks from that party say that he and the deceased were pretty cozy. His girlfriend storms out of the party because he's paying too much attention to the deceased, and the doorman at her building claims he didn't see your client leave that night. Of course, your client claims the doorman disappeared conveniently just as he was walking out.

"I'd say we've got plenty of reason to hold him, wouldn't you, Counselor?"

Smith smiled. "I'd say you have reason to consider him a person of interest, Morrie, but hold him? No. He's a respected member of the community, used to work for a congresswoman, now a lobbyist. If he agrees to provide a DNA sample, it's all right with me. But the questioning stops unless you charge him with something."

"How about double homicide?"

Smith's smile vanished. "I've always appreciated cops' sense of humor. I saw the TV reports this morning of the woman who fell from her apartment. From what I heard, it looks like a suicide."

"Could be. I just find it interesting that your client shows up at two unnatural death scenes, and lies."

"Maybe he's not lying."

"He says he was never inside the Simmons house, but his prints on a glass, and his hair in a bathroom, say otherwise. Forensics don't lie. People do."

"Some people. I'll go back and tell him to let you swab his mouth for DNA. After we leave, Morrie, you can always reach him through me as his attorney."

"Good to see you again, Mac Smith. I thought you'd packed in your law practice to teach a whole new gang of defense attorneys over at GW. What brings you out of retirement?"

"Jonell Marbury is a friend."

"He's lucky. Okay. He submits to a DNA sample, and he walks out of here with you. His lady is out front. We'll want to talk to him again."

"Of course."

A swab from Marbury's cheek was taken, and Smith escorted him to where Marla waited. After she and Jonell embraced, and she'd wiped tears from her face, they left headquarters and went to Smith's car.

"We can't thank you enough," Marla said to Smith.

"Happy I could help," Mac said. "Now let's go to my apartment where you can tell me everything, Jonell—and I mean everything."

⁂

Rotondi caught a few updates on Camelia Watson's death from TV news, but there wasn't much additional to report. As he was about to call for a taxi to take him to Reagan National Airport, Rick Marshalk's face appeared on the TV screen, interviewed by a reporter.

"Camelia's death is a true tragedy for all of us at the Marshalk Group," Marshalk said solemnly. "She was an outstanding young woman with a great future."

The reporter said, "The police are saying that it's an apparent suicide. Did you see signs of despondency in her recently?"

"Unfortunately, I did. Of course, you never think that someone who appears to be depressed will take his or her own life this way. But yes, she'd been depressed lately. I asked her about it and offered to help, but she said she was fine. All I know is that we will miss her greatly."

Another story followed.

Rotondi made his call and went to the kitchen to take pain pills before heading for the airport. He pulled a glass from a cabinet, filled it with water, and downed the capsules. He placed the half-empty glass in the sink and started to walk away. But he stopped, returned, and retrieved the glass. Everything in Emma's home kitchen came from her catering business—glasses, silverware, plates, cups and saucers, pots and pans, table mats, carving knives, serving spoons, toothpicks, and wooden skewers, all nontaxable perks. He held the glass up to the light coming through a window and frowned as he ran his fingertips over the surface, tracing the almost indiscernible indentations on it. He didn't know why, but that particular water glass had meaning to him at that moment.

He continued to ponder it until he heard a blowing horn from outside. He placed the glass back in the sink, grabbed his overnight bag, roughed up Homer's coat and kissed him on the snout, and left.

&

"Aren't you going to work?" Alexandra Simmons said to her husband, Neil, that morning. It was ten o'clock and he was still in nightclothes.

"No."

"Why not?"

"Because I don't want to. I can't believe this has happened—first Mom, now Camelia. I just want to crawl under the covers and stay there."

"You were with her last night. Did she seem suicidal to you?"

"No. She was never suicidal. I mean, I didn't stay long at the party, just long enough to make an appearance. She seemed fine."

"You never can tell about people," said Alex. "Remember that woman, Jacqueline, from up the street? She was the happiest person you could ever want to meet until she ran a hose from the exhaust of her car into it. You just never can tell."

He sat glumly at the table.

"What did Rick say when he called?"

"What?"

"Rick," she snapped. "You never listen to me. I asked what Rick said when he called with the news."

"Oh, sorry. Rick said that he'd been noticing for a while now that Camelia was depressed. He said he was worried and even talked to a friend of his, a psychiatrist, about her. He was sure I'd noticed the same thing."

"But you didn't."

"No. Absolutely not. I mean, I knew that she was unhappy working at Marshalk and wanted to go back to her job at Justice. That's what she decided to do, which would have made her happy, not depressed."

"Well," said Alexandra, "it's too late for any psychiatrist to do anything for her now. Poor thing. I don't think I could ever kill myself by jumping off a high place." She grimaced and shook her head.

One of their sons came into the kitchen. "Is Daddy sick?" he asked Alex, noticing his father's attire.

"Yes, Daddy's sick," she said.

"I'm not sick," Neil said angrily. "I'm—I'm—I'm sad, that's all. Why wouldn't I be? Jesus, try and understand."

The boy pouted and left the room. Alex got up from the table and rinsed out the coffee carafe, saying as she did, "I have girls' day

today, Neil. They're coming for lunch. I really don't want you hanging around all day in your pajamas."

"All right," he said. "I'll be gone by then."

He went to the bedroom, closed the door, and climbed into bed.
The news of Camelia's plunge to her death had short-circuited him
that morning. Not that he wasn't already in a fragile emotional state.
As potent as the news of his mother's murder had been initially, the
reality and weight of it seemed to increase as the days passed; time
was not healing all wounds, as some claimed. There were physical
manifestations, too. His legs had become heavy and unsteady, like an
old man who has lost muscle mass, or alcoholics who seem to search
for the ground with each unsure step. His convictions were as unsteady as his gait. He couldn't identify anything in which he believed.
Nothing mattered. *Whatever* had become his most frequently used
word since the murder of his mother. Want to watch something on
TV? "Whatever." Potatoes or rice with dinner? "Whatever."

He'd tried to codify his feelings, to make sense of them. He'd even
resorted to writing down his inner thoughts as a means of structuring
them. A business writing class he'd taken at his father's school, the
University of Illinois, had stressed that often the act of writing helped
clarify thinking, rather than thinking being a prerequisite for clear
writing. Horse before cart? He'd been bored in that class, as he had
been in most classes, his GPA reflecting it, mediocre at best but
enough to graduate.

As he cowered in his king-size bed, legs drawn up in the fetal position, the covers pulled up to his chin, he tried to cry but couldn't.
His reservoir of tears was empty. He wanted to cry out but the energy
wasn't there.

He wanted to die, but didn't have the will to bring about his
death.

He hadn't meant harm to come to anyone as a result of what he'd
done.

It seemed so right at the time, so noble.

And it had turned out so wrong.

TWENTY-THREE

The taxi driver dropped Rotondi at the general aviation section of Reagan National Airport, where a sleek, twin-engine Gulfstream III jet aircraft stood waiting on the tarmac. Senator Simmons's chief of staff, Alan McBride, and Press Secretary Peter Markowicz were already inside the operations building when Rotondi walked in.

"Where's the senator?" Rotondi asked.

"On his way," McBride said. "Should be here any minute.

"Is Polly coming?" McBride asked Markowicz.

"She begged off," Markowicz replied. The men exchanged knowing glances.

"Polly was supposed to be with us?" Rotondi said.

"Yeah," said Markowicz. "The senator thought she'd enjoy a day in Chicago. Didn't work out."

They looked through a window as Senator Simmons's black Mercedes pulled up, Walter McTeague at the wheel. The senator got out, said something to McTeague, and strode into the building.

"Good morning," Simmons said. "Looks like a nice day for a flight."

"Couldn't be better, Senator," McBride agreed.

"How are you this morning?" Simmons asked Rotondi.

"Just fine. You?"

"Must have slept wrong," Simmons said, rotating his head. "I've got a crick in my neck."

The flight's captain led them to the plane, where his first officer was conducting a last-minute walk-around visual check.

"That's a mean-looking machine," Simmons commented.

"Top of the line," the captain said. "Ready to board?"

"Yes, sir," said Simmons. "Let's go."

The interior of the sleek business jet was all leather and chrome. It looked to Rotondi that it would seat a dozen people, and he wondered whether others would join them. The closing of the passenger door answered that question. There would be just the four of them in the back, with the two-man crew up front. The first officer came to where they'd chosen their overstuffed, swiveling tan leather club chairs and announced that he'd be back to serve coffee and pastries once they were at cruising altitude. "There's a bar, too. Help yourselves. It's fully stocked."

Rotondi was impressed with the aircraft's power as it lifted from the runway, the nation's capital falling away below. They soon reached their assigned cruising altitude, and the first officer fulfilled his promise of a continental breakfast. Markowicz, who sat next to Simmons, said, "How about moving to the rear, Senator? There're some things to discuss."

Simmons replied, "Anything can be discussed in front of Phil, Peter. He knows why we're going to Chicago."

"Fair enough," Markowicz said, smiling at Rotondi. He said to the senator, "Some press has gotten wind of the meeting and the reason for it."

"Who?"

"I got a call this morning from a reporter at the *Post*. She wanted to know who would be attending the meeting, and whether they'd signed on to your campaign."

Simmons laughed. "Campaign? What campaign? I haven't announced anything. I assume you straightened her out."

"I don't know whether she's straightened out or not, but I told her that you were going to Chicago to attend a fund-raiser for your next senatorial run. I don't think she bought it."

"What about the Chicago press? Do you think they'll be on it?"

"Beats me" was Markowicz's response. "I'm working with our PR people there. They've got their finger on things. We won't be blindsided."

As Simmons and his two top staff people continued to discuss the upcoming meeting and possible media interest in it, Rotondi reclined his leather chair and contemplated where he was and why he was there. Should he, Philip Rotondi, son of a shoemaker from Batavia, New York, feel privileged to have been included in this inner circle, seated next to a possible future president of the United States and listening to conversations to which few were privy? The most influential journalists in the land didn't enjoy this level of access.

His overnight bag sat on the carpeted floor next to him. In it was the file Jeannette had given him when they were together on the Eastern Shore. There was a certain irony, he knew, in having such damaging information within a few feet of the man who might one day end up in the White House. He'd considered pulling Simmons aside and laying it all out for him, and knew that the time would probably come when he would do just that. But at this stage, he preferred to keep his friend's confidence and to wait until he'd had a chance to learn more about the source of the salacious, damning material. That's why he'd agreed to accompany Simmons to Chicago. The answers to his questions, he now knew, were in the Windy City.

As he sat in the opulent private plane flying at thirty-one thousand feet, the whoosh of its twin jet engines the only ambient sound, he shifted his attention between what Simmons and his aides were discussing, and his own thoughts about everything that had transpired since receiving Lyle's phone call announcing that Jeannette had been killed. Had his friend of so many years played a role in his wife's murder? There was certainly speculation about that around Washington. The senator's own daughter harbored such suspicions. Was she right? He knew he had to consider the source, a free-spirited, iconoclastic daughter estranged for years from her powerful father. Still, one had to at least not arbitrarily rule it out, nor summarily dismiss anyone else in the Simmons family with the exception of Polly, who wasn't anywhere near D.C. the day of the murder.

He glanced over at Simmons, who'd slipped into his lecture mode, with McBride and Markowicz his eager students.

If Lyle Simmons had nothing to do with his wife's death—and Rotondi fervently hoped that was the case—what kind of president would he make? Rotondi had abandoned interest in the political scene since leaving the U.S. attorney's office in Baltimore. Not that he'd ever been a keen observer of it, or participant in it, even back then. He didn't trust politicians. As far as he was concerned, their only interest was retaining power, loftier societal needs be damned. He realized that his disdain for elected officials represented a level of cynicism that was probably uncalled for, and sometimes wondered whether he should change his tune. It hadn't happened, and he remained content to be an onlooker, regular voting serving as his conscience salve.

The Gulfstream landed smoothly at Chicago's Midway Airport, where a stretch limo awaited them. They were whisked to the Ambassador East Hotel, home of the famed Pump Room bar and restaurant. Rotondi had been treated to evenings there by Lyle's father and mother when the two college students visited the Simmons home on the city's Near North Side. On many occasions, they were seated in the famed Booth One on the east wall, mirroring the elder Simmons's stature in Chicago. Myriad high-profile celebrities had enjoyed the vantage point of that booth; Bogart and Bacall celebrated their wedding in Booth One, as did Robert Wagner and Natalie Wood. Sinatra held court there on many nights, John Barrymore roared for more

champagne, and noted Chicago columnist Irv Kupcinet used Booth
One as his office away from the office. It was a heady, albeit uncomfortable experience for the college-age Phil Rotondi to be seated there
as part of the Simmons family.

"Afraid you're on your own, Phil," Simmons told Rotondi as they
headed for their rooms. "I'll be tied up in these meetings all afternoon. Meet you in the Pump Room at five for a drink before the
fund-raiser."

"Sounds good to me," Rotondi said, meaning it.

After being shown to the small suite to which he'd been assigned,
Rotondi sat at the desk and placed a phone call. Kala Whitson answered on the first ring.

"Hi, Kala. It's Phil."

"My gimpy friend made it," she said in a husky voice. "Nice
flight?"

"Fancy private jet, all the comforts of home. No, better than
home."

She laughed. "Sounds like you're selling out, Phil. Private jets
were never your style."

"They still aren't, but when in Rome—"

"Don't go getting literary on me, pal. Are we on for this afternoon?"

"I hope so. I have to be back at the hotel by five. I'm free until
then. Where and when?"

"My apartment. I don't think it's bugged, although everyplace
else seems to be. The war on terrorism and all . . . or is it the war on
the Constitution?"

Rotondi smiled. His friend from the Baltimore U.S. attorney's
office hadn't changed a bit since being transferred to the Chicago
office ten years ago. They'd worked closely in Baltimore on some of
the toughest prosecutions, and he valued her no-nonsense, take-no-
prisoners attitude. They'd stayed in touch after her transfer and his retirement, sending amusing e-mails back and forth, making fairly
regular phone calls, and swapping books they knew would interest

each other. Kala was an avowed, prideful, unabashed lesbian, as comfortable in her skin as any heterosexual. She looked mannish. She wore her hair in what could only be described as a designer-styled crew cut, and was fond of tailored black suits that tended to slim down her square body. She talked tough and had a raspy voice, enhanced by chain smoking. She also possessed the most beautiful green eyes Rotondi had ever seen—and his deceased wife, Kathleen, had a pretty spectacular set of green eyes herself.

Kala Whitson was one of his favorite people.

"I assume you've come up with what I need," he said.

"Of course I have, Philip. What the hell did you think I was doing, inviting you to my apartment to seduce you?"

"I was hoping."

"Hope on, my friend. Maybe you noticed you're not my type. Two o'clock?"

"On the button."

Rotondi carried the envelope containing the damaging material about Lyle Simmons and the Marshalk Group with him to the Pump Room. He sat at the bar and enjoyed a beer and sandwich. The doorman hailed him a cab, and he arrived at Kala's apartment building in the Old Town Triangle section of the city, adjacent to Lincoln Park. It had been settled in the mid-1850s by German immigrants and remained a German American enclave until an influx of other nationalities created a melting pot of Germans, Hungarians, and Russian Jews. Gentrification followed, and real estate prices soared, forcing out many of its original residents. Kala bought her condo there because she enjoyed the ghosts of what had been, including saloonkeeper aldermen like Mathias "Paddy" Bauler, who was fond of telling reporters, "I'll talk about anything with you, as long as the statute of limitations has run out." Kala was right for the neighborhood, and the neighborhood was right for her.

Kala and her two rescued stray cats welcomed Rotondi to the apartment. "Drink?" she asked.

"Please."

"Still drinking Scotch?"

He nodded and followed her into the kitchen.

"I hope you know how much I appreciate this, Kala."

"You'd better appreciate it, Philip. My neck's way out on this one."

"I know."

"When you called and told me what you had, I was ready to kill the little weasel, only somebody beat me to it."

"Who is this weasel?"

She handed him his Scotch over two cubes and led him back into the living room.

"Show me the stuff you ended up with," she said, lighting a cigarette.

He opened the folder and laid out its materials. She rifled through it for thirty seconds, shoved the papers back, said, "Yeah, the same stuff."

"Gathered by a weasel?"

"A no-good, rotten little double-dealing weasel. I'd use some other words to describe him, only I wouldn't want to offend you."

"Thanks. So, tell me."

She took a long, sustained drink of club soda, sat back, fired up another cigarette, and said, "Where do I begin? Okay. We flipped a guy who was inside one of our fair city's leading crime families. Despite all the Russian and Jamaican and Haitian mobs, we still have the Eye-talian variety, not as powerful as they used to be but still with plenty of fingers into everything, mostly construction and trash hauling, with side ventures in prostitution and drugs. This guy we flipped, Joey Silva, started bringing us the sort of material you have in the folder, links between his crime family and a certain U.S. senator who happens to be an old friend of one of my favorite prosecutors, now happily retired. At first, the info was sketchy, and it was tough to connect the dots. The route the money took to the senator was convoluted, no straight lines, which you would expect from somebody as smart as your college buddy. But the more Silva gave us, the more the picture started to take shape. The family used front companies that moved the money from their hands to a middleman, namely a lobbying firm in D.C. headed by a gentleman named Marshalk."

"A familiar name," Rotondi said.

"Another familiar name is president of Marshalk, Simmons's kid. But of course, you already know this."

"Everything but the weasel. Go on."

"The weasel, Mr. Joey Silva, lowlife that he is, kept hitting us up for more money. Every time he did, he said he had more and better information, so we went along. The little bastard was getting rich off us, but he was delivering the goods." She tapped the file folder on the coffee table. "Juicy stuff, huh, Philip?"

"Not for the senator and Marshalk."

"Who cares about them? Oh, you do, of course."

"Not Marshalk. Simmons? Yeah, I care about him."

"Are you trying to protect him?"

Rotondi shook his head and sipped his Scotch. "I'm not out to protect anybody, Kala. I just need to know the truth. Simmons's murdered wife, Jeannette, and I were close."

"Oooh," she said with a deep, provocative laugh. "Tell me all about it."

"Another time, Kala. Get back to the story. Who sent this material to Simmons's wife? This weasel, Silva?"

"Looks like it." Another cigarette was lighted. By now, a gray haze had engulfed the room, stinging Rotondi's eyes. "After you called," Kala said between drags, "I checked with the FedEx office in the neighborhood where Silva lives. They pulled the records for me—I have a friend there—and she comes up with the shipping forms that coincided with the dates you gave me. Sure enough, Silva sent a package to Mrs. Simmons. The stupid bastard didn't even bother to use a phony name."

"He was working both sides of the street," Rotondi said.

"That's right. Where's the honor, Philip? He wasn't satisfied getting paid by us, he has to try and extort money out of the senator's wife, too."

Rotondi remembered what she'd said when he first arrived—that she'd wanted to kill Silva but someone had beaten her to it. He asked about it.

"It would have been my pleasure to waste Silva myself," she said, "but one of his spaghetti-bender friends must have gotten wind of his deal with us and shut him up for good. Slit throat, tongue pulled through the slit, classic."

"The pictures, Kala," Rotondi said. "They set Simmons up?"

"They sure did. He'd been bedding down this broad here in Chicago for a while now. We all knew it, and we didn't care. No crime in shacking up, although I'm sure his wife wouldn't have been as understanding. This lady is cozy with some of the mobsters here in Chicago. When they knew she was warming the sheets with a United States senator, they went high-tech and videotaped them in the throes of passion, with her permission, of course."

"Did anyone from the mob tell the senator about the photos?"

"Not according to the weasel. He said they were holding on to them in the event the senator decided to not play ball with them any longer. An insurance policy. So tell me, Philip, how close you and the deceased Mrs. Simmons really were. Must have been damn close for her to entrust you with what's in that folder."

"Close enough that she trusted me, Kala. I guess I have a trustworthy face or something."

"Probably the *something* you have was most important. Speaking of that, how's your love life?"

"Good. She's a D.C. caterer."

"Smart move. You never have to worry about a meal. She own a liquor store, too?"

"Not yet."

"What about the senator's son?" she asked. "You close with him, too?"

"I know him."

"Who back in D.C. knows about the stuff you have in that envelope?"

"No one. Jeannette Simmons was going to talk to her son about it, but I'm not sure she ever did prior to her murder."

"What are *you* going to do with it?"

"I don't know. What are you going to do with what you have?"

"The way it looks at this juncture, nothing."

"Nothing?"

"The long reach of Senator Lyle Simmons and the Marshalk gang extends beyond Washington, Phil."

"The fix is in?"

"Sure is. The powers that be in the AG's office here are sitting on the information about Simmons and Marshalk. Ask them why and they say they don't have enough to go forward with indictments. You know what I say? Bull! Simmons was instrumental in getting them their jobs here, and they're not about to lose what they have. They'll keep it under wraps until he makes the White House and they need something from him. Business as usual. Sweet, huh?"

"Sour is more like it."

"Want a tip, Philip?"

"Sure."

"You might as well do what my esteemed leaders are doing, buy a good shredder and get rid of that stuff. You might end up hurt by hanging on to it. The senator and his friends at Marshalk play rough."

"Thanks. How's yours?"

"How's my what?"

"*Your* love life."

"Boring. I'm thinking of the convent."

"You'd hate it. They have vows of silence and a no-smoking policy."

"I suppose you're right. I have to get back to the office. Any other questions?"

"No. I really appreciate this, Kala."

"The leg's bad, huh?" she said as they said good-bye in front of the building.

"There are moments."

She kissed him on the mouth and said, "Take care of yourself, Philip. You're one of the white hats."

TWENTY-FOUR

"How did your meetings go this afternoon?" Rotondi asked Simmons when they met in the Pump Room.

"Good, Phil. The brain trust feels that the time is right for me to announce my candidacy."

"Will you?"

"I still haven't made up my mind. Jeannette's murder has muddied things." A thoughtful expression crossed his face as he finished what was left of his bourbon. "What do you think?"

"About announcing your candidacy?"

"About running at all."

"My opinion about something like that is irrelevant, Lyle. I'm illiterate when it comes to politics."

"That's a cop-out, Phil. You know me better than any other person in this world now that Jeannette is gone. Has her murder tainted me?"

Rotondi looked quizzically at him.

"You know what I mean, Phil, the rumors that are swirling around that the marriage was on the rocks, that I had a mistress in Chicago, trash like that. The situation with Polly doesn't help, that's for sure. I asked her to come with me to Chicago this trip and join me at the fund-raiser. Naturally, she refused. I don't know how to get through to her. I love her, Phil. I'm sure you know that."

What Rotondi knew was that Jeannette had told her husband that she wanted a divorce.

"Running for president won't help the situation," Rotondi said.

"I suppose not. I hate to bring this up, Phil, but I'm curious about that trip Jeannette took to the Eastern Shore not long before she was killed. She was a different person when she came back."

"In what way?"

"I don't know, more distant, uncommunicative. There was already a gap between us that was growing. I admit that. But she was—" His laugh was rueful. "I've always wondered whether you'd get even with me one day for stealing her from you at school, you know, try and bed her down."

Simmons's comment was, at once, hurtful, infuriating, and sad. Rotondi thought before responding. "I'm going to let that pass, Lyle."

"Hey, no offense," Simmons said, placing his hand on Rotondi's shoulder. "To be honest, I'd deserve it for what I did back at old U of Illinois. That you chose to remain friends with me after it says something wonderful about you. I'm not sure I could have done the same."

"That's old news, Lyle. And no, Jeannette and I didn't sleep together that weekend."

"You're a quality guy, Phil."

"Shouldn't we be heading for your fund-raiser?"

Simmons looked at his watch. "I suppose so. Meet you in the lobby in half an hour."

Rotondi watched Simmons exit the bar and chewed on the conversation they'd just had. He knew that if he'd ever wanted to "get even" with his college roommate for wooing Jeannette away from him, sleeping with her would have been minor compared with what he could do with the information upstairs in his room.

CRU

The fund-raiser was held in a ballroom at the Hyatt Regency Hotel in downtown Chicago, just off the Magnificent Mile. A few hundred well-heeled supporters laid out three hundred dollars apiece for a meal, a chance to hear their senior senator opine about his vision of the future for Illinois and the nation, and a moment's press of his flesh.

Seeing Simmons deliver his after-dinner speech brought back memories for Rotondi of their college days together. Lyle had always been good on his feet, a natural performer, confident and comfortable in front of a microphone. Rotondi had come to appreciate the power and potency of a gifted public speaker, someone who could set agendas and garner support through words and the smooth delivery of them, particularly when the audience was already in his corner, or dissatisfied with the status quo and seeking answers. Hitler came to mind, for one.

Simmons had the party faithful in the palm of his hand as he spun his tales for the evening, self-effacing at times, boastful at others, his engaging smile brought to bear like a laser pointer, softening the hard messages and cuing the audience when it was time to smile or laugh. It was a masterly performance from a man whose wife had only recently been violently murdered, and who would return to Washington to lead a memorial to her.

The handshaking ritual followed, one person after the other jockeying for position to squeeze his hand, slap his back, and whisper in his ear. The senator treated each one as though he or she were the only person in the room, a gift unto itself. Some women were openly and inappropriately flirtatious, which Simmons handled with characteristic aplomb. It wasn't his good looks that invited such behavior, Rotondi knew. It was the power he exuded. Kissinger had been right. Power was, indeed, a mighty aphrodisiac.

Like everyone else in the room, Rotondi found himself at times swept up in his friend's oratory. But now and again he would remember the file of destructive information sitting in a drawer in his suite, concealed beneath shorts and socks. His conversation with Kala Whitson had put things in better perspective for him. According to her, the Justice Department was poised to come down on the Marshalk Group, and by extension his friend the Illinois senator. There was nothing he could do to head that off; nor was he sure he would if he could. Obviously, he could share what he had with Simmons and at least give him a heads-up, providing him some time to plan a counteroffensive. But there was more than a few people's political future at stake.

There was Jeannette's murder.

What part did the package of material Jeannette received from Joey Silva, "the weasel," play in her murder? Rotondi had been grappling with that question since the day she was killed. Who would be hurt the most should that information become public? The choices were easy. Her husband, certainly. Rick Marshalk and his lobbying firm. Neil Simmons.

The next question was: Who knew Jeannette had come into possession of the photos and documents? According to her, she hadn't told her husband, but had intended to talk with Neil about it. Which didn't mean that the senator didn't know. It was conceivable that his son had brought it up with him, or that Jeannette had done the same but chose to not tell him, Rotondi, that she had. Too, mobsters behind the laundering of money through Marshalk and one of its eventual recipients, Senator Lyle Simmons, had executed Joey Silva because of his double-dealing. They certainly had reason to make sure Jeannette never had a chance to reveal the material about their connection with her husband and the Marshalk Group. Had they dispatched someone to silence her? The more Rotondi thought about it, the more plausible it became.

He joined Simmons and his two staff members in the limo for the ride back to the Ambassador East. McBride and Markowicz were, of course, generous in their praise of the boss's performance that night.

"What did you think, Phil?" Simmons asked.

Rotondi smiled. "You were great, Senator. Not good but great."

Simmons suggested getting together for a nightcap but Rotondi declined. They were scheduled to fly back at seven in the morning, and his leg had been particularly bothersome that night. He stripped down to his shorts and turned on the TV. After a few local stories, the anchor shifted to Washington:

"We've just learned that the police investigating the murder of the wife of senior Illinois senator Lyle Simmons have come up with what an anonymous source says is a 'major development in the case.' Senator Simmons was here in Chicago tonight addressing a fund-raising dinner. In an unrelated story, we have learned that Simmons spent this afternoon huddled with political advisers about his expected candidacy for president. A spokesman for the senator, his press secretary Peter Markowicz, denied that the meeting was for that purpose. In other news—"

Rotondi called Emma, who'd just returned from that evening's job.

"How's it going?" she asked before he could pose a question.

"Here? Fine. Hey, I just heard on TV that the police are announcing some sort of news about Jeannette's murder."

"I heard that, too, but I don't know any more than you do. Hold on a sec. There's a message on my machine."

Her answering machine sat next to the phone, and he could hear the incoming voice: "This is Mac Smith, Emma. I know that Phil is in Chicago with the senator, but it's important that I speak with him. If you are in touch with him, please have him call me. I'll be up until midnight, and here all day tomorrow." He left his number slowly, and repeated it. Among many life's annoyances for Mackensie Smith were people who rattled off their phone numbers when leaving messages.

"I'll call him when we get off," Rotondi said.

And he did.

TWENTY-FIVE

Mac Smith had spent that afternoon grilling Jonell Marbury. His fiancée, Marla, tried to not interject but failed enough times to prompt Smith to ask her to leave the room on one occasion. They were joined later in the day by Annabel, who'd been at her gallery in Georgetown processing recent purchases of several pre-Columbian artifacts.

"Go over it again," Mac said to Marbury. "I know, I know, you don't feel there's anything left to tell. But sometimes repetition generates information that was forgotten in previous versions."

Marbury sighed.

"More coffee?" Annabel asked.

"Please."

Marla, who'd returned, paced the room as a substitute for intervention into the conversation.

"I'll start from the beginning again," said Marbury. He recounted his visit to the Simmons house to deliver the envelope given him by his boss, Rick Marshalk.

"Mrs. Simmons answered the door?" Mac said.

"Right. I'd never met her, so I introduced myself and said I had an envelope from Rick Marshalk for the senator. She thanked me, took the envelope, and closed the door."

"And you don't know what was in the envelope?" Annabel asked. Marbury said, "I have no idea."

Annabel said to Mac, "Do we know whether the police took that envelope from the house?"

It was Mac's turn to indicate a negative response with a shake of his head. "I'll ask," he added.

Marbury continued chronicling his activities on that afternoon. When he was finished, Mac shifted the topic to Camelia Watson and her plunge to death the previous night.

"Like I said, I saw her walk into the elevator at her apartment building, and I left. That's the last time I saw her. She was fine, maybe a little tipsy. No, let me correct that. She *was* tipsy when she left the Fly Lounge. But after we sat and talked for a while, she'd sobered up. At least that's the way I remember it."

"Why didn't you tell me that you drove her home?" Marla asked.

"Because—because I didn't want to add fuel to the fire, Marla. I just wanted to square things between us after our spat at the party. Driving her home meant nothing. There never was anything between us."

"You should have been honest with me," Marla countered.

"This is a subject that you two can hash out later," Smith suggested. He said to Marbury, "If what you say is true, Jonell—and I'm not questioning your veracity—it means that someone has framed you regarding the Simmons murder. This tragedy with Ms. Watson represents lousy timing and coincidence. Who would do that? Frame you?"

"Whoever killed Mrs. Simmons," Marbury replied, stating the obvious.

"Who has it in for you?" Annabel asked.

"I can't think of anyone," Marbury said. He asked Marla if she had any ideas.

"Someone from Marshalk?" she said.

"Why?" Marbury said.

"Who else?" Marla said.

"Someone from when you were on the congresswoman's staff?" Mac suggested.

Marbury scrunched up his face in thought. "You always make a few enemies in Congress," he said, "but I can't think of anyone who would both murder Mrs. Simmons and try to set me up like this. Sorry. I can't come up with anyone who makes sense, Mac."

"It has to be someone from Marshalk," Marla said with conviction.

"If that's so," said Annabel, "it means that the murderer is from Marshalk, too."

They continued their discussion until late in the afternoon. Mac informed Jonell and Marla that while he'd been happy to jump into the breach and represent him that day at police headquarters, he wasn't prepared to handle his defense should things progress to that stage. "But I'll bring in a top defense lawyer, Jonell. I've worked with the best."

Marla cried, and Annabel put her arms around her. "Chances are what Mac said won't be necessary," she told her, "but it's always prudent to anticipate the worst."

"I know," Marla said, accepting a tissue from Annabel, "but I can't believe we're sitting here talking about Jonell needing a defense lawyer. He hasn't done anything wrong."

"Maybe if I'd gone to the police right away," Marbury mused, "this wouldn't be happening." He glanced at Smith, who refrained from giving him an *I-told-you-so* look.

Throughout the questioning, Smith kept thinking about the lunch he'd had with Phil Rotondi, and what the former Baltimore prosecutor had told him. He decided to raise it with Marbury without being specific.

"Jonell, are you aware of any damaging material about the Marshalk Group that might be circulating?"

"I don't think so. Well, that's not exactly true. There have been rumors that the Justice Department is getting ready to charge the firm with something, but I don't know anything more specific than that. Why do you ask?"

"Just something I've heard around town."

"There is a lot of dissatisfaction at work, however. I know that Camelia was leaving because of what she felt was a pending problem. And I had a long talk with Neil Simmons the other day. To be honest, I've been thinking of bailing out, too, and I had the feeling that Neil might be contemplating the same thing."

"I imagine that Mr. Marshalk wouldn't be happy having his top people leave, knowing where the skeletons are hidden," Smith said.

"No doubt about that, Mac. Camelia told me—" He glanced at Marla, whose expression was blank. "Camelia told me that Marshalk threatened her before she left."

"*Threatened?*" Annabel said. "Physically?"

"According to her. He said something like he wouldn't want to see anything bad happen to her. He also tried to buy her silence."

"Silence about what?" Annabel followed up.

"About what she knew. She used to work for Justice, and she was going back there. He handed her an envelope with a check for fifty thousand dollars in it, a going-away bonus."

Mac whistled. "That's a hefty severance."

"She wouldn't take it, gave it back to him."

"I don't imagine he was pleased with that," Mac said. "You told me that Marshalk tried to convince you to not go to the police about having been at the Simmons house that day."

"Right."

"But according to the police, he says just the opposite, that he told you to come forward."

"That's a lie, Mac, an out-and-out lie."

"I believe you. Look, Jonell, right now all the police have is your fingerprint on a glass, and the possibility of one of your hairs in the house. I have no doubt that you're being set up. What we have to do is come up with the person or people who are behind it. Absent that, the police are likely to decide that those two pieces of forensics are enough to charge you."

"You can't let that happen, Mac," Marla said.

"I'll do all I can to prevent it, Marla. Why don't you two go on home and salvage what you can of the day."

"I didn't go into work today," Marla said.

"Neither did I," said Marbury. "I should have called, only I had other things on my mind."

Smith half laughed. "I'd say that's an understatement, Jonell."

After they'd left, Annabel said to Mac, "I feel terrible for them."

"Everybody's worst fear, to be accused of a serious crime you had nothing to do with."

"Have you talked with Phil again?"

"No. He's in Chicago. He said he had a source there who might be able to fill him in on who sent that package to Mrs. Simmons." He checked his watch. "I don't know where he's staying. I'll call Emma."

❧

Lyle Simmons was somber on the flight back to D.C. the following morning. McBride and Markowicz read their boss's mood and kept their distance, and Rotondi picked up on the atmosphere. Walter McTeague was waiting at the general aviation area of Reagan National when they landed and drove them into the city, dropping Rotondi off at Emma's house before proceeding to the Dirksen Senate Office Building. Rotondi thought Emma might still be sleeping, but she was up, showered, and dressed when he came through the door. Homer leaped off the couch and slapped his paws on his master, who returned the enthusiastic greeting.

Emma's greeting was as wholehearted as Homer's but her paws were smaller, and softer. "Good trip?" she asked.

"Yeah, it was fine. Good catering job?"

"Basically tasteless food but I tried to spice it up a little. Everything went smoothly. You talked to Mac Smith?"

"I called him right after we talked. He wants to get together with me today."

"About the murder?"

"You might say that. That new development the press is talking about hits close to home. They're suspecting Jonell Marbury of the murder."

"*What?*"

"And they think the young lady's fall from her balcony might not have been an accident. Jonell is involved in that, too."

"Welcome home," she said. "Got any more bombshells to share with me?"

"No."

"God, Phil, I'm speechless. Where did you hear this?"

"Mac Smith. That's why he wanted to get ahold of me last night. When the police took Jonell in for questioning, his fiancée, Marla, called Mac. They went together to police headquarters and arranged for Jonell to walk, at least for the moment. But according to Mac, the cops are convinced they have a case against Jonell. They found his fingerprint on a glass in Jeannette Simmons's kitchen, and a hair in one of the bathrooms that came from an African American. Jonell claims he never set foot inside the house, which as far as the police are concerned brands him a liar."

"Do you think—?"

"That he *is* the murderer? Beats me. He didn't come off like one when we met. Mac's convinced he's being framed by someone. My question is . . ."

Emma waited for him to continue.

"Look, Emma, there's another dimension to this that I haven't shared with you."

"Oh?"

"Sit down and I'll run through it with you. It's sensitive stuff, Emma, *really* sensitive."

cR.

Neil Simmons was about to leave the house when his father called.

"Hi, Dad. You're back?" His voice was flat.

"Yes, I'm back. I'd like an update on the memorial service."

"Everything's in order, I think."

"You *think*? I expect better than that, Neil."

Neil held in check what he was about to say. Instead, but more firmly, he said, "Everything is set, Dad. If you'd like, I'll come by today and show you the plans."

"Come at noon. I'll have some time then."

"All right. Noon."

"Run by the house before you come and pick up some briefing papers I need this afternoon. They're in my tan briefcase next to my desk in the library."

"All right."

"Who was that?" Alexandra asked as she came down the stairs.

"My father."

"What did he want?"

"I'm meeting with him at noon about the memorial service."

"I haven't the slightest idea what to wear. I suppose it will have to be black."

"I really don't know what color you should wear, Alex. I have to go. I might not be home for dinner tonight."

cR.

Rotondi finished his "briefing" of Emma.

"And you've had the papers and photos all this time?"

"Since that weekend with Jeannette."

Emma smiled. "I won't ask what happened that weekend, Phil."

"Between Jeannette and me? Nothing happened, aside from hearing her story, and being handed the envelope with enough ammunition to blow Lyle's presidential hopes out of the water, to say nothing of sinking the Marshalk Group."

"I believe you," she said.

"As long as we're in this confessional mood, I should also tell you about the relationship I did have with Jeannette."

"Relationship? Romantic?"

"Yeah. Back in college. Want to hear?"

"Only if you want me to."

After he'd recounted for her the story of how he'd been dating Jeannette in college, and the way Lyle stole her away, Emma's expression morphed from intense interest to anger. When he was through, she glared at him.

"You're mad," he said.

"You bet I am."

"It was a long time ago, Emma."

"I don't care how long ago it was, damn it. How could you have remained friends with this bastard all these years? That's what I'm mad about."

Rotondi shrugged. "That's me, Emma. I don't hold grudges."

"The hell you don't. And if anybody ever deserved to have a grudge held against him, it's your friend Simmons."

"I didn't want to tell you because I didn't want to taint your opinion of him."

"*Taint* my opinion? I can't find the words to tell you how *tainted* I am."

"Well," Rotondi said, "I'm glad you know everything, my history with Lyle and Jeannette, the package Jeannette received, all of it."

"And you believe that the material you have is connected in some way with her murder?"

"I don't know for certain, Emma, but I think it is. I have to run."

He got up from his chair, grabbed his cane from where it leaned against the chair's arm, and started for the stairs leading up to the bedrooms.

"Phil."

He turned. "What, babe?"

"I love you. I've never loved you more."

Neil Simmons stopped by his office before going to his father's house to pick up the papers he'd been asked to collect. Camelia Watson's death had cast the expected pall over the workplace. He muttered responses to comments about it, closed the door to his office, and sat heavily behind his desk. He'd made a list of things to be accomplished concerning his mother's memorial service. He saw that there were still a number of loose ends to be resolved. He called Polly at the Hotel George but received only the hotel's message service. He didn't bother leaving one.

He realized as he looked out his window over Washington, D.C., that he'd become unraveled. He seemed incapable of making even the most minor of decisions. His father was fond of saying, "Any decision is better than no decision. At least you have a fifty-fifty chance of being right." Good advice, except that when you were paralyzed, any chance of being wrong was anathema.

He was immersed in his fog when a knock snapped him to attention. Rick Marshalk opened the door and said, "Got a minute?"

"Sure, Rick. Come on in."

Marshalk, dressed in white shirt, wide floral tie, and suspenders, took a chair across the desk. "Man," he said, "when will it stop?"

"What? Oh, the rain?"

"No, not the rain. What's been happening around here. First your mother, now Camelia."

"It's terrible news," Simmons said.

"You've got that right. But wait'll you hear this next bit of terrible news, Neil."

Simmons stared blankly.

Marshalk came forward in the chair. "Catch this. The police think Jonell might have killed your mom."

Simmons gasped and swallowed wrong, causing a coughing spasm. He got it under control and said, "That can't be."

"Hey, you're preaching to the choir, Neil, and I'll do everything in my power to help Jonell get through this."

"Why do they think that?" Neil asked.

"The rumor is that they found some forensic evidence at your mom's house that belongs to Jonell—a fingerprint, I think, maybe more." He slid even closer to the desk. "And I'm afraid there's speculation that Jonell might have had something to do with Camelia's fall."

Simmons kept shaking his head back and forth, as though motion would dispel what he'd just heard.

"I know, I know," Marshalk said, standing. "Just thought you'd want to know. He drove her home last night, and we all know he and Camelia were getting it on."

"I don't think that's true, Rick."

"Well, no matter. I just thought you'd want to know. Just remember one thing, Neil. Jonell is innocent until proven guilty. That's one of the most important safeguards we have in this great country of ours. How are plans coming for the memorial service?"

"I'm, ah—I'm working at it. I'll be gone most of the day handling last-minute details."

"Take all the time you need. Family rules, Neil. Family trumps. *Ciao.*"

Neil watched the door close and slumped in his chair. Jonell a murderer? Jonell his mother's killer? Jonell responsible for Camelia's fall from her balcony?

"It can't be," he said aloud. "It can't be."

He turned on a small TV in his office and watched the news. A report on his mother's murder mentioned only that an anonymous source in the police department said there had been significant progress in the case. No mention of Jonell. Where did Marshalk hear it?

He clicked off the TV and went to Jonell's office, where his secretary sat glumly.

"I just heard," Neil said.

She burst into tears. "It can't be true," she said through them.

"Have you spoken with Jonell this morning?"

"I called. I got his machine at home. Oh, God, say it isn't so."

"How did you hear about it?" he asked.

"Rick."

He continued down the hall to Marshalk's corner office.

"Yes, Neil?"

"There's nothing on the news about Jonell, Rick. Where did you hear it?"

Marshalk grinned crookedly. "I have my sources, Neil. You know that. Let's just say that a little bird flew down on my shoulder and whispered in my ear."

"A little bird my—"

"Just kidding, pal, just kidding. I heard a rumor, that's all. I know it's a hell of a blow to you, with you and Jonell working together and all. Let's just hope there's nothing to it."

"Okay, Rick. Thanks."

Back in his office, he tried Polly again at the hotel. No luck.

He took the to-do list he'd created for the memorial service and drove to St. John's, where he went over some of the details with a layperson responsible for the logistics of special services, particularly high-profile ones.

As he stood outside the church, he was almost overwhelmed by the need to go home and go to bed. But that was out of the question. He'd promised to pick up papers for his father and meet in his office at noon.

He took a long, circuitous route to the house in which he'd grown up. He was in no rush to get there. Walking into the foyer where his mother's lifeless body had been found posed a challenge. The simple act of opening the front door was a daunting physical and mental exertion.

He eventually reached the house, pulled up the circular drive-way, and parked directly in front. A series of deep breaths gave him the fortitude he needed as he got out of the car, climbed the front steps, and inserted his key into the lock. The door swung open. He was relieved that the alarm wasn't on. He'd gone blank on the code to deactivate it.

He stepped inside and blinked to acclimate to the change in light from outside. It was, he thought, deathly still in the house, and cold. The AC was cranked up full-force. He walked quietly into the library, taking careful steps so as not to disturb anyone—the spirit of his mother, the dominating aura of his father? He saw the tan briefcase, but instead of picking it up and leaving, he sat in his father's chair and looked about the darkened room.

It occurred to him that he had few memories of growing up there, as though a portion of his life had been skipped over, fast-forwarded. There were happy times with Polly, two kids giggling together at their parents' perceived foibles, and pleasant recollections of summer cro-quet matches in the rear yard. *But surely there's more to remember about childhood than that.*

He closed his eyes and dozed off for a minute. He awoke with a start. "Have to get going," he said, standing, grabbing the briefcase he'd come to retrieve, and walking to the door. He stopped and raised his head, his face, his nose. The scent of perfume was distinct. Now another memory came to him. It was a perfume of which his mother was fond; she wore it virtually every day while he was growing up. There were times when she would hug him, and the scent was so overpowering it made him sneeze and pull away. Had the scent been there when he entered the house? He didn't think so, although it might have been.

He went to the foot of the stairs and looked up. Was the smell of perfume stronger now?

He started up, taking the same sure, silent steps as when he'd ar-rived, stopping now and then to breathe in sweet wisps of perfume. He stopped at the landing and cocked his head, heard nothing. He continued. When he reached the carpeted second floor, he looked at the various bedroom doors that lined the long hallway. They were all closed, with the exception of his parents' room. He approached it, closed his eyes, opened them, and took the final steps that allowed him to see into the room. At first, what he saw—what he *thought* he saw—was so shocking that he looked away, like someone shielding eyes from a gruesome movie scene. He forced himself to look again. Seated at his mother's dressing table was—

Mother? he mouthed without sound.

The woman, whose attention was focused on the dressing table mirror, had been unaware of his presence. She was observing herself in the glass from different angles, moving her head this way, then establishing another vantage point. He stared in disbelief. The perfume was overwhelming. He coughed against it.

The woman turned. "Neil, darling," she said in an exaggerated southern drawl. "How wonderful to see you."

Marlene Boynton now turned to face him. She was heavily made up, her lips oversize with a heavy application of bloodred lipstick.

"What are you doing here?" Neil asked weakly.

"Why, ahm getting made up, silly. A woman has to look her best at all times, don't you agree?"

Neil was aware that he'd allowed his mouth to hang open, and he closed it. He shifted from foot to foot and cleared his throat several times in anticipation of speaking, but said nothing.

"Don't just stand there like that, Neil. Come in and give me a hug, a great big hug."

"This is—I thought—this is Mom's room and dressing table. Why are you sitting there using her makeup and . . . ?"

She stood and turned slightly to admire her body in a full-length mirror next to the dressing table. She wore one of Jeannette's favorite dressing gowns over her clothing, pink silk with a small, darker pink lace collar.

"Have you spoken with your father today?" she asked, slowly crossing the room in his direction.

"I think you should leave, Aunt Marlene," he said, trying to force conviction into his voice.

"I thought I'd wait until your daddy came home. I always like to look good for him. Or . . . do *you* think I'm sexy?"

He backed to the head of the stairs and almost stepped off the landing. He grabbed the banister and righted himself. She continued to stand in the bedroom doorway, smiling, a hand on her hip.

He ran down the stairs, glancing back a few times. He reached the foyer and started for the door. But he realized that he'd carried his father's briefcase upstairs with him and had dropped it to the floor outside the bedroom. He ascended the stairs as fast as possible. The briefcase was a few feet from Marlene. He reached for it as though going after something from a very dangerous place, grabbed it, took a final look at her, bounded downstairs, and stumbled out the door.

TWENTY-SIX

"I'm here to see Detective Crimley," Rotondi told the desk officer.

"Is he expecting you?"

"Probably."

"Probably?"

Rotondi gave him what passed for a grin. The officer frowned. "You are—?"

"Phil Rotondi."

The uniform placed a call. "He's in a meeting, but he wants you to wait. He'll be free in fifteen minutes."

"Thanks," Rotondi said, limping to a wooden bench and picking up a dog-eared copy of *People* that had been discarded there.

⬥

Morris Crimley was conferring with the Simmons case task force, which now consisted of six detectives, including detectives Chang and Widletz.

"The presumptive blood test on the hammer Mr. Lemón stole

from in front of the Simmons house came up negative," Crimley announced.

"He wants a reward," Widletz said through a chuckle.

"A reward for what?" Crimley asked.

"For showing us where he dumped the hammer. He thinks he's solved the murder."

"I suggest that we wait until more definitive tests are done on the hammer before releasing him," Chang proffered.

Crimley's shrug was noncommittal. He drummed his fingers on photographs of evidence on his desk. "Let's talk about Marbury," he said. "What bothers me is why he lied about being in the house. I mean, if he'd said Mrs. Simmons had invited him inside for a drink of water, or to use the bathroom, it would make sense. But—"

"It's possible that someone is framing him, Morrie," said Widletz.

"You sound like a defense attorney," Crimley growled. "Go over again for me what they said at Marshalk."

Chang, who with Widletz had interviewed employees at the Marshalk Group, consulted his notes. "Mr. Marshalk claims that he encouraged Mr. Marbury to come forward to the authorities about having been at the residence the day of the murder. He further stated that Mr. Marbury and the deceased, Ms. Watson, had been engaged in a romantic relationship during her employment at the firm, and that Mr. Marbury was affectionate with Ms. Watson at the party held for her departure from the firm. In addition, Mr. Marshalk says that Mr. Marbury had, on occasion, demonstrated a temper that, as Mr. Marshalk put it, 'threatened to get out of hand and to erupt.' That observation was corroborated by the firm's vice president of security, Mr. Jack Parish."

Crimley chewed his cheek. "Marshalk is no friend of Marbury," he said.

"I disagree," said Chang. "He said repeatedly that he would do anything to help Mr. Marbury, but wanted only to be truthful with us. His firm put up a fifty-thousand-dollar reward for information leading to the apprehension and conviction of Mrs. Simmons's murderer."

"So I read in the papers," Crimley said. "Good PR, huh?"

"Have you gotten any more info on the possible Chicago connection?" one of the other detectives asked.

"No. I'll try Bergl again later today. He's still stonewalling on this." Crimley yawned. "Let's get back on it. We'll hold Lemón another day or two. I want you to talk to the handyman again, Schultz, and Senator Simmons's driver, McTeague. See if they remember anything else about that day and night."

They filed from the room, and Crimley called to the front desk to have Rotondi brought to his office.

"So, how was the Windy City?" Crimley asked after Rotondi had settled in a chair.

Rotondi sat up a little straighter and frowned. "How did you know I was in Chicago?" He didn't need an answer. Obviously, Crimley had decided to keep tabs on his whereabouts.

"I don't know where I heard it."

"It was lovely," Rotondi said. "Beautiful city, nicely lighted at night. The breeze off Lake Michigan is always bracing, and the drinks at the Pump Room are still top-notch."

Crimley couldn't help but laugh. "You talk like you went there as a tourist."

"That's right."

"You and the senator taking in the sights?"

"You might say that. Thanks for letting me barge in on you like this, Morrie."

"I have ulterior motives."

"Why am I not surprised? I understand that you're focusing on Jonell Marbury in the Simmons murder."

"Word gets around. What's your source?"

"His attorney, Mackensie Smith."

"Ah, yes, Mackensie Smith. One of my few favorite lawyers."

"No argument from me. You have Marbury's print from inside the house?"

"I'll be damned," Crimley said. "Whatever happened to attorney–client privilege?"

"I'm on the team, Morrie."

"Congratulations."

"What about the African American hair?"

"There is one."

"Belong to Jonell?"

"You sound as though you and Marbury are friends."

"We've met. He doesn't strike me as the murdering kind."

"People change. Model citizen gets screwed by somebody and snaps, and doesn't take kindly to a pretty young thing saying no."

"Camelia Watson. You suspect him of having something to do with her death?"

"We're interested in him. He drove her home, was the last person to see her alive."

"Emma catered the party Ms. Watson was at the night she died."

"I know. We'll be talking to your lady friend about it. Your buddy, Marbury, and Ms. Watson were having an affair."

"That'll be news to his fiancée."

Crimley glanced down at a yellow legal pad on his desk that was covered with notes. "Ms. Marla Coleman," he read. "His fling with the deceased has been confirmed by people at Marshalk Group."

"How would they know?"

"The Marshalk gang is a pretty close-knit group. Those things are never kept secret for very long."

"Like squad car romances," Rotondi said.

"Exactly! What did you do in Chicago?"

"Played listening post to the senator."

"You hook up there with any of your old friends from Baltimore?"

Okay, Rotondi thought, *you know about Kala Whitson.*

"As a matter of fact, I did. Kala Whitson is an assistant AG out there. We worked together in Baltimore before she moved to Chicago. We got together for old times."

Crimley's raised eyebrows suggested that Rotondi elaborate.

He didn't. He was tempted to mention the materials Jeannette Simmons had received from "the Weasel," but resisted, for two reasons. First, he didn't want to lose control of the material. Give it to the police and chances were good that it would be leaked to the media by morning. The second reason was more pragmatic. He'd been sitting on potentially valuable evidence, incriminating or exculpatory, in a murder case. You could go to jail for that, he knew only too well. He'd put away a few such offenders himself.

"By the way, Morrie, I rendezvoused with Kala Whitson in her apartment. Juicy stuff, huh?"

"No comment. What do you know about a possible Chicago connection to Jeanette Simmons's murder?"

"Chicago connection? Like in the mob?"

"Yeah. Speaking of juicy stuff, the senator's extracurricular love life with a mob-connected Chicago woman has me wondering."

"What the senator does behind closed doors, Morrie, is none of my business."

"Even if it might have had something to do with his wife's murder?"

"Do you think it did?"

Crimley's large shoulders moved up and down. "Did your buddy, Ms. Whitson, have anything interesting to offer about their investigation?"

"What investigation?"

"Ah, come on, Phil, don't treat me like an idiot. We know that the Chicago U.S. attorney has been looking into Senator Simmons and his connections with certain folks with crooked noses out there."

"Why don't you ask them?"

"We have. I've talked to Bergl here in D.C., who promises to bring us into the loop. He hasn't. Justice is treating us like second cousins. No, worse than that. They won't share a damn thing."

Rotondi was tempted to suggest that the MPD's penchant for leaking information was a good reason for other law enforcement agencies to keep their sensitive investigations close to the vest. He didn't bother. Crimley didn't need to be reminded of it.

"Can we talk about Jonell Marbury?" Rotondi asked.

"Sure. Since you've joined the Mac Smith team, ask away."

"Did your people take from the Simmons house the envelope that Jonell delivered that afternoon?"

"No. Chang started to go through some of the stuff in the senator's library—there were envelopes piled everywhere—but the senator's people complained that some of it might be top secret and jeopardize national security. The usual bull. It didn't matter. What's in those envelopes is irrelevant to the investigation. Marbury admits delivering something for the senator, and Marshalk confirms that he sent him on the errand."

Rotondi came forward in his chair, moved his injured leg with his hand, and looked through the evidentiary photos on the desk. He picked up the picture of the water glass taken from the Simmons kitchen, on which a fingerprint was identified as belonging to Jonell Marbury. "Nice glass," he said. "Notice those little indentations around the middle? Hard to see in this picture, but they're there."

"So?"

"Emma's kitchen cabinet is filled with them. She had those particular glasses custom-made for her catering service. The indentations provide a surer grip, fewer glasses slipping from people's hands and breaking."

"Interesting," said Crimley, "only I don't know why." As he said it, he remembered Chang's comment that the glass with the fingerprint didn't match any of the other glasses in the Simmons kitchen.

"Wouldn't be hard for someone to take one of Emma's glasses at a catered event, have Jonell use it and leave his prints, and place that glass in Jeannette's kitchen."

"You're not the first person to raise the possibility of a frame, Phil. Some of my detectives are doing the same thing. The question is, *who?*"

"Somebody at Marshalk. Emma caters all their parties."

"They're her only clients?"

"Of course not. She caters a lot of events on the Hill, agencies, fund-raisers."

"And Marbury worked on the Hill before coming to Marshalk. I imagine he made a few enemies over there."

Rotondi stretched his arms out in front of him, and sighed. "You accused me the last time I was here of being all take, no give. I don't like that reputation."

"I'm listening, Phil."

"What would you say if there was a sheaf of papers and pictures that are not only damaging to Senator Simmons, but also damning to the Marshalk Group?"

"Is there such a thing, and why would it matter?"

"If there was such a thing—and I'm not saying there is—and somebody wanted to make sure that the information never became public, anyone in possession of it would be at risk."

"All right," Crimley said. "Who *was* in possession of it?"

"I didn't say that such material existed, Morrie. Strictly hypothetical."

"Right. And there's no such thing as global warming. Come on, Phil, level with me. Do you know that the sort of material you mention—hypothetically, of course—was in the possession of someone connected with the Simmons murder, and maybe the Watson death?"

"I'm working on nailing it down," Rotondi replied. "When I do, you'll be the first to know. Thanks for the time, Morrie."

Crimley walked him to the lobby. "Man," he said, "you are really in pain, aren't you?"

"Some days are worse than others. This is not one of the better ones."

"Mind a word of advice, Phil?"

"Shoot."

"Withholding evidence is a serious crime."

"That it is."

"It's nothing you don't already know, but sometimes we lose sight of things—exceed our ego boundaries, as the shrinks like to say."

Rotondi nodded.

"If you have the sort of material you mentioned, don't sit on it, Phil. Your friendship with the senator ain't worth it. I'd hate to be the one who has to haul you in."

Rotondi smiled. "I promise I'll spare you that pleasure, Morrie."

⁂

Neil Simmons's encounter with his aunt Marlene had unnerved him. He sat in his car in front of the house and tried to bring his breathing under control. He felt like a bug in a swimming pool about to be sucked into the skimmer. He kept looking back at the house, hoping she wouldn't come through the door. He'd seen Marlene act out strange fantasies before, but nothing like this. She'd obviously gone off the deep end. She was totally mad. The last time she'd been hospitalized, she'd slipped into a deep depression; it took powerful medications to bring her out of it. This time, depression would have been welcome.

The relationship between Marlene and her sister had never been good. Marlene's mental problems contributed to that unfortunate situation, although Neil also knew that his father's reaction to it exacerbated the tension between the sisters. Senator Simmons had little patience with Marlene's antics, and avoided any personal interaction whenever possible. His answer was to shell out whatever money it took to fence her off from Jeannette and the family, happy to pay for her condo and car and daily living expenses, as well as whatever out-of-pocket costs her hospital stays incurred. Jeannette, on the other hand, frequently reached out to her sister behind her husband's back. But on occasion, even she became exasperated and verbally lashed out at Marlene. *Dysfunctional* was the word that came to Neil's mind.

When he felt he was sufficiently calmed to drive safely, he started the engine and pulled away, not sure where he would go next. He checked his watch. He was due at his father's office at noon. It was eleven. He pulled off the road and called Polly on his cell phone. This time, she answered.

"Polly, it's Neil."

"Hi."

"I have to see you."

"Why? Is something wrong?"

"Yes. I can be there in fifteen minutes."

"Neil, what's going on?"

"I'll tell you when I get there."

Polly had come down to the lobby to wait for him. He burst through the hotel's entrance and approached her; she put down her magazine.

"Are you okay?" she asked, aware of his agitated state.

"Let's go to your room."

Once there, he said, "Have you spoken to Marlene recently?"

She thought for a moment. "I called her yesterday."

"Was she—what I mean is, was she okay? Sane?"

His comment brought forth an involuntary laugh from Polly. "Yeah, she sounded sane. Why?"

"I just came from the house. She was up in Mom and Dad's bedroom, sitting at Mom's dressing table putting on makeup. She had on Mom's favorite dressing gown. Christ, she thinks she *is* Mom!"

"That's ridiculous, Neil."

"No, it's not. I was there. I saw it. Do you know what she said? She said that she wanted to look nice for when Dad came home."

Polly scrutinized him in an attempt to decide whether what he'd said was credible, made any sense. She decided it did.

"Did you talk to her about it?" she asked.

"No. I went there to pick up some papers for Dad. I got out fast."

She'd sat on a small couch while he paced the room. Now he joined her and grabbed her hand. "Do you know what this means?" he asked.

"I'm afraid to ask," she said.

"She must have killed Mom."

His words jolted her.

"She's always been jealous," he went on, squeezing her hand harder. "Polly, she killed our mother so that in her twisted mind she could take Mom's place."

The blood drained from Polly's face. She withdrew her hand and looked toward the windows.

"Are you listening to me?" he said. "It's so obvious. Aunt Marlene snapped and killed Mom. Jesus!" He got up and resumed pacing.

She faced him. "What do you think we should do?" she asked.

"I don't know. I've got to tell Dad what to expect when he goes home. Maybe we should go to the police and tell them what we know."

"No," she said, her voice steady now. "That would be a mistake. What about Phil?"

"Rotondi?"

"He'll know what to do. I mean, Neil, this might all be a mistake. Maybe you misunderstood her."

His face reddened, and he held his fists at his side. She sounded to him like Alexandra, always questioning him. "I did not misunderstand her," he said.

"Okay, okay," she said, aware of his pique. "Let's get ahold of Phil and see what he thinks."

"Maybe you're right," he said. "Do you have his number?"

She fished his cell number from her purse, along with her phone, and made the call. "Phil, I'm with Neil at my hotel. We need to speak with you."

"Sure. Now?"

"Yes. Can you come to the hotel?"

Neil said, "Not now, Polly. I have to get those papers to Dad, and go over plans for the memorial service. Tell him to come later. Two o'clock."

"Can you come by here at two?" she asked.

Rotondi agreed and they hung up.

"I want to go to the house," Polly said.

"Why?"

"To talk to Marlene before we go spreading poison about her."

"Polly—"

"You don't have to come, I'll take a cab."

"No, no, it's okay," he said. "I'll call Dad and tell him I'll be late."

"Damn!" she said.

"What's the matter?"

"I have an appointment for a manicure and pedicure in fifteen minutes."

"Cancel it," he said, not adding what he was thinking—that getting your nails polished was frivolous under the circumstances.

She made the call, and they headed for the house.

✿

Rotondi clicked off his cell phone. Why did Polly and Neil want to meet with him? Polly's voice had sounded urgent. Had something developed that had a bearing on their mother's murder? He'd have to wait until two to find out.

He drove to the Watergate complex, found a parking spot, and called Mac Smith's apartment. Annabel answered.

"Mac and I planned to get together this morning," Rotondi told her.

"Hold on, Phil. He's just getting off the other line."

"Hello, Phil," Smith said.

"I'm around the corner," Rotondi said. "Any chance of getting together now?"

"It's fine with me, Phil. I'll come down. I'd rather talk away from here."

"I'll be in the lobby."

Smith arrived ten minutes later and suggested they walk through the public area separating the Watergate Hotel from the apartment complex. It was a fat day, as Smith was fond of terming days with sunny, cool, breezy weather. They sat near a large fountain that created a pleasant background rush of water.

"What's up?" Smith asked.

"I went by MPD today and talked with Morris Crimley."

"Anything new on their end?"

"No. He says they didn't remove any envelopes from Lyle's library. He's not the neatest of people. He's got magazines and envelopes and God knows what else piled up everywhere in that room. I want to see what was in the envelope that Jonell delivered that afternoon."

"For what purpose?"

"Just curiosity. I raised the question with Crimley about the glass with Jonell's print on it. Although it's hard to make out in the photo, that glass looks like the ones Emma uses in her catering business. Catch this, Mac. Morris told me that some of his own detectives are raising the possibility that Jonell was framed. That's exactly what must have happened, and it has to have been Marshalk who's behind it. He sends Jonell on an errand that places him at the scene of the murder. They have a glass from one of their parties that Emma catered and arrange for Jonell to pick it up somewhere along the line and leave his prints. They plant a hair from him. And Marshalk counsels Jonell not to go to the police about having been there. That puts Jonell in a further bad light with the cops."

Smith listened impassively, an occasional grunt his only verbal response. When Rotondi was finished, Smith said, "The question is *why?*" He looked at the manila envelope Rotondi carried with him. "Is that the material you've told me about?"

"Yes."

"You think it might provide a motive for Mrs. Simmons's murder?"

"Yes."

"Time for me to look at it, Phil?"

"Yes."

Rotondi handed the envelope to Smith, who slowly opened it and looked at one piece at a time, carefully removing each paper or photo, examining it, and replacing it before extracting another. The process took ten minutes. He secured the clasp when he was through and handed the envelope back to Rotondi.

"What are you going to do, Phil?" Smith asked.

"Show it to Lyle at some point."

"Well," Smith said, "you know what he'll say. He'll tell you to burn it."

"I know." Rotondi leaned back and looked up into the pristine blue sky and puffy white clouds that drifted by. "The senator's daughter, Polly, called me a little while ago. She sounded upset. I'm meeting with her and her brother at two."

"Maybe you should run that stuff by them before going to the senator," Smith said.

Rotondi pondered the suggestion. "Maybe. Jeannette said she was going to talk to Neil about it."

"Did she?"

"I don't know. Neil has never mentioned it, and I haven't brought it up. It's time I did."

"Your call," Smith said. "I'll be home all afternoon if you need me. I'm meeting with Jonell and the attorney I've brought in to officially represent him."

"Do me a favor," Rotondi said. "Ask Jonell what the envelope looked like, the writing on it. It'll help me identify it when I go there."

Smith's final words came as they parted ways in front of Smith's apartment building. "If Mrs. Simmons was killed because she had that material in her possession, Phil, anyone else having it could be in jeopardy, too."

Rotondi got the message.

Neil and Polly pulled up to the house in which they'd grown up. Neil turned off the ignition and stared at the front door.

"Coming?" Polly asked as she opened the door on her side.

"Yeah, sure," Neil said, not sounding convincing.

He used his key to gain entrance. They stood silently in the foyer and strained to hear any sounds coming from upstairs.

"Smell that?" Neil asked.

Polly raised her head and sniffed. "Perfume," she said. "Mom's favorite."

"See? I told you."

Polly took deliberate strides up the stairs. She paused at the landing and looked back at her brother, who stood as though paralyzed. Polly waved, and he began a slow ascent. She waited on the second floor until he'd joined her. They went to the open door to the master bedroom. There was no one there. Polly went to the dressing table and looked down at the array of cosmetics. She turned to Neil. "I don't see any sign that she was here," she said.

Emboldened, he entered the room and stood at her side. "She was here, Polly. You can smell the perfume, can't you?"

"Yes, I smell it. Let's go to her place."

"I'd rather not," he said. "I say we go right to the police and let them know that she probably killed Mom."

Polly fixed him with a quizzical stare. "You sound as though you *want* her to be the one, Neil."

"Oh, no, that's not true. It just makes sense, that's all. We all know how sick she is, Polly. At least the police should be made aware of what I saw."

"We'll see what Phil thinks," she said with finality. "We don't do anything until we talk to him."

"Phil's not God," he said.

Polly ignored him and went down the stairs and out the door, with Neil close behind. "If you won't take me to Marlene's place, I'll go myself," she said.

"All right," he said.

They said little on the drive. Polly rang Marlene's doorbell. Marlene answered. She was dressed in a designer set of pink sweatpants and sweatshirt with small green-and-yellow birds embroidered on the shirt.

"Hello, Polly," she said pleasantly. "What a nice surprise." She looked past her niece to where Neil stood. "And Neil, too. This must be my lucky day. Come in, come in. I have iced tea and lemonade and—"

"Aunt Marlene," Neil said, "why were you at Mom's house today?"

Marlene's eyes widened in surprise. "I don't understand," she said. "I haven't been at Jeannette's house since—" She pressed her hand against her lips and said, "Since that dreadful day."

Neil stepped forward. "Marlene," he said, "I was there. I saw you in Mom's bedroom and—"

"I have never heard such an outlandish thing," Marlene said, a smile returning to her heavily made-up face. "All this heat must be having a bad effect on you. Now, you two come in and enjoy the cool and a nice cold drink."

"We can't," Neil said. "We have to go. I have an appointment."

"Well, now, this is certainly strange," Marlene said, "stoppin' by this way and not bein' gracious enough to accept my hospitality." She'd slipped into her southern belle mode.

"Neil is right, Aunt Marlene," Polly said. "We just wanted to say hello and make sure you're all right."

"Ah've never been better, you two sillies. Come back when you have some time to spend with your aunt Marlene. Ah insist."

Neil drove Polly to the Hotel George. "I have to go see Dad," he said. "He'll be angry that I'm late. I wasn't imagining that Marlene was there, Polly."

"I believe you, Neil," Polly said. "But that doesn't mean she killed anyone."

"I'll be back by two," he said, and drove off.

*

Rotondi finished lunch at the Blue Duck Tavern in the recently renovated Park Hyatt hotel and dialed Mac Smith's number.

"Mac, Phil Rotondi here. Have you had a chance to ask Jonell about the envelope he delivered?"

"No, but he's here, just arrived." He put Jonell on the line.

"Hello, Jonell. I need something from you."

"Anything," Jonell said. "Mac tells me you're working with him on my behalf."

"Not much I can contribute, but I'm trying. Jonell, that envelope you delivered the day of the murder. Can you describe it to me?"

"Sure. Eight-by-ten, manila with a clasp. Rick Marshalk wrote the senator's name on it in big purple letters."

"Purple letters?"

Jonell laughed. "Yeah, it's one of Rick's many idiosyncrasies. He's always writing things with a purple Flair. He's flamboyant that way."

"Okay, thanks. Hope your afternoon goes well."

"I'm in good hands," Marbury said. "The best."

⟡

Neil arrived at the Hotel George fifteen minutes late. "Sorry," he said. "Dad was tied up and—"

"No problem," Rotondi said.

"I can't stay long," Neil said.

"Go ahead, Neil," Polly said. "Tell Phil about Aunt Marlene."

Rotondi listened as Neil recounted his confrontation with Marlene in Jeannette's bedroom. When he was through, Rotondi said, "It's not news that Marlene has mental problems, Neil, but that doesn't necessarily translate into her being a killer."

"That's what I said," Polly chimed in.

"I know that," said Neil, "and I know you both view Marlene as being a harmless kook, but as far as I'm concerned she's crazy enough to do anything. Look, I have to go. Polly wanted to run this past you, Phil, and get your advice on what to do with it."

"*My* advice?" said Rotondi. "What do *you* think should be done, Neil?"

"I want to go to the police and at least make them aware of the possibility that Marlene killed Mom."

Neil looked to Polly, and then to Rotondi.

"Sure," Rotondi said. "Go to MPD and give them the benefit of your thinking. But don't expect anything to come out of it. Aside from Marlene's aberrant behavior, there isn't one iota of evidence pointing to her as your mother's murderer."

Neil was aware that while what Rotondi had just said supported what he, Neil, wanted to do, the tone in which he'd said it testified to a different interpretation.

"Thanks for your advice," Neil said, and shook Rotondi's hand. "Sorry I have to run. Thanks for coming."

When her brother was gone, Polly said what she'd been holding back while he was there. "Do you know what this is really about, Phil?" she said.

Rotondi's cocked head invited her to explain.

"Neil will do anything to get Dad off the hook. I'm surprised he isn't pointing a finger at me as Mom's killer."

Rotondi let the comment slide, and asked, "Feel like doing me a favor, Polly?"

"If I can," she said.

"I'd like to go to your house."

"Why? To smell the perfume?"

"To find an envelope with purple writing on it."

She laughed. "Okay," she said. "Whatever you say."

TWENTY-SEVEN

"**W**hat's this all about?" Polly asked as a taxi took them to the house.

"The police have focused in on someone in your mom's murder," he replied, leaning close to her ear to avoid being overheard by the driver. "Maybe you heard on TV when the cops announced that they had a break in the case."

"I don't watch TV."

"Have you heard of Mackensie Smith?"

"No."

"He's a former top defense lawyer who's helping this person. They're friends. I've recently met him at Smith's house."

"Who is this person," she asked, "this break in the case?"

"I'll tell you about it later. For now, let's just say that he didn't kill your mother, or anyone else for that matter, and I'm trying to help Smith prove that. The envelope I'm looking for—"

"With purple writing."

"Right. It might prove useful in establishing his innocence."

"How?"

Rotondi grinned. She had a question for everything, accepted nothing at face value, like a good trial attorney.

"I don't know," he said, "but I'm curious to see what the envelope contained. This fellow delivered it to the house the afternoon of the murder."

"It was for my mother?"

"No, your father."

"From the Senate?"

"No, from the Marshalk Group."

"Neil sent it?"

"No, his boss, Rick Marshalk. This man—all right, his name is Jonell Marbury—he works for Marshalk."

"You're sure he didn't do it, Phil?"

His attention was diverted as the driver turned a corner into the street on which the house was located.

"Go up the driveway," Rotondi instructed. "That one over there."

"Should we have him wait?" Polly asked.

"No. We'll call another. Got your key?" Rotondi asked as the driver drove off.

"Yup."

She unlocked the door, and they stepped into the foyer.

"I feel like I was just here," she said.

"You were," he said.

He entered the library off the foyer and snapped on the overhead lights.

"What a mess," Polly said, referring to the piles of material stacked on the hardwood floor.

"Your dad's never going to win the Senate's annual award for neatness," Rotondi said. He went to the pile nearest the desk, took the chair, and started pulling things from that stack. He'd reasoned that if the envelope was still there, chances were that it wouldn't be buried deep. Jeannette had probably tossed it on top of one of the piles. In the five days since the murder, Lyle had spent very little time at the house, making only brief stops to pick up clothes to take to the suite at the Willard that had become his second home.

His hunch was right.

Polly stood over him. "There it is," she said.

SENATOR SIMMONS in bold purple strokes was on the sixth item he picked up.

Rotondi looked up at her, nodded, and turned the envelope over. The flap had not been sealed by its glued surface. Only the small metal clasp secured it. He opened it, reached inside, and withdrew six pieces of paper.

"What are they?" Polly asked.

"I'm about to find out."

The first three papers were on the Marshalk Group's letterhead. He scanned their contents, laid them on the desk, and examined the remaining three. They were virtually blank except for some scribbling that didn't seem to make any sense. He retrieved the three letters and looked at them more closely this time. "Hmmm," he said.

"What?"

"Look at the dates."

She leaned closer. "They're old," she said.

"Yeah. These letters are from last year."

"Is that important?"

"Maybe," he said, placing the papers in the envelope, folding the clasp, and standing.

"That's it?" she asked.

"That's it."

"I like being here with you, Phil," she said. "For some reason the house isn't as forbidding as it's been."

"It'll be a long time before you'll be comfortable here, Polly."

"This man they think killed my mother. Why do they think he did it?"

"Some forensic evidence," Rotondi said. "They found his fingerprint on a glass in the kitchen, and a hair in the bathroom belonging to an African American."

"He's black?"

"Yes."

"Why was his fingerprint here? Was he a friend of Mom's?"

"No. He says he'd never met her before, and that he'd never set foot in the house."

"How can that be if his fingerprints and hair were here?"

"I'll explain on the way back. Call a cab."

⬧

Senator Simmons's receptionist told Neil that the senator had just been called into an important last-minute meeting, and she didn't know how long he'd be.

"Maybe I'd better leave and—"

The door to the inner office was flung open and the senator stood in the doorway.

"Hi, Dad."

His father turned and disappeared back into the office. Neil followed.

"Close the door," Simmons said.

Neil did as instructed. He handed the tan briefcase to his father, who dropped it to the floor behind his desk.

"What's new with the memorial service?" he asked as he sank into his large, leather swivel chair. He looked exhausted to Neil, puffy dark circles defining his eyes, his developing jowls more pronounced.

"Everything is in order."

"Good."

"Dad, I have to talk to you about something."

The senator looked up at a wall clock. "I have a meeting to get to in five minutes, Neil. Make it quick."

Neil collected his thoughts. He hadn't expected to have only a limited time to say what was on his mind. "When I went to the house today to pick up those papers for you, Aunt Marlene was there."

"What was *she* doing there?"

Neil made a false start.

"Get to it, Neil."

"She was in your bedroom pretending to be Mom."

Simmons opened his mouth to say something but closed it before words escaped. Finally, he said, "That's ridiculous."

"I know it sounds that way, Dad, but I swear that's what happened. She was at Mom's dressing table wearing one of her robes, the pink one, and—"

"What did she say?"

Neil hesitated. "She said she wanted to look nice for you when you came home."

Simmons's sigh was deep and prolonged.

"She's insane, Dad. Polly and I went to her condo after I told Polly about it. Marlene acted as though she'd never been at the house."

The senator's brow became deeply furrowed, his lips pressed tightly together.

"Do you understand what this means, Dad? Aunt Marlene killed Mom."

Simmons said nothing.

"There's no other conclusion to come to. In her sick mind, she killed Mom so she could take her place. She's always been jealous of Mom, always thought she was the one who should be married to you."

"Who have you told about this, Neil, aside from Polly?"

"Phil."

"Why did you tell him?"

"Polly wanted his advice before we did anything. He came to the hotel and met with us."

"I'll talk to Phil."

"All right, but I don't know why you'd bother. He didn't think it was a big deal. Frankly, I don't understand why everything has to be run past him."

Simmons gave another look at the clock. "I have to leave. Keep this between us, Neil. *I mean that.*"

He got up, took his suit jacket from an antique clothes rack, slipped it on, glanced at himself in a full-length mirror, and walked to the door.

"Dad."

The senator stopped. "What?"

"I need to talk to you."

"Another time, Neil."

"Were you and Mom going to get a divorce?"

Simmons looked down at his shoe tops, then up at his son. "It really doesn't matter anymore, does it, Neil?"

Alone, Neil stared straight ahead, his mind a blank. He'd wanted to ask his father about the material his mother had claimed to have in her possession that would be destructive to his Senate career, and to Marshalk. Had she told him? Did he realize the jeopardy he might be in—that his political career and presidential aspirations could be at stake? He wanted to tell him that he intended to resign from the Marshalk Group, and that he was sorry for the mistakes he'd made, and . . .

Another time, Neil.

His eyes took in the photographic history of his father's career that filled the walls of the office, this man who, with his mother, had brought him into the world, handsome and self-assured, shrewd and successful, his smile beaming out from picture after picture, an arm around a famous celebrity, shaking hands with world leaders, ruler of his domain, Senator Lyle Simmons, potentially the next leader of the free world.

Neil closed his eyes, clenched his teeth, and felt the pressure build in his eyes and throat.

"Can I get you something, Neil?" the senator's secretary asked from the doorway. He had to confront his father as soon as possible.

"What?" Neil said, his eyes snapping open.

"Can I get you something?"

"Oh, no, thanks," he said, not turning to have her see the tears on his cheeks. "I'll be leaving in a few minutes."

❧

Mac Smith and the criminal defense attorney he'd brought in to represent Jonell Marbury were wrapping up their meeting with Jonell when Rotondi called. "Mac," he said, "I've got to see you."

"Sure." He told Rotondi who was there.

"Have him stay. I'll be fifteen minutes."

Rotondi arrived. He greeted Marbury and Smith, and was introduced to the attorney. He laid the envelope on the table.

"That's the one I took to the Simmons house," Jonell said.

"I know," Rotondi said. "Fortunately, the police didn't think it was important to their case. I just came from the house— I found it there."

"This is the envelope that Rick Marshalk told you to deliver to the Simmons home?" Smith said.

"That's it," said Marbury.

"Did you know what was in it?" Rotondi asked Marbury.

"No," Jonell replied.

Rotondi opened the clasp and laid out for them the six pieces of paper, which they passed around.

"I'm not sure I see the relevance of this," Jonell said.

"I do," said his attorney. "These papers are worthless, junk, nothing but filler."

"Why would Rick tell me to deliver worthless documents?" Jonell asked. He didn't have to wait for their answer because it came to him without prompting. "He sent me there to put me at the house the day she was killed."

"Looks that way, doesn't it?" said Smith.

"But the glass and my hair and—"

"All part of the frame-up," Rotondi said. "Marshalk made you a patsy."

Marbury, who'd been seated on the couch next to Smith, smiled, got up, and clapped his hands. "This proves I had nothing to do with the murder," he proclaimed ecstatically.

"Not so fast," said Smith. "While this looks to us like a classic frame-up, proving it is another matter."

Marbury's smile faded. "If you take this to the police," he said, "surely they'll agree."

"I'm afraid we'll need more than this," Marbury's new attorney said.

"How do we get more?" Jonell asked, his voice less exuberant than a moment ago.

Rotondi answered. "Let me talk to Neil Simmons. He's been at Marshalk throughout this period. I don't know how candid he'll be, but I somehow have the impression that he's disillusioned with Marshalk. It's worth a shot."

"Give it a try," Smith said. "In the meantime, having this envelope and its worthless contents might be enough to convince the MPD to back off a little where Jonell is involved in case they decide to get more aggressive. Before we break this up, however, there's the added question of the death of your friend Ms. Watson, Jonell."

"Do you think her death is connected with Mrs. Simmons's murder?" he asked.

"It might be nothing more than coincidence," said Smith, "but maybe not. Jonell, you told me that she was leaving Marshalk because she was concerned about illegalities there."

"That's right."

Mac looked at Phil. Should he bring up the material in Rotondi's possession? He decided not to—yet.

"I'm going to try to catch up with Neil when I leave," Rotondi said. "I'll get back to you if it results in anything useful."

Marbury shook Rotondi's hand. "I know we've just met," he said, "and that you don't have any reason to be trying to help me, but I want you to know how much I appreciate it."

Rotondi shrugged. "I spent my professional career pursuing justice, at least as I saw it. You don't retire from that commitment. Besides, I have a stake in this, too, Jonell. Jeannette Simmons and I were close. I loved her, and I want whoever killed her to pay. Hang tough. This will all work out."

Rotondi rode the elevator down to the lobby, where he called the cell number he had for Neil.

"Oh, hi, Phil," Neil said.

After leaving his father's office, Neil had taken a walk, ending up at a small neighborhood bar and restaurant that looked inviting. He'd gone in, taken a stool at the bar's far end, and ordered a bourbon-and-water. The room was dimly lighted; soft rock music came from a speaker above his head. The barmaid ignored him after serving his drink and engaged in conversation with a couple at the other end.

"Neil," Rotondi said, "can we get together tonight?"

"Tonight? I don't know, Phil, I—"

"It's important, Neil. Very important."

"Is this about Dad?"

"I'd rather discuss it in person. Dinner? My treat?"

"I suppose so, but it will have to be a quick one. Alexandra doesn't like me to be too late. I like to be home to help put the kids to bed and—"

"We'll make it an early dinner, Neil. Any preference?"

"No."

"Where are you now?"

"A bar on Capitol Hill. I needed to relax and—"

"Tell me where it is. I'll meet you there."

Neil looked down at the bar napkin on which the establishment's name and address were printed and read it to Rotondi.

TWENTY-EIGHT

"**I**'m nervous about the memorial service," Neil said to Rotondi as he joined Simmons at the bar.

"They're always tough, Neil. Emotions run high, feelings run low. Everybody'll get through it."

"Sometimes I can't believe what's happened. I mean, people get murdered in other families, not your own."

Rotondi tasted his Scotch.

"I'm worried about Dad."

"He'll be fine."

"I saw him today, just a few hours ago. He didn't look good."

With Rotondi enjoying another sip, he took in his surroundings. It was the sort of small, worn, nondescript place that inspired songs—Billy Strayhorn's "Lush Life" or "Something Cool" sung by June Christy—a place to escape from whatever blows you'd been dealt that day and to put things in perspective with the help of alcohol and anonymity.

"I assume you told your dad about Marlene," Rotondi said.

"Yes, I did. He was running off to a meeting so he didn't really have time to talk about it."

A group of six men and women came through the door.

"Let's take a booth," Rotondi suggested. "You wanted a quick dinner. Why don't we eat here? It's early but—"

"Sounds good," Neil said.

The barmaid insisted upon the drinks being paid for at the bar before the men took a table, and Rotondi obliged. They chose a booth at the rear of the place, and she brought them menus.

"I'll get to the point," Rotondi said after they'd chosen pasta dishes and salads, which seemed safe. "You know that Jonell Marbury is under suspicion in your mother's murder."

Mentioning that seemed to have a physical effect on Simmons. He made a sound as though he'd been poked in the ribs, and slowly shook his head. "When I heard about Jonell, it was almost as much of a shock as when Dad called me about Mom's death," he said. "Jonell and I have been friends ever since he came to work for Marshalk."

"He didn't do it, Neil."

"I hope not." A second thought came to him. "How do you know?"

"I've been working with Jonell's legal counsel. Somebody set him up."

"You mean like framing him?"

"That's another way to put it."

"Who would do that?"

Rotondi waited a beat before answering. "Someone at the Marshalk Group."

Again, Neil reacted physically, lowering his head and splaying his hands on the table. "That can't be," he said.

"Why not?"

Simmons sat back. "Why would anybody at Marshalk want to frame one of its employees? That doesn't make any sense."

Rotondi let enough time to pass to allow Simmons to answer his own question.

Neil faced Phil. "If that's true," he said, "it means that somebody at Marshalk killed Mom."

Rotondi locked eyes with him.

"No," Neil said. "You're wrong. Maybe Jonell did do it. What about Camelia Watson?"

"What about her?"

"He was with her the night she died. He was having an affair with her."

"I don't believe that," Rotondi said, not aware that Neil didn't believe it, either. "Let me show you something, Neil." He pulled the six pieces of paper from the envelope Marbury had delivered to the house and handed them to Neil.

"What's this?"

"This is the envelope that Rick Marshalk asked Jonell to deliver to the house the day your mother was killed."

Simmons handed them back.

"No," Rotondi insisted, shoving them into Neil's hands. "Look at them, Neil. They're worthless pieces of paper. The letters are a year old. Marshalk sent Jonell to the house to establish that he was there close to the time of the murder. Why else would he have Jonell deliver worthless documents?"

Simmons gave the papers back to Rotondi, who returned them to the envelope. "I'm sorry, Phil, but it couldn't have been somebody from Marshalk. What about Marlene? I told you what she did, believing she's my mother."

Rotondi decided not to debate that scenario. Instead, he said, "Neil, I wanted to talk to you because of something I've come to learn about the Marshalk Group—and about your father."

"What's that?" Simmons asked as their salads were served, along with beers.

"Did your mother discuss with you a package she'd received from someone in Chicago?"

Rotondi's question obviously took Simmons by surprise. His eyes mirrored that surprise, as well as concern.

"I believe that she did, Neil," Rotondi added.

"How would you know about that?"

"She told me she intended to."

"You know about that package?"

"Yes, I do. In fact, I have it."

"*You* have that package?"

A nod from Rotondi.

"Mom gave it to *you?*"

"Yes."

"I can't believe she'd do that." He shifted his position as though to create distance between them. His level of agitation was palpable. "What was in that package?" he asked.

"Damaging material about your father and the Marshalk Group." He didn't wait for Simmons to respond. "Did you share with your father what your mother told you?"

Simmons's awkward silence testified that he had.

"So he knew," Rotondi said. "Who else knew?"

"No one."

"What was your father's reaction when you told him?"

The pasta arrived. Neither salad had been touched. "Is something wrong?" the barmaid asked.

"No, everything is fine," Rotondi said. "We'll have it with our pasta . . . Neil," he went on, placing his hand on Simmons's arm, "I want to know who killed your mother as much as you do. I don't care how it ends up as long as there's justice. Who else did you tell about your mother having that package?"

"No one. I told you I didn't say anything to anybody except Dad."

Rotondi closely observed Simmons. He didn't buy his answer. "What was your father's reaction?" he repeated.

Neil gathered his thoughts before replying. "He said it was nothing to worry about and that he would take care of it."

"Meaning what?"

Neil shrugged. "I don't know."

Rotondi speared a piece of pasta. The red sauce was sweet, too sweet.

"You hate my father, don't you, Phil?" Neil said almost under his breath.

It was Rotondi's turn to be surprised. "Why would you say that?" he said. "Your father and I have been friends for a very long time."

"You hate him because of what he did to you in college, stealing Mom from you."

"That's—that's not true, Neil. Your father told you about that?"

Neil shook his head. "Polly did. Mom told *her*."

"That's water over the dam, Neil, and you're wrong. I don't hate your father and never have. Was I in love with your mother once? I sure was. And I continued to love her but in a different way. If I hated your father, I would have turned the material over to the police, or to some reporter. I haven't done either. But I am convinced that your mom was murdered because of what's in that package, and I intend to prove it."

"I don't want to see my father hurt."

"Neither do I. I understand wanting to protect him, Neil, but what about the people at Marshalk? Do you have that same need to protect them?"

"Of course not. I mean, I wouldn't want to hurt them. Rick Marshalk has been good to me, Phil. I'm sorry, but suggesting that Rick or someone else there might have had something to do with Mom's death is ridiculous. They wouldn't do anything like that."

Neil's desire to protect his father came across as sincere and credible. Marshalk was a different story. What Neil said sounded forced, a denial rammed through reality.

The barmaid passed the booth and observed that their pasta and salads had barely been touched. Rotondi smiled at her. "It's good," he said. "We're not as hungry as we thought."

She continued on her way without comment.

"Phil," Simmons said.

"What?"

"Could I see what Mom gave you?"

"No. It wouldn't serve any purpose."

"I don't care if it's offensive or harsh. I just want to see it for myself. Mom never showed it to me and—"

"For good reason," said Rotondi.

"I should be the judge of that."

"Sorry, Neil, but it remains with me."

Up until this point, Simmons had been low-key, almost lethargic. He spoke without animation or emotion, his face unexpressive. But a flush of anger was now evident. "I really resent this, Phil. What are you going to do, blackmail my father over that garbage?"

"That's not worthy of an answer, Neil."

"You really do hate him." Rotondi started to respond, but Simmons continued. "You come off like some saint, some holier-than-thou person. You limp around with that cane so people cut you some slack, but what you really are is a goddamn Judas. Whatever Mom had belongs to me, not you. Who the hell do you think you are telling me I can't see it? Give it to me!"

He'd become loud, which caused people at the bar and in a nearby booth to turn in their direction.

"Calm down," Rotondi said.

"I'll make you give it to me," Neil said, sliding from his side of the booth. He now stood over Rotondi. "I'll get a lawyer and make you give it to me. You have no right to do this."

A man appeared through a door beyond the booths. "Is there a problem?" he asked.

A red-faced Simmons responded, "Yes, there is," before walking through the bar area and out the door.

"There's something wrong with the food?" the man, who'd said he was the manager, asked.

"No, the food was fine," Rotondi said. "The conversation wasn't. I need a check."

༄

Rotondi stood in front of the restaurant and looked for Neil on the street. There was no sign of him. He hadn't had time to react to Neil's charges inside, but now that he did, he ran a gauntlet of responses. There was anger, of course, but that quickly dissipated. What was left was more pity than ire. He wondered whether his friend's son was teetering on the verge of some form of breakdown. He'd been through a lot. He was the son, conceived out of wedlock, of one of the Senate's most influential members, a domineering, overbearing man who wasn't likely to win the father-of-the-year award. His mother had become a browbeaten semi-recluse who'd turned to the bottle for solace. His sister had fled at the earliest possible moment and harbored a continuing resentment of her father and what he stood for. Aunt Marlene was mentally unbalanced. He knew little about Neil's marriage to Alexandra. He'd attended their wedding, a happy, festive, albeit tense event as many weddings can be. Lyle had dropped hints that he didn't approve of his son's choice in a mate, and had made similar remarks long after the wedding and the birth of their two sons. Too, Neil worked in a high-pressure environment at the Marshalk Group where, as far as Rotondi could ascertain, he was still nothing more than a figurehead, one whose sole contribution was his relationship to Senator Lyle Simmons, possibly the next president.

Not a life to be envied.

He decided to walk until his leg protested. As he did, he focused on Neil's admission that he'd discussed with his father the material Jeannette had received from the weasel in Chicago. Lyle had never let on that he was aware of it; nor had he shared with Rotondi any discussions of divorce. Not that he would be expected to. While close friends share many intimate secrets, some remain off-limits.

He stopped at a corner when a particularly sharp pain shot up his leg and caused him to grunt in protest. He waved down a taxi and gave the driver Emma's address in Foggy Bottom.

"Hi," she said as he came through the door. Homer got to his feet and wagged his tail.

"Hello," Rotondi said, dropping into a cushioned chair.

"How was your day?"

"Okay. You have a gig tonight?"

"Yeah," she said. "Can you believe—another Marshalk party."

"What's the occasion?"

"A reception for a couple of congressmen and their fat-cat supporters." She disappeared upstairs, returning minutes later with freshly applied makeup. "Sorry to run out, Philip, but duty calls."

"Where's the bash?"

"National Building Museum. One of my favorite venues. Cocktails and dinner. I'll be late. Don't wait up. There's a killer lasagna in the freezer and a Caesar salad in the fridge." She kissed the top of his head and was out the door.

He went upstairs, opened a closet door, and rummaged through a succession of shoe boxes on the floor until coming up with the envelope he'd been given by Jeannette Simmons. He returned downstairs and took the envelope to his car, where he did what Jeannette had done: He hid it in the trunk beneath a pile of things he thought he might need on the road one day, and that he hadn't used since putting them there. He returned to the house and the chair and used the remote to turn on the TV. A rerun of *Law & Order*, one of his favorite shows, had just started. He watched a few minutes before leaning his head back and falling asleep.

He'd dozed through the first commercial break, and would have continued sleeping had his cell phone not sounded.

"Phil, it's Lyle."

"Oh, hi."

"You sound sleepy."

"I conked out. A power nap as they say."

"I need to see you tonight."

"What's the occasion?"

"Does there have to be an occasion, Phil? I need your counsel."

Rotondi's antenna went up. He'd learned over the years that when Lyle claimed to need "his counsel," it more than likely meant a large favor.

"Sure," Rotondi said.

"I have a fund-raiser in an hour, a quickie, a drink and out of there. Come to the hotel. I'll be back by nine. We'll order up."

"Okay, Lyle."

While Rotondi watched the end of *Law & Order*, the senator returned to where Neil waited in the bedroom. "He's coming here at nine," Simmons said. "I appreciate you bringing me this information."

"You can't trust him, Dad. He's not the friend you think he is."

Simmons said nothing.

"He'll blackmail you, Dad. He's got that material and he'll hold it over your head."

"I'll take care of it, Neil."

"I'm glad I found out that he had it."

"Yes, that was good, son. Good job. I have to leave now."

"I have to go, too. Rick is hosting a fund-raiser. I need to stop by."

"You go on then," said the senator. "I'll be in touch with you in the morning."

Father and son left the Willard together. The senator got into the Mercedes driven by Walter McTeague, and Neil hailed a cab to take him to the National Building Museum where Emma Churchill's catering staff was receiving last-minute instructions from her, the "battle plan" for the evening the basis of her comments.

"Good to see you again, Emma," Rick Marshalk said after she'd dispersed her crew.

"Hello, Mr. Marshalk. Always a pleasure catering one of your events."

"If you're going to throw a party, always go with the best," he said, flashing a wide white smile and patting her back.

She watched him head to where a contingent of men and women were arriving. The group included a familiar face to Emma from watching C-SPAN's gavel-to-gavel coverage of the House of Representatives, a veteran congressman from California who'd recently been the target of a well-covered investigation into campaign finance irregularities. Marshalk warmly greeted the congressman and his friends, and waved over a server carrying a tray of hors d'oeuvres. Emma had to admit to herself that since Phil told her about the materials he'd been given by Jeannette Simmons, her view of Marshalk—of all lobbying firms for that matter—had changed.

Lobbyists who exploited loopholes in ever-changing campaign finance laws—lawmakers seemed to leave such loopholes in every piece of legislation—certainly were nothing new. They'd been snidely known for years in Washington as "the fourth branch of government," so pervasive was their influence on lawmakers and the laws they passed. Much of it was unsavory and cynical, politicians' unquenchable thirst for money creating conflicts between big-money interests and sound public policy.

But if what Phil had said was valid, the Marshalk Group made other controversial lobbying firms look like bastions of morality and pristine ethical conduct. They'd become a sophisticated money-laundering conduit between organized crime in Chicago—and undoubtedly other places—and Senator Simmons. Were other politicians the beneficiaries of the mob's largesse? she wondered. A more chilling question was whether someone at the Marshalk Group, aware that Jeannette Simmons had possessed the sort of information that could destroy them, had ruthlessly silenced her.

And would they do the same to whomever else held the power to bring them, and Lyle Simmons, to their knees?

Someone like Philip Rotondi.

Since he'd shared the information with Emma, she hadn't taken the time to appreciate the danger he might be in. Of course, she rationalized, it wasn't established definitively that the Marshalk Group had been behind the murder of Jeannette Simmons.

But someone had.

Jonell Marbury had been framed via a glass with his prints that matched the glassware she used in her catering business; an African American hair belonging to Jonell; and his being at the scene that afternoon to deliver an envelope. Nicely packaged forensic evidence but, as Phil had pointed out, all easily choreographed to point a finger elsewhere.

Am I feeding food and drink to murderers?

She forced that grim contemplation out of her mind and got busy helping her staff serve the increasingly large crowd. She was checking with one of her bartenders when she saw Neil Simmons come through the door. He headed directly for the bar and ordered a white wine. Emma had met him half a dozen times, fleeting occasions, and wondered whether he would recognize her. He didn't. He accepted the glass from the bartender and walked toward Rick Marshalk, who was entertaining a group of people with a story that had them laughing. Marshalk spotted Simmons and waved him into the conversation. Emma continued to observe. While everyone else laughed as Marshalk continued with his humorous tale, Simmons stood quietly, a stony expression on his face. Emma sauntered in their direction. But when the punch line had obviously been delivered—the laughter erupted then faded away—Marshalk and Simmons left the knot of happy people and headed for an unoccupied, dimly lit corner of the vast party room. Emma considered for a moment trailing behind them and getting close enough to eavesdrop. But she scotched that notion. She was a caterer, not a private eye. She went in the opposite direction and contented herself with standing where the piano-and-bass duo wove popular melodies as background for the guests. As she allowed the soothing sounds of their playing to wash over her, she saw another man heading toward the corner where Marshalk and Simmons had gone. She remembered him from a previous party; he'd been introduced as the Marshalk Group's chief of security, a name like Parish, she thought, a former MPD officer.

"We're running low on shrimp," one of the catering staff said to Emma.

"Can't have that happen," she said. "I have more in the kitchen. Come with me."

Had Emma stayed where she'd been, she would have seen Marshalk, Simmons, and Parish leave their secluded corner and head for the door. Simmons and Parish continued through it while Marshalk said something to a senior lobbyist from the firm, who nodded his understanding. After a few additional stops to slap a back or whisper in an ear, Marshalk joined the other two outside the building.

"Are you sure, Neil?" Marshalk asked Simmons after a few minutes of conversation dominated by Simmons.

"I'm sure."

Marshalk motioned for his driver to pull to where they stood. The driver opened a rear door of the stretch limo and Marshalk, Simmons, and Parish got in.

"The office," Marshalk instructed the driver.

"I don't want to cause trouble," Simmons said. "I just want to—"

Marshalk gave his president, the son of Senator Lyle Simmons, a reassuring pat on the knee. "Don't worry about a thing, Neil," he said. "We'll go back where we can be comfortable and talk privately. Everything will work out just fine, Neil. Trust me."

TWENTY-NINE

Rotondi stayed at Emma's house until quarter of nine, when he called a cab to take him to the Willard. He'd noticed earlier that Homer was limping again, and questioned whether he should find an emergency vet service open at that hour. He decided it wasn't necessary. Tomorrow would do. He massaged the dog's hindquarters, which resulted in a lot of licking of Rotondi's hands and face. He washed up, gave Homer his usual cheery good-bye, and climbed into the taxi.

After Lyle's call, Rotondi had had second thoughts about agreeing to meet with him. According to Neil, he'd discussed with his father the Chicago documents and photographs that Jeannette had received. That meant that the senator was well aware of the threat to him and to the Marshalk Group from the Chicago AG's office, and from whomever had the copy that had ended up in Jeannette's possession.

Kala Whitson had told Rotondi that political pressure had put a tight lid on what the informer had delivered to the Chicago AG. Did

Lyle know that? Had that pressure come from Simmons himself, or from someone working on his behalf?

These sorts of political machinations were anathema to Rotondi. He'd seen plenty of them in the Baltimore office, although nothing to rival this situation. He'd realized shortly after becoming an assistant attorney general that he would never progress very high up the ladder of responsibility and status. One of his earliest cases had been shelved because of politics. The target was a city official with strong ties to the sitting administration in Washington. Rotondi had the goods on him, an especially strong case that would have been, to use a now familiar bit of slang, a slam dunk. But the case was dropped at the last minute, allegedly because his boss decided there wasn't enough credible evidence to go forward. When Rotondi confronted him about the decision, he was given a lecture on political reality and the need to work as a team. Following that conversation, Rotondi was assigned only to criminal cases that did not include political overtones, which was fine with him.

Politics was for politicians.

For the Lyle Simmonses of the world.

But as the time to leave for the Willard grew closer, Rotondi's attitude changed. He was now anxious to lay out on the table for Simmons what he knew, and how he knew it. While he was not out to derail his friend's political future, he wouldn't let that stand in the way of getting at the truth about Jeannette's murder. If the envelope secreted in the trunk of his car held the answer, so be it. Chips could fall where they may.

Lyle Simmons was waiting in the suite when Rotondi arrived. He'd been sitting in a red-and-gold wing chair by the window. A glass of whiskey rested on a small table. The senator had rolled up the sleeves of his white shirt and discarded his tie. He'd removed his shoes; a hole in the sock on his right foot allowed the end of his big toe to poke through, unusual for someone as fastidious about his appearance as the senior senator from Illinois.

"Grab a drink at the bar," Simmons told Rotondi. "There's a room-service menu there, too. Order something for both of us. I don't care what it is."

Rotondi got the drink but ignored the menu. He took a matching chair across from Simmons.

"You've been a busy boy, haven't you, Phil?" Simmons said in a flat voice.

"You might say that, Lyle. You look beat. Tough day?"

"They're all tough. But I had one piece of good news today. That son-of-a-bitch detective, Chan or whatever his name is, is off the case."

Rotondi looked at him quizzically.

"I called Chief Johnson myself and told him his guy was rude, nasty, unprofessional, and inept, and that I wanted him gone."

꩜

Crimley had been summoned to the chief's office late that afternoon and was instructed to remove Detective Chang from the Simmons case.

"Why?" Crimley had asked. "He's doing a good job."

"Let him do a good job on another case, Morris," was the chief's response.

"I still want to know why," said Crimley, afraid he probably already knew the answer.

"Senator Simmons called. Evidently, Chang has been rude and unprofessional in the way he's handled things."

"Bull! Charlie's not the most likable of cops, but he's good."

"Please, Morris, don't argue with me about this, okay? I'm not about to buck a U.S. senator. Assign Chang to another team. End of discussion."

Crimley tried to mount a further argument but Chief Johnson cut him off by standing, slipping on his uniform jacket, and heading for the door. "Pick your fights, Morrie," he said on his way out. "This one's not worth it."

Rotondi shook his head. "So a suspect in a high-profile murder case, who just happens to be a United States senator, doesn't like the detective investigating him and plays the eight-hundred-pound gorilla to get him off the case."

"Offends your sense of justice, doesn't it, Phil?" Simmons said.

"I just wish it offended yours, Lyle."

Simmons changed subjects. "I keep thinking of what Walter told me when he dropped me at the house that night, that Jeannette and I should get away for some R-and-R. I could use some right now."

Rotondi shifted his posture to look out the window. The light in the room was low, table and floor lamps the only illumination in the large, handsomely furnished and decorated space. Outside, lights on government buildings further glorified them. Washington, D.C., was a beautiful city, with its wide avenues and gleaming marble edifices; its visual grace befit the nation's capital. It was what sometimes went on inside those places that could detract from their beauty.

Simmons seemed folded within himself, his face expressionless, eyes drooping from fatigue and alcohol. Rotondi had never seen him look this tired—or defeated.

"You know about the envelope," Rotondi said, breaking a silence that had descended upon the room.

"Yes, I do, Phil. I understand it's ended up in your hands."

There was no need for Rotondi to acknowledge it.

"What you have in your possession, Phil, can destroy a lot of people."

Beginning with you, Rotondi thought. *Especially you.*

Simmons's lip curled into what could be taken as the beginning of a rueful smile. "Ironic, isn't it?" he said.

"What is?"

"How after all these years, you end up with my life in your hands.

You used to seem content to play second fiddle to me. Philip Rotondi, the straight arrow, always taking the moral high road as you defined it. I used to admire you for it, Phil. I don't anymore."

"How you view me is irrelevant."

"I know that," Simmons said. "For me, it's always been more important how you viewed me. I don't know why. Hell, I've done pretty well for myself. Why I should give a damn what my college friend thinks?"

"It doesn't make any sense to me, either," Rotondi said.

But it did. Lyle Simmons needed a conscience, an external one to compensate for the lack of an internal moral compass. Still, Rotondi wasn't about to play shrink. He said, "I admire you, Lyle, for what you've accomplished."

"*What I've accomplished*," Simmons muttered. "I have a wife who became so unhappy that she turned to the bottle. My daughter has an even lower opinion of me. No, that's an understatement, and I know you're not a fan of understatement. My son is weak, no backbone. And I got caught with my pants down in Chicago because I'm human."

Simmons got up and refreshed his drink at the rolling bar. He didn't ask Rotondi whether he, too, wanted a refill, which would have been declined anyway.

"You said on the phone that you wanted my counsel," Rotondi said. "That's why I'm here."

"That's right, Phil. You're here as my friend. You've always been there when I needed you." He raised his glass: "Here's to friendship, Philip. Nothing more fulfilling than having good friends."

Rotondi had seldom seen Simmons drunk. Lyle always enjoyed his drinks, and there were a few times over the years that the alcohol's effect became apparent, but never to the point of inebriation. Rotondi wondered whether this night was about to become an exception.

Still standing at the bar, Simmons said, "Are you satisfied, Phil, now that I've admitted to you my failures and weaknesses?"

Rotondi started to say that he took no pleasure from hearing it, but Simmons cut him off. "It's good for a man to come clean once in a while," he said. "But once you have, there's no sense in dwelling on your failures. You know what I find interesting about you, Phil? You've never reached very high, which means you've had less to lose, not as far to fall." The senator resumed his seat. He leaned forward, an elbow on his knee, and extended the glass of whiskey as though it were a finger. "I haven't gotten to where I have without taking chances and cutting deals. That's what politics is, risk and deals. You wouldn't know about that because Philip Rotondi doesn't cut deals. Philip Rotondi doesn't negotiate."

"I've done plenty of negotiating, Lyle," Rotondi said, not especially pleased at his need to defend himself.

Simmons drank. "Let's get down to it, Phil," he said. "I've known about that garbage from Chicago for a while now. Has it caused me to sweat, to lie awake nights? It hasn't, because I know that nothing will ever come of it. Neil told me that Jeannette became aware of it and threatened to do something stupid, like give it to someone who could use it against me." He forced a guffaw. "Naturally, I wanted her to give me the copies she'd received. She wouldn't. I searched the house for them, Phil, looked in every place I could think of. Nothing. I wondered whether she was just blowing smoke, trying to use it as leverage against me. She wanted a divorce."

"I know."

"Of course you do. The farther Jeannette and I drifted apart, the closer she got to you. You know what I should have done, Phil?"

"Tell me."

"The day Jeannette and I decided to get married back at good old U of Illinois, I should have dropped you for the loser you are. But I didn't because I figured I owed you for the way things worked out with Jeannette and me. I'm loyal to my friends, Phil. I've always had a soft spot for you, which was a mistake, a big one. You don't get to where I've gotten by being soft. You get soft and they take you down and chew you up, spit you out like a piece of rotting meat."

Rotondi's stomach growled. He thought of Emma and the party

she was catering for the Marshalk Group, wondering idly what was being served, food and otherwise.

Simmons read his mind. "Hungry, Phil?" he asked, "or have you lost your appetite for breaking bread with your old college chum?"

"Did you have Jeannette killed, Lyle, because she knew about you and your Chicago connections?"

Rotondi's directness had an impact on Simmons. He looked quizzically at his old friend.

"Did you?" Rotondi said again. "She was killed by someone who had a lot to lose if she'd ever gone public with the information. You had plenty to lose, Lyle."

Simmons took a deep breath, stood, and came around behind Rotondi. He placed his hands on Rotondi's shoulders and dug in with his fingers. "You think I killed Jeannette, Phil?"

Rotondi didn't move. "I asked whether you had, Lyle."

"You're right, pal. I did have plenty to lose—and still do." He removed his hands and walked to the bar, where he picked up the menu. "Steaks?" he asked. "Or maybe you'd prefer quiche."

Rotondi was poised to get up and leave. He'd found the exchange deeply distasteful. Simmons's demeaning remarks, while not as hurtful as he might have intended them, still nettled. Instead, he sat back, smiled, and said, "Make it a steak, Lyle. I'm interested in hearing more."

༄

Rick Marshalk, Neil Simmons, and Jack Parish were in Marshalk's office on K Street. Marshalk sat in his red, high-backed, tufted leather office chair, which rested on a small platform, assuring that he always looked slightly down at whomever was on the other side of his oblong, tempered-glass desk.

His tone had been soft and conciliatory at the beginning of the meeting. He'd encouraged Simmons to expand on what he'd said at the National Building Museum, which Neil did in bursts, tossing out a sentence and then retreating, going to extremes to clarify what he'd said to avoid confusion on the part of Marshalk and Parish, and to avoid adding to his own confusion.

"So tell us again about Rotondi," Marshalk said softly. "He's your father's best friend. Your dad has mentioned him a few times."

"He was," Simmons said. "Dad's best friend. He's not! I think that he wants to blackmail him." Perspiration appeared on Neil's forehead. "What I mean is, why would he be holding on to the papers and photos unless he intended to do something with them? Dad's always trusted him. I did, too. I mean, he comes off like a nice guy and all but—"

"Go over again for me what he said to you, Neil," Marshalk suggested, with a smile to indicate that he was only trying to be helpful.

"He said he only wants to get to the bottom of Mom's murder. He said . . ."

"Go on, Neil. It's important that I fully understand what we're dealing with here."

Simmons made a false start, ran his index finger across his forehead, and said, "He's never forgiven Dad for stealing my mother from him back at school. I think Phil and my mother were lovers."

"Back at school?"

"And after."

"A real friend wouldn't have done that to your dad."

"I don't know. I mean, I just think that . . . My mom was having some problems the last few years, drinking—I already told you about that—and troubles with Dad. She wanted a divorce."

"Yes, I recall you saying that when you came to me about the package she'd received. I want you to know, Neil, how much I appreciated you coming forth with that information. As you know, we have a lot at stake here. You're the president of this firm. You have a fine future with us. I trust I've made that abundantly clear over the few years that you've been here."

"Of course," Neil said, "and I hope *you* know how much I've appreciated it."

Marshalk had listened with his hands formed into a tent, his chin resting on it. Now he lowered his palms and leaned forward, resting them on the glass surface. "I've been hearing rumors lately, Neil, that you might be thinking of leaving us."

"That's not true," Neil said, his voice cracking. "That's just not true."

Marshalk went back to his original position. "So, tell me more about this Rotondi fellow. He's married?"

"Not anymore. He has a girlfriend here in D.C. She's a caterer, Emma Churchill. She caters all our events."

"Of course. She's the best in the city." He took a business card that had been on the desk and handed it to Simmons. "Her card," Marshalk said. "It has her home address on it. I've kept it in case I wanted to have a personal, private party catered by her. This Rotondi, he lives with her?"

Simmons tossed the card back on the desk in front of Parish, who sat slightly behind Neil. "Sometimes, I think. He has a house or a condo somewhere down on the Eastern Shore. He stays with her when he's in town."

"And he's in town now."

"Of course."

Marshalk gave an understanding nod. "And you say he has the envelope that your mother received from someone in Chicago."

"He told me about it in the restaurant tonight. Like my mom did. Horrible stuff that claims that Dad is on the take from the mob, and that we're laundering money for the mob here at Marshalk and funneling it to Dad for his campaigns. As I told you when I came and mentioned what my mother had said, I don't want to see us or Dad hurt in any way. That's why I urged you to cut off any ties with people in Chicago—if it was true—and clean house, make sure everything is on the up-and-up."

"If you'll recall, Neil, I assured you that we had nothing to hide, nothing to *clean up*, as you put it."

Simmons looked down while deciding what to say next. As he did, he never noticed Parish quietly get up and leave the room, Emma's business card in his hand.

"I don't understand about Jonell," Simmons said to Marshalk. "Rotondi claims he's been framed by someone here, and that—"

"And that someone here killed your mother," Marshalk said, finishing Neil's thought. "I suppose he's accusing us of having something to do with Camelia's death, too."

"That's right," said Simmons.

"This guy is sick, Neil. He's got a screw loose."

Simmons swallowed hard against a developing nausea.

"Are you all right, Neil?" Marshalk asked.

Simmons looked to where Parish had been sitting. "Where's Jack?" he asked.

"He's on his way back to the party at the museum."

Simmons drew a deep, prolonged breath before saying, "I know you didn't have anything to do with Mom's death, or Camelia's, but I have to hear you say it, Rick."

"If that will make you feel better, Neil, and put your mind at rest, I'll be happy to say it. I had nothing to do with either of those unfortunate incidents. Absolutely nothing! Feel better?"

Simmons nodded. "Thanks, Rick. I think you're right. Rotondi has a mental problem. Dad has to get away from him, and fast! He's a danger to him, and to us."

"You're right," Marshalk said, standing and coming around the desk, where he patted Simmons's shoulder. "Look, I have to get back to the party, too."

"I'll come," Neil said.

"Not on your life," said Marshalk. "You have a lot on your mind, Neil, including the memorial service. You've been through a lot lately, and I need my president to be hale and hearty and rarin' to go. We have some big things on the horizon. I need you with me all the way. You go on home now to that wonderful family of yours. We'll touch base in the morning."

Marshalk watched Simmons slouch from the room. He turned out the lights and headed downstairs, wished the security guard at the lobby desk a pleasant evening, and stepped outside to K Street, where his car and driver waited.

༜

Emma Churchill had gone outside for some air; she'd just returned inside when Rick Marshalk came through the door.

"How's everything?" he asked pleasantly.

"Wonderful party," she replied.

"It always is with you providing the food, libations, and your radiant personality," he said, laughing.

"Thank you," she said. She glanced at her watch.

"Looks like things are winding down," he said. "You go ahead and take care of business. I have a few people to say good-bye to before this breaks up."

She watched him join a group and slip into the conversation they'd been having as smoothly as though he'd been there all along. She realized as she walked in the direction of the kitchen that she hadn't seen him for a while, but chalked that up to the size of the party, and her attention being focused elsewhere. Forty-five minutes later, as she was leaving with some of her crew, Marshalk intercepted her.

"Thanks again, Emma, for a splendid job."

"My pleasure, Mr. Marshalk. Anytime."

"Heading home?"

"After I drop the van at the office. Then it's home, shoes off, feet up, and a stiff drink."

"Enjoy it," he said. "You've earned it."

He kept his eyes on her as she went through the door before walking to a secluded area of the large hall. He flipped open his cell phone, and pushed a rapid-dial number. "She just left," he said.

THIRTY

It was Emma's intention to follow her usual routine: Drive the van to the small industrial building in which she maintained her office, storeroom, and kitchen, refrigerate what perishables were left over, and leave the rest for the morning. But one of her servers, who'd been with her since Emma started the catering company, insisted on helping unload everything.

"Okay," said Emma. "Means I can sleep in tomorrow morning."

As they brought things in from the van, Emma thought of Phil. What was he doing at that moment? she wondered. She knew that although he'd shared a great deal with her about the envelope and its contents, he'd kept his most private feelings to himself. She'd grown certain that however things were resolved, his relationship with Lyle Simmons and the Simmons family would never be the same. On the one hand, she would be sorry to see that happen. The unraveling of friendships of such duration was always sad. On the other hand, she wondered what price Rotondi had been paying to maintain the relationship.

"Thanks, Imelda," she told her employee after they'd emptied the van. "Drop you home?"

"No, thank you, Emma. I called my husband. He's on his way. You go. Go on. Go home and rest."

Emma got in her car, started the engine, closed her eyes for a moment, opened them, and pulled away. She was exhausted, physically and mentally. Engaging in pleasant chitchat with Rick Marshalk had been a chore because of what she knew about the allegations raised by Rotondi.

She turned on the radio, tuned to a classical music station, and played Beethoven's Fifth loud, very loud, to drive those thoughts out of the car through the open windows.

Would Phil be there when she reached home?

She assumed he would, and that contemplation brought a smile to her face.

THIRTY-ONE

Jack Michael Albert Parish was named after his mother's brother. That was before Uncle Jack was sent away for thirty years for aggravated assault with the intent to kill. Young Jack's mother once confided in a neighbor and close friend—as well as their local Catholic priest, who advised that exorcism probably wouldn't work—that her son, then fifteen years old, had inherited Uncle Jack's genes. She'd arrived at the conclusion after Jack had been picked up by the police again for vandalism. Previous brushes with the law had involved assault on a classmate, a girl, and breaking into a local soda fountain. Jack's father, who was fairly well connected in town, managed to negotiate with the victims and their families to drop charges in return for restitution, and none of Jack's transgressions appeared on any police record.

He graduated from high school near the bottom of his class and worked a few menial jobs until hearing that the Washington police were actively seeking recruits in the face of rising crime in the nation's capital. He applied, and to everyone's surprise was accepted. He became a cop.

His twenty-year-stint on the force was not without incident. Parish was known as a hothead who too often took it upon himself to mete out his own brand of justice. He wasn't unique within the department. There were a number of rogue cops who crossed the line, particularly with low-level drug dealers and other public nuisances, who tended to find themselves with bruises and broken bones after being confronted by Parish and those sharing his views. He'd been brought up on charges a few times, but nothing stuck. There were also rumors—and nothing more than that—that he'd killed a drug dealer during a confrontation in a deserted alley. Parish had called dispatch to report that he'd come across the body of an unidentified male. Why Parish had been in that alley raised all sorts of speculation, although there was no physical evidence to point to him as the one who'd crushed the dealer's head. Those beat cops who worked closely with Parish over the years were convinced that he'd avoided the revolving-door justice system and rid the city of one of its less desirable citizens. Parish denied any involvement, of course, but when kidded about it by fellow officers, he'd smile his crooked smile and wink.

The truth was, Jack Michael Albert Parish enjoyed hurting people, and after twenty years on the force, his superiors were glad to see him gone.

He'd hooked up with Rick Marshalk two years ago through Senator Simmons's driver, Walter McTeague, also a former D.C. cop. There had developed in Washington a club of sorts, its "members" retired police officers offering their services as private drivers and bodyguards. McTeague knew little of Parish's reputation as a cop, just a few vague rumors that faded with time. When the senator made McTeague aware that Marshalk was looking for a driver who could also provide personal security, McTeague mentioned that Parish, who'd been doing part-time work in those capacities, might be available. He was, and he signed on. Six months into his employment,

Marshalk called him into his office and announced that he was making him his vice president of security, with a salary to match the title. Parish's grin had never been bigger, or more slanted, than on that day. As far as he was concerned, Rick Marshalk was the smartest, savviest, greatest guy in D.C. and beyond, and he pledged to him on that day that he would do anything Marshalk expected of him. "I'm yours, Rick," he said as they shook hands on the deal. "Anything you need, just name it."

This night, after leaving Rick Marshalk's K Street offices, he took a cab to Foggy Bottom, where he instructed the driver to let him off two blocks from Emma Churchill's home. He stood in the shadows of a boutique hotel until his cell phone rang.

"She just left," he heard Marshalk say.

He walked the two blocks to the address on Emma's card, stood in front of the house, and took in his surroundings. It was a quiet street. He saw no one. Satisfied that he wasn't being observed, he took quick steps down the driveway, passing a Subaru Tribeca parked off to one side. He proceeded to a door at the rear of the house and peered through one of its windows into a small kitchen illuminated by lights beneath a microwave installed over the stove. The parked Subaru concerned him. Did it belong to this guy Rotondi? Was he inside?

He tried the door. Locked. He removed a set of jigs on a metal ring from his pocket. He chose one and used it. The door unlocked easily. He slowly pushed it open and focused his hearing. No sound. He quietly closed the door behind him and was about to move to another room when Homer appeared in the doorway.

"Well, what do we have here?" Parish muttered as he pulled his semi-automatic from its shoulder holster.

Homer barked twice.

"Calm down," Parish said. "You want to go out, huh? Is that what you want?"

He took a few steps back and opened the door. "Come on, baby, go on out for a walk. Nice night out there."

Homer limped toward the door. Parish stepped aside. The dog

looked up at him, barked once more, and went outside. Parish quickly shut the door and drew a deep breath. He hadn't expected to be confronted by a dog. He would have hated to shoot the animal. He liked dogs.

He found the room off the kitchen to be empty. He explored other rooms. The house was his alone. All he had to do now was wait.

⁂

Emma turned down the radio's volume as she turned onto her street. She noticed as she pulled into the driveway that no lights other than what she'd left on glowed through the windows. Rotondi wasn't there yet.

She parked next to his car, turned off the ignition, and went to the back door. She inserted her key but saw that the door was already unlocked. She shook her head at her failure to lock up before leaving, and entered the kitchen. It didn't surprise her that Homer didn't greet her. His hearing had been failing; it took louder noises and voices to rouse him these days.

She tossed her handbag on the counter and flipped on the overhead lights. Leaving her shoes in the kitchen, she went to the living room and turned on lights there, then headed upstairs to change into pajamas and a robe.

As she stepped into the bedroom, she paused. She hadn't seen Homer downstairs and wondered where he'd elected to sleep that night. She was about to retrace her steps down to the living room when a strong hand from behind clamped over her mouth. The sound she emitted was a combination of fright and pain. Parish's fingers dug into the flesh around her mouth as he used his other hand to grasp her left arm and yank it behind her.

She struggled, but he was stronger. He brought her down to the floor on her stomach, his knee rammed into her lower back. "You gonna calm down, lady, or do I have to snap your neck?"

Up until that point, she'd thought only of fighting him off. Now reason replaced valor. She forced herself to relax, which prompted him to loosen his grip. He placed the muzzle of his weapon against her temple, slid off, and turned her onto her back.

"What do you want?" she managed, fighting to inject calm into her voice. "You want money. You can have it. Just don't hurt me."

"I don't want your money," he said. "Your boyfriend has something I need. He's got an envelope that he shouldn't have. You tell me where it is and I go on my way. You don't—"

"I don't know what you're talking about," she said.

He slapped the side of the automatic against her face, cutting her cheek.

"Where is Rotondi?" he asked.

"I don't know."

He threatened to strike her again.

"I don't know where he went tonight. I swear it. And I don't know about any envelope."

The weapon's barrel was pushed into her temple again. She squeezed her eyes shut in anticipation of having her brains blown out. As she did, the sound of a car door being slammed shut in front of the house reached them.

"Sounds like your boyfriend's home," Parish said.

Emma looked up into Parish's face. His mouth was a slash, a cruel smile that at the moment was more frightening to her than the gun.

Parish got up, the weapon still pointed at her. "Come on," he said. "Time to greet your honey."

Emma slowly pulled herself to a sitting position. She touched her cheek and observed the blood on her fingertips.

"Don't hurt him," she said, standing unsteadily.

He came around behind her and again jabbed the gun into her temple. "Let's go downstairs," he said. "It's showtime."

⁂

Rotondi walked up the driveway toward the rear of the house. He saw Emma's car and was pleased she was home. He had a lot to tell her.

⁓

The extended time spent with Lyle Simmons in his suite at the Willard had been a roller coaster of emotions and debate. It was as though Simmons had crashed against a wall that he'd always previously managed to circumvent. Over steak dinners delivered to the room, he and Rotondi talked of many things, of their years in college, the situation with Jeannette, Rotondi's steadfast determination to go his own way, Kathleen Rotondi's tragic slaying, Polly's estrangement from her father, and Neil's meandering adult life. Simmons ricocheted from one extreme to the other. He was, at times, maudlin and filled with remorse about certain aspects of his personal life. Then, without warning or smooth transition, he became belligerent and critical of Rotondi's life choices, of his rigidity and deep convictions. Rotondi did little talking. His role was as it often was when alone with Simmons—foil, audience, superego.

There came a time when Rotondi brought the dialogue around to Jeannette's murder.

"Marshalk arranged for her killing, Lyle, and framed Jonell Marbury," he said bluntly.

"I don't know this Marbury fellow," Simmons retorted, "and I have serious trouble believing that anyone at the Marshalk Group would have murdered Jeannette." When Rotondi started to follow up, Simmons said, "But if what you say is true, whoever was behind it should pay."

"What about Neil?" Rotondi asked.

"Are you suggesting that he was a part of it?"

"No, I'm not, Lyle, but he is the president of the firm. It will impact him, too."

"And you intend to take that information Jeannette got from Chicago, including those disgusting photos, to the police?"

"I've thought a lot about that, Lyle. I don't see how the photos are relevant to the murder case, unless they provide a motive for you to have had Jeannette killed. I don't believe that you did."

"Then I'd like you to give me those photos, Phil."

Rotondi didn't commit.

"Neil thinks you intend to blackmail me about them, along with the other accusations about Marshalk funneling dirty money into my campaigns."

"Neil is wrong."

"Then give the pictures to me. I think I can ride out the laundering charges. Hell, I don't know where most of my campaign money comes from. I leave that to other people. If someone connected with my campaign knowingly took mob money from Marshalk, I'll have his head."

There he was, Rotondi thought, playing the politician to the hilt. As long as there was someone else to blame, politicians could always feign ignorance and faulty recall to get off the hook. Sadly, there was never a shortage of lackeys willing to take the rap to protect their superiors, good soldiers with skewed senses of duty.

"I intend to go to the police in the morning," Rotondi said, "and lay out for them what I believe. I may need that envelope and what's in it to help make my point."

Simmons finished his drink, patted his mouth with a napkin, got up from the table, and walked to the door. "You do whatever you think you have to, Phil. Not that you need my permission. I just ask that you remember how much we've meant to each other over the years."

Rotondi left, his mind filled with nothing but.

❧

He reached the end of the rear of Emma's house and turned in the direction of the kitchen door.

"Homer?" he said. The dog sat on the steps wagging his tail at seeing his master.

"What are you doing out here?"

Emma's car was there. She was home. She never would have let Homer out without having him on a leash. Rotondi was adamant about that, obsessive when it came to protecting Homer from harm.

What was going on?

A long wire lead used to tie Homer outside was attached to a tree ten feet from the door. Rotondi quickly clipped the dog's collar to the lead and returned to the driveway, this time staying close to the house as he moved toward the street. He stopped. A pretty fabric shade Emma had purchased just that week was raised a few inches off the sill. Rotondi peered through the opening into the living room. At first, he wasn't sure what he was seeing. Emma was standing in a corner of the room. With her was a man—holding a gun to her head. Rotondi blinked to clear his eyes. He looked again. He wasn't seeing things.

He backed away from the window, went behind one of the trees that lined the driveway, and dialed 911: "There's a woman being held at gunpoint in a house in Foggy Bottom." He gave the address. The 911 operator tried to ask for additional information, but Rotondi had clicked the phone closed. He opened it again, dialed Emma's home number, and returned to the window, the phone to his ear.

He could see from his vantage point that Emma said something to the man holding her hostage. He couldn't tell what she was saying but assumed it had to do with the ringing phone. The man with the weapon shoved Emma across the room, and she fell on the couch. Rotondi ducked away as the man came to the window and lifted the shade. Rotondi was inches from his face. Parish's eyes darted back and forth before he allowed the shade to fall again. Rotondi raised his head at the distant sound of a siren. He moved as quickly as his lame leg would allow to the street and was standing there when the marked squad car came to a screeching halt. Two uniformed officers jumped out, leaving their doors open.

"What's going on?" one of them asked Rotondi.

He gave the officer a fifteen-second précis.

"Who's the woman?" the cop asked.

"My fiancée," Rotondi said, a word he'd not used before when describing Emma. "I'm going in," he added as two more cars arrived, each occupied by a pair of officers.

Rotondi didn't wait for a response. As the cops fanned out around the house, Rotondi went to the rear door, opened it, and stepped into the kitchen. "Hey," he shouted, moving to the doorway to the living room. Emma cowered on the couch while Parish stood over her, the gun pointed at her head.

"I don't know who you are," Rotondi said, "but the house is surrounded. There are cops everywhere. Drop the gun and—"

Parish's face mirrored his genuine puzzlement. He lowered the gun. Rotondi reacted instantly. He lunged at Parish, his cane extended in front of him to shorten the distance between them. The point of the cane caught Parish in the eye and sent him sprawling on top of Emma on the couch. Rotondi closed the gap between them and twisted Parish's wrist violently, sending the weapon to the floor. Phil kicked it across the room and pounced on Parish, his hands closing around his neck, guttural, animal sounds erupting from his throat.

The kitchen door was flung open and police rushed in. They'd watched the fracas through the same window Rotondi had peered through. Parish was jerked to his feet, pushed to the floor, and cuffed.

"Are you okay?" Rotondi asked Emma as they got to their feet.

"Yeah, I'm okay," she said. "You?"

"Fine. I'm fine."

She looked at the six uniformed officers who now crowded the room. "How did they know?" she asked. "How did *you* know?"

"A four-legged friend named Homer."

THIRTY-TWO

ONE MONTH LATER

"**I** stand here today with a heavy heart as I announce that I will not seek my party's nomination for president of the United States, nor will I seek reelection to the United States Senate."

Illinois senator Lyle Simmons faced a sizable crowd of journalists and supporters in the rotunda of the U.S. Capitol. Dozens of microphones jutted up from the lectern on which an American flag had been carefully affixed. A bevy of TV cameras ringed the rear of the crowd. Standing next to Simmons were his daughter, Polly; his press aide, Peter Markowicz; and his chief of staff, Alan McBride.

"I think of what Theodore Roosevelt once said: 'Death is always and under all circumstances a tragedy, for if it is not, then it means that life itself has become one.' A man is meant to absorb only so many personal blows without sagging beneath the weight of such burdens, and that is true of this man. The tragic deaths of my beloved wife, Jeannette, and my beloved son, Neil, have forced me to look deep inside myself for the strength and courage to weather these tragic losses. I believe I have done that, but at the expense of the energy necessary to continue representing the state of Illinois, and the American people in the United States Senate, or in any other position of public trust and extreme responsibility. After many years of dedicated public service, I find it extremely difficult to come to this decision. But I must, for my own sake and for the sake of my daughter, Polly, who stands beside me today."

He looked at her and managed a smile. Her expression didn't change.

"While I shall no longer seek elected office, I intend to commit myself as a private citizen to such good acts to which I am able to contribute something positive. I do this in the name and spirit of Jeannette and Neil Simmons, whose love shall always sustain me. Thank you for your years of support. It has been a profound privilege to have served the American people. God bless America!"

As grieving father and daughter turned from the lectern, McBride whispered to Markowicz, "Nice speech, Peter."

"He delivered it well," Markowicz replied as they fell into step behind Lyle and Polly.

◈

Phil Rotondi and Emma Churchill watched Simmons's televised farewell in her Foggy Bottom home. They hadn't spent much time there during the month following the incident with Jack Parish. After meeting with Morris Crimley the following morning at MPD headquarters, where they gave formal statements and Rotondi laid out for the detective his take on the Jeannette Simmons and Camelia Watson murders—and after Emma had arranged for some of her upcoming catering jobs to be handled by Imelda, her loyal and longtime employee—they packed Homer and some of Emma's clothes into Phil's SUV and headed for the Eastern Shore in search of what solitude and peace they could manage.

It hadn't been easy for Rotondi to not attend Jeannette's memorial service, but he decided that she would understand his absence under the circumstances. Chances are she would have skipped it herself. He watched portions of it on TV and cried.

"I feel bad for Lyle," Rotondi said after turning off the TV.

"He brought it on himself," Emma said.

"True," Rotondi said, "but let's not be so hard. He played the game his way and lost. Everything in his life, personal and political, has come crashing down around him. I don't wish that on anyone."

✿

Within days of being incarcerated, Jack Parish had cut a deal with prosecutors. In return for turning state's evidence against Rick Marshalk, the Marshalk Group, and by extension Senator Lyle Simmons, he was promised minimal jail time and an eventual place in the federal Witness Protection Program.

"Not a bad deal for a guy who murdered two people," Emma said after Rotondi had been filled in about the deal over the phone by Crimley, *entre nous*, of course.

"It's the system," Rotondi said.

He fell silent.

"What?" she asked.

"I'm just thinking that what happened at your house wasn't all bad."

"You're joking! That scum Parish almost killed us!"

"I don't mean it was good what happened to you, Emma. But the way it turned out, I didn't have to reveal anything from that envelope. I didn't have to contribute to bringing Lyle down. There were plenty of others to do it."

Swarms of law enforcement agents had invaded the Marshalk offices and removed anything of potential evidentiary interest. The raid, which quickly uncovered the link between Marshalk and Simmons, prompted a change of heart in the Chicago AG's office. The damaging material about Simmons, kept under wraps theretofore thanks to political pressure, was released to various law enforcement agencies—which meant, of course, that it soon found its way into the press, including two of the photos, which ran in a tabloid publication. Federal indictments would soon be coming down against Simmons, according to Rotondi's sources.

◦

Rotondi and Emma sat in the kitchen of his condo on the Eastern Shore drinking coffee and passing pieces of that day's newspapers back and forth.

"I hope he wins," Rotondi muttered.

"You hope *who* wins?"

"The Asian American detective who got booted off the Simmons case. Charlie Chang."

"What is he trying to win?"

"A sense of justice for himself and the system. I don't think I ever mentioned that Lyle brought pressure on Chief Johnson to get rid of Chang. The chief caved and told Morrie Crimley to transfer him to another unit. Crimley was boiling mad about it, but with retirement on the near horizon, he played good soldier. Chang quit the force and has brought a suit against MPD for racial discrimination."

"You don't think Lyle wanted him gone because he's Asian, do you?"

"No. I think he didn't like that this Chang refused to kowtow to him. Crimley says that Chang never did fit in and was tired of the way other detectives were treating him. According to Crimley, Chang has a master's degree and is going after a Ph.D. He's better off gone."

◦

Jeannette Simmons's memorial service wasn't the only funeral that Rotondi had elected to avoid during the past month.

Neil Simmons's service was held in a small church near his home. According to Polly, it was sparsely attended: "His wife and kids seemed to hold up okay," she reported during a call to Phil that afternoon.

"How are you doing, Polly?" he asked.

"Confused, so confused. God, Phil, poor Neil. He said in that note he left behind that he'd killed Mom by going to Marshalk and telling him of the damning information she had against them. All he wanted was for them to do the right thing and clean up their act. Mom. Camelia Watson. And now Neil. Marshalk sure left a trail of bodies, didn't he?"

A vision of Neil Simmons sitting in his car in a closed garage, a hose from the exhaust pumping noxious, fatal fumes through a small opening in the window, flooded Rotondi. He willed the grim visual away. "How's your dad?" he asked.

"Okay, I guess. I haven't spoken much with him. He asked me to stay around D.C. until he makes his announcement about not running—for anything. I said I would. Have you spoken with him?"

"Yes, once."

☙

Rotondi hadn't tried to contact Lyle, but had received a call from him just a few days before his announcement that he was abandoning politics.

"Hello, Philip," Simmons had said, his voice strong. "How goes it?"

"Just fine, Lyle. You?"

"Under the gun, but I'll come out all right. Phil, the reason I'm calling is to see if you'd be interested in working with me on a committee I'm thinking of launching."

"What sort of committee?"

"A private organization made up of concerned citizens who are fed up with the way lobbyists run the show in Congress. It'll take outside pressure, I'm afraid, to force the House and Senate to come up with any meaningful legislation." Simmons laughed. "I'm the perfect one to spearhead such a movement, don't you agree? I'm trying to make something positive out of all this, Phil."

"That's good, Lyle. I'll think about it."

"Of course you will. Get back to me about it, Phil. We make a hell of a team. We always have. Stay in touch."

❧

Rotondi hadn't stayed in touch but knew he would, not to become involved in any committee, but to maintain contact with his former college roommate and friend of so many years. Whether he'd ever see Polly again was pure conjecture. And Marlene? He doubted their paths would ever cross again, either.

The phone rang. It was Mac Smith.

"How are things?" Rotondi asked.

"Good. You?"

"We're doing all right, Mac. How's Jonell Marbury?"

"He's landed a new job, White House liaison for a Wisconsin congressman."

"Good for him. He deserves the best."

"And he and Marla have set the date."

"Nothing but positive news," Rotondi said. "I like that."

"Staying in Washington for a while, Phil?"

"As little as possible. Emma's second-in-command is doing a bang-up job, so we can spend more time down at the shore."

"That's why I'm calling. Annabel and I are thinking of spending next weekend there—you know, some sun, sand, get our toes wet. We'd love to catch up with you and Emma."

"It's a date," said Rotondi.

They promised to follow up with details later in the week.

"Time for Homer's walk," Rotondi said. He yelled the dog's name, which awoke him from a deep, fidgety sleep. "Come on, buddy, time to fertilize the grass."

As man and beast were about to go through the front door, Rotindi turned and said, "Do you know what I said the night Parish was here?"

"No, what?" Emma asked.

"When the cops arrived, they asked who the woman was being held inside the house."

"And?"

"And—I said it was my fiancée."

Emma laughed. "Remember our deal," she said.

"I'm remembering," he said, "only as I get older, my memory isn't as good as it used to be. Back in a minute."

She smiled and went to the kitchen to fill the dishwasher. As she did, she found herself singing, for no discernible reason, the old Doris Day hit, "Que Sera, Sera."

"Que sera, sera, whatever will be will be, the future's not ours to see . . ."

Come to think of it, her memory wasn't what is used to be, either.

ABOUT THE AUTHOR

MARGARET TRUMAN has won faithful readers with her works of biography and fiction, particularly her ongoing series of Capital Crimes mysteries. Her novels let us into the corridors of power and privilege, and poverty and pageantry, in the nation's capital. She is the author of many nonfiction books, including *The President's House*, in which she shares some of the secrets and history of the White House, where she once resided. She lives in Manhattan.

ABOUT THE TYPE

This book was set in Electra, a typeface designed for Linotype by W. A. Dwiggins, the renowned type designer (1880–1956). Electra is a fluid typeface, avoiding the contrasts of thick and thin strokes that are prevalent in most modern typefaces.